THE ANATOMY OF COURAGE

Peter Cawdron

thinkingscifi.wordpress.com

Disclaimer: No Artificial Intelligence (AI) was used in the creation of this story. Some would argue that no intelligence was used at all. I'll leave that for you to decide.

Core Art: **War Casualty** by Adrian Hillman. Used with permission from iStockPhotos 150379142.

Subscribe to my email newsletter to learn more about my writing, special deals and upcoming releases.

Imprint: Independently published

ISBN: 9798883705952 — Paperback

ISBN: 9798883708168 — Hardback

Much of the evil in this world
is due to the fact that man, in general,
is hopelessly unconscious.
Carl Yung

A man of character in peace is a man of courage in war.
Lord Moran

Mud

Doctor Christopher Walters sits at a desk made out of old wooden crates. A gas lantern hisses softly, hanging from a wooden beam running through the middle of the dugout. The light cast around the stone walls is warm rather than bright, although warm is a description of its color and not any heat. Vapor forms on his breath in the bitter cold. A candle burns beside him on the desk. Wax drips into a steel tray. Its light is pitiful compared to the gas lantern, but the flicker helps ward off the shadows cast by his own hands. He has a battery-powered LED light on his helmet, but batteries need to be saved for the battlefield, so the light within the dugout is dim.

Doc has a pen out and is writing on a piece of paper torn from the back of his leather-bound journal.

My dearest Jean,

I miss you deeply and cannot wait until this dreadful war is over. After four months of working in a field hospital, this is my first rotation to the Front. Six weeks here. Six weeks back at the hospital. And then I get two weeks of furlough before doing it all again.

I don't know what you hear on the News, but you probably know far more than I do about the actual fighting. We are starved of information in the trenches. The war on the Western Perimeter has stalled, with the aliens pushing south and east. I cannot tell you exactly where I am, but not because of any clandestine security requirements.

I simply do not know. We've been stationed in the lines between Chelyabinsk and Omsk. The Novos will lock in on any kind of electromagnetic signal, even something trivial like a smartwatch. Small diesel pumps go undetected, but not the engines in cars, so the trucks dropped us off in Kurgan, and we walked from there.

We walked for days without end. From the road, we could see thousands, perhaps tens of thousands of soldiers and peasants digging trenches and lining them with wood from the forest. These are our fallback positions should the Novos swarm to the west.

The trenches are long, often running for miles and branching in different directions, but their width, their depth—it's as though they're a grave awaiting a coffin. They're cut into the clay and mud and reinforced with timber. And then there's no man's land, a strip of bloody earth separating our trenches from those dug by the Novos. At a guess, no man's land is several hundred yards wide and pockmarked with shell holes. Honestly, it terrifies me.

Everything in this war is about anticipating the enemy and keeping him boxed in. The thought of being overrun by those damn things is scary as hell. If those fallback trenches are ever used, I fear I will be, too. We're told there are reserves held back to reinforce the line as needed, but as everyone's on foot and the ground is muddy, nothing happens quickly out here. Our food, our water, our medical supplies and ammunition are brought in by mule. I cannot see a counterattack being mustered in anything less than a day. That's the frustrating part of the war. Artillery can breach the line, but not tanks. There are no helicopters, no planes, no missiles, no drones. The Novos simply bring them down with lightning.

There's shelling outside. Occasionally, the barrage lands close enough to shake the ground. It's more like a heavy truck rumbling across an overpass than an earthquake. The Novos counter with their own fire. Ours sound like distant thunder. Theirs crackle like lightning. There will be clear blue sky above, but it sounds like a storm is rippling overhead. They throw boulders at us. Some of them as big as houses.

If you check the satellite view online, this part of Russia looks as though it has been shelled by giants in wars gone by. There are lakes everywhere. They look like gigantic craters. The water table is so shallow here that our dugouts are always muddy, even when there's snow outside. Water seeps through the walls, which means we can't lean against them, not without setting up plastic or canvas. My boots are caked in mud. I clean them off whenever I can, scraping the soles against the side of the trench when the weight gets too much, but it is an endless battle and one as exhausting as the Novos themselves.

Please give my love to all. Tell them not to worry. We're here for the good of humanity. If I die—and I have no such plans—remember me fondly.

Lovingly yours,

Chris.

There are no envelopes at the Front, so Doc uses the back of the paper as the outside of an informal envelope. He folds his letter with precision, sealing it with a few drops of wax. Then, he pushes the end of an empty shell casing on the wax instead of a seal. Doc writes an address on it and writes the word *FREE* where the stamp would normally be placed. He slips the letter into a ziplock plastic bag to protect it from moisture. There's no need for stamps. The US Army will ensure it gets to his fiancé.

"Sir?" a voice says as a silhouette blocks the natural light coming from the entrance. "Your protection detail is outside."

"Of course," Doc replies. He holds his arm out, handing the letter to the corporal. "See this goes out with the dispatches."

"Yes, sir."

Doc stows his journal in his bag and slings the grimy canvas bag over one shoulder. He snuffs the candle and blows out the lantern. Mud squelches beneath his boots as he walks on the half-sunken boards toward the entrance. Thick timber beams frame the doorway.

Doc steps up from the dugout into the sunlight. The trench is eight to nine feet deep but only a few feet wide at this point. It's reinforced with wooden poles holding back the dirt and rock.

"Staff Sergeant Meyers," a lanky soldier says with a helmet that seems two sizes too big on his head. His clothing hangs off him, hiding his thin frame. Meyers is gaunt. His cheeks are long, while his hair is straggly, poking out from beneath the molded Kevlar. A chin strap hangs idly from the side of his helmet. Were he to run a hundred yards, his helmet would beat him to the finish line, bouncing off his head as he ran.

Meyers comes to attention while Doc is looking for a handshake.

"Ah, yes. Of course," Doc says, stiffening in response. "No salutes either, huh?"

"Not while we're out in the open," Meyers says.

"Okay," Doc replies sheepishly.

"Delta Foxtrot 3 Squad reporting for duty, sir. 4th Infantry. 23rd Regiment."

Beyond Meyers, the other members of the squad have spread out within the cramped trench. They're curious, wanting to see their principal—the person they're tasked to protect on the battlefield. Several of them are clinging to the side of the trench, having climbed up on the logs to get a better look at him.

A woman at the front says, "You got dawg food!"

Doc is confused. His brow narrows.

"It's the squad name," Meyers says by way of explanation. "DF3 is known as the Dog Food Squad."

"Oh," Doc says, reaching out and offering to shake the woman's hand.

"Aw, hell no," she says, pretending to accept his hand and quickly withdrawing her fingers, running them up through her purple hair. "And this is the chump we're gonna die for?"

"I, um," Doc says, taken aback by the bluster unfolding within the squad.

"Where are you from?" one of the other soldiers asks. He's wearing glasses, but they're dirty. Smudges cover the cracked lenses. A wad of

4

tape holds the rims together.

"Chicago," Doc says. "I was a—I *am* an ER trauma surgeon."

"*Shikaakwa*," a soldier with distinctly Native American features says, using the city's *Algonquin* name. He's tall and thin, standing behind the others. His skin is soft brown. He has no facial hair beyond his eyebrows. It's not that he's freshly shaven. His skin has the complexion of a child.

Meyers says, "Well, you're in the Mud City now, Doc," also alluding to another nickname for Chicago. "Let me introduce you to the squad."

"Oh, yes. That would be wonderful."

From the back, one of the soldiers calls out, "Ain't nothing wonderful at the Front, Doc. You best get used to that."

"That's Leech," Meyers says, pointing him out. Leech is pale, with acne breaking out on his face. He looks sickly.

"Leech? That's your surname?"

"Ain't none of us use our real names, Doc," Leech replies. "None of us are gonna last that long out here on the Front. Makes it easier if there are no names."

It's only then that Doc notices Meyers is the only one wearing a name tag velcro'd on his uniform. The others either don't have them or have their nicknames handwritten with a black marker.

Meyers says, "And that's Mouse at the back next to Leech."

"Mouse?" Doc replies, looking at a six-foot-six linebacker who barely fits into his uniform. His broad shoulders and biceps strain against the material. He's got a small head relative to his thick chest and huge arms.

"As quiet as," Mouse replies with a smile, revealing missing teeth.

"Hawk," Meyers says, pointing at the Native American. "He's *Navajo*."

Hawk doesn't say anything. He keeps his face stoic and simply lifts his chin slightly in acknowledgment of his name.

"You've already met Lavender," Meyers says, gesturing toward the brooding woman with purple hair.

"Oh, yes."

"William Sunday," another woman says, standing opposite Lavender, only she's genuinely friendly, reaching out her hand to shake his. Doc accepts. Her accent is Russian. English is a second language. Although she's part of the US Army, Doc doubts she's ever been outside of Russia. With the war in meat grinder mode and an apathetic population back in the States, locals have informally joined the army. Once someone's in a body bag, it makes no difference which country they came from, so no one at the Front cares about nationalities.

"And your name? William Sunday?"

"William was my brother. He died out here on the day I arrived at the Front."

"And Sunday?"

"Sunday was the day I arrived," she replies as though that should have been obvious.

"Just call her Sunny," Meyers says.

Given the scowl on her face, Doc isn't sure if he's being sarcastic, but he goes with it, saying, "It's nice to meet you, Sunny."

"Where's Happy?" Meyers asks the squad, craning his neck, trying to spot someone at the back. "Happy. Are you there?"

A hand protrudes from behind Mouse, squeezing past Hawk's waist, reaching for Doc.

"Ah, hi," Doc says, stepping forward and shaking cold fingers.

"Nice to meet you, Doc," Happy says from out of sight. "It'll be a pleasure dying beside you."

Meyers says, "Happy's our optimist."

"Oh," Doc says, releasing Happy's hand.

"Mouse, let Happy through."

Mouse turns sideways within the trench, which doesn't seem to help as he's so bulky it makes almost no difference. Happy waves from the rear. He's short, probably around five-foot-six, and is utterly dwarfed by Mouse. At a guess, Mouse is two to three times the weight of Happy.

"Okay, get your kit ready," Meyers says. "We've got a raiding party going out at twenty-two hundred. Get some sleep if you can, 'cause you won't be gettin' none tonight."

There's grumbling from the Dog Food Squad. They turn and make their way down along the muddy trench.

"And Happy. Take Doc's kit. Get him stowed."

"Me? Why me? It's always me," the short man says, squeezing forward and taking Doc's bag from him.

"The squeaky wheel gets the grease," Meyers replies as Happy wanders off after the others.

Doc is perplexed. He asks Meyers, "We're going out tonight?"

"Yep."

"They told me there were only one or two missions a month."

Meyers laughs. "More like one or two a night. You're going to be busy, Doc. Come on, let's get you to Command, so they can brief you."

The two of them head along the trench. Every fifty yards, the line turns but by only roughly ten degrees, ensuring no one section of the trench is dead-straight. The zigzags are confusing, but they center on a straight line. There must be some logic to it, Doc figures, like limiting the line-of-sight view of the Novos if they breach the Front, but he finds it disorienting. There are signs with arrows pointing toward places called Red Lake, New Town, and Devil's Lake.

They reach an intersection. The trench widens, giving soldiers somewhere to congregate. Vape floats in the air, along with the smell of freshly burned coffee.

There's a sign with an arrow pointing away from the Front that reads: *South Dakota this way.* They turn and begin walking on another set of wooden planks that flex and squish in the mud.

"South Dakota?"

"Don't you know, Doc? We're at war with Canada."

7

"Canada?" a visibly surprised Doc says, turning to face him as they trudge through the mud at the bottom of the trench. "But we're in Russia."

Meyers laughs. "The Front is aligned with a map of the US. We're in North Dakota. The Novos are in Canada. The East and West Coast are our flanks. Our command post is in Standing Rock, while our reinforcements are stationed in Lincoln."

"Nebraska?" Doc asks, wanting to make sure he understands the logic correctly.

"Yep. That's about ten to fifteen miles that way. Then you've got CentCom in Wichita."

"Ah, right. So, the Marshall Field Hospital—where I was stationed? Where's that?"

"That's down in El Paso. Right on the border."

"The border of what?"

Meyers looks at Doc with a bewildered look of surprise on his face. "The real world, Doc."

"Oh, yes. Right."

"Defense-in-depth," Meyers says. "Or at least, that's the plan. In the early days, the Novos would surge, and we'd scramble, losing miles trying to contain them. Now, we make them pay for every yard. And we keep a damn good buffer between us, them and the civvies."

"Huh."

"Besides, it confuses them."

"How?"

"They're smart, Doc. But they're too smart. Everything's got to be logical, but we're not. We're human. We're a mixture of emotion and logic."

"Mostly emotion," Doc says.

"You got that," Meyers replies as they continue on along the muddy trench leading away from the Front. The wall has collapsed on one side, forcing them to clamber over sticky clay and mud. There's a detachment of soldiers fixing the rockslide, but only a couple of them are actually moving mud and debris. The others are standing around vaping or leaning against the remaining wall, drinking coffee. One soldier is crouching, taking a shit in the mud. Steam rises from the fresh lumps falling into the dark water. Doc looks away.

"So we've taken a map of the US and turned it sideways. North is east. West is north. East is south. South is west. Fucks with their minds."

"Fucks with my mind," Doc says.

"Just remember Canada. We're fighting Canada. You're either going toward Saskatchewan or Manitoba on our stretch of the Front."

"And how do the Canadians feel about this?"

Meyers laughs. "They said it was about time the US invaded."

Doc shakes his head. With a Canadian mom, he can't help but grin at that comment. He's sure she'd disagree—and with a flourish of expletives thrown in with her various objections to make the point clear.

Eventually, Meyers leads him to a dugout with a broad entrance. Gas lanterns hang from the ceiling. Wooden crates line the floor, keeping them well clear of the mud.

"I'll wait outside."

Doc wants to say he doesn't have to, but he gets the impression that Meyers knows the drill. He wants to ask him how many doctors he's brought here for their induction, but professionalism gets the better of him, and he bows his head, ducking beneath the wooden beam as he steps down into the dugout. Adjustable steel props support the ceiling, allowing the command center to span easily fifty feet. Maps cover tables that have been strategically placed to catch the lantern light.

"Captain Christopher Walters?" an officer asks, looking at the name tag on his chest. "We've been expecting you."

"Ah, yes," Walters replies. His rank is honorary rather than earned. Being a civilian doctor, the thinking is to give him enough authority to get things done without getting in the way. Everyone knows it's a fake rank. He's not actually expected to or capable of commanding soldiers beyond his squad. Meyers will have been told to humor Doc

9

while steering him toward correct decisions. Doc's role is to save lives. His rank is like a scalpel or an IV line; it's a means of getting the job done in the chaos of battle.

"This way, sir," the officer says, leading him to the back of the dugout where a gruff old man sits puffing on a vape. "Colonel, Med-Cap Walters to see you."

Being in a dugout, Doc salutes out of respect.

"Yes, yes. Of course," the colonel says, not bothering with a salute in reply and barely looking up from his paperwork. He gestures to a makeshift chair. "Sit. Please."

Doc sits on a rickety crate with his hands in his lap.

"First time at the Front?"

"Yes, sir."

"Hmm," the colonel says. "Listen, Chris. I need you to understand why you're here."

The colonel has addressed him as Chris. Not captain or doctor. It's not a mistake. It's a ruse. Doc understands that. The colonel is trying to disarm him and help him relax, but relaxation is an enigma at the Front.

Doc fights the reflexive and somewhat cliched response, *yes, sir.* He simply nods and listens. For him, that's always the challenge. Listening to understand, and not simply listening to reply. Doc genuinely wants to understand the colonel's position.

Having majored in English at college before pursuing a career in medicine, Doc is very aware of the power of words—and their limits. Words are linear. For every word spoken or written, there are hundreds of others that fall by the wayside. As effective as speech and language have been for humanity, it is impossible to express ideas in any other way than with one word following another. But ideas are bigger than words. Ideas span more than sentences. They capture emotion, history, intent. Words are blunt. Ideas are fragile. The wrong words, or even just imprecise, clumsy words, can kill an idea before it has a chance to germinate.

Doc has been in a similar position to the colonel, where his authority within the hospital demanded words spoken with precision. In an emergency, it's impossible to say everything that needs to be said without clutter. Words need to be wielded like a scalpel, not an ax. Not everything needs to be said, but what is said needs to be precise and carry weight.

Doc can see the machinations of the colonel's mind as he considers his words in those few fleeting seconds. He's got roughly six thousand soldiers under his command. He relies on the command structure to overcome the impersonal nature of his authority. At any one time, he's balancing dozens of priorities from his standing orders to logistics and resupply to intel on the enemy's movements and his mission planners looking to exploit weaknesses in the Front. The last thing he needs to be doing is sitting here talking to a doctor. As his brow narrows, he's trying to condense what he needs Doc to understand into as few words as possible.

"Do you know what my soldiers need?" the colonel asks.

Doc doesn't answer. He understands that the colonel's question is rhetorical. If he knew, the colonel wouldn't need to ask. He shakes his head softly. To reply with a clichéd answer about ammo or more ethereal notions such as morale or leadership would be insulting.

"Hope."

The colonel draws in long and hard on his vape. To either side, there's a pile of messy papers of roughly equal height. A red marker sits on the desk in front of the colonel. The pile on his left is a combination of handwritten notes and typed pages. The pile to his right is covered in brutish red comments, often underlined. His notes are rough, being written over the text rather than in the margins. He's making command decisions in bombastic style not because he's bombastic himself but because that's what he needs to send ripples through the chain of command.

"When an attack is ordered, my troops need to know that going over the top is not a death sentence. They need to believe they're coming back. They need to know that if they take a hit out there, someone—*you*—are coming to get them."

Doc nods.

The colonel picks up the red marker and scrawls a note on the piece of paper he was reviewing when Doc sat down. He shifts it to the completed pile. His mind is running on multiple levels. His note reads: *Fuck them. I want it yesterday!*

"But you, Doc. I need you alive. I do not need you dying out there on some fool's errand. Do you understand?"

Doc grits his teeth. He nods.

"Don't go getting all sentimental on me out there, Doc. War is triage. You understand that, right? You save those you can. Those you can't, you let go. You turn your back, and you walk away."

He picks the next piece of paper up from the pile and draws a large X over the five paragraphs he never read. Doc wonders about the emotional toll weighing down on the colonel. Army officers are taught to compartmentalize their emotions and separate them from their decision-making, but no amount of drills or marches while sleep-deprived can ever turn humans into machines. Whoever wrote that submission will assume it was given full consideration and not a fleeting glance. Or perhaps the large X will tell them to be more succinct as they resubmit, increasing the colonel's paperwork once more.

"Any questions?"

"What's the average?" Doc asks. They both know that no further qualification is needed.

"For you? Twenty, maybe forty ops before you get sloppy and take one to the back of the head."

The colonel picks up his vape and draws in on it long and hard, saying, "My advice: don't get sloppy."

Doc nods but doesn't reply.

"And for those going over the top? Five to ten. But averages are misleading. A lot of wets don't last more than one or two ops, leaving the vets to clock up thirty or forty before rotating out."

Doc nods, appreciating the colonel's honesty while hating his indifference.

"We all die, Doc. It's just a question of when and where. Oh, hell. We all wanna hit a hundred, but it makes no difference. Thirty years and a shell hole or a ton and a hospital bed. All that ain't nothing when compared to 13.8 billion years. Might seem like a big deal to us, but it ain't. Better to fight for the future than die cowering in a hole."

Doc doesn't say anything, but they're cowering in a hole in the command center. Would the colonel be so cavalier if he were going over the top each night?

"And you," the colonel says, pointing at him with the red marker. "Don't think I'm getting all sentimental wanting to keep you alive. I ain't. A doctor's death is bad for morale, so make smart decisions out there. Understood?"

"Understood."

"That is all, Chris."

"Thank you, sir," Doc says, getting to his feet.

No sooner have those facile words left his lips than he regrets saying them. *Thank you* is a cliché, making it meaningless. *Sir* is groveling obedience to someone who only ever referred to him informally. Doc said what he was supposed to say, not what he felt, not what he meant. He said what the colonel wanted to hear. Doc is roleplaying like all of them in this theater of death. But what other possibilities are there? Stand and fight is the only option in battle. That then leads to the need for structure and efficiency. War is a machine. Coal needs to be shoveled into the furnace. The wheels are greased with the blood of men and women who would otherwise be buying a six-pack of beer in preparation for the weekend.

War is an altar to an angry god—one that doesn't exist.

One future is sacrificed for another. They'll be remembered, or that's what they're told. In reality, an abstract will be remembered. Even those who knew them well will forget them. They won't want to. They won't mean to, but who really knows anyone well enough to really remember them for years? Decades? Their relatives will remember the way they felt when they found out they died but little else.

Doc hangs his head as he walks past the maps that spell out death for soldiers standing outside in the sunshine. But what other options are there? They can't surrender to the Novos. The choices in war are only ever between degrees of suffering.

Doc steps up into the trench. Meyers is waiting to one side. He rushes over.

"Are we good?"

"We're good," Doc replies, realizing his idealism has just been shattered.

"Let's get you back to Westhope."

"Westhope?" Doc says, feeling startled by the similarity in that name. Did the colonel know where Doc was stationed? Is that why he used the term hope?

"Yeah, it's on the Canadian border," Meyers replies.

"Of course it is."

William Sunday

With no electronics and only the hiss of a gas lantern to break the silence, the night seems endless. Dog Food is sheltering in a dugout on the front line. They're considered an auxiliary squad, so they don't have to be in the trenches with ladders in place, ready to go over the top. From where Doc is, he can see legs walking past the entrance. Boots splash in the mud. Occasionally, snowflakes drift through the air, making their way into the dugout before melting on the floorboards. Shadows rush back and forth along the trench. Orders are given. Soldiers steel themselves.

Meyers sits by the entrance. He seems interested in the discussions unfolding outside and is trying to gain a glimpse into any recovery mission that might unfold.

After a while, Doc realizes there's an interesting dynamic within the dugout. Doc pulls out his journal and makes notes, observing the behavior of the squad before deployment.

Mouse is asleep. He's propped himself up in the corner, wearing his wet weather gear to ward off the moisture seeping through the gaps between the rocks and stones. He may be dry, but he cannot be warm.

Hawk has his battlefield kit laid out on a tarpaulin and is cleaning the already meticulously clean equipment. He's the comms specialist, so he'll carry several rolls of wire to lay out a temporary phone line, giving Dog Food the ability to talk to Command. It's ancient tech. There are no batteries as such. Rather, the handset has to be cranked to produce enough electricity to power the line. It's low-tech and slips under the

Novos. Talk too long in any one location, though, and there's the risk of being targeted. Communiques need to be short and sharp.

Lavender is playing solitaire with a pack of dirty cards on an upside-down crate that doubles as a desk sometimes and a chair others. Not only are the cards grimy and muddy, they're distasteful, with pornographic images on them. Topless women and swinging dicks adorn the cards.

Doc is curious about Lavender. She could involve the others, but she seems to want to remain distant. She flips cards, rearranges piles, grimaces and then smiles, content with her play. Then she shuffles the deck and starts again. Like William Sunday, her face is painted with disruptive patterns. Black smudges and grey marks hide the outline of her eyes, nose and lips.

William Sunday looks nervous. She's sitting opposite Mouse, leaning against the other corner of the dugout, and is also wearing her wet weather gear, but she's not trying to sleep. Doc notices she's wearing orange earplugs even though there's barely any noise seeping into the dugout. She's got a pair of standard-issue sonic foam earplugs. Although these are passive, they dull noises above eighty decibels, allowing soldiers to talk while firing their weapons.

Happy is reading a book, but he hasn't turned a page in almost ten minutes. He stares at the novel, seemingly lost in thought, but he's neither reading nor contemplating what he's read. He's going through the motions of reading by the gas lantern, but why? Is he trying to fool the others or himself? Doc suspects he's staring through rather than at the ragged pages of the paperback, lost in memories rather than thoughts. Every now and then, his face grimaces. His cheeks rise, and his eyes squint, but not in response to anything he's read—unless he's reading the same thing a dozen times.

Happy, Hawk and Mouse are all introverted and tend to be quiet, but for different reasons. Doc is worried about Happy, and he's only known him for about seven hours. It's not just that Happy's putting on a facade, but that whatever worries lie behind his eyes, they're tormenting him. His thoughts are dark. Suppressing his emotions is not healthy.

16

Doc makes notes in the back of his journal. He divides the two pages facing him up into equal sections and writes code names for the squad. They have real names, which are unknown to him, and nicknames. Now, he's giving them cryptic pseudonyms so he can make notes over time without fear of anyone reading and deciphering his comments. It's important that they don't realize he's observing them in preparation for writing a book about the war.

Mouse is Road. The link won't be obvious to anyone but Doc, but to his mind, Road is phonetic for rode—as in rodent. Lavender becomes Silver because although the lavender plant has purple flowers, its leaves are a silvery green. William Sunday becomes Weak, a play on the first letter of her name and the fact her last name describes a day of the week and not that he thinks she's in any way weak. If anything, she seems mean. Leech is sitting opposite Doc, flicking pebbles into a cup for sport. He becomes Muscles in Doc's notes because he has none.

Hawk notices the way Doc looks around the dugout. He seems to suspect the notes Doc's taking are personal. He stops what he's doing and stares at him. Doc smiles in reply, refusing to be intimidated, knowing any apparent sign of guilt would be interpreted by Hawk as hostile. Doc writes down the name Knives, thinking if Hawk could, he'd use a knife instead of a gun on the battlefield. The intensity in Hawk's gaze is such that it seems he'd relish getting up close to one of the Novos.

Happy becomes Hope for the sake of Doc's notes. For Doc, these observations are personal. And in Happy's case, he seems hopeless. He's so caught up in himself that he's unable to see his way clear of his own shortcomings. Doc, though, doesn't think he's a lost cause. And he wants his notes to reflect that.

Meyers is perhaps the simplest of the soldiers to analyze. While the others have their quirks, Meyers seems settled. He's a classic combat soldier. Rather than retreating into a persona to deflect the mental trauma he's experienced, he's grounded. Doc is curious about him. His notes on Meyers go under the pseudonym Cat, being a play on the Dog Food squad Meyers heads up. Doc can't help but think Meyers is hiding behind his professionalism instead of a quirk of his personality like the others. Hiding, though, heightens trauma rather than dealing with it. Although Meyers seems solid, Doc has his doubts. He writes "*five to ten years for emergence*" in his notes, predicting that, once the war is over and Meyers has returned home, that's the timespan in which PTSD or Post-Traumatic Stress Disorder will emerge.

And what about him? What about Doc himself? He knows he's not immune to the stress of war. He may think he is, but that's a lie. People think lies are fibs they tell someone else, but Doc knows better. The most effective lies are the ones people tell themselves. And Doc knows he's not immune to PTSD. For all the scorn heaped on sociopaths and psychopaths, the one advantage they have over regular folk is that they're not subject to PTSD. Not caring has its benefits. Doc uses his journal to channel his thoughts and stop emotional trauma from building pressure like molten lava beneath Vesuvius.

Reluctantly, Doc makes notes about himself under the pseudonym Joshua. To anyone finding his writings after he's killed—*if* he's killed, he mentally corrects himself—there won't be an obvious correlation. Joshua was the actual name of Jesus. Few people realize Jesus would have been known to his Judean followers as Joshua ben Joseph of Nazareth or Joshua the son of Joseph from the village of Nazareth.

Jesus was a Greek name that didn't come to prominence among Christians for a couple of hundred years after his death and resurrection. Being Judean, the historical Jesus would have spoken Aramaic and Hebrew. He would have been known to his family and followers as Joshua. The Greek name Jesus would have sounded as strange to him as Pierre would to someone named Peter. Doc settles on Joshua for himself in his notes because it's a not-so-subtle reminder that he, Dr Christopher Walters, is *not* the Messiah. Doctors are sometimes criticized for playing God, but the truth is, they're just trying to do what's right. Often, though, there is no right decision, there's just a bunch of shitty options. Doc uses Joshua to remind himself he's not above suffering from PTSD. The more he's aware of that, the better he can manage his own mental health.

Doc came to the war wanting to make a difference. He's not naive. He's seen enough gunshot wounds in Chicago to know even survivable injuries can be crippling—and often for life. Scars run deeper than the mere scar tissue on the skin. And then there's the mental scars that linger. Being a trauma surgeon, he was initially assigned to a field hospital, but the intent was always to have him in the golden hour—and that meant on the battlefield. Shock kills more soldiers than blood loss. Stabilizing wounded soldiers and getting them to surgery within an hour of contact increases their survival rates by 500%. Dog Food's job is to keep Doc alive long enough to save others.

"Whatcha writing?" Meyers asks.

"Oh, uh... a book," Doc replies, being caught off guard. He was so focused on his observations that Sergeant Meyers took him off balance. He didn't mean to be quite that honest about his notes.

"A book?" Lavender asks, looking up from her card game. "What? Like some sci-fi crap?"

"Aw, hell, we're living that shit!" Leech says before Doc can reply.

Around the cramped dugout with its low ceiling, the squad comes to life, but in entirely different ways. Mouse opens one eye before closing it again. He's not asleep. He seems content to listen without contributing.

William Sunday scrunches her legs up in front of her, wrapping her arms around her knees. To call her motion a defensive posture is an understatement. Her body language screams of being hurt, but not physically. The way she clenches her hands over her forearms suggests she's shutting herself off, protecting herself emotionally, but from the war, not from the squad. She pops out one of her earplugs, making her intent clear. Like the others, she's curious about the newcomer. She wants to hear what's being discussed with Doc.

Hawk repacks his field kit, but like Mouse, his motion is a bluff. He's listening intently, pretending to be busy, allowing Meyers, Lavender and Leech to carry the conversation. Happy looks angry. The introverts are sheltering behind the extroverts.

"Ah, it's nothing, really," Doc says, closing the leather-bound journal and clutching it in his hand a little too defensively. William Sunday isn't the only one that wants to hide.

Meyers speaks. His voice conveys genuine support for Doc as an author. There's no judgment in his words.

"I think that's cool. Writing ain't easy. Trying to capture all those damn thoughts and arrange them in a logical manner. Ah, I think I'd give up after a few days."

"What's it about?" William Sunday asks, surprising Doc. She's taken out both earplugs now. The fluorescent orange plastic is squished between her fingers.

Doc can't lie to them. These soldiers are about to follow him onto the battlefield and protect his life while he triages the wounded. They deserve honesty.

"It's about the war... as seen from the perspective of a doctor."

"What's it called?" William Sunday asks, raising her chin out of interest.

Doc really wasn't prepared for this level of disclosure. Not so soon. He wanted to quietly observe not only the squad but life in the trenches for his book. The idea was to observe soldiers without being seen—like a conservationist in a hide watching ducks on a pond.

"*The Anatomy of Courage.*"

Doc is expecting a flurry of scorn from the Dog Food Squad, especially from Lavender and Leech, but there's quiet admiration. Even Hawk nods.

"And what is it?" Meyers asks. "What is courage?"

"Well, it's difficult to describe in a few words," Doc replies, feeling exposed. "That's why I'm putting it into a book. Oh, you've got your dictionary definitions and action-heroes in movies running around with guns blazing, but I think courage is something that has to be lived rather than defined."

No one responds to that point. The silence is strained. Doc feels awkward. He feels as though he has to say something authoritative on the subject.

"Ah, okay. So... Aristotle said virtues lie between the extremes of various vices. He thought of courage as lying somewhere between fearful and foolhardy."

"I like that," Mouse says, keeping his eyes shut.

"Duty," Lavender says. "That's what it is for me. I don't see courage in the trenches so much as honor and duty. We do what we have to, not what we want to."

"Courage is going over the top," Hawk says in a whisper. "Stepping into the darkness, not knowing if you're coming back but pushing on regardless."

William Sunday keeps her arms wrapped around her legs. Her head rests on her knees. She says, "Courage is being afraid but doing what needs to be done anyway."

"And there are lots of loudmouths out there," Leech says, pointing at the doorway. "They hide behind the bluster of courage. Anyone who talks a big game is a small-time bit player. They want everyone to think they're brave, but they're little children on the inside."

That Leech has focused on the negative is telling for Doc. Leech is bitter, but why? Is it his nature or because he's been emotionally hurt? Is this how he protects himself?

William Sunday replies to Leech, saying, "We're all little children on the inside."

"We are," Mouse says. "No one ever sees you for who you really are—only who they want you to be."

For someone of his bulk and stature, it's a remarkable insight. It's easy to see Mouse as strong because he's so physically imposing. Doc's sure Mouse could bench press him a dozen times without breaking a sweat, but that Mouse recognizes his physical strength throws out a stereotyped persona is quite profound. Only Mouse knows what lies in the depths of his heart, and he knows others can only guess at his reality. He knows what unravels in the darkness of his soul, and that takes courage to accept. It would be easy for him to ride on his physical strength and keep up a facade, but it wouldn't be honest. Doc respects his openness.

Leech says, "We're zombies, man. I mean, think about it. We

spend a third of our time asleep, a third in the trenches, and a third zoning out to escape this horror we call life. What is that? Cause it sure as hell ain't living!"

Happy is silent. He's the only one that hasn't said anything.

"What do you think?" Doc asks Happy, wanting to pry open his defenses.

"Oh, I... I'm not sure anyone wants to know what I think."

"Sure, we do," Lavender says, although Doc would have rather she remained silent and let him continue talking. Happy's fragile. Doc can see it in his eyes. There's what he feels he should say and what he desperately wants to say—and they are not the same thing. His eyes dart around, looking for someone else to speak and move the spotlight onto another person or another topic.

"It's okay," Doc says. "You're among friends."

Happy narrows his gaze, looking intently at Doc. He clenches his fists. His knuckles go white. Doc offers nothing but a warm smile in response, wanting to disarm him. Doc is reasonably sure he knows what Happy is thinking: *if we were friends, we'd be friendly, and we'd know each other's actual names.* Happy may not consider his squad to be friends, but camaraderie is all that holds them together out in no man's land. It's one thing to come to war for ideals such as protecting Europe, fighting the enemy or freeing the land, but all that dissolves when the people around you start dying.

War is little more than an abstract idea for most of humanity. It's news reports from among the ruins, accompanied by images of shell holes and bloodied clothes. But war isn't something that goes away when the television is turned off. Doc understands war becomes goddamn personal when the person next to you gets blown apart. Dog Food has lived this for over a year now.

"War," Happy says. "I—I'm not sure it can be described in terms of fear or courage or bravery. War is hell."

"War is worse than hell," Doc replies. He regrets his comment as soon as those words leave his lips. He's right, but he should have listened

22

rather than spoken. He should have encouraged Happy to elaborate. He should have drawn more heart out of him. Instead, he's inadvertently diverting the conversation away from Happy, which is precisely what the scrawny man wants.

"What do you mean, Doc?" Meyers asks.

"Ah, back in the Korean War, there was a field hospital just a few miles from the front line. They saw it all. Wounded soldiers from both sides, along with civilians, elderly men, women and children. I forget the name of the surgeon, but he was talking to a priest in the operating theater. He made the point that, in the Bible, hell is reserved for sinners. War, though, knows no such bounds. War will happily consume the innocent as well as the guilty, and that makes war worse than hell... We make the devil look tame."

"We do," Leech says.

"Not just us, Doc," William Sunday says. "Not anymore. The Novos will kill anyone in their way."

"Yep," Doc concedes, nodding.

Doc can't help but notice that Happy has used the discussion to hide once more. The others don't realize it, but Happy is struggling. He can't maintain eye contact with Doc.

Doc wants to rewind the conversation, but a high-pitched whistle breaks through the air, followed by a thundering impact that shakes the ground. Within seconds, hundreds of shells are falling all along the Front. There has been sporadic shelling throughout the day, but most of it fell well beyond their portion of the front line. Now, though, shells fall without pause, thundering into the earth.

The artillery barrage is designed to soften the ground, making it difficult for the Novos to advance and hide. They know humans come at night, but they don't know where they'll emerge from their long lines. The shells offer no clues, pummeling the hills and fields all along the Front. Dirt rains down within the trench from a nearby explosion. Whether it was deliberately dropped that close is hard to tell. It could have been a misfire. It could be part of the deception, misleading the Novos on where the trenches are located and which trenches are occupied.

William Sunday holds her hands over her ears. She must have her earplugs back in, and yet they're not enough to block out the thunder echoing around them. Physically, they would dull the noise, but she's reacting emotionally to the barrage.

Outside, it sounds as though the gods are unleashing a vicious storm, punishing humanity. Flashes of lightning accompany the explosions, but this is from the Novos intercepting shells in midair. The sheer number of shells fired by the US Army ensures the majority get through, but the Novos match the army's ferocity with jagged streaks of lightning cutting through the night. From within their trench, eerie blue lights flicker across the wooden beams.

Dust falls from the ceiling as a shell apparently lands on top of them. In practice, it wouldn't be a direct hit, or they'd be dead, but to Doc, it feels as though the high explosive shell struck immediately above the thick wooden beams supporting the roof. It's then he realizes the shells that fall short must have been struck by the Novos' lightning weapon. The physics of momentum keeps these shells flying forward, but whatever energy is imparted by the lightning itself either redirects them or causes them to fall short.

William Sunday is shaking. She has her head down, with her face buried in her knees. The others are all staring at the ceiling, waiting for a stray shell to burst through the wooden timber and end the war for them.

Doc gets up. He rests his hand on her shoulder, saying, "Hey."

William Sunday reacts as though she's been struck by the Novos' lightning weapon. She jumps as if shocked by electricity, but she keeps her arms wrapped around her legs. Her face is pale. Her eyes are bloodshot. Tears stream down her cheeks.

"Leave her," Meyers says, standing beside him.

Doc is already crouching, wanting to get on the same level as William Sunday, trying to connect with someone who's overwhelmed with panic.

"It's okay."

"No. It's not," she spits back at him. "It'll never be okay."

Doc is taken aback by the venom in her words, but he keeps his hand on her shoulder, knowing touch speaks louder than anything he could say. William Sunday hasn't shrugged him away. She could, and he'd respect that, but she seems to warm to his touch. Her breathing slows beneath his fingers. She might not say anything, but she seems to appreciate him breaking through the social taboo of touch between soldiers. The army would have them operate as machines, but Doc knows they'll always be human.

Meyers speaks softly amidst the staccato of hundreds of shells raining down in no man's land.

"She was there... in *Novosibirsk* when they landed."

"You've seen them," Doc mumbles.

William Sunday nods but refuses to acknowledge him beyond that. She keeps her head facing toward the far wall where Mouse is sitting quietly, listening intently to their conversation. Tears continue to roll down her cheeks. She makes no attempt to wipe them away.

Doc has seen satellite surveillance photos and mock-ups of the Novos, but very few people have seen the aliens up close and lived to talk about them. Little is known about these creatures beyond their aggression and the way they seek to displace Earth's ecosphere with their own biosphere. Far from being a single species, like *Homo sapiens*, they're composite beings. In a similar way to how humans are made up of organs and limbs working together as an intrinsic whole to form a body, the Novos are formed by combining seemingly independent creatures. And their body parts are interchangeable based on need. They can have two, three, or even eight arms, depending on what they're trying to accomplish. They can run on two legs, four or six if they need to carry heavy loads. And there seems to be some kind of psychic link between their parts. They can separate to accomplish a goal and then recombine, with each individual part acting autonomously. The closest terrestrial analog is the octopus, where each arm has its own brain and can act independently while still coordinating as part of a whole.

No two Novos are the same on the battlefield, making them insanely difficult to combat. And they mimic human tactics. Humans build trenches and dugouts, so the Novos build canals and tunnels. Humans shell no man's land to deny them access to the battlefield, and the Novos respond in kind, hurling boulders upwards of forty miles. No one is sure how they accomplish that without chemical propellants, but as it matches the distance of the best howitzers of the US Army, it means the two armies are kept at bay by heavy weapons.

Meyers says, "She'll be fine once the shelling stops."

"No, she won't," Doc says. "She's suffering from severe PTSD. She needs to be evac'd from—"

Doc doesn't get to finish his sentence. William Sunday wheels around and grabs his shirt by the collar. She yanks Doc toward her, pulling him so close they almost touch. At this distance, his eyes can't focus on hers.

"I—ain't—going—nowhere. Got it?"

Reluctantly, Doc nods.

She releases her grip, and he slips away from her, stumbling back to his feet. William Sunday breathes deeply. She wraps her arms around her legs, hugging her knees against her chest once more. Her eyes, though, are no longer full of tears but rather fury.

"It's personal, Doc," Meyers says.

"Oh, yeah, I got that," Doc replies.

Both of them are still standing beside William Sunday, knowing she can hear everything they say and knowing she doesn't give a damn.

Meyers says, "I know you mean well, but you've got to understand, out here, we deal with trauma in our own way. We take it over the top."

"I'm not sure that's—"

"No, it ain't healthy," Meyers says, cutting him off. "It's war. Nothing about war is healthy. It's about holding the line. It's about protecting others. It's about surviving."

"I know. I know."

Meyers isn't finished. "We're out here so those goddamn things don't tear through Chelyabinsk the way they tore through Krasnoyarsk and Irkutsk because, if they do, the next stop is Moscow, Warsaw, Berlin and then Paris. As for London and Washington... I don't know about you, Doc, but I wouldn't bet on the ocean stopping these fuckers."

"This is our planet," William Sunday says with pale cheeks and snot running from her nose. She still isn't facing them. She's looking at Mouse as she speaks. She points at the bench in front of her, pointing down at the ground. "We stop them here."

"We do," Meyers says, backing away, and Doc gets a glimpse into how he's held the squad together. At first, Doc saw Meyers as a grunt. He thought of him as a sergeant only as a means of providing structure to the team. Now, he realizes he's the glue that holds them all together. Doc follows his lead, leaving William Sunday with a grim look on her face. The pain she holds inside must be tearing her apart, but she's right. For her, being on the Front is a way of dealing with the loss of her home and her family. It's not anger or hatred that stirs within her, but rather defiance.

As Doc sits back down at his makeshift desk, he's acutely aware that the eyes of the others are on him. It's tempting to feel shame and a sense of inadequacy. He blundered while trying to help William Sunday, but mistakes made out of kindness are easily forgiven and mostly forgotten. He can see that in the eyes of Lavender and Leech. Neither is shy of voicing an opinion. Their silence is respect.

Lavender gets up quietly and sits behind William Sunday, who's still sitting with her legs up in front of her and her arms wrapped around her knees. Lavender reaches around, hugging her. William Sunday buries her head into Lavender's forearm. They're close. They understand each other. In the midst of the war, there's love. Doc is fascinated to see how Lavender drops her extrovert persona, matching William Sunday's demeanor and providing comfort. The two women are at peace in the midst of the bombardment. They appreciate each other.

As the shells rain down outside, thundering into the ground like giants trampling the land, Doc slips his journal into his pack.

He's taken enough notes for one day.

No Man's Land

After what seems like hours, the shelling stops. Rather than slowing to a trickle, the bombardment thunders into silence, with the last dozen or so shells all falling within seconds of each other all along the Front. Once the tremors have passed, an ominous silence falls.

"Here we go," Leech mumbles.

The sound of whistles echoes along the trench. The nearby screeches are loud but only in short bursts. A clear signal is repeated up and down the line. It's coded, being blown in Morse Code. The Novos can hear it as well as the humans, but it replicates for the whole one hundred and fifty miles that span the front lines. Multiple incursions will have been set by military planners for a variety of reasons, not all of which are known to those going over the top. Out in the trenches, most squads will be stood down. The unlucky will be given their orders and sent up wooden ladders. All Doc knows is that some poor bastard from their stretch is going to be mowed down up there in no man's land, and Dog Food has been tasked with finding them and dragging them back.

Doc has been reading up on the stats. During the battle for Fallujah in Iraq, one of the bloodiest fights since World War II, the casualty rate was five percent, while the fatality rate was just under one percent. Against the Novos, it is almost twice that, with one in ten soldiers being wounded during a raid. Those aren't the kind of odds that inspire gallantry. Before the advent of field evacs being undertaken by specialist teams like the Dog Food Squad, the fatality rate alone was five percent. Almost half of all those wounded would die in the mud and grime of no man's land. Field evacs took that down to less than one percent, which helped restore morale.

Outside, boots thunder up rickety ladders. The shelling begins again, but it's no longer like torrential rain. The Novos know humans are coming, so the second wave of artillery has two goals. The first is to protect advancing troops by walking the barrage forward in front of the soldiers as they cross no man's land. The second is to confuse the Novos, walking shells forward in front of no one at all to hide the point of attack as long as possible.

"All right," Meyers says. "Get your shit together."

William Sunday looks strangely relaxed. It must have been the frequency and intensity of the shelling that triggered her PTSD. To Doc, the sporadic shelling is just as terrifying, but she seems calm. She has her backpack on and is ready to go, sitting on the edge of the bench seat next to him.

Doc opens his medi-kit on a crate. It has only just been delivered by the quartermaster and is fully stocked, but Doc wants to familiarize himself with the layout. Working in the dark, with shells falling around him, he has to be able to find whatever he needs quickly and efficiently.

"What's that?" William Sunday asks, pointing at a white tube roughly two feet long with a diameter of half a foot. Velcro straps hold it in place, but it takes up almost a third of his pack, limiting the supplies he can carry.

"Bulky," Doc replies. "That's what it is. The damn thing takes up too much space."

"Is it an EPR?"

Doc looks at her, surprised she recognizes the unusual medical device. "Yes, it is." He rests his hand on it. "It's an Emergency Preservation and Resuscitation unit undergoing field trials."

"They told us something like this was coming."

Doc is intrigued by her curiosity. "Ah, it's experimental. The challenge is how to run it without electronics. Back in the US, these are computer-controlled. Out here, it's mechanical, so it doesn't attract Novo attention."

"How does it work?"

"Well," Doc says. "It's designed to fit as a sleeve over the arm or thigh and cool the blood to about 60 degrees."

"Sixty?" a surprised William Sunday says. "That's hot!"

"Oh, in Fahrenheit. Not Celsius. In Celsius, it's about 15 degrees."

"Ah."

"In theory, it will extend the survivability of a patient with severe blood loss from two minutes to two or three hours."

"But?"

Doc taps two old-fashioned thermometers on the outside of the EPR. They're positioned next to a bulky, chrome-plated flask. "This is the nitrogen store. It's a vacuum flask cooled to negative three hundred. It'll last for about four days without a recharge, but every twelve hours, any gas needs to be vented. That's what this pressure gauge here indicates."

"And the other thermometer?"

"That's the patient's blood temperature."

"But won't they die if they get that cold?" she asks. It's a good question. It's a better question than any of the questions he asked during training.

"At this point," Doc says, "They're already dead."

"They're dead???"

"If they're not already dead," Doc says, "then I have to kill them by stopping their heart."

William Sunday's eyes go wide.

"This is the end of the road," Doc says, patting the EPR. "If you see me strapping this on to someone, they're effectively dead. This baby, though, can keep the body cool enough that the brain is able to survive. Get them into an ER within an hour or so, and we can bring them back."

"Cool," William Sunday says.

"In more ways than one," Doc replies.

"But you don't like it?"

"Oh, I love it. The problem is that it takes up space. And it's heavy. And that means I don't have as much room for plasma and bandages and can only carry one oxygen cylinder."

"And?" William Sunday says. Doc is impressed by the young private. She's perceptive. There's something in his tone of voice or perhaps his body language that suggests he's holding back, and she's not afraid to pry and ask why.

"And it's one shot. If there are two or more soldiers with severe blood loss, I have to play God and decide who survives."

He hangs his head, looking down at the backpack. For Doc, playing God is horrifying. Far from feeling powerful, he feels sick when he has to make life-and-death decisions. In medical school, he was drilled to remain impersonal and make clinical decisions without second-guessing himself. In practice, it's never that easy.

Doc's fingers run over the contents of the pack, feeling for the surgical scissors, clamps and single-use, disposable scalpels, memorizing their location and feel. He notes the position of clotting sponges, chest seals, splints, pain management medication and circulatory support drugs. These have been mounted with velcro on the inside of the pack.

"You're not playing God," William Sunday says, "You're being human. You're giving us a chance."

Doc nods but doesn't reply. It's strange. She's made him uncomfortable when, a little over an hour ago, he was trying to comfort her.

"You'll do good out there, Doc," she says, getting up and tapping the EPR.

She walks over to join Lavender. Doc continues going through his pack. He doesn't need to, but it's a way of quelling his nerves. Lavender and William Sunday laugh about something. They're jovial, which for Doc seems surreal when they're all about to head into no man's land.

Hawk walks outside into snowflakes falling lightly from an

overcast sky. He stands in front of the entrance to the dugout, listening to the sounds of battle in the distance. If he has any fear, it doesn't show.

Meyers is still sitting beside the entrance within reach of an old-fashioned telephone. The handset is made from thick, durable plastic. There are two brass bells above the phone. A small hammer set between them is attached to a solenoid, ready to strike the bells repeatedly as soon as the faintest electrical impulse comes down the line.

Mouse gets up and joins Hawk outside. He's so tall he can't stand upright within the dugout and has to crouch going through the doorway. His backpack has several folded aluminum stretchers strapped to it. He's the pack mule of the squad.

Time crawls. Sporadic gunfire breaks out. Shells continue to fall. Lightning ripples across the sky, but not from the low-lying clouds.

Lavender looks at Doc. "Nervous?"

Doc won't lie. "Yes."

"Good. Nerves will keep you alive up there."

Doc nods. He knows she's right. The stats are clear. The first few excursions into no man's land have the highest fatality rate. He's not sure why front-line experience plays such a big role in survivability, but it does. He's determined to follow whatever advice the squad provides.

William Sunday says, "Don't worry, Doc. We've got your back up there."

Doc nods. The transformation in William Sunday's demeanor is stark. Her professionalism is beyond dispute. It's as though he's dealing with an entirely different person.

Leech says, "Remember. Stay low. Keep to the shell holes. Don't stand upright. Move in short bursts. And if we come under fire, move, move, move! You're going to want to hide, but don't. You're going to want to stay where you are, but don't. You'll give them an easy target. Stay close, and we'll get you back here, okay?"

"Okay," Doc says, rubbing his sweaty hands together. He fixes a lanyard to his glasses, looping it over the back of his neck so if they fall from his nose, they won't tumble into the mud.

Happy's the only one who hasn't switched gears mentally. He mumbles to himself as he swings his pack up on his back and picks up his rifle. Without saying anything to the others, he heads out to join Mouse and Hawk in the trench.

"You should take a piss," Lavender says rather unceremonially.

"I—uh."

"It doesn't matter whether you need to or not; you should empty your bladder. 'Cause once you get to the top of that ladder, your body is going to tell you that you need to go."

"Right. Of course," Doc says.

The lowest corner of the dugout contains a latrine bucket. Throughout the night, various members of the squad have used it. Privacy isn't a concern, as no one cares. Doc gets up and relieves himself with a trickle rather than a flow. Some kind of blue liquid in the bucket acts as a sanitizer of sorts. As he's shaking the last few drops, the bells on the phone sound behind him. A tiny hammer strikes the brass with a burst of noise that startles him. Within a fraction of a second, Meyers has the handset up against his ear.

He listens for a moment before replying, "Dog Food is clear for Charlie-Seven."

Doc has seen the codes laid out on the map of this part of the Front pinned to the wall. Someone's used a ruler to scribe charcoal lines on the map, dividing it up like a chess board or perhaps like some more exotic fantasy role-playing game. Charlie is the third square along, while Seven is the seventh square into no man's land. As their dugout is in Echo, they need to go several hundred yards west and then north, which is to their left and then over the top into no man's land.

"Seven," a concerned Lavender says. "That's deep. I was hoping we'd get something a little closer for Doc's first jaunt."

Although Doc can see the seventh square in the Charlie column, it's only now that it clicks that the wounded are seven hundred yards away from the trenches. Seven hundred yards is a helluva long way to go through shell holes and muddy fields. The Novos are at ten to twelve.

34

Dog Food is going to be a mere three hundred yards from the enemy position.

Doc swallows the lump rising in his throat, knowing he could die out there. Tonight. Death is always a possibility in life. No one wants to acknowledge that, but humans are only ever a heartbeat away from death. Whether it's in a heart attack, a car accident, drowning in the lake, or falling from a ladder, no one wakes up thinking they'll die on any given day, and yet people do. For Doc, it's sobering to know his odds could be settled with the roll of a couple of dice.

And the problem with statistics is that they're generalizations drawn from past activity. They're a rough guide, nothing more. Doc would like to see stats based on the distance from the front lines. No, he decides. He wouldn't. The survivability from five is probably twice that at seven, if not more. The closer they get to the Novos, the worse their odds become.

Doc grabs his pack and joins Dog Food as they form up in the mud. Meyers stands on one of the logs lining the trench, allowing him to tower over them.

"Mouse."

"Got it," Mouse replies, and Doc feels his medical pack lifting off his back.

"What? No," he says, turning side on as Mouse plucks his medical kit from his shoulders. "I can carry my fair share."

Meyers says, "We need you alive out there, Doc. And in one piece."

Doc tightens his lips. As much as he doesn't want to agree with Meyers, the sergeant is right. Keeping him fresh is more important than any notion of fairness. Since when has being fair been a consideration in war?

Mouse wears Doc's medical pack on his front, carrying it over his chest.

"All right. Here's what we know. A snatch-and-grab has gone bad. We've got forty out there spread over two squares. They're reporting three wounded, so we've got three WIA we need to haul back here."

Happy mumbles, "So far..."

"And KIA?" William Sunday asks.

Doc is fascinated by how freely they used these terms, pronouncing the acronym WIA as wire and KIA as though it fell somewhere between tire and mire. Back in the hospital, the team he worked with spelled out the acronym each time, accentuating each of the letters. On the Front, these terms have become words of their own.

Meyers seems reluctant to reply to William Sunday. His jaw tightens as he clenches his teeth, struggling with what to tell them about those killed-in-action.

"Seven."

"Fuck. So that's ten in all? Ten out of forty?"

"Yeah, it's bad out there. Okay, we need to roll."

With that, Meyers drops into the trench and starts a light jog along the boardwalk. Soldiers press themselves against the muddy walls of the trench, making room for them as they pass. They lower their eyes. It's not difficult to understand why. Not everyone's coming back.

Doc jogs alongside William Sunday. Under his breath, he asks, "Ten is bad, huh?"

"It reduces their fighting capability," she replies with her pack bouncing on her back. "And that fragments both offense and defense. They've lost a quarter of their fighting force. They'll hold out as long as they can, but those numbers are only going to go up. At some point, they need to cut and run."

"At what point?" Doc asks as they cross a T-intersection in the trench. Mud splashes from their boots as they jog on.

"Conventional wisdom," William Sunday says between breaths, "is to pull back when you hit ten percent. Fifteen max... They should have retreated with four or five soldiers down. Sounds like they got hit hard and fast."

Doc doesn't reply. The attacking force is already down by 25%. The implication is that Dog Food could get out there to find the troops pulling back, leaving the severely wounded to die. And then what? What can a squad of eight do where forty failed? They'll also be recalled, having risked their lives for nothing.

Meyers comes to a halt beside a wooden ladder leading up out of the trench. He stands at the bottom, hitting each of his soldiers on their packs and yelling, "Go. Go. Go!" as they thunder up the rungs. Mud and slush spray from their boots as they rush up the ladder.

Doc reaches the rickety wooden ladder. Meyers drags him to one side, allowing William Sunday to climb first. It's not until the last soldier has cleared the top of the trench that Meyers pushes Doc forward, slapping him on the shoulder.

"Go!"

On either side of the ladder, regular soldiers stand on raised wooden platforms, peering into the night from behind sandbags. They have rifles leveled at the darkness. Doc tries to rush up the ladder, but it shakes and flexes beneath him. He pushes on, aware of the need to get over the top as quickly as possible to reduce his profile against the night sky. He swings a leg up over the last rung, looking at the mud and dirt on the other side, when a hand grabs him and hauls him over the edge, dragging him down into the shadows.

"Mouse?" he says, surprised by the strength with which he was manhandled.

"William," is the soft, feminine reply from the darkness.

Mud squelches beneath another pair of boots. Meyers sinks into the shell hole beside him. From where they are, Doc can't see anything beyond the rim some twenty feet away. Brackish water sits at the bottom of the crater. It stinks. Rats scurry through the shadows. Dog Food edge their way around the shell hole, following muddy boot prints, keeping to the lowest path between craters. They move in silence. Above them, lightning crackles through the clouds, casting an eerie blue glow over the battlefield. Unlike terrestrial lightning, it lingers for almost a minute, slowly fading.

The squad marches in silence, staying low, keeping to the shadows. Nothing could prepare Doc for the devastation in no man's land. They creep through the basement of a collapsed house, stepping

37

over fallen beams. Snowflakes drift by innocently, coming down from above with a sense of calm that is entirely misplaced. Ice forms on the top of puddles, cracking beneath their boots. A collapsed wall gives them passage back to the battlefield. Bricks have been stacked by soldiers to form a makeshift set of stairs that wobble beneath them.

Doc reaches up and tightens the strap on his helmet. A direct hit from one of the alien energy weapons will slice through the Kevlar like soft butter, but at least death will be instant. The helmet's value comes from protecting him from the rocks and dirt thrown up by the artillery being used by both sides.

The ground shakes under a nearby impact. The flash of the explosion briefly lights up the night. Doc reaches out a gloved hand, taking hold of a tree root within the crater to steady himself. Dirt showers the squad. Rocks pelt them, raining down from a darkened sky. It's only then that Doc realizes he's taken hold of the rear leg of a dead horse. The animal is mostly buried. Its bloated stomach protrudes from the soft dirt. Its head is missing, having been severed halfway down its broad neck. Blood soaks its mane. Doc lets go as abruptly as he grabbed the hoof.

"Damn, that was close," Meyers says from two soldiers ahead of him. "Where are we on the order of attack?"

Another explosion rocks the night. A wall of dirt is thrown into the darkness, coming down on them like hail.

"Fuck," Happy cries aloud, crouching and trying to make himself as small as possible.

A few red headlights on helmets illuminate the shadows. Lavender has a wax-covered map out. It's folded and covered in markings and timings written with a grease pencil. Arrows and numbers show exit and entry approaches.

"We're in the right place," she says, pointing at the map. "Right time. Those fuckers back there, though, don't know shit about barrage accuracy."

Meyers says, "Hawk. Let them know they're dropping early in Charlie-Three. Tell them we're crossing to Delta-Three, then back to Charlie-Four."

"Jesus," William Sunday says from beside Doc. He didn't even see her moving up in the shadows within the crater. "It's one thing to get fucked up out here, but by your own goddamn artillery—that sucks. They don't know what the hell they're doing."

Happy says, "They don't care."

Hawk winds the crank on the side of a black box and raises the headset. He has to tilt his helmet sideways to get the receiver to his ear. As he's sending their position and movements, another shell explodes. This one is so close that a wall of dirt rushes over the shell hole they're crouching in like a wave at the beach. Rocks rain down on them as smoke billows into the sky. The sound is deafening, leaving Doc with ringing in his ears.

"Yes," Hawk yells into the phone. "That was you, you dumb fuck! You're dropping short, goddamn it."

He hangs up, packs up his phone and fiddles with the wire spool, making sure it's free-flowing as they continue on.

Meyers falls into the side of the shell hole beside Hawk, almost directly opposite Doc, having crept back after conferring with Happy and Lavender over the map.

"What did they say?"

"They said we're running off yesterday's order of battle."

"And are we?"

"No, they're using tomorrow's charts."

"Fucking idiots!"

"They know now," Hawk says. "We should be fine from here."

William Sunday says, "When you pay peanuts, you get chimps."

Leech says, "We need to keep moving before they drop one right on top of us."

"Yeah," Lavender says in response to him. "I don't trust those fuckers back there."

Meyers says, "Happy, Lavender. You're on point at a separation of twenty meters. Mouse and Leech. You're out wide at fifty, back twenty.

Doc is in the middle with Sunday. I'll bring up the rear with Hawk. Okay, we've got some ground to cover. Let's get this done."

Doc looks back at the front line. He can just make out the silhouette of guards on the edge of the trench roughly a hundred yards away. As exposed as he felt back there, the trench seems idyllic by comparison.

Flashes of light rip across no man's land as shelling continues along the Front. It's impossible to know if the Novos are on the move as well. The aliens have raided trenches before, but a war of attrition has set in, with both sides digging in for the long haul.

Dog Food follows Lavender, who's working from the map, leading them through gaps in the razor-sharp concertina wire. They cross wooden bridges spanning abandoned trenches. Bodies lie in the mud. They're little more than silhouettes in the darkness.

Lavender is deft, seemingly drifting above the ground rather than touching it. She moves with grace. Doc watches as she crouches in a shell hole ahead of them, briefly turning on her red headlamp and checking the map before leading them hard left. A few minutes later, shells rain down on the muddy hill they just skirted. With no electronic devices, there's no way to use GPS to track their movement. Lavender works off landmarks, matching them to her map.

They reach the remains of a forest. Wooden boards have been laid down to allow soldiers to cross a swampy section before emerging within a stand of dead trees. The trunks have been denuded. Most of the trees have been severed at a height of ten to fifteen feet, with their trunks being splintered like matchwood. Shrapnel has been embedded in the wood, making it look as though the trunks are covered in thorns. They're in a depression, which gives them more visibility than the high ground as they can see the approaches from all directions without being exposed to enemy fire.

Lavender comes to a halt beside an overturned wooden cart with old-fashioned spoke wheels. She crouches, using it for cover as she checks the map.

William Sunday tugs softly on Doc's sleeve, urging him down.

"What?" he whispers, crouching beside her. She doesn't reply. Her eyes, though, peer hard to the right, out beyond the cart where Lavender is sheltering. There's movement on the ridge. Doc blinks, trying to make sense of what he's seeing. If he were asked to describe the creature, he'd swear it was made up of tentacles rather than arms or legs. Given the briefing he had back in the states and the intelligence photos he's seen, the view before him is confusing. The Novos look nothing like he imagined. Peering through the shattered stumps of dozens of darkened trees, the Novo seems to move by creeping forward rather than stepping.

Happy is out in front of the squad. He's exposed. He's within ten to fifteen yards of the creature on that flank. He has his back to a tree trunk, keeping it between him and the alien. He's got his rifle up in front of him, ready to swing to either side and fire. His eyes, though, are on Meyers, looking for guidance. William Sunday is down in a kneeling position, with her rifle pointing at the creature. Her elbow rests on her knee, allowing her to steady her aim.

Happy stays still as the creature passes. He's blind to the alien's movement, hiding behind the shattered trunk. Meyers uses short, sharp hand signals, telling Happy when to step sideways so as to keep the dead tree between him and the Novo. Meyers keeps his hand in front of his chest so the motion is only visible to someone specifically looking for it in the dark. With his camouflaged uniform, the staggered signals could easily be mistaken for a scrap of cloth blowing in the wind or the motion of a rat creeping through the shadows.

Hawk is on the phone, talking to someone back at Command.

William Sunday taps Doc on the shoulder. She's pointing well behind and beyond Happy. Several more Novos are moving through the decimated forest, using it for cover.

"We're fucked," she whispers. "We are so totally fucked."

"What? Why?" Doc asks in a hushed reply, at least wanting to understand the reason he's about to die.

"They're a flanking squad. They're trying to get around our boys and set up a crossfire or perhaps an ambush during their retreat."

"What are we going to do?"

"Nothing. I make eight to ten. There's probably more. There are too many of them to engage."

From the shallow, muddy shell hole they're crouching within, William Sunday looks back at Hawk. She may not say anything, but Doc knows what she's thinking: their only option is to bring in an artillery strike directly on their position.

"Oh, no," Doc whispers.

Seconds later, a high-pitched whistle echoes across the battlefield.

"Incoming," William Sunday says.

She grabs Doc and pushes him face-first into the mud at the bottom of the shell hole, smothering him with her body. Filthy water swirls up over his face, covering his mouth and seeping into his nose. Doc struggles, but William Sunday holds him still. He can't breathe. She doesn't care. He twists and turns, wanting to get his head above the putrid water. William Sunday uses her forearm and elbow to pin his head in the mud as shells thump into the ground around them. Then, the world turns white.

Doc doesn't hear the shell that explodes next to them, but he feels it. Several explosions thump through his body in rapid succession, shaking his bones. The ground moves like the sloshing wave of someone jumping in a swimming pool, rising and falling as though it were on the ocean. Rocks and boulders fly through the air. William Sunday is blown off Doc. Her body tumbles across the battlefield, kicking up mud and colliding with the stump of a tree.

A wave of heat washes over Doc, searing the skin on his face. A fireball rises into the night, lighting up no man's land with a deathly yellow glow. Flames cling to shattered trees. Someone's yelling, but all he can hear is muted tones. It takes Doc a moment to realize he's the one who's screaming. He's sitting in the mud, surrounded by blue alien blood. A severed spider-like leg writhes near his boots.

A muddy, gloved hand wraps over his mouth but not his nose, silencing him. William Sunday has blood dripping from a gash on her forehead. Smoke rises from her smoldering backpack.

"Shhhh," she whispers, holding a finger to her lips. She lets go of his mouth.

Doc is in shock. His ears are ringing. Ice water has seeped inside his uniform, wetting his thermal underwear and chilling him to the bone. He shivers, but whether that's from shock or the cold, he's unsure. Perhaps it's both.

Fires have broken out across no man's land, burning in pockets and lighting up the muddy shell holes.

"Stay here," William Sunday whispers. "I'm going after Leech."

Doc hasn't given any thought to anyone other than Happy out in front of them, but Mouse and Leech were out wide on their flanks. The barrage came down right on top of them.

William Sunday slips her pack from her back and staggers on with her rifle pressed hard into her shoulder. She stabs at the dirt with her boots. William Sunday is walking on unsteady legs. It's as though she's drunk and fighting to walk in a straight line. Her rifle, though, remains perfectly steady as she creeps on. Fires flicker around her, lighting up her face. Her helmet is gone, having been blown off her head. Her hair has been singed.

Hawk appears beside Doc, moving in complete silence like a ghost. He follows William Sunday into the darkness. Meyers splashes through the mud, rushing up to Doc. He grabs his arms, feeling them for breaks and checking Doc's physical response, looking for any grimace from pain. Meyers moves down to his hips and legs, squeezing hard to feel through the thick material.

"I'm good. I'm fine," Doc says.

William Sunday staggers back through the haze and smoke, dragging Leech with her. She has his right arm draped over her shoulder. He shuffles, barely able to walk. His boots kick at the dirt. Hawk helps her down the side of the crater.

Mouse comes in from the other flank.

"My pack," Doc says as William Sunday rests Leech on the side of the shell hole. Doc's boots slide into the muddy water, but he's beyond caring. Mouse dumps his pack in the mud.

Doc rummages around in the medical pack. It's been carefully designed to treat major trauma injuries on the battlefield and unfolds into four parts when unzipped, laying out the equipment and supplies he needs as effectively as any nurse in the ER. Doc reaches up and switches on the LED light on his helmet, turning it from red to white.

"Keep it red," Meyers grumbles.

"I need to see what I'm doing," Doc replies, ignoring him.

William Sunday opens Leech's jacket and unbuttons his shirt, exposing his chest. Vapor rises from his warm skin.

"Fuck, fuck, fuck," Meyers mumbles, getting up and grabbing his rifle. "Keep it short."

"Understood," Doc replies.

Meyers addresses the others. "Hawk. Mouse. Lavender. Happy. Spread out. Search the area. Make sure we have clean kills out there."

No one replies. The soldiers vanish like phantoms, disappearing into the shadows. Occasionally, a single shot rings out nearby as they kill wounded Novos.

Doc adjusts his light, pointing it down at an angle. Battery-powered LEDs are some of the few electronic devices the team can use on the battlefield. It's the simplicity of the circuitry. Low current. Simple, steady electrical drawdown. LEDs are as close to organic as anything electronic can be, but even they need to be shielded and used sporadically. Get too close to a Novo, and the aliens can smell the LEDs burning through electrons.

Doc pulls off his leather gloves, tucking them in his jacket pocket. As Leech isn't bleeding, he doesn't bother with sterile disposable gloves. He touches lightly at Leech's ribs, starting from up beneath his armpits and working down his side. Leech flinches. Purple welts have already formed on the private's stomach, but Doc ignores that for now, checking the shape and position of his ribs and touching his sternum.

Doc's fingers brush against Leech's stomach. The private flexes in agony, pulling away from him.

Doc turns off his light.

"Okay, you've got a few cracked ribs, but they haven't separated. And they haven't broken, so you're in no danger of a punctured lung. Your spleen, though, and possibly one of your kidneys, has ruptured. You're bleeding internally. How bad? It's impossible to tell. We need to get you back to the line."

"Not without a WIA," Leech says.

"You *are* a WIA," Doc counters, matching Leech's pronunciation as wire, even though his training has him wanting to spell out the acronym W. I. A.

"I'm okay."

"No. You're not. You can't go on, Leech. You'll die if you go forward."

"And I'll die if I go back," Leech replies through gritted teeth.

"There ain't a lot of options out here, Doc," William Sunday says. "Leech knows the odds. If he heads back now, he goes alone. We need everyone else for the rescue."

Leech spits dark blood from his mouth. "And if I collapse on the way back, you'll never find me. No, my best chance is to continue on and stick with the squad."

He bites on a morphine stick, chewing on it.

"Sweet Jesus," Doc says, prepping a syringe with an experimental circulatory support drug designed to slow internal bleeding. Leech grimaces as Doc injects it just below his ribs. "Listen. I'm going to wrap a compression bandage around your abdomen. That'll help hold things in place. The pressure will reduce the internal bleeding and buy you some time, but we need to get you into surgery."

"Ain't happening," Leech replies.

"What else, Doc?" William Sunday asks. "What else can you do for Leech?"

The look in her eyes is one of longing. She's hoping for a miracle, but there are none, not here, not in the middle of no man's land. Not as shells rain down along the Front. Not as lightning ripples through the clouds. Not as monsters stalk them in the dark.

"Ah, the cold," Doc says. "We need to keep you cool. It'll slow down the bleeding."

No sooner have those words left his lips than William Sunday has Leech up and leaning forward. She strips his jacket from him along with his shirt. Moisture rises from his skin into the night, drifting like the smoke from newly formed shell holes. Purple bruises mar his pale skin. Doc binds his chest and abdomen with two elastic compression bandages. It won't do much beyond restricting the movement of his cracked ribs, but he can see Leech gaining strength. William Sunday helps him stand.

"I'm good to go," Leech says as Doc repacks his medical kit.

"I don't like this," Doc says, feeling conflicted, knowing his priority has to be the injured in the raiding party.

William Sunday says, "None of us like this, Doc. Not a single one of us."

As they climb out of the shell hole, a wounded Novo squirms, half-buried beneath the dirt. Only one of its spider-like legs is visible. William Sunday points her rifle down and fires. The shot is deafening, causing Doc to flinch. The alien convulses and shakes before falling still.

Doc feels sick.

Waking the Dead

As they approach Charlie-Seven, the crack of gunfire can be heard over the shells falling along the Front.

Meyers slides into a shell hole, kicking up dirt as he comes to a halt beside Leech.

"How you holding up, soldier?"

Leech doesn't reply. His head hangs low. He's got one arm wrapped around his ribs, clutching at the bandages. He offers a thumbs up. It's a lie, but one no one is going to question.

Meyers addresses Doc and William Sunday.

"Listen, there's a collapsed trench about thirty yards to your right. That's the triage point. Alpha Kilo's medic has dragged the dead and dying there. Time to do your thing, Doc. I'm going to move up in support of Alpha Kilo along with Lavender, Happy and Hawk. We'll provide you with cover fire. You'll have Mouse and William Sunday on stretcher duty along with whoever else is in the trench."

"And me," Leech manages with a grimace. Although Meyers doesn't specifically address his comment, he nods in passive agreement. No one is fooled by Leech's bravado. In reality, he should be on one of those stretchers.

"I'll see if I can get a couple of stretcher-bearers from Alpha Kilo. Get the wounded stabilized and on the move. We'll lay down suppressing fire once you're ready to roll. Got it?"

"Got it," Doc replies.

Meyers scrambles up over the dirt embankment and disappears into the low-lying fog hanging over the battlefield. Doc peers beneath the bandage on Leech's abdomen. His stomach is almost black with bruising. Leech needs to be in surgery.

"This way," William Sunday says, hoisting Leech's good arm over her shoulder and dragging him on.

Explosions flash across no man's land, lighting up the battlefield. There's no flat ground anywhere. So many shells and boulders have fallen that the earth has been turned as if it's been plowed in preparation for sowing seeds in the field of a giant. With each step, Doc's boots either slide in the soft dirt or splash in stagnant puddles. Snow and ice clings to the mud. Scraps of concertina wire protrude from the mud, along with the occasional blackened arm or a boot still attached to a bony leg.

Doc swallows the lump in his throat. Working in the ER back in Chicago, he's seen death, and not just any death, not simply the death of someone succumbing quietly to old age, but the death of a child hit by a car or a teen shot by a stray bullet. Death is always heartbreaking, but here on the battlefield, it's raw. It's profane. It's an insult to life.

Rats scurry through the darkness. A pack of wild dogs scavenges among the dead. Their silhouettes sulk along the ridge before disappearing into the night.

A skull protrudes from beneath a helmet, half buried in sludge. The bone has been picked clean by something, probably a bird. An arm protrudes from freshly turned dirt. The skin is still intact and appears pale in the flashes of light rippling across no man's land.

Doc is struck by the reality that these soldiers were once where he is now, and they're now as he will one day be. Whether it's here at the Front or back in the US, death will come calling. As utterly repulsive as it is to see a rotting corpse lying face down in the muddy water at the bottom of a crater, death is never graceful. Death is always repugnant. Far from being the antithesis of life, death is simply the chaos into which all life eventually descends. Whether that's in a hospital bed or a muddy crater makes no difference. And it's at that point Doc realizes the only difference comes from what he does between now and then, whenever then may be. Has he got five minutes, five years or five decades left? As a physician, he's taken an oath to preserve life, to rally against death rather than surrender to it, but he can't save everyone. And no one lives forever, but he can extend life and reduce suffering. And that's why he's here. His goal is to reduce the number of those rotting in the mud, but having seen the devastation on the battlefield, he feels inadequate.

William Sunday creeps forward through the slush and grime. She keeps to the leeward side of the craters, keeping a wall of dirt between them and the battle whenever possible. She darts across open ground, staying low and ducking behind a fallen tree trunk before turning to make sure Doc is in lockstep with her and Leech.

They reach the collapsed trench. A gash opens out in the Earth, stretching for forty to fifty feet. Bodies lie piled to one side. The rats won't wait. They're already scurrying through the shadows, squeezing between corpses and winding their way over crumpled arms and broken legs. Bile rises in Doc's throat. It's all he can do not to throw up.

A medic shuffles between five wounded soldiers. IV lines have been set up on the dirt. Without a metal stand, they've been mounted at the top of the trench with their thin plastic tubes unfurling into the wrists of the patients. Mouse is already there. He's set up the four stretchers, leaning them against the opposite, steep wall of the trench.

Doc drops into the mud and slush. As tempting as it must be for the medic to grab some of his own men and get them carrying the wounded back to the front line, bitter experience demands proper triage. Soldiers die unnoticed while bouncing around on stretchers. Doc's role is to assess the injuries and provide specialist care if needed to improve the survival rate. In the darkness, he's being asked to see the kind of subtle details that would normally only be visible under surgical lights, in X-rays or in the dark smudges of a CT scan. It's an impossible task undertaken in absurd circumstances.

The medic snaps. "Where the hell have you guys been?"

"We got here," Doc says. His voice trails away as he sees blood clinging to the side of the medic's face. "As... soon..."

"Ah," the medic says in a manic panic, spitting blood with his

49

words. "We've got five WIA and twelve KIA."

Wires and kires. These are terms that will haunt Doc's nightmares.

The skin on the right side of the medic's face has peeled down from his forehead, exposing his cheek. Blood seeps from the corner of his right eye, which remains stationary as he looks around with his left eye. He's been blinded in one eye. Whether he realizes that or not isn't clear. He's in shock and running on adrenaline.

"We've got four stretchers," Doc says, pointing out the obvious. He's still coming to grips with the bitter reality of battlefield triage. He wants to treat the medic first, but only because the man's facial injuries look so hideous. As the medic is conscious and capable of functioning, the rules of triage put him last.

"We can double-up on one," Mouse says. "Just give me the word, Doc, and I'm on the move."

Mouse has dumped his pack and weapon. From the way he's abandoned them, it's clear he has no intention of taking them with him. He's stripped down to his undershirt in the cold. His biceps flex. He mashes his fist into his palm.

"Who can I take?" he asks the two of them.

"Ah, Phillips and Smithy are stable and ready to go," the medic says, pointing at two bloodied soldiers. They both have tourniquets around their thighs, stemming the blood loss from severed legs. They're conscious, but barely.

Doc checks their pulse. Given the physical trauma their bodies have been through, their heartbeats are surprisingly regular and not unduly elevated. In practice, that means the meds the medic has administered are working and suppressing physiological shock. That won't last, though.

"They're good to go," Doc says, confirming the medic's assessment.

Mouse picks up the first soldier and spins him around, laying him on one of the stretchers leaning on the other side of the trench. He loops a strap beneath the soldier's arms, holding him in place and preventing him from sliding down. The soldier groans. Mouse grabs the second soldier, who's lost both legs and straps him to the same stretcher.

Doc examines the third wounded soldier. He's been struck with something in the left chest. He's pale, sweating, and his breathing is labored. Doc opens his shirt and listens to his heart with a stethoscope, moving it around his chest. Shells rain down like the frantic beating of the man's heart, thundering into the dirt and shaking the ground. Doc wants to question the medic about this soldier, but time is of the essence. That the medic hasn't provided pain relief speaks loudly. He doesn't know what the problem is and doesn't want to mask the symptoms by hiding them behind a narcotic gaze, where the glazed look in the patient's eyes makes it seem as though they're okay.

"Punctured lung," Doc says, pushing his mind to make quick, accurate assessments. He rummages around in his medical pack, lying it on the dirt. "Sounds like a tension pneumothorax. Left lung. I'm inserting a chest tube to release the pressure."

The medic offers a slight nod, acknowledging Doc's assessment.

Standing there in the filthy, muddy water up to his ankles, Doc dons plastic gloves and rubs the man's chest with an alcohol swab. Fragments of ice float around his boots. He inserts a needle with a wide bore, pushing it between the man's ribs. Trapped air rushes out, and the soldier's breathing becomes less labored. Blood oozes up, bubbling as it runs over the soldier's chest before mixing with the mud in the trench. Doc gives him a shot of painkillers and uses a sharpie to write the name in shorthand on the soldier's forehead, along with the dosage and time.

FxH 200mg/14:20

"Ah, he's good to go," Doc says, standing up and wiping his forehead with the back of his hand. "Only him, though. You can't stack anyone on top of him."

"Got it, Doc," Mouse says, grabbing the young soldier as though he weighs almost nothing and swinging him around onto one of the other stretchers. Mouse straps him in.

"He needs to be in surgery within the hour."

"On it."

Doc moves on to the next soldier. He's expecting William Sunday and Leech to grab the second stretcher and head off with Mouse, but the big guy climbs up on the edge of the trench alone. He reaches back with both of his massive hands and grabs the aluminum cross member on each of the stretchers. Mouse hunches his back. He hauls the two stretchers up, dragging them behind him like a pack animal as he disappears over the lip of the trench. Four muddy trails follow him as the handles of the stretchers are pulled through the dirt and rocks.

"Is he going to be...?"

"He'll be fine," Williams Sunday says. "We'll catch up to him."

Leech collapses next to one of the remaining stretchers, but he doesn't fall onto it. He positions himself next to it, still clutching his side while setting one hand on one of the handles. He shuffles his fingers to the middle of the crossbar. His hands shake, but he's ready to carry it from that hollow beam. Unlike Mouse, he's not going to be able to drag the stretcher, but he and William Sunday will be able to carry it between them. Movement hurts, but he repositions the stretcher beside the next wounded soldier.

The fourth soldier is conscious and breathing in short bursts. He has makeshift splints supporting his legs.

"He was hit by flying debris," The medic says. "Fractured fibula on the left. Clean break through the tibia and fibula on the right."

Doc nods, knowing how a clean break would be easy to spot, but not the fracture. The medic is clearly experienced.

Doc addresses William Sunday as he examines the swelling on the soldier's right leg. "Get him strapped in and ready to move."

Leech helps William Sunday lift him onto the stretcher.

"Are we good to go?" William Sunday asks, grabbing the handles.

"Not just yet," Doc replies, wanting to examine the last wounded soldier.

As tempting as it is to simply send off the wounded in the order they're laid out within the trench, number four might be in agony, but his leg wounds are easily survivable. Doc needs to understand what's wrong with number five before sending Leech and William Sunday scrambling over the dirt with a stretcher.

At a glance, the fifth soldier couldn't be more than fifteen years old. He's got to be a local volunteer like William Sunday. An oxygen cylinder lies next to him in the mud. His face is covered by a transparent mask with a mechanical valve, regulating and mimicking the rhythm of his natural breathing. "What have we got here?"

"Not sure," the medic says. "He's unresponsive. I mean, there are no breaks. I can't see any injuries, but he's just not there. No response."

"But you've got him on forced oxygen?" Doc says.

"His breathing. It was shallow. Failing. I don't know. I've never seen anything like this before."

"Shell shock?"

"Dunno. Maybe."

Mud and dirt cascade down the side of the trench as two soldiers come scrambling into the far end.

"We heard you need stretcher bearers."

Doc doesn't even look at them. His focus is on the fifth soldier. He points at the fourth soldier with the broken legs lying on the stretcher, saying, "Take him."

Leech and William Sunday step back, allowing the soldiers from Alpha Kilo to carry away their comrade. They haul him up over the side of the trench and disappear into the dark of night.

Doc turns on his headlamp, temporarily flicking it to white instead of red, and sways his head back and forth, catching each of the soldier's dilated eyes individually. He sways across the soldier's face from different sides. There's no response beyond a few blinks. He checks his pulse.

The soldier's neck moves, but there's something unnatural about the way it tilts. Rather than being a muscular response, the motion comes from the shifting dirt slipping down into the mud as William Sunday kneels beside him, wanting to help.

"Jesus," Doc mumbles, switching off his light and grabbing the soldier's head. He pulls it back gently into the mud.

"What?" the medic asks. "What is it?"

"Spinal injury. At a guess, C3. Perhaps even C2. Fuck. He's in there. But he's trapped and unable to speak."

"From a spinal injury?" the medic asks.

"There may be bruising around the brain stem," Doc replies. "That would leave him mute, at least temporarily."

He looks around. "Boots. Get me a boot. William Sunday, position yourself above him and gently take the weight of his head. Don't pull, but don't let his head sag, either. We've got to protect his spinal cord."

William Sunday moves cautiously. Dirt slides from beneath her boots. She takes over from Doc, holding the soldier's head with care.

"He's blinking. Rapidly."

"He's talking," Doc says. "He's trying to tell us we're right. He's paralyzed. I doubt he can feel anything from the neck down."

"Easy, buddy," William Sunday says, leaning over his face and speaking tenderly to him. "We're going to get you out of here. We're going to get you back to the lines. I promise."

Doc fumbles with his equipment, mumbling to himself. "If we can minimize the damage, stem cells can repair his spinal cord. We just have to get him out of here in one piece."

The medic pulls a muddy boot off one of the corpses. He splashes through the puddles at the bottom of the trench, breaking through the thin ice that's formed on top, and hands the boot to Doc.

Doc uses a pair of heavy-duty trauma shears to cut through the thick leather. He separates the shaft from the heel and cuts around beneath the eyelets. Rather than unlacing the boot, he simply cuts through the laces, allowing the boot to fall open. His motion is frantic. Little thought is given to precision. The leather hide is frayed and torn, but he separates it from the sole of the boot.

Doc looks at William Sunday. She has tears in her eyes. Given all she's seen on the battlefield, the helplessness of this wounded soldier has struck deeper than any other. Given that the most common injury is the loss of a limb, it's the invisible wounds that seem to leave her distraught. It must be the sense of uncertainty that comes with them. Tourniquets can't be applied to internal bleeding or a damaged spine.

"Listen," Doc says, shaving away a few bumps on the remains of the boot with the shears. "I need you to hold his head perfectly still. I'm going to dig beneath him and hollow out the dirt. That will allow me to slide this in place and use it as a neck brace. I need his skull and neck supported by his shoulders for the journey back—and this should do the trick—hopefully."

William Sunday nods.

With his blue, disposable, once-sterile muddy gloves still on, Doc begins clawing at the dirt with both hands. He tunnels beneath the soldier's neck. William Sunday is like a statue, leaning over the soldier from above. As the dirt falls away from beneath the soldier's head, her hands remain steady and firm. The medic helps, clearing away dirt from the other side.

"Okay," Doc says, wiping his gloved hands on his shirt in a feeble attempt to clean off the mud. "I'm going to slide the brace in place and secure it with an elastic compression bandage."

Doc wraps a stretchy bandage around the paralyzed soldier's neck, fixing the severed boot in place beneath his skull and jaw. There's a slight gap as the two sides of the makeshift brace, marked by the eyelets, don't quite reach. Doc's not too bothered by that, though, as he can position that gap immediately over the soldier's throat, keeping pressure off his airway. Leech positions the stretcher next to the soldier, butting it up against his limp arm.

Doc turns to William Sunday, saying, "Ideally, we should have a back brace as well, as there's no way of knowing if there's any additional damage to his spine. Once you're out of here, you need to be quick. And gentle. He needs to be in traction and on the operating table like, I dunno, ten minutes ago."

The four of them lift the soldier onto the stretcher, laying him gently on the canvas.

"We've got him, Doc," Leech says with tears streaming down his cheeks. He's in excruciating pain.

"Do you need anything?" Doc asks, gesturing to his medical pack and offering him some painkillers.

"I'm fine. We need to go."

"Okay. Go. Go."

"And you?" William Sunday asks.

"I'll be right behind you. Just packing up my gear."

William Sunday pauses, standing ankle-deep in the muddy water at the bottom of the trench.

"Go. I'll catch up."

She grabs the handles of the stretcher. Like Mouse, Leech grabs the crossbar rather than the handles, but for him, it's out of necessity. His other hand is held across his chest as he tries to reduce the movement of his ribs and reduce the spasms of pain he's feeling.

"You should go with them. Help them," Doc says to the medic.

"No, I need to stay with my unit."

Doc doesn't agree but nods anyway. "Let me look at your face."

Reluctantly, the medic slumps to the dirt, sitting on the side of the shell hole.

William Sunday clambers up the fallen side of the trench with her pack on her back and her rifle slung over her shoulder. She keeps her head low as she carries the stretcher behind her. Leech struggles to match her pace at the rear. His steps are sudden, stabbing at the ground.

Doc figures he'll pack his gear and catch up with them to relieve Leech, as the wounded soldier is probably not going to make it back to the Front carrying that stretcher.

As the soldiers leave and the water at the bottom of the slit trench falls still, the rats emerge. They can smell the fresh blood and are moving in before the dogs arrive. Doc is disgusted, but what can he do? Whenever they can, soldiers will retrieve their dead, but the ferocity of the battle unfolding beyond the trench makes that impossible. The various squads out there are falling back while trying not to sustain any more injuries or fatalities. Doc doesn't know what the goal of this incursion is, but the death and misery he's witnessed makes it seem pointless.

Doc applies an antiseptic cream with a topical painkiller to the medic's face. He tapes a gauze pad over the medic's cheek, gently covering his motionless eye. The medic is quiet but seems agitated. His fingers twitch. Given all he's been through and the severity of his own injuries, that's hardly surprising.

With his pack folded and the clips in place, Doc swings his medical kit up onto his back and trudges toward the narrow end of the trench. The medic is already up by the rim, peering across the battlefield.

Rats swarm over the pile of bodies. To Doc's horror, one of them bites at a hand, and it reacts.

"Wait," he says as the medic flexes, readying himself to dash out into no man's land and rejoin his squad. Doc says, "Someone's alive in there."

"What? No!"

Doc dumps his pack on the dirt. He kicks at the rats. They bite at his boots, not wanting to surrender their prize. Doc drags two bodies down into the muddy water, wanting to reach the survivor. Fingers twitch in the shadows of a blue bolt of lightning as it arcs its way across the sky.

"No one's alive," the medic says, staying high on the rim of the crater and not coming back to help him.

"This man is alive," Doc replies, grabbing the soldier and dragging him away from the corpses. Rats snarl, hissing at him, refusing to give up their conquest. Doc brushes them away, and they scurry back to the corpses.

"Corporal Sanderson," the medic says, recognizing the soldier in the shadows. "No pulse."

Doc pushes his fingers hard up into the carotid artery, palpating the pulse below and to the left of his jaw, feeling beneath the bone. He

57

moves his fingers around. Nothing.

"Too much blood loss," the medic says, but his clipped sentences are telling. He's stressed. He's fatigued. He's running on empty. It's all he can do not to flee from the horror of war.

Doc grabs two of the abandoned IV lines still lying in the trench and attaches one to each of the soldier's arms, fixing them with tape. Deep down, he knows it's hopeless, but he can't give up, not while there's a chance. It would take hours, perhaps days, to replace the blood loss this way without a transfusion. He needs whole blood. The soldier's abdomen has been ripped open, leaving a bloody mess of fat and pulp where his stomach should be.

"He's hemorrhaging. His body is in shock, but we can save him."

"We?" the medic asks. "No, we can't."

The medic points at the sky. At first, Doc is confused. Is he religious? Is he suggesting the soldier is beyond help and only divine intervention would make a difference? It's then Doc notices. The sky is lightening. It's no longer pitch-black. They're still at least an hour from dawn, caught somewhere in the astronomical twilight, but the sky has a slight tinge as though it were navy blue rather than pitch black.

"We need to get out of here before the sun rises," the medic says. "If we're caught out here in the open—"

Doc snaps, "I'm not leaving him."

He throws open his pack and rummages around, looking for the freeze-dried plasma. As tempting as it is to apply the EPR and cool the soldier's body, the extensive intestinal bleeding needs to be stopped first. There's no point in cooling blood that's simply going to leak out into the dirt without actually cooling his brain. Doc has to try to stabilize him first.

Doc grabs a yellow bag that could easily be mistaken for urine and crunches it beneath his hands, breaking up the crystals. Then he snaps open a vial of sterile water and pours it into the bag.

"I need you to apply a major trauma dressing to his wound," Doc says, kneading the plasma. "Start looking for severed arteries."

"I—I can't," the medic says. "He's—He's all but dead. It's only a matter of time. I—I'm sorry."

With that, the medic slips over the edge of the trench. Dirt cascades down into the muddy water, having been dislodged by the medic's boots. Rats scramble between bodies.

"Fuck," Doc mumbles, using his teeth to bite open a plastic gauze pad. He's trying to multitask and needs more hands. He fumbles with an auxiliary port on the IV line and attaches the plasma, setting it running into the soldier's veins. Above him, the sky lightens.

"Fuck, fuck, fuck," Doc mumbles, opening the soldier's ripped, bloodied shirt. The seemingly dead soldier's stomach has been torn open. In the bitter cold, sweat forms on Doc's forehead. He leans over the soldier and turns on his headlamp. Doc rummages around within the soldier's abdomen with dirty fingers, looking for severed arteries. He pushes in a few clotting sponges, trying to see beyond the blood pooling in the wound.

"What a goddamn mess," he mumbles, grabbing clamps and fixing them in place. He checks for a pulse. It's faint, but the soldier is alive. Doc finishes up with clamps and butterfly clips, doing his best to repair the arteries, but the soldier needs proper surgery. He sticks a large gauze pad over Sanderson's stomach, using it to hold the soldier's intestines in place.

Doc is torn between options. The textbook approach would be to put the soldier into a controlled death using the EPR, stopping his heart and pumping his blood manually with the EPR lever, cooling him to sixty degrees, but that will take time—time Doc doesn't have. And time lost here is time that could be used in the Emergency Room of the triage center back at the Front.

Clouds high in the stratosphere light up in blood red.

Doc has to make a decision. He wants to go with the EPR. He knows that's what his instructors back at the base hospital would recommend, but with shells raining down and bullets flying, he's also concerned for his own life. The longer he's trapped here near the Novo lines, the worse his odds of survival become.

"Fuck," he says, punching the dirt, hating the choice before him. EPR might help Corporal Sanderson to survive if Doc can administer it correctly with his trembling hands, and if he can make it back to the lines as dawn breaks. Those are two damn big ifs. But if he leaves with Sanderson now, he can probably get back before the sun comes over the horizon. His odds of survival go up while Sanderson's drop. But what hope does Sanderson have with an EPR strapped to his arm if Doc takes a Novo bolt to the back of his head in no man's land?

The smart decision is to leave Sanderson to die. The medic was probably right. Even with the IV and the plasma, the amount of physiological shock Sanderson is in could still overwhelm his body. He could be dead before Doc makes it back to the lines. No one would blame Doc for leaving the corporal. No one would know. And this is precisely the kind of scenario the colonel wanted him to avoid.

"Don't you die on me," Doc mumbles. "Don't you dare."

Doc takes off his helmet and opens his jacket, knowing he's about to fire up his own internal furnace in spite of the cool wind, the vapor on his breath and the snowflakes drifting through the air.

Doc grabs the soldier by his arm and leg and hoists him up over his shoulder, leaving his medical pack where it lies in the dirt. Given the extent of the man's injuries, Doc has to be strategic with how he holds him. He rests his chest on his shoulder, reaching his arm up over and around the man's ribs. He's got to keep pressure off the wound. Doc reaches down and drags the IV bags and the plasma bag over to him, hauling them up and hanging them over his shoulder along with the soldier. He presses the bags into the side of his neck, wedging them between himself and the soldier to keep them higher than the man's arms and so still feeding down into his veins. Then he wraps his other arm around the man's legs, holding them firmly in front of him. The soldier's ass juts out ahead of him. Limp arms knock against Doc's lower back.

"Stay with me, Sanderson."

Doc staggers up the side of the trench. His boots slide in the soft dirt. He keeps his legs wide, desperately searching for firm ground. On reaching the top, the sky provides him with a sense of direction. He needs to head away from the rising sun—and fast. Shells rain down on the battlefield, crashing around him and shaking the ground like an earthquake. Mud and rocks are thrown into the air. Dirt rains down on the two of them. Doc can see soldiers ahead of him, firing back behind him. They must have passed him as he treated Sanderson in the trench, not realizing he was still down there.

Doc staggers on. His thighs burn. His lungs scream for oxygen. He can barely keep his head up. It's all he can do to watch the shadows and place his boots one in front of the other. Rather than keeping to the craters, he stays high on the rim. It's not a smart move, but it's the fastest. It's the only option open to him. With the sky lightening, he's out of time. And Sanderson doesn't have time. His life is measured in minutes, not hours.

Doc pauses to catch his breath in the shattered remains of the forest. He hoists Sanderson higher on his shoulder and continues on. The soldier groans.

"Good sign," Doc says between breaths. "Keep groaning, buddy. Keep complaining. *Your feedback is important to us!*"

When Doc reaches the wooden planks spanning the swampy ground, he picks up his pace, rushing along them even though they shift and move beneath his boots, threatening to topple him into the quagmire. He's breathing hard. His heart is racing.

Doc stumbles past the torn remains of the Novos that were shelled by Hawk. Their blood is phosphorescent, glowing blue as it mixes with the mud.

Lines of concertina wire bar his path.

"Goddamn it," he mumbles, looking up and down the line, trying to find a way through to the trenches. Dozens of bootprints in the mud lead to his left, so he follows them, tracing the steps of retreating soldiers. His knees feel as though they're going to give at any moment.

The dead horse. He remembers the dead horse.

"This way," he mumbles, trying not to slide as he descends into a shell hole, following the trail of the soldiers before him. "Almost there, buddy. Hold on. Just a little longer."

By his calculations, Doc should have reached the front line by now. He's anxious. He's confused. He's dehydrated and sore. His muscles are cramping. Shadows stretch across no man's land, changing its appearance and making the ruins seem elongated. Nothing looks familiar. Light returns to the battlefield. The sun hasn't risen, but the murky, indistinct bumps and blotches he saw on the way out resolve into smashed wooden carts, concrete horse troughs, a collapsed church and an overturned car. These are relics from when the battlefield was once farmland dotted with villages.

"Where the hell is everyone?"

Doc staggers up a rise. The trenches should be here. They should be right in front of him, but there's nothing beyond shell holes and craters stretching into the distance. The crumpled brick wall of an old farmhouse is the only shelter he can see. Its roof has been burned in a fire. The tiles have collapsed in on themselves. Perhaps he can rest there. He'll survive the day hiding. Sanderson, though, won't.

It's then Doc hears a voice yelling somewhere to his right.

"Hey, there's someone still out there!"

Doc turns and looks. To his dismay, he's been staggering alongside the trench for the past few minutes, having lost his sense of orientation.

Doc wheels around and stumbles forward. Soldiers rush out of the trench and grab him, hauling him and Sanderson back to the front line. Flashes of blue lightning ripple around them, shooting past them. One of the bolts passes so close that the radiant heat warms his cheeks. Doc, though, is oblivious to the danger. His only concern is his patient.

"Easy, careful," he says, gesturing for the soldiers to be gentle with Sanderson. One of the IV lines drags along the mud.

Meyers rushes out and grabs Doc. He helps him turn and descend the wooden ladder into the safety of the trench.

"They told me you were back already."

"Couldn't leave him," Doc replies, barely able to speak.

Already, three medics have Sanderson on a stretcher. They're checking his pulse and reinserting an IV line. Within seconds, they jog away, rushing to get him to one of the triage centers. From there, he'll be stabilized and transferred to the rear before being sent to the local field hospital. Given the extent of his injuries, Sanderson will probably be medi-evac'd to the US military hospital in Germany. One of the medics jogs alongside the stretcher, carrying the two IVs and the bag of plasma.

"Sweet Jesus," another medic says. "How is that guy even alive?"

Doc pushes his head back against the side of the trench, breathing deeply. He looks up at a sunrise that, in Chicago, Illinois, would be stunning. Here, it's misguided. Beauty torments him. Pinks, reds, and yellows spread across wispy clouds high in the stratosphere as the sky fades from black to blue. A couple of birds soar through the air. It's as though nature missed the memo about the war.

"And Leech?"

"He collapsed in no man's land," Meyers replies. "William Sunday left him and the soldier in a crater and went to get Mouse. Together, the two of them dragged them back to the line. Leech is in a triage station, but I suspect he'll be moved to the hospital in El Paso."

Doc is exhausted. He slumps to the wooden floorboards running through the trench. Soldiers step over him. Meyers sits beside him and offers him a canteen. Doc drinks. The fluid contains electrolytes mixed with water. At that moment, it tastes like champagne.

"Damn crazy night, huh?" Meyers says.

"Damn crazy war," Doc replies, looking at his trembling, muddy hands.

The Killing Hour

Doc crashes on his bed in the squad dugout. The shelling during the day is less intense but still annoying and loud. Occasionally, he's awakened by a tremor shaking his wooden cot from a nearby explosion.

The canvas within his aging Russian cot bed sags, so it's reasonably comfortable. Turning over in a sleeping bag while surrounded by thin wooden support beams requires the kind of gymnastics that should be confined to the Olympics. He ends up shuffling from side to side.

Mouse snores. He's loud. It's as though a chainsaw started up and someone's cutting wood. Doc, though, is too tired to care. As their cots are lined up next to each other, being separated into groups of two with a narrow aisle in between, every now and then, Lavender thumps Mouse with a pillow. He grumbles and then resumes snoring.

Doc wakes around four in the afternoon to find all the other cots have been packed away. The squad members sit around the dugout, chatting quietly, playing cards or reading mud-stained books.

"Morning," Meyers says.

"Morning," Doc replies, sitting up and ruffling his hair, willing himself awake. All his muscles ache. He unzips his sleeping bag and turns sideways on his cot, slipping on a fresh pair of socks and then pushing his feet into his unlaced boots. Socks are one of the oddities of the war, any war, but especially one fought in trenches. Wearing fresh socks every day seems like overkill to Doc, but he's been assured his feet are his greatest asset. As a surgeon, he thinks it's his hands, but he understands how easy it is for bacterial infections to take hold. Damp, sweaty socks are a microbial paradise. He's noticed Meyers changes his several times a day.

Doc relieves himself in the latrine bucket, which has a layer of ice on the surface. His urine cuts multiple holes in the ice, which is surprisingly fun until the stench reaches his nostrils. Doc makes a mental note to be a little more conservative next time and pee around the edges.

"Coffee?" Lavender asks as he walks back into the main area. Mouse has already rolled up Doc's sleeping bag and packed up his cot bed, stacking it in the storage area at the rear of the dugout.

"Ah, yes. Thanks."

Doc sits on the bench seat running around the dugout and warms his hands around a fresh cup of coffee that tastes as though it's three days old. The smell, though, is invigorating and inviting, as is the sight of vapor wafting from his cup into the air.

Doc opens his journal and makes a few notes about last night's excursion into no man's land. It's not that he thinks he'll forget what happened, but as the days roll by, it will be easy to confuse and merge details with other events. He wants his observations to be pristine and laid out in chronological order.

"Well, congratulations," Meyers says. "You managed to piss off the top brass on your first day."

"What???"

"The colonel is livid. News of your antics has already reached the Press Corps. They're calling you a fiver."

"Fiver?"

William Sunday says, "That's how many days they think you'll last."

Hawk says, "The bookmakers have you at twenty-to-one odds of dying in your first week."

Mouse says, "I'll take those odds."

"Mouse!" William Sunday says, scolding him with a glare that could kill.

"I don't understand," Doc says.

"Sanderson," Meyers replies. "He was too far gone. You were supposed to leave him, not save him."

"But—"

"Oh, it doesn't worry me," Meyers says, holding up a hand in fake surrender. "And the rank and file love you for getting him into surgery, but the brass hates it. They don't want you taking unnecessary risks. Dead doctors are bad for morale. The grunts, though, well..."

He points at a crate by the entrance to the dugout. It's full of chocolate ration bars. As he's speaking, a soldier briefly appears in the opening, blocking the natural light as he drops a chocolate bar onto the pile. There are easily a hundred chocolate bars sprawling on top of each other.

"It's their way of saying thank you."

"But I'm lactose intolerant."

"I'm not," William Sunday says.

"Me neither," Mouse says.

"Don't tell them," Lavender says.

"And the colonel?" Doc asks.

"He gave you *the talk*, right?"

Doc nods.

"Well, he wants you alive. He's already dressed me down and told me to pull you back sooner next time."

"And will you?"

Meyers shrugs.

"How did you do it?" Happy asks. "How did you survive the killing hour?"

Doc scratches a quick note in his journal, saying, "The killing hour?"

"The hour before dawn," Lavender replies. "We're not sure if it's because of their anatomy or biological clocks, but that last hour has the highest rate of Novo activity. And they love nothing more than catching stragglers in no man's land."

"I guess I was lucky."

"If you're lucky, then I want to pair with you," William Sunday says. "No, wait. Standing next to someone that's lucky increases your odds of being hit, right? If they're lucky, you're unlucky. You've got to be. Everything has to even out."

She looks genuinely flustered, overthinking something that doesn't exist.

"There's no such thing as luck," Hawk says.

"Maybe they took pity on me," Doc says.

"Pity?" Happy spits his coffee back into his cup. He shakes his head. He's on the verge of laughing, but there's bitterness in the lines on his face.

Lavender says, "Ain't no such thing as pity in war, Doc. You kill them the first chance you get, or they kill you the first chance they get. That's it. Them's the rules. There is no chivalry, no code of honor."

"She's right," Happy says.

"But a doctor with a wounded man slung over his shoulder?"

"Makes no difference," Lavender replies. "Because that guy you're carrying could be back tomorrow to put a bullet in their head."

Doc is curious. He asks, "Would you shoot someone in the back?"

"Yes," William Sunday says without hesitation.

Doc is interested to note that Meyers is listening and observing without offering an opinion one way or the other. Mouse nods but doesn't contribute. Hawk looks disinterested, but he's not. He's keeping his thoughts to himself, but he has his own opinion. It's the way his eyes narrow at William Sunday's reply that gives away his agreement. There's a slight nod from his head, but it could easily be just the way he exhales.

"Isn't that murder?" Doc asks.

"Nope," Happy replies. Out of all of them, he and Lavender are the most vocal.

"War is the absence of civilization," Lavender says. "War is what happens when there's nothing left but you and them—and they mean to kill you."

"But what about civilians?"

"They don't have any," Lavender says. "And neither do we, not this close to the Front."

"So we're just animals?" Doc asks.

"Not animals," Happy replies. "Worse. Animals hunt for food. We hunt for scalps."

William Sunday says, "We're fighting for our way of life."

Doc has his notebook out in his lap. He jots down comments, wanting to capture the conversation so he can review it later and think more deeply about their logic. He finds it interesting to observe the different rationales they're clinging to. Happy is pragmatic. William Sunday is idealistic, clinging to an abstract notion of their way of life that simply does not exist in the mud and grime of the trenches.

"Whatcha writing?" Happy asks.

"Oh, just jotting down notes."

"Courage, huh? You still think this is about courage? You've been out there, Doc. You've seen what it's like. You've seen men shit themselves when their legs are blown off. Fuck that for courage!"

Doc stops writing. He rests his pen in the middle of his journal, but he doesn't close the book.

"There ain't no courage," Happy says. He's bitter. Angry. Sad. "My boy, my best friend from college. He's a runner. He *was* a runner. Mitch was eight thousand yards from the Front. Eight goddamn thousand! He was running notes from Iowa to Nebraska, only the trenches don't align. They date back to the early part of the war. No one was thinking straight back then. They just dug in and prayed as the shells whistled overhead. Rather than fall back through Missouri, he cuts across open ground. Stays low. But it's the killing hour. He's quick. He darts between fallen buildings and ditches. The last stretch is over a rise. It ain't more than thirty yards. They call it home plate 'cause everyone slides the last ten, slipping into the trench like it was a stupid game of baseball or something. Mitch, though. He rests his hand on the remains of a brick wall. He tenses his legs, ready to spring out. He raises his head, and—*wham*—a bolt of that blue lightning shit strikes him before he can take his first step. Hell, they were shooting over the goddamn horizon at him."

Around the dugout, heads are bowed. Happy is fighting back tears.

"Took his head clean off his shoulders."

Happy shakes his head slowly. His eyes glance up at the wooden beams forming the ceiling. He's not lost in thought so much as reliving a moment he never saw and only ever had recounted to him, but he's been there. In his mind's eye, in the dark of night when everyone else is asleep, he pictures what happened to Mitch. Doc can see that in the single tear that rolls down his cheek. If he notices, he doesn't wipe it away. Doc desperately wants to make notes but doesn't. Now is the time to listen.

"They got their goddamn dispatches," Happy says. "They waited a few hours and then sent some other poor sap crawling across the battlefield to get them. He told me Mitch's body was still leaning against the bricks. His head was thirty feet away. And that poor sap? He had to bag him. He shoved Mitch's body in a black plastic bag and dragged it back to the trenches like it was garbage."

Happy sniffs.

"But do you know what?" Happy asks, raising a finger and shaking it slightly. "Do you know what's worse? I read the letter they sent his folks. His Mom took a photo of it and emailed it to me while I was on R&R back in Kyiv. She was so proud. But the letter? It was full of lies."

Happy wipes his nose with the back of his hand.

"*Your son was brave. He was courageous. He did his duty. He gave his all in service to our freedom.*"

Happy pauses. No one speaks.

"Bull—*fucking*—shit! He was terrified, like all of us. He was tired. He was cold and wet. His feet ached. He was hungry. He was lonely. He was living for just one more day. Hoping, praying he'd make it to

70

tomorrow. Hell, I don't think he'd ever even seen a Novo. And now? He's a number. He's a *fucking* statistic. He's a name engraved on a memorial wall. He's a gold star service flag hung outside his parents' home."

Happy looks Doc in the eye. As uncomfortable as it is, Doc refuses to look away. He understands the raw hurt behind those eyes. He knows Happy needs to feel release. Happy needs to unpack the pain within his soul.

"And courage? Do you want to know what courage really is, Doc? Courage is the lie we tell ourselves to make ourselves feel better about the stupid *fucking* waste of life around us. We want to find meaning in tragedy, but there's none, so we tell ourselves Mitch was courageous. Well, I don't want to be courageous. I want to be alive."

Happy knocks back the last of his coffee, which must be cold by now.

"And I ain't no coward. But I ain't no fool either. I know how they use courage. How they use bravery. How they use duty. These are weapons our own leaders use against us."

Doc looks around at the Dog Food Squad. Not only have they turned their eyes down, they're staring away from Happy, looking at the way mud has smeared on the wall or at bootprints on the wooden floorboards. Doc's not sure whether they agree or disagree. Perhaps it's a sense of shame that has them looking away because they sense a hint of truth in his voice.

Happy points at the light streaming in through the opening of the dugout.

"You don't see *them* venturing into no man's land. You don't see *them* facing off against the Novo. No, it's just us '*courageous*' fuckers that get that honor. Shit. And yet, we'll go back out there tonight. Not because we're brave. Not because we're courageous. Not because we're doing our duty. You want to know why we do it? Because we love those we've left behind. Because if we don't make a stand here, sooner or later, the Novos will march into our hometowns and kill everyone we care about."

William Sunday nods.

Under his breath, Mouse mumbles, "Yeah."

Dog Food

Doc is fascinated by Hawk. He's the strong, silent type; only that stereotype is a lie. It's easy to project strength by hiding. On one level, it's a coping mechanism, allowing an introvert like Hawk to absorb the stress that's thrown at him, but that strategy only works for so long. Like the fault lines between two tectonic plates, stress can only be held to a certain point. Stress has to be released, either bit by bit or in something sudden and catastrophic, like an earthquake. Either way, stress cannot be contained. It has to be dealt with. Hawk may think he can bottle it up, but he can't. Superman is a myth best left to comic books and movies.

Mouse prepares dinner, cooking a stew over a portable stove. White hexamine tablets burn with a blue glow that is all too reminiscent of the alien lightning, but no one other than Doc seems to notice that. The tablets are set on a raised metal tray, keeping them off the crate, but there are scorch marks on the wood from the hundreds of meals cooked here in the shadows. Mouse stirs an aluminum pot set above the hex stove. Steam rises along with the smell of meat boiling.

William Sunday helps Mouse by chopping up vegetables. Lavender jokes around with her. She's playful. She reaches out and tickles William Sunday, touching her hips and causing her to grimace. William Sunday turns toward her with the knife, laughing and telling her to stop. Lavender's face is lit by the gas lantern. Her cheeks are rosy. She's full of life and enjoys teasing William Sunday.

As the sun sets, Hawk steps out of the dugout. Doc sees an opportunity to talk to him alone.

"Gonna get some fresh air."

No one replies. Meyers is asleep. Happy is flicking playing cards across the dugout, trying to land them in a rusty frying pan.

Doc steps up onto the boardwalk, leaving the dugout behind. It feels good to walk out under a clear sky, even if he's still in a muddy trench. Soldiers mill about. There's no urgency. They're conserving their energy. Two women share a can of tuna, picking pieces of fish out of the brine using the tips of their combat knives.

Hawk is sitting on one of the logs supporting the trench. As the trench is V-shaped, being wider at the top, by propping himself up there, he allows the foot traffic to pass him by. He keeps his head below the sandbags. Doc is expecting him to be reading or perhaps writing a letter back home, but Hawk is whittling away at a piece of wood.

"Hey. Can I join you?"

Hawk points with his knife at the log beside him. Doc climbs up and sits sideways, facing him.

"Beautiful sunset, huh?"

"What do you want, Doc?"

"Nothing. I just want to talk. To get to know you. That's all."

"Nothing to know," Hawk replies, avoiding eye contact. He's carving a piece of wood that's roughly six inches square. That he's carving the head of a majestic eagle, proud and bold, speaks loudly to Doc. It's in the style of a raised relief, meaning rather than trying to carve a three-dimensional head, he's capturing it in side profile. The beak and eyes appear finished, at least to Doc, and he's working on the feathers that adorn the bird's head.

"It's beautiful," Doc says, painfully aware he's used that term twice within a minute. Perhaps that says something profound about him. Doc's looking for some kind of solace in the heartbreak of life at the Front when there's none to be found.

"Hmm," is all Hawk says in reply.

"Who is it for?"

Hawk stops carving. Doc has struck a nerve. For all his gruff exterior, this is personal. The others within the Dog Food squad must have seen him working on this carving for weeks. Doc's sure they would have commented on the image, but it seems he's the only one who's asked about the recipient. They see the physical item, the carving. Doc, though, is trying to peer beyond the mere wood to understand what makes Hawk tick.

"My daughter."

"How old is she?"

"Five."

With just a handful of words, Hawk has bared his soul. Like Doc, most of the soldiers on the Front are single. Some have girlfriends or wives back home, but few of them have children. Doc's engaged. His fiancé didn't want him to go to war, but Doc had to be part of the resistance. He saw the war with the Novos as the defining challenge of his generation and something he couldn't sit out.

There's no draft. Not yet. Volunteers tend not to walk away from families, especially with young kids. That Hawk has made no mention of his daughter's mother or any other children is equally telling. Hawk may not mean to disclose this, but Doc gets the feeling his marriage or perhaps his de-facto relationship with her mother has broken down.

"What's your daughter's name?"

"Heather."

"Heather's a beautiful name."

Doc has got to stop using the word beautiful. It reveals far too much about the longing in his soul and his desire to find meaning in the insanity of war.

Hawk continues carving. "You trying to get inside my head, Doc?"

"I'm already in there."

Hawk smiles. He tries not to laugh. He shakes his head, asking, "And what do you see?"

"Atlas—carrying the world on his shoulders."

Hawk is quiet.

"I see someone unlike anyone else here. Someone who knew *precisely* what they were getting into and came anyway. Someone that's trying to bend the war to their own will."

"You don't know shit," Hawk replies.

"We all do it."

"Do what?" Hawk snaps, which for Doc is telling. He may not mean to, but he's lowering his guard.

"Try to control the chaos. It's what we all want in life. Control. But we can't have it. We can't bend reality to our will. The desire for control is understandable, but it's always beyond us. We like to think we're in control of our lives, but we're not. None of us are. Certainly, not up there. Not on the battlefield. Not when facing the Novos."

"Control?" Hawk asks. From the look in his eyes, he genuinely wants to understand what Doc has observed about him.

"It's the way you clean your equipment. The way you pack your bag. The way you prepare for contingencies. Everything is double and triple-checked."

"And that's bad?"

"I didn't say it's bad."

"What are you saying?"

"You're hyper-vigilant."

"Vigilance is good. Vigilance keeps me alive."

Doc is brutal. "Vigilance keeps you from life."

Hawk falls silent.

"Hyper-vigilance is a substitute for living life to the fullest. Everything's calculated. You can't take any risks, and yet, every time you go over the top, you're rolling the dice. You're trying to shape life when it's life that shapes you. Embrace the chaos. Don't try to control every aspect of your life, or you'll miss life entirely."

"You sound like Marie," Hawk mumbles.

There's heartache in his voice. Hawk doesn't need to elaborate. Marie is his ex, and Doc senses she left him, not the other way around.

She took control away from him. As much as he doesn't want to admit it, Doc can see he's reacting to that, trying to claw back some semblance of control over his own life.

Hawk clenches his jaw. Attempting to control all the variables in his life is an admission of failure in itself, admitting that there are things he wants to control but can't. Marie made a decision. Regardless of the reasons, it was hers to make, and he cannot change that through strength of will alone. At a conscious level, he must know that. His subconscious, though, longs for more and drives him on, demanding he take control of anything and everything.

Hawk wants to cry, but he can't. It's the way his dark eyes narrow that betrays his emotions. It's not that Hawk is holding back tears but that his heart won't allow him that indulgence. Doc wants to reach out and touch him, but for a man's man, it would be too much. Doc watches as Hawk swallows the lump rising in his throat. He continues carving the feathers on the eagle's head. His silence screams in anguish.

Doc says, "Look. It's your life. I'm not going to tell you, do this or don't do that, but I will listen. If ever you want to talk, I'm here for you."

With that, Doc rises from the log. He looks down at the muddy boards running through the trench, picking the spot where he'll land when he jumps down.

"Hey, Doc."

"Yeah."

"You ever feel like you're not good enough?"

"Me? Oh, yeah."

Doc sits back down, propping himself sideways on the log.

Hawk says, "My dad. He was strict, you know."

Doc is silent.

"He, uh... He hit me. He hit my brother. My sister."

Doc lowers his gaze, looking down at the carving. The blade of Hawk's knife flicks at the wood, cutting out chips and leaving the impression of feathers on the wood.

"He hit my mom."

Doc swallows the lump welling up in his throat.

"It was the booze. Dad worked on the roads. He was in the sun all day, digging trenches, laying down gravel, pouring concrete. On Saturdays, he worked half a day. Half days were the worst. Dad would spend half a day in the blazing sun and half a day watching sports on TV while drinking rum. You don't need much to get drunk, and he'd damn near empty the bottle."

Hawk pauses as Happy walks past. He's quiet, waiting until Happy is well out of earshot before continuing.

"You could set your watch by my dad," Hawk says. "Four-thirty on a Saturday afternoon, and he'd start yelling and cussing, but the violence didn't hit until around six. And me? I'd stay low. I'd try to stay out of his way. But everything, absolutely everything I did was wrong. I *breathed* wrong."

Doc purses his lips, wishing there was something he could do for Hawk, but there's nothing he can do to help him other than listen. Hawk needs to work through the trauma for himself.

"Me. My brother. My sister. We'd go to our auntie's house. Or we'd go to a friend's house. But they were older. They left home as soon as they could, and then there was just me, Mom and the dog. Most Saturday nights, I'd ride my bike down to the high school. There was no one there. I'd just walk around the grounds alone. Or I'd sit on one of the benches with the dog beside me. I couldn't leave him. Dad would have killed him."

Doc nods, knowing what's coming next.

"I—I tried. But I couldn't. I could never please him. I could never... And then, one day, one of the neighbors had enough. They called the cops. And the cops shot him on our front lawn. And me? I wasn't there. I heard the gunshot echoing over the suburb from the empty bleachers on the high school track field. If I had been at home, perhaps I could have talked him down. Perhaps I could have talked to the police. Helped them see..."

Doc wants to speak, but now is the time for silence.

"I—I couldn't control him. I couldn't change what happened on that hot summer's eve. I couldn't control anything in my life. Nothing. Not a goddamn thing. Nothing I did made any difference. And there he was. Dead. His life soaked into the grass."

Hawk works with the tip of the blade, etching fine lines on the feathers at the back of the Eagle's head. His craftsmanship is exquisite. His control of the knife is like that of an artist with a fine paintbrush.

"I loved my dad."

"I know," Doc says.

"And then Marie. She made me so angry... No. No. She didn't. It was me. The anger. I got so angry. And I... And I hit her. And it was then I realized I'd become him."

A single tear rolls down Hawk's cheek.

"I can't be him."

"You're not."

Hawk wipes away the tear. His face, though, doesn't betray him. To anyone walking past or watching from a distance, there's no emotion there at all.

"Courage, Doc. That's what you're writing about, huh?"

Doc nods.

Hawk says, "Coming here didn't take courage. Not for me. No. For me, it will take courage to go home."

Doc nods. "It takes courage to talk about these things."

"It does," Hawk replies.

Even though he barely knows him, Doc can see Hawk's a man of honor. He prides himself on being principled, but it's a defense mechanism. It's a way of hiding from his own flaws.

"Everyone makes mistakes," Doc says. "But it's not our mistakes that define us. It's what we do about them."

"She will never forgive me," Hawk says, hanging his head.

"She doesn't need to," Doc says. "You have to forgive yourself. You can't change the past. But you can change the future. Your future."

"And her?" he says, fighting to swallow the lump rising in his throat.

"You have to let her go. She has to live free. You've got to let her make her own decisions in life. You can't control her. You shouldn't even try."

"And that takes courage, huh?"

"It does," Doc replies. "It takes more courage than facing Novo bolts up there in no man's land."

"Damn you, Doc," Hawk says. He spits into the walkway. "Fuck you... Fuck you for being right!"

Although it sounds aggressive, Doc understands his intent. Doc hasn't told Hawk anything he doesn't already know in the depths of his soul; he's simply forced him to face up to the hurt buried so deep within.

"Fuck me," Doc says. "I've got nothing. I haven't got any answers for you. I haven't got any solutions because there are none. Not everything can be solved. Not everything can be fixed."

Hawk says, "Not everything can be controlled."

Doc nods.

Hawk stutters. "But I—I—I love her. I still love her."

Doc says, "I know it hurts, but the most loving thing you can do for her is to let her go."

Hawk sobs. He pushes his fingers up into his eyes, trying to prevent the tears from flowing. His chest heaves.

Happy walks back along the trench. He makes eye contact with Doc, who shakes his head softly. Doc tightens his lips. His jaw clenches. His body language screams *keep walking*. Happy lowers his head and walks past without saying a word. Hawk doesn't notice him. He looks up at the sky. Wisps of cloud sit high in the stratosphere, shining like gold, catching the last rays of sunlight.

Hawk composes himself. He wipes his eyes.

"Do you know where it comes from? Our squad name? Dog Food?"

He's shifting the subject, which Doc finds peculiar. As much as

Doc may have wanted to talk to Hawk about bottling up his trauma, it seems there's something Hawk wants to talk to Doc about, something he considers important out here in the trenches.

"Uh, no," Doc replies. "I just figured it came from the designation DF."

"Delta Foxtrox. Doesn't Forget. Dumb Fuckers. Dead Freaks. Disco Fools."

Doc laughs. "I like that last one."

"We're called Dog Food because one wrong step out there, and that's all you are."

"I saw them," Doc replies. "The wild dogs."

"They'll attack you. Don't let yourself get isolated. They'll take down a lone soldier."

Doc nods, adding one more hazard to his mental checklist when scrambling through no man's land.

"My advice, Doc. Don't get too close to anyone—we're all just dog food in the end."

Doc shakes his head in disagreement. "I... I can't do that. I can't lose my humanity out here."

"You'll get hurt."

"I'd rather be hurt than alone."

Hawk's nostrils flare. He's not angry so much as challenged by that notion. Hawk has used isolation as a way of protecting himself, and now he's being forced to rethink his position.

Doc says, "No one wants to get hurt by losing someone, but it's better to be hurt than hardened. I mean, what are we out here for if it's not to fight for *our* humanity? Not humanity in some general sense of the people crossing Trafalgar Square to get to work or rushing through the rain to get to their offices among the skyscrapers of New York. Our humanity. Ours. It's us, Hawk. We matter. Out there. On the battlefield. All we have is each other."

Hawk reaches out and places his hand on Doc's shoulder.

"You must come to the reservation when this is over. And we will sit and talk and laugh with the elders, sharing stories of this time with the next generation."

"I would be honored," Doc replies.

William Sunday bounces up next to them in the walkway. Her hair is spiky. She's washed it, allowing her natural blonde highlights to come through. Her face is clean. She looks entirely out of place in the filthy, muddy trench. A smile lights up her lips. Her eyes sparkle. She's effervescent with life. At that moment, Doc decides she doesn't belong here in the war zone. She should be in Rome or Paris, sitting in a café or dining in a fancy restaurant. She should be wearing a beautiful evening dress, not combat fatigues. And yet he knows she wouldn't be anywhere else. They're all fighting for the future.

"Dinner is served," she says with bubbly enthusiasm, holding two square aluminum bowls. Vapor drifts from the stew. Bits of carrot float on the surface. Lumps of meat rest on the bottom, forming clumps beneath the gravy-like stew.

"Oh, thank you," Doc says as Hawk echos his comment.

They take the bowls from her, and she rises on her heels, saying, "Enjoy!" before disappearing down the trench. She skips rather than thuds on the muddy wooden planks.

All along the Front, shells fall, but their rhythm is hypnotic. They're the distant rumble of thunder on a hot summer's evening. The snowflakes drifting through the air put lie to that idea, but it's easy to block out the sound.

"What about you, Doc?" Hawk asks, taking a bite of the stew. "What brought you here?"

"That," Doc says, pointing at him with his spoon. "That is a very good question."

Doc takes a bite of meat. Stew dribbles down his chin. He wipes it away with the back of his hand. Hawk eats quietly. If Doc didn't know better, he'd think he was being played by a psychiatrist understanding the importance of silence following a probing question. For Hawk, this is natural, almost instinctive. It leaves the onus on Doc to respond.

"Wide-eyed optimism, I guess. At least, initially."

Hawk is silent. His steely gaze is intimidating, leaving Doc feeling awkward. It's as though he can see through him. Honesty is what's needed, not lies. Doc might tell himself he came here because he believed in the cause and wanted to help, but his motives run deeper than perhaps even he realizes. Currents swirl beneath the surface of his mind. He's tempted to be dismissive, but Hawk opened his soul. To do any less in response would be insulting.

"Life's messy, you know."

"I know," Hawk replies.

"There are the reasons I tell myself. The reasons I tell my friends and my parents. And then there's the real reason."

Hawk nods.

Doc chews on a piece of meat. It's surprisingly tender and juicy, distracting him rather conveniently.

"Hey, I didn't think we'd get fresh meat this close to the front. What is this? Chicken?"

Hawk smiles. "Rat."

Doc stops chewing. "Oh."

He chews a little slower, struggling to overcome his sudden sense of revulsion. He's fighting a lie, and he knows it. He was quite happy eating the meat before he knew what it was. What difference does it make now? As if to challenge him, Hawk picks a small bone out of his stew and bites on the cooked meat hanging from it. Pretense is a bitch. Doc is at the Front. Nothing matters anymore. This may well be the last meal he ever eats. He might as well enjoy it. He does offer himself a little respite, though, fishing out a piece of carrot to follow on from the meat.

"And the reason?" Hawk asks.

"Ego."

Hawk offers a solitary "Huh."

"Yeah, pretty dumb, huh?"

Hawk smiles. "Yes."

"I mean, it's not now. Oh, ego gets squashed pretty damn quick as you approach the Front. Back home, though, they flattered me. The doctors. The nurses. I don't think it was intentional on their part, but they fed my ego. I felt proud to be doing my part. The big man's going to make a difference."

"Sounds familiar," Hawk says, nodding.

"It does, doesn't it? We're not that different, are we? None of us."

"Nope."

"And then you get here, and you see the carnage, the utter waste, the futility. Death is all around us. There's nothing glorious about the fight. We're barely holding on, that's all."

Hawk says, "We're barbs of wire holding back the horde."

"We are."

Doc turns his attention back to his stew, which has cooled. He eats. There's silence between them, but it's not strained. Out of all the members of the Dog Food Squad, Hawk is the last one Doc thought he'd ever be able to relate to. Not only are they ethnically and culturally different, but their demeanors and personalities are like north and south on a compass, and yet, Doc feels an affinity with Hawk.

As night falls and shadows stretch across no man's land, burying the trenches in darkness, the barrage increases. Explosions thunder along the Front.

"Thank you, Doc," Hawk says, resting a firm hand on his shoulder as he stands on the logs supporting the trench. Hawk drops down onto the boardwalk. Mud squelches beneath his boots, spraying out across the wooden supports on either side of the walkway. Hawk leaves Doc with his stew and his thoughts.

Doc feels uncomfortable being alone. He needs others around him, or so he thinks. Extroverts like Doc feed off others, but deep down, Doc knows he needs to be comfortable with himself. As much as he'd like to keep talking to Hawk or join him walking back to the dugout, this is where he needs to be. It's strange, but as the sky darkens and stars appear, Doc is content. The cold of night descends, chilling the air and causing vapor to form on his breath, but Doc feels warm. He's not sure how long he sits there, but he's eaten his stew, having chased the last few bits of carrot around the edge of the tray.

Soldiers walk past, ignoring him, as they should. Who is he? No one. He's just another chump at the Front. He's no better or worse than any of them. Oh, he's a surgeon, but that's a function, a specialty. His ego is as dead as the bodies strewn across no man's land. As flattering as it was with everyone giving him their chocolate rations, for once, Doc is quietly happy being lactose intolerant. The whole squad risked their lives out there on the battlefield. They should all share in the chocolate.

The cold seeps into his bones. It's time to go inside.

"Are you finished?" a familiar voice asks, and Doc turns to see Happy with a bunch of steel bowls stacked on top of each other. He must be on cleaning duty.

"Sure," Doc replies, handing him his bowl. "Thanks."

"The squad's prepping for deployment."

"Oh, right," Doc replies, dropping down onto the walkway.

"Hey, Doc," Happy says, stalling for a moment before walking away. Doc grimaces, not wanting Happy to bring up the conversation with Hawk. Discretion is needed, not gossip, but Happy says, "When we get back, I need to have one of those talks with you."

"Sure," Doc replies.

Crossing the River

As night falls and the barrage outside increases, William Sunday retreats into her own world. She sits huddled up at the back of the dugout with her legs up in front of her, hugging them to her chest. She has her day-glow earplugs in and stares at Mouse, who's sitting opposite her once again. She mumbles softly. Doc's not sure, but he thinks she's singing quietly to herself.

Lavender and Happy are playing *Snap*. They're using a regular deck, ignoring the suits and racing to slap the slow accumulation of cards any time there's a duplicate. Lavender is slightly quicker, but Happy compensates by holding his hand low, hovering, ready to strike. Occasionally, one of them slaps in time with a nearby shell falling and they laugh at each other.

Hawk is relaxed. Instead of cleaning his already immaculate equipment or methodically laying out his pack, he's sitting there working on his carving. He briefly makes eye contact with Doc and offers a slight smile. For Doc, there's a wonderful sense of irony in how Hawk has taken control of his life by not trying to control everything. He's content.

"That's really good," Mouse says, watching Hawk with interest.

"Thanks."

Leech walks in.

"What are you doing here?" Meyers asks. "You're supposed to be on R&R."

"Oh, I couldn't let you fuckers have all the fun," he says. "Besides, a bit of stem therapy, and I'm good to go."

Doc has been writing in his journal, using his codenames to capture the salient points in the various discussions he's had with squad members. He closes the book and places it on the crate he's using for a table.

Lavender gets up and rushes over to hug Leech. Doc notices that Leech tries desperately hard not to flinch as she grabs him, but he can't help it. Doc also hears the telltale rattle of pills in a plastic bottle. He's got to be doped up to his eyeballs.

"Ah, were you cleared for deployment?" Doc asks, knowing that even with stem cell therapy, his ribs cannot have healed in that time, let alone the internal bruising and bleeding he sustained.

"I'm cleared," Leech says, waving away any concern from Doc.

Meyers says, "You're not deploying with us tonight."

"But—"

"Nope. That's an order."

William Sunday pulls her earplugs out and says, "Hey."

"Hey," is the reply from Leech. Nothing else needs to be said between them.

"You can warm my sleeping bag," Lavender says.

"Now, that I can do," Leech replies, grinning.

"And mine," William Sunday says before putting her earplugs back in.

"Want me to deal you in?" Happy asks, gathering up the cards and shuffling them.

"Sure."

Doc is fascinated by the dynamic within the squad. Leech could have had up to five to ten days at the rear. He may have even been able to apply for leave while recuperating and remained away from the Front even longer, but he didn't. From the way he jokes with Lavender and Happy, it's clear the squad forms an intricate part of his identity. Friendships aren't an accessory to him so much as an extension of his own soul. He needs them. As angry as he may be about the war, Dog Food is family to him. Leech sits on the bench seat. He reaches out, and Mouse gives him a high-five followed by a fist pump.

"You da dawg, man," Mouse says. "You da dawg."

Leech nods. There's a shared sense of respect between them.

The phone rings.

Meyers rushes to the dugout entrance. Everyone turns and looks. No one speaks. No one moves.

"Yes... Understood... We are India in close support."

Meyers replaces the receiver in a daze. His mind is clearly trying to process the orders that have been passed down to him. Doc is confused. It's too early in the evening. They haven't had the thunderous barrage yet or the whistles blowing along the trench.

"What's happening?"

"We're getting royally fucked," William Sunday says, holding her earplugs in her hand. "That's what's happening."

"I don't understand," Doc says.

Meyers doesn't reply. He's looking at the map of the Front, tracing his hand along the various routes that go north from India. Although in this context, India doesn't describe the country, it's 'I' in the NATO phonetic alphabet, being the square grid placed between Hotel and Juliette. And north is east. Whatever's happening, they're going to be trudging through the trenches for a while to get to India before heading over the top and into no man's land.

"We don't do close support," Happy says. "We're medical reserve. We're only supposed to be called out of the trenches if the squad medic is overwhelmed."

"But?" Doc asks.

Lavender replies, "But when command knows they're sending out a Sierra mission."

"A suicide mission," Mouse says, cutting in.

"Then they have us in close support. Basically, we walk behind the troops, mopping up the dead and dying."

"It's a snatch-and-grab," Meyers says.

"It's *always* a snatch-and-grab," Happy says. "Only they never snatch anything other than a bolt to the head."

"They're deploying two hundred soldiers."

Between Lavender, Leech and William Sunday, they each speak one word, saying, "Two—*fucking*—hundred!"

William Sunday shakes her head. She asks Meyers, "And the attrition rate?"

"A third."

"Sixty casualties? They're expecting sixty dead or wounded?"

"We can't cover sixty," Lavender says, shaking her head.

"We're deploying with two other medic units. Delta Hotel 2 and Delta Golf 2."

"That's still twenty each," an incredulous William Sunday says. "And that's assuming the Novos play nice and scatter casualties evenly."

Hawk says, "That's four or five stretcher runs between the trench and the battle."

Meyers hangs his head. "I know. I know."

"What the fuck?" Happy says.

"And there's no rolling barrage," Meyers says.

To which William Sunday says, "It really is a suicide mission."

"I—I don't get it," Doc says, not understanding the significance of the lack of a barrage.

"Novos dig," William Sunday says. "Sending out a rolling barrage ahead of advancing troops limits the Novos ability to crawl and hide in the dirt."

Meyers says, "Command wants a surprise attack."

"Oh, it's going to be a *fucking* surprise all right," an outspoken William Sunday says with indignation. "It'll be a surprise if any of us make it back."

"Objections noted," Meyers says. "I'll put your comments in the Suggestions Box back at Command."

In unison, Lavender and Happy say, "*Your ideas and feedback are greatly appreciated.*" Mouse laughs. It seems their sarcasm is a running gag for the squad.

Doc leans forward and whispers to William Sunday, "Is there really a Suggestions Box back in Command HQ?"

With a straight face, she replies, "They use it for toilet paper."

Meyers calls out over the various discussions unfolding within the dugout. "We roll in five. Get your shit ready."

Doc pushes two crates together and unfolds his replacement medical pack. It came with a stern warning from the quartermaster that the next lost pack would be deducted from his pay, which got a round of laughs from the squad. Mouse said they're all in the red for lost equipment. Happy joked that it's tough collecting debts from a dead man.

Doc checks the pouches and pockets, making sure the pack has been stocked correctly and nothing has gone missing. He has a locked box of additional supplies under the bench seat. He dumps a few extra vials of Oxycodone in his pack, along with large absorbent gauze pads and elastic bandages. He shoves them in the EPR, making use of the hollow insides of the tube for extra space.

"You good to go, Doc?" Mouse asks, hunched over and peering at the pack.

"Ah, yeah."

Doc closes the medical kit. Mouse takes it from him. As much as Doc appreciates the big man's strength, he hates being the exception within the squad. He'd prefer to carry his own pack, but he understands the rationale is to keep him as fresh and nimble as possible. Doc's never been one to shirk his duty. It feels wrong.

Outside, it's a bitterly cold evening. There's no moon, which is probably why mission planners are pushing for the attack. Clouds blot out the stars. Explosions rock no man's land, but these are part of the regular bombardment. Someone somewhere is peering through binoculars, picking out targets and calling in the artillery. Most of the time, the gunners won't know what they're shooting at beyond a few coordinates. Spotters will target shadows. And they get bored. There's a quota to meet, so they'll shell dogs scavenging on the battlefield. Doc talked to the gunners when he was back at the field hospital. They pride themselves on what they call their speed of delivery. Several of them have adopted names such as *Uber Eats* and *Door Dash*. If only they could drop off a few hot meals now and then.

The Dog Food Squad marches along the interconnected V-shaped trenches winding along the Front. Soldiers stand on the sides of the trench with rifles resting on sandbags, but it's rare for them to fire as their line of sight is only a few hundred yards. If the Novos ever got that close, all hell would break out along the line. For the most part, it's humans that probe the battlefield. The Novos are more interested in defense than attack, although when they do attack, they come in relentless waves.

Part of the main trench has collapsed, having been hit by the Novos with boulders. Soldiers work into the evening, digging with shovels. Sandbags are filled with wet clay and stacked high on the brim. From the way the soldiers handle them, it's as though they're filled with lead.

A temporary trench has been dug around the back of the fallen trench, but it's barely three feet deep. Soldiers crouch, rushing across the raised ground and darting between boulders. Bolts of Novo lightning whip past close enough to the ground to leave streaks of dry clay and cracked mud on the surface. Scorch marks from old hits blacken the rim of the trench.

William Sunday points at one of the black patches on a sandbag, telling Doc, "They know the trench is gone. They've got a sniper out there in no man's land, targeting this region, looking for anyone that's careless."

"How much has collapsed?" Meyers asks the corporal overseeing the dig.

"About fifty to sixty yards. There are a few shell holes you can shelter in, but it's pretty nasty up there."

"What's the plan?" Lavender asks, being unusually aggressive. It's her way of making her displeasure known. Being an easy target for Novos weighs heavily on everyone's mind. It's one thing to venture into no man's land; it's another to be target practice for a bolt of lightning. If they're ordered to go over, they will, but Doc can see Lavender is trying to influence Meyers. Technically, as his rank is captain, Doc could pull rank on Meyers and demand they take the long way around, but that would ruin their working relationship. Meyers looks at the squad. Their faces scream in anguish without words crossing their lips.

"We'll double back and box the fallen trench."

"Sounds like a plan," Lavender says, and Doc wonders if she needed to say anything at all. Would Meyers have risked their lives? She clearly felt so. Doc, though, trusts Meyers. He's settled. Out of everyone in the squad, he's grounded. Meyers avoids swinging between extremes like William Sunday. He's able to navigate the madness that leaves Happy depressed. And he doesn't get manic like Lavender.

Meyers leads them back to the previous T-junction, and they head away from the Front. On reaching the next intersection, they turn parallel with no man's land, but this trench has been mined to buy humanity some time if the Front is overrun. Wooden spikes point upwards at an angle, facing the direction from which the Novos and any retreating humans would come running. Dive into the trench to escape the bombardment, and they'll be impaled. Claymore mines run along the slope, facing the Front. They've been set in rows, probably so they can be detonated sequentially, giving the defenders the ability to trigger multiple detonations in the same place at different points in time. There are no soldiers in this trench. And why would there be? It's wired to explode. And yet, it's a better option than cutting across the fallen trench at the Front.

Every forty yards or so, there's a wooden ladder spanning the trench, having been laid flat and level with the ground. From where Doc is on the boardwalk, they appear like bridges, and their intent is clear.

Retreating soldiers are supposed to fall back across these rather than drop into the trap. Doc makes a mental note to watch his step during any retreat.

After a hundred yards of ducking and weaving through the forest of wooden stakes, claymores and mines, they reach another T-junction and turn back toward the Front.

"Well, that was fun," William Sunday says, grinning.

Doc finds William Sunday perplexing. She's soft-spoken and petite. And she's young. At a guess, she's barely twenty. This is the last place on Earth she should be, but the loss of her family drives her on. It is interesting, though, that she chose a medical support team rather than a combat unit. She's not here out of a sense of revenge. It seems she doesn't want anyone else to go through the heartache and loss she's experienced. Regardless of how arduous and physically demanding a mission is, she never seems to tire.

On returning to the front trench, Meyers picks up the pace. Doc can keep up by widening his stance and quickening his stride, but William Sunday has to jog with her backpack and rifle dwarfing her shoulders. In the low light, it's easy to lose one's footing on the slippery boards. Several of the squad have their soft red LED headlamps on, but most of them are saving the batteries. Doc trips when stepping from one set of boards to another in the darkness. William Sunday grabs him by the arm before he falls, preventing him from slipping into the muddy gutter running along the far side of the trench.

"Careful, Doc."

Her speed and strength are deceptive.

"Thanks."

It's over an hour before they reach the staging area in the India segment. Then, the waiting begins. Dog Food lean their packs against the wooden support beams within the trench and sit on them.

"It's always like this," William Sunday says from the shadows. "We're always in a hurry to go nowhere. Then we wait. And wait."

Lavender says, "Maybe one in three missions is scrubbed."

"Yeah. The longer we're sitting here, the better the odds of a scrub," William Sunday says. "We may yet get a good night's sleep."

Meyers moves down the line in the darkness, talking softly. He reaches the three of them and says, "One-twenty-seven, one-thirty and one-thirty-three are over the top. We're up once one-thirty-five is on the move."

Doc feels his heart race. It's strange, but it's the lack of heavy shelling, the lack of gunfire, the lack of Novo bolts, and the lack of any soldiers rushing around that causes anxiety to well up within him. As chaotic as the previous night was, there was no time to think. They rushed along the trenches, up the ladder and into no man's land. Sitting here makes it worse. The anticipation is killing him. It's as though humidity is building on a stinking hot summer's day, and dark clouds are rolling overhead, threatening to rain but never unleashing their fury. At some point, he knows the deluge will come.

In utter silence, the members of the Dog Food Squad get to their feet and don their packs. Mouse grabs Doc's medical kit. The ladder is only a few feet further along the trench, but Doc didn't see it in the pitch-black of night. One by one, they climb the rungs and slip over the sandbags, dropping into a ditch on the other side. Doc loses his footing. A hand grips his jacket, grabbing it in the middle of his back, between his shoulder blades and lifting him before he tumbles. Doc wants to turn and thank William Sunday, but thanks isn't required. Silence is what's needed.

Meyers speaks softly. "Okay, we're four hundred up and hold. Lavender, keep us on track. Hawk, there's a helluva lot of concertina wire in this channel. Watch for snags. I don't want to lose comms with command."

"Understood," Hawk says.

"We're moving in an arrow formation. Happy, you're on point. William Sunday, you're left flank. Lavender, you're on the right. Mouse, you're ten yards back in support of Happy, providing cover fire as needed. Doc and I will be twenty yards back. Hawk, you're bringing up the rear while laying wire."

With barely any noise, Happy, William Sunday, Mouse and Lavender creep up and over the side of the ditch. There are no comments and no complaints. Their silhouettes remain low, barely breaking the ridge. Flashes of blue lightning ripple past, but the shots are high and not directly overhead. Further along the battlefield, flares light up no man's land, casting ghostly shadows over the landscape, but they're a diversion, falling over empty ground.

"Stay close behind me," Meyers says to Doc. "Step where I step."

Doc understands. Meyers is using his body as a shield to protect him. They scramble up the bank and then down into the next shell hole. Ice has formed on the muddy water at the bottom of the crater. Several dead dogs lie half-submerged in the thick mud. They've been shot while scavenging.

Meyers has the agility of a rabbit. He scrambles around the shell hole, peers over the edge and then disappears over the loose rubble. He's not babysitting Doc. There's an assumption that Doc will keep pace. Even without a backpack, it's not easy as dirt slips beneath his boots.

Doc is breathing heavily as he comes up behind a low brick wall beside Meyers. He looks around for the rest of the squad but can't see them in the darkness. Meyers seems to read his mind. He points ahead and then slightly forward and to either side. If Doc strains his eyes, squinting, he can just make out movement in the shadows.

William Sunday is light on her feet. She seems to drift above the debris, darting through crumpled buildings. She appears in a doorway of the only remaining wall of a nearby store. Doc blinks, and she's gone. Ahead of them, Mouse moves like a wraith through the ruins. He's there, and then he disappears, blending in with the shadows. Try as he may, Doc can't spot Lavender anywhere. She's out there, but she might as well be a ghost.

The squad has emerged in a small, decimated Russian town. Slabs of upturned concrete that once formed the main street rise like gravestones on the edge of shell holes. Buildings have collapsed, forming mounds of bricks. The squad picks their way around rather than over the rubble.

Meyers is quick. He darts between rusted cars and crushed buses. Broken glass crunches underfoot. Somehow, the broad metal frame of a billboard is still standing about fifty yards ahead of them. It's been reduced to a skeleton. The billboard is devoid of any of the panels that once tried to sell new cars or promote the latest smiling politician to a skeptical public. Being so visible, it's become a rallying point. It's something that can be seen for hundreds of yards in either direction. Several soldiers have set up a field command post beside the central support. Meyers joins them with Doc out of breath behind him.

"DF3 medical," he says to someone not wearing any sign of rank so as not to attract Novo attention.

"Good, Good," the officer replies. "You're currently at three-fifty. My soldiers are approaching five hundred without contact. Move up to four-fifty and hold."

"Copy that," Meyers replies. He sulks away, staying low. Doc copies him. His eyes are on the footfall of Meyers' boots. He's taking Meyers a little too literally, but for him, it's a way of staying focused. If Doc looks around, he finds the devastation overwhelming.

The plastic head of a doll has been stuck on a reinforced steel bar rising out of a broken cinder block wall. Like the billboard, it's a waypoint. It's an easily identifiable position to which soldiers can fall back and regroup. Doc wonders about who once played with that doll. Was it abandoned, or was it dragged along by an anxious child desperate to hold on to something familiar in the chaos of war? His heart breaks as he spots a tiny skeleton on the other side of the bricks. The child has been buried by rubble, but a bony hand and part of their skull protrude from beneath the broken bits of brick. At a guess, he'd put their age at five or six.

Rats scurry in the shadows as they creep past the remains of a gas station. A collapsed bridge marks the outskirts of the town. The river is still visible from the way it meanders through the land, but the water no longer flows. Instead, it's clogged with debris, forming stagnant pools. Shattered tree trunks, crushed cars, railway carriages, and bits of buildings, such as walls with doorways and window frames, have dammed the river. Ice clings to the muddy banks. The far side of the river has a steep berm, hiding the soldiers from sight. The Novos would have to come over the bank to be able to see them from their side of no man's land.

Several makeshift bridges have been built, allowing foot traffic either way. They're little more than planks spanning the remains of the bridge footings. A single rope sways above the wooden boards, being a token gesture to help with balance. Meyers darts across. The planks shake and flex, wobbling beneath his boots as he jogs over the makeshift bridge, but it doesn't seem to bother him.

Doc hesitates. The thought of plunging into the icy cold water, being swamped by debris and dragged down by the weight of his water-logged uniform and combat boots is not in any way appealing. Drowning is a bitter way to die.

Hawk comes up beside him, saying, "Do you trust me?"

Doc may nod, but it's a lie. His eyes go wide with fear, betraying his doubts. Fear is amplified by uncertainty. The idea of being struck by Novo lightning is an abstract. Falling into the dark water is real, and it terrifies him.

"Trust me," Hawk says. "Run... Don't stop. Don't walk. Keep your hand on the rope and your legs pumping. The faster you go, the more stable you will be. It's about rhythm. Don't fight the flexing boards beneath you. Move with them. If you go slow, you're more likely to fall, and you're an easy target. Understand?"

Doc understands. Intellectually, what Hawk has said makes sense. In practice, Doc is terrified. It's one thing to hear those words and agree with them in principle. It's another to ignore the adrenalin surging through his legs, causing them to shake.

"Think of it like learning to ride a bike. Go slow, and you'll wobble and crash. The faster you go, the more stable you are."

Hawk pats him on the back, saying, "You'll be fine. Trust me. Go fast, and you'll be okay."

Doc swallows the lump in his throat. He places a boot on the first board, feeling it flex under his weight, and grabs the rope with his gloved hand. From the far side of the river, he can see Meyers in the shadows, waving for him to follow.

Hawk slaps him on the back, saying, "Go. Go. Go!"

Before Doc has time to think, he's sprinting along the first board. The shock of being struck by Hawk overwhelms his reluctance, and within a fraction of a second, he finds himself several feet from the river bank behind him and running hard.

The planks are held together with braces nailed beneath them. There are four boards between him and the first concrete pylon. The further he gets away from the bank, the more the planks flex beneath his boots. As he pushes off, the plank sinks away from him, but Hawk is right; by running, he remains level regardless of the way the boards flex. By the time the plank has rebounded back to where he is, his next boot is landing, again pushing it away from him. The rope slides within his open, gloved hand. At the halfway mark between the bank and the first pylon, the boards are wobbling and flexing like a rubber band. They sway and reverberate, traveling easily two feet beneath his thundering boots, but with each step, they rebound, slamming into his soles.

Doc reaches the first pylon. He throws his arms around the remains of the concrete and reinforcing steel rising from the footing of the bridge, hugging it for dear life. His heart is beating out of his chest.

"I—I made it," he says, panting.

"Again," Hawk calls out, and it strikes Doc that he's now stuck. He's raced to the first pylon and celebrated his success, but he's nowhere. Planks and ropes trail behind him and lead in front of him to the next pylon. He has no option. As safe as it feels to be standing on the concrete, he's stranded in the middle of the river. He has to overcome his hesitation again. He doesn't want to. Once was enough, only it's not. He has to push on. Although he may think he has a choice, he doesn't. He can't stay here forever.

Doc stares across the gap in the center of the river. There's a stretch of open water surrounded by ice. The boards in this section look smaller. They're not, but they are crooked, having twisted and shifted under the boots of hundreds of soldiers. The rope seems too high. Even before he sets out, it seems as though the boards will flex well below the rope.

Doc does not want to be here. Of everything he's seen in no man's land, this makeshift bridge terrifies him most. Who the hell thought of this? Why couldn't they send up the Engineer Corps and build something more robust?

Behind him, wood flexes. Boots pound on the planks. He turns and looks. Hawk is running hard with his rifle in one hand and the rope in the other. His head is down, lowering his profile. He charges across the gap. Instead of slowing as he approaches the pylon, he thunders into it, swinging around as he grabs a reinforced steel bar on the other side of Doc. As the pylon is only a few feet in diameter and crumbling, there's barely room for the two of them.

"Fun, huh?" Hawk says.

"Yeah," Doc replies, but he doesn't sound convincing. "Ah, you go first."

"Oh, no, Doc. It doesn't work like that. I'm not leaving you here. You need to move on."

Doc swallows the lump in his throat, looking down at his boots on the shattered concrete. Loose bits of stone fall into the dark water as he shuffles around the pylon. He edges toward the next plank.

"Courage, Doc. That's what you're writing about, huh?"

Doc nods.

"Well, consider this the practical part of the exam."

Doc shakes his head in disbelief. Hawk is right, though. It's one thing to pontificate about the nature of courage and what it means to be brave. It's another to step out on a flimsy wooden plank with icy cold water swirling in the darkness. This time, there's no slap on the back. It's almost as though Hawk is coaching him, telling him he no longer needs a push to get going.

Doc rocks back and forth, building his resolve, thinking about the rhythm of his boots. He bolts out into the void. The concrete pillar falls away behind him. Planks flex beneath his boots. He keeps his eyes on the next pylon, refusing to look down. Doc was right about the rope. Long before he reaches the middle, it's above his head. He's still got a hold of it, allowing it to slide through his gloved hand, but his arm is high above his helmet. Were he to fall, were he to slip and lose his footing, there's no way he's holding onto the rope with just one hand. The thought of plunging into the dark water terrifies him.

Wood groans. Boards flex, threatening to break, but then they spring up beneath his boots. One foot in front of the other, and on he runs. As he approaches the next pylon, the rope becomes lower, which is reassuring. Running uphill along the planks is easier than running down. Somehow, he feels more stable approaching the far pylon.

Doc reaches the second concrete pillar, but he doesn't stop. He wants to, but he can't. Momentum is more than physics: momentum is a mental state as much as a physical one.

"Don't think," he tells himself. "Just do."

Doc steps around the pylon and grabs the next rope. Meyers calls him on, but he doesn't need encouragement. He needs this to be over. From here, it's all downhill as the wooden boards lead to the far bank. He grabs the rope and runs along the planks. The boards no longer rise to meet him. Instead, his boots fall away from him, and it's all he can do not to tumble into the water as he rushes to the other side of the river.

Meyers has his hand out. He's standing on the bank, holding on to the anchor point and reaching out for Doc. Their fingers touch, and Meyers pulls him in.

Doc collapses on the muddy slope, catching his breath. Seconds later, Hawk joins them. He's running a wire behind him from a spool. He started with eight spools and is down to three. In the gloomy half-light, Doc can see the way the thin wire rests on the ice and sends out ripples in the open water. He loses sight of it draped across the half-sunken tiled roof of a farmhouse that has washed down in a flood, but the wire must span the entire river. Doc didn't even notice Hawk laying it down as he ran.

"Are you good?" Meyers asks.

"I'm good," Doc replies. He wants to ask how they handle stretchers across the river, but he doesn't. They'd go slower and would wobble around. As scary as it is, Doc would much rather run across the planks. It's then he spots a set of twin ropes further along the river, spanning the gap. There's a pulley. They must hook them up and haul them over to stretcher-bearers on the other side.

"Well, congratulations," Meyers says. "You're officially halfway. You get to do this all again in a few hours."

"Great."

"If it's any consolation, it never gets any easier."

"That's not what I wanted to hear," Doc replies to a grinning Meyers.

The three of them scale the bank. Although the bridge and approaching road have been destroyed by shell fire, the upturned sections make the climb easy. Rather than scrambling over loose dirt, they follow a trail that winds along the cracked slabs. Happy waits for them in the shadows, having fallen back to talk to them.

"What are we dealing with?" Meyers asks.

"Nothing. I'm not seeing any Novo activity at all."

Happy offers Meyers a set of binoculars. They have a periscope-like attachment reaching up less than a foot, which allows Meyers to observe no man's land without exposing himself to any alien snipers that might be looking for easy targets. A prism built into the top of the binoculars and open to the sky allows ambient light in to naturally amplify the image.

"And our troops?" Meyers asks.

"One-thirty-five is off to the left, about sixty to seventy yards up. Look for the fallen fast-food sign."

"Okay, I see them."

"One-thirty-three is directly ahead. By my reckoning, they crossed the first line about half an hour ago."

"They're at the Novo trenches???" Meyers asks, surprised.

"They're beyond the first trench. The Front is narrow here."

"And there's no Novo activity?"

"None. Our guys are easily a hundred yards behind the lines and nothing. Not a goddamn thing."

"Something's wrong," Meyers says, handing the binoculars back to Happy.

"No shit," Happy replies. "It's quiet out there. Too damn quiet."

"And we are vulnerable as *fuck* on this side of the river. Hawk, get on the horn. Tell them we're across the river but worried about an ambush."

"On it," Hawk says, attaching a handheld receiver to the wire spool on his hip. He talks in rushed but hushed tones.

Happy peers through the binoculars. Meyers must be nervous. He nudges him, and Happy surrenders them to him again.

Meyers peers through the binoculars, using the periscope to scan no man's land. Doc can't help himself. He sees a gap between two fragments of concrete. The way the shadows fall tells him he'll get a clear view without exposing his head. He creeps up and peers across no man's land. With the town behind them, the ruins ahead are of farms and scattered homes. There's a rural church with a graveyard. The tombstones are chipped and broken. Further ahead, denuded trees rise to form a forest. Although the trunks are thick, none of them reach up more than twenty feet. It's as though a gigantic scythe has swept through the air, cutting down the forest as though the trees were nothing more than blades of grass.

A hand on his shoulder pulls him back. Meyers isn't impressed by his curiosity, but if Doc's going to die out here, he'd like to see death coming.

Happy says, "I've got Mouse holding by the tractor. William Sunday is providing cover from the church. Lavender is prone in the field. None of us are happy."

"I know. I know," Meyers says, turning to Hawk. He ends the call and packs up the receiver.

"Command says continue on to the church and set up a triage point there."

"Triage?" Happy asks, raising an eyebrow. "They know no one's wounded, right?"

"Oh, they know," Hawk replies.

The Church

Doc follows Meyers over the edge of the riverbank and into a shell hole, sliding back out of sight. Hawk follows them, looping the wire around an upturned tree root. Happy walks ahead of them, following the edge of the shell hole. He's got his rifle slung over his shoulder and isn't crouching or running. He looks relaxed. Far from slinking between shell holes, he's walking proud.

"What the hell are you doing?" Meyers calls out.

"Testing a theory."

"What theory?"

"That there's no one out here but us."

"Sweet Jesus, Happy. Get in a goddamn shell hole. That's an order."

"Sorry, I didn't catch that," Happy says, walking off along the edge of a broken concrete slab. A collapsed house lies to one side. Its brick chimney still stands firm, reaching up toward the dark sky.

Meyers darts to one side, ducking into a drainage ditch that once ran alongside a now nonexistent road leading into the countryside. They follow it to the church, occasionally dipping in and out of shell holes but remaining below ground level. Happy is in no rush. He walks on with no regard for his own safety.

William Sunday has taken up a position behind the crypt of some wealthy local family in the church cemetery. Whereas most of the gravestones reach up to waist height, the crypt is a concrete building set above ground and wide enough to inter several coffins on raised stone benches. The quarter-inch steel plate door has been ripped off and leaned against a bunch of headstones to provide additional cover.

The crypt is peppered with holes, but the statue of an angel still stands on its roof, missing half a wing. It's a good location to set up triage as it's easy to move around without being seen from the battlefield. The crypt itself is empty. The flat slabs inside reach up roughly three feet, being ideal for treating the wounded, although it won't be comfortable for anyone lying on the cold stone.

"Hey," Doc says, coming up beside her and seeing his medical backpack leaning against a gravestone. Mouse must have dropped it off before moving over to the tractor to set up for covering fire if needed. Meyers and Hawk shelter beside the cemetery's crumbling stone wall. Hawk has the receiver out and is talking to Command. Happy walks up. He towers over William Sunday and Doc, standing in plain sight.

"Will you get down?" William Sunday says.

With a sigh, Happy slumps to the ground and leans against a gravestone.

"What is wrong with you?" William Sunday asks.

"Me?" Happy replies, pointing at himself. "What's wrong with all of you guys? You've walked into a trap, and you don't care. You're pretending everything's normal. It's not."

"What are you talking about?"

"This whole thing," Happy says, waving his arms in the air. "They're inviting us in, and any moment now, they'll spring the jaws on this bear trap." He claps his hands. "And we're dead. Not just a few of us. All of us."

"You're being paranoid."

"Am I?" Happy asks. He turns to Doc, saying, "You're an intelligent man, Doc. What do you think? Am I overreacting?"

Doc doesn't know. This is only his second foray into no man's land.

"I—ah... It does seem unusual that there's no enemy fire."

"They're drawing us in," Happy says.

106

Meyers comes over and crouches, saying, "Don't get too comfortable. Command wants us to move up to the abandoned Novo line and set up there. One-thirty is already in the second row of trenches and recovering a lot of good intel."

"See?" Happy says, holding his hands out.

Meyers looks confused, not having heard Happy's earlier comment.

Doc looks at Meyers and says, "We're going to be an awful long way from our own lines."

"You have your orders." Meyers creeps across the sodden field beyond the cemetery to brief Mouse, who's crouching behind the rusted remains of a tractor half-sunk in the mud.

"We're fucked," Happy says. "We are so fucked."

Without any words passing between them, it's clear Doc and William Sunday agree with Happy, but what can they do? They can't prove anything's wrong. Nothing's wrong. That's the problem. They're in a war zone, but there's no fighting. Far from being an opportunity to advance, the silence should scream at them in warning.

The three of them grab their packs. Mouse looks over from the tractor. Doc signals "*No*" with a wave of his hand. He can take his pack from here. Mouse nods.

Meyers and Hawk creep forward to the edge of the cemetery. Lavender is already on the move, darting over toward a fence post leaning on an angle on the other side of the decimated road that runs in front of the church. Mouse hunches, rushing between shell holes in the field on the far side of them.

Happy walks tall. He has no intention of creeping up to the empty enemy trench. William Sunday walks beside him, defiant. Fuck it, Doc thinks. He clambers out of a shell hole and joins them. The three of them walk along the broken slabs of concrete that once made up the road.

From the ditch, Meyers calls out, "Get into cover."

None of them so much as turn to acknowledge him. They walk on, making their way around the shell holes that have punched through the road.

As Doc steps from the crushed rubble to a concrete slab the size of an upturned kitchen table, he comes to a halt, looking down at his boots. William Sunday senses his unease. She stops as well.

"What's wrong?" she asks.

Doc crouches. He picks up a handful of dirt, letting it run through his gloved fingers.

"Strange."

"What's strange?" Happy asks, standing on the slab and looking at the mud on the edge of the broken concrete.

Doc stands and turns, looking back the way they've come. He spots similar mounds scattered around the edge of various craters and fallen buildings. If they continued creeping through shell holes for cover, he would have never noticed, but from where he's standing, he gets a good view of the battlefield. There are freshly turned piles of dirt spread roughly forty to fifty feet apart on the edge of the concrete, next to the numerous shell holes.

"Ah," he says softly. "We really shouldn't be out here."

"What do you see, Doc?" William Sunday asks, alarmed. She raises her rifle to her shoulder and scans the area, peering through her starlight-enhanced sight, but, like the others, she's overlooking the ruins. She's looking for Novos creeping forward to attack, but there's no movement.

"We're surrounded," Doc says. His hands tremble at the realization of how close they are to being slaughtered.

Meyers comes to a halt near enough to hear them talking. He's still in the ditch, but he doesn't seem angry. He's curious about what's got the three of them to stop in the middle of the decimated road.

"What is it, Doc? What's got you spooked?" William Sunday says, turning and looking behind them as that's the way Doc is staring. Happy scans ahead of them with the scope on his rifle. Doc is petrified.

Doc takes his time answering William Sunday, but not because he doubts what he's seen. He pauses because he's looking for cover.

"Fresh dirt."

"There's always fresh dirt," Happy says.

"Not when there's been no bombardment," Doc replies, pointing at the dirt beside the cracked concrete slab.

"Fuck."

William Sunday crouches. With the butt of her rifle, she gently pushes the topsoil to one side, slowly burrowing beneath the freshly turned earth. Happy holds his rifle hard into his shoulder and points the barrel down at the dirt, barely two feet in front of his boots. His finger is on the trigger.

Meyers clambers out of the ditch and joins them, staring at a patch of freshly turned earth beside the concrete slab. He knows. He communicates with hand signals, clenching his fist, but not just to ensure the three of them are quiet. He's signaling the whole squad. He repeats the gesture, holding his fist up high and then uses two fingers to point back toward the church. In the shadows on either side of the road, Mouse and Lavender begin pulling back.

William Sunday stops shoveling. She's cleared less than a foot of soil from the top of the broad mound. A neon blue glow seeps through from beneath the dirt. Novos are lying in wait all along the trail, buried just out of sight, waiting for the signal to spring their ambush.

Meyers points at Hawk in the ditch and then pinches his fingers together, holding them toward the sky before opening them out, mimicking an explosion on the ground. Hawk attaches the receiver to his wire spool and talks softly to Command, passing them coordinates.

Doc's legs are shaking. He needs to pee. His bladder feels as though it's about to burst.

Meyers taps Doc on the shoulder, quietly signaling for him to join the others and withdraw to the church and then the river beyond that, but Doc is paralyzed with fear. Death lies at his feet. Meyers grabs him by his pack and drags him away, pushing him toward the church. Doc looks. There are at least five freshly turned mounds between him and the wall of the cemetery. He can skirt them, but how many lie within the graveyard itself? And what will trigger them to wake?

One by one, the soldiers retreat along the decimated road. Happy is the last to leave the slab, keeping his rifle aimed at the faint blue glow in the shadows.

Meyers mumbles, "Fuck, fuck, fuck."

Meyers, William Sunday and Doc are facing back toward the cemetery and the river beyond that, but Happy doesn't take his eyes off the freshly turned dirt. He's got his rifle set hard against his shoulder. He scans from side to side, alternating between the three closest mounds as he steps slowly backward, feeling for the ground beneath his boots.

Once they're back at the crypt, Meyers says, "Spread out and search the grounds. If those fuckers are in here, I need to know where. The last thing we need is for one of them to spring out of a goddamn grave."

Lavender and William Sunday scour the ruins of the church along with the graveyard. Happy checks the brick wall surrounding the yard.

Mouse crouches in front of Doc, asking, "Are you okay? You look like you've seen a ghost."

"I have," Doc replies. "Mine."

Mouse laughs, slapping him on the shoulder. "You're all right, Doc."

Meyers takes the receiver from Hawk. Although Doc can only hear one side of the conversation, it's clear Command doesn't believe him.

"You're not listening to me," he says, holding the phone with an iron grip that threatens to crush the molded plastic. His knuckles go white. "We are surrounded by Novos. Dozens of them are buried north of the river. We need an immediate barrage, or no one north of here will be able to fall back to the front line... I know, I know, no one else has reported Novos in this sector. If they had, we wouldn't have been sent forward, but I'm telling you, the ground is riddled with them... Why didn't anyone else spot them? I don't know. They weren't looking for them, I guess. Hell, we almost stepped on one before we saw it... No, it didn't react... Yes, I'm sure... Jesus Christ. This is going to be a goddamn massacre... Do something, damn it!"

He ends the call by handing the receiver to Hawk in disgust.

Lavender and William Sunday dart between gravestones as they move back to the crypt.

"What did you find?" Meyers asks.

William Sunday says, "Three Novos. One in the northwest corner. One in the rubble of the church."

"And one on the southwest corner," Lavender says.

"We've set trip wires and grenades. When they emerge, they're gone."

"And we'll know it," Lavender says.

"We certainly will."

Happy asks, "What's the plan, Sarge?"

"Command wants us to continue moving up to the Novo line."

"Well, fuck that," William Sunday says, beating everyone else to that sentiment. "They're crazy!"

"They're overstretched," Meyers replies. "They don't doubt we found a buried Novo, but they don't believe my estimate of how many are out there. And they want coverage during the retreat. We're supposed to head up to the line while DG medical holds here."

"Fuck that shit," Happy says.

"Fuck that shit indeed," Meyers says. "We're not a military unit. We're medical. We can't hold off dozens of Novos popping out of the dirt. We're pulling back to the river. We'll provide cover fire from there."

"And our troops?" Mouse asks, looking toward the Novo lines.

"If we go up there, we'll die with them," Meyers replies. "The best thing we can do for them is to provide cover fire from the river bank."

Mouse lowers his head. He doesn't like what he's hearing, but like all of them, he knows there are no other options. They're too small to fight anything other than a few Novo stragglers.

"What are they waiting for?" Doc asks

"As many as they can get in the net," Meyers replies. "Command said they'll drop in a barrage to support retreating troops if needed, but to fire now will give away the mission and strand the advanced teams on the wrong side of no man's land. The mission is too—"

"The *fucking* mission?" Lavender says, cutting him off. "The goddamn fucking mission is now a body bag count."

"By the time the Novos trigger the ambush, our boys will have to drop shells right on top of their own troops," a frustrated William Sunday says.

"I know," Meyers replies, shaking his head. "I told them they need to clear the land now before our troops fall back, but they're nervous. They still think they can pull this off."

"Bastards," Happy says.

"All right, we are pulling back using a reverse arrow."

"A shovel," Happy says. "Call it a shovel."

"Because it's going to bury us," William Sunday says.

Meyers ignores them. "Hawk, you and Doc will take the lead. I'll be in the middle. Mouse, I want you on the two-oh-three at the rear. If we have contact, get those grenades flying. Lavender and Happy, you're on the flanks."

"And me?" William Sunday asks.

"You're paired with Doc. You're never more than two feet from him, understood?"

"Understood."

Before they move out, the lead scout for the DG squad arrives at the rear of the graveyard. Meyers takes him and the squad sergeant to one side and briefs them.

Doc hears, "Well, *fuck* that," drift on the breeze.

Both squads pull back to different ends of the riverbank, with DG heading toward the western edge and Dog Food heading diagonally to the east. As they approach the bank, there's an explosion. Doc turns to see a puff of dust rising from one corner of the graveyard.

"Down," William Sunday says, pushing his helmet so hard she forces him to his knees. Doc slides into a shell hole as she turns with her rifle already up and pressed hard into her shoulder, peering at the church from over the edge of the crater. Two more explosions break in rapid succession as the other booby traps go off. Whether the first was accidental or not is difficult to tell, but once it went off, the Novos awoke.

All across no man's land, blue glows erupt from the battlefield. Gunfire breaks out. Flashes of blue lightning tear through the air.

Blue Blood

Across the battlefield, there's yelling and screaming in between the cracks of lightning and the bursts of machine gun fire. Novos rise from the freshly turned earth like zombies. Dirt tumbles from their torsos. Mouse is firing his grenade launcher. Each shot comes with a distinct *Ka-Thonk,* followed barely a second later by the detonation. Depending on whether the grenade landed in mud or on a slab of concrete, there's a chesty thump or a resounding *boom!*

William Sunday slides into an old crater with Doc. She pushes his head beneath the lip of the dirt. Although she's keeping him safe, she's also inadvertently preventing him from seeing what's unfolding, which is even more terrifying. In his imagination, a Novo is about to appear on the edge of the shell hole at any moment, and he'll be trapped, unable to run.

William Sunday returns fire. Empty shell casings bounce off Doc's helmet. He moves away from her, working his way around the other side of the crater. At a guess, they were less than fifty feet from the riverbank when all hell broke loose. That's three, maybe four craters they need to traverse.

From the far side of the shell hole, Doc can see the tip of the church steeple leaning on an angle and a distant rise, but most of no man's land is still hidden from sight by the far edge of the crater. As tempting as it is to creep higher, Doc resists his curiosity. On the distant hillside, though, he catches glimpses of Novos disappearing from sight. Although they naturally glow in a neon blue, their skin is like that of a cuttlefish. They can blend in with the background. Their limbs can become all but transparent, with only their skeletal structure being barely visible, making them difficult to see. As effective as their camouflage is, though, it has its limits. They can't sustain it forever, so they wink in and out of existence like fireflies. Perhaps it's like breathing, and they can only hold their breath for so long before returning to neon blue again. At a guess, Doc would put the frequency at about 45 seconds. Also, the flat, open ground doesn't suit them, which is why humanity has engaged with them on the plains of southern Russia. It was the American Expeditionary Force that scorched the forests in this region, denying them the ability to blend in with the trees.

From an evolutionary perspective, humans are predators, meaning their sight is based on detecting movement, which counts against the Novos. They may be able to turn translucent, but the motion of their limbs betrays them. The soldier's disruptive camouflage might be primitive by comparison, but it's effective, distorting shapes and causing the Novos to second-guess their shots.

The Novos on the hill adopt brown camouflage to blend in with the mud around them, but their silhouettes are exposed when seen from a prone position.

Gigantic rocks begin falling before any shells land. Boulders the size of cars pound the bank, causing sections to collapse and slide into the river. The Novos at the rear, firing their equivalent of artillery, aren't trying to hit anyone so much as to cut off any retreat, trapping the medical squads between them and the river.

William Sunday scrambles over the loose dirt within the crater.

"What are we going to do?" Doc asks as mud rains down upon them.

"We need to go sideways," she replies, pointing. "Get out of the kill zone."

"Okay," Doc says with eyes as wide as saucers.

"There's a crater ten feet that way," she says. "I'll be right behind you. Go. Go. Go!"

William Sunday turns, firing back across the shell hole at advancing aliens. Like the humans, they use shell holes for cover, darting in and out of them with astonishing speed. Between this and their camouflage, they're almost impossible to hit.

Doc scrambles out of the crater and along the edge of a narrow ditch. His boots pound on slabs of broken concrete. He runs for twenty feet, thirty, forty. There are no craters. There's nowhere for him to dive for cover. He staggers on in the darkness, clambering over a fallen fence that threatens to entangle him in loose strands of wire.

"Sunday," he yells over the thunder of the battle breaking around him. "William Sunday. Where am I going?"

There's no reply. To his right, the riverbank explodes as boulders slam into the slope. He can't go that way. It would be suicide.

Wooden weatherboards slip beneath his boots, threatening to topple him, but still, there are no craters. He scrambles over the crushed remains of a house. A wrought iron bathtub stands on a flat expanse of tiles, being all that remains of what was once an ornate bathroom. The white enamel paint is chipped. The plug is out. A thin sliver of mud lines the bottom, but most of the rainwater has drained away.

Doc climbs into the bathtub. It's no crater, but it will allow him to hide until William Sunday catches up. He curls his legs, lying on his backpack, looking at the dark clouds rolling across the sky. Bolts of blue lightning crisscross the night.

Shells fall. Explosions rock no man's land. Clods of dirt and rock are thrown in the air. The bombardment is deafening. Doc clasps his hands over his ears, trying to block out the sound. The ground shakes. Rocks pepper the bathtub, striking it like the *ratatat* of a machine gun, but the wrought iron holds. A shell lands nearby. The compression wave rippling out causes the air around him to thicken. Dents appear on the inside of the tub. If Doc had been in the open, his legs would have been torn to shreds by the red-hot shrapnel.

White flares are fired, illuminating the night. They linger, drifting on tiny parachutes with smoke billowing behind them as they descend, allowing the soldiers to target Novos on the battlefield.

The air is electric. Static causes his damp uniform to cling to him. Lightning surges, rushing across no man's land.

From somewhere to his left, shells begin raining down in quick succession. They pound the ground like an angry giant. Roughly fifty miles behind the Front, someone has given the order to walk a series of high explosive shells in a line, probably in response to a request that has come from a spotter like Hawk. Doc can feel them moving toward him. There's nothing he can do. Each impact strikes closer. He wants to clamber out of the bathtub and run, but where? Being caught in the open when shells land is a death sentence, forcing Doc to hold his nerve.

A wall of dirt sprays across him, landing in the bathtub as a nearby shell decimates what little remains of the house he scrambled over. Doc never hears the next shell. The world around him goes white. The bathtub is lifted off the tiles and sent tumbling through the air. Doc falls. He's thrown free from the tub and ends up rolling on the dirt. Another explosion rocks the ground. He feels it rattle his bones, thumping through his chest.

Doc scrambles forward on his hands and knees. Blood drips from cuts on his face. A piece of shrapnel is embedded in the side of his neck. As he moves, blood rushes from the wound. He tumbles into a shell hole and slides toward the muddy water at the bottom as another explosion rocks the Earth. Dirt cascades over him. Rocks pelt him. And then there's silence. In reality, the battle continues to unfold, but the shells falling fifty yards away are quiet by comparison. His ears are ringing. His uniform is torn. One sleeve has been ripped away, exposing his arm to the cold of night.

Doc slumps against the side of the shell hole. He feels weak. He has no idea how much blood he's lost, but it doesn't take much to lose consciousness. Shock is more than a mental state. It's a physiological reaction to a severe injury. He knows his mind is trying to protect itself by shutting down and shutting out the overwhelming sensations assaulting his body.

"Stay awake," he scolds himself. "You're okay. You've got to focus. Be present. Stay with me. You're going to be fine."

Doc reaches up and touches the shrapnel in his neck. It's warm. Blood trickles beneath his uniform, running down the side of his chest.

"Half a pint," he mumbles to himself. "Got to keep the loss to under a pint."

Fresh dirt slides down around him. Electricity crackles along the loose dirt within the shell hole. Neon blue goo drips on his shoulder. It runs down his front, causing him to freeze in panic. Something touches his helmet, rocking his head to one side. A Novo clambers across the edge of the shell hole.

Doc springs around the inside of the crater, twisting and turning as his boots sink into the soft soil. He's facing a Novo. It's injured, but that's not what distracts him. The alien is nothing like the images he was shown before deploying to the Front. There are none of the segmented, multi-part creatures he saw in dozens of classified images. Doc got a glimpse of the Novos on his first night, and it confused him back then as well. From a distance, in the darkness, the Novos look terrifying, but up close, it's clear there's a torso surrounded by numerous appendages that, to his mind, resemble baby elephant trunks. Those beneath the creature carry it on like legs. The feet taper to a point. Those around the torso act like the arms of an octopus. They search the air, sampling it. Blue lightning crackles between them, dancing across pale skin. Dozens of dark eyes peer at him. He blinks. He's looking at a massive compound eye in the middle of the creature, but it's segmented with multiple lenses.

The wounded Novo reacts to Doc. It fades, blending in with the dirt on the side of the shell hole for a moment, all but disappearing were it not for the indentation of its legs in the soft mud. One of its arms, though, has been severed near the creature's torso and weeps blue blood that cannot be hidden.

"Easy," Doc says. He's got one hand on his wounded neck and the other out, trying to still the alien as though it were a wild horse.

He swings his pack down off his shoulder, resting it on the side of the crater.

The Novo reacts. The arms facing Doc stiffen as electricity builds. Sparks arc through the air.

"No," Doc says, holding out both of his arms and pleading for the alien not to fire. Blood drips from his fingers. "I'm unarmed."

Whereas moments ago, the electrical charge was building, now it wanes. That could be because the alien is succumbing to its injuries, but Doc suspects there's more to its response.

"You're injured. You're hurt. I am, too."

The blood running down the inside of his uniform is soaking into his trousers.

"I—I don't have long. Neither of us do. But I can help."

With one hand still held out with a flat palm, appealing for time, Doc reaches down with his other hand and slowly unzips his backpack.

"I'm a doctor," he says, gesturing to his medical kit. "Not a soldier. I'm sworn to save life, not kill."

Blue lightning crackles across the arms of the Novo, centering on one elephantine-like trunk as the charge builds. Under ordinary circumstances, the monster would have fired by now, but being wounded, the alien can't summon all its strength.

"I—I'm dying. Like you. I'm losing blood. If I don't stem the flow, you won't need your lightning weapon."

Doc slumps backward, sitting in the dirt. His boots slide into the muddy water.

"I can help. Please. Let me help you."

For Doc, his plea is a survival strategy. If he's a threat, the alien will kill him. If he can help it, maybe, just maybe, it will let him crawl out of this shell hole and through the mud back toward the river.

Doc's talking more for himself than the creature. He doubts it can understand him. If the Novos have the ability to speak, it's not apparent. Given that the evolutionary differences between them span not only billions of years but trillions of miles as well, their means of communication are probably entirely different.

"Look. I'll show you what I'm going to do. I'll treat myself first."

Doc flips open his backpack, allowing it to unfold into four sections. The Novo flinches, unsure whether such an action poses a threat. And it's at that moment that Doc understands what's transpiring between them.

"Trust," he says. "I get it. We're at war. We're enemies. There is no trust. But not you and me. Them. Out there. They're shooting at each other. But not us. We're hurt. We're injured. Look. I'm bleeding, too."

He reaches up, unclips his helmet and tosses it in the muddy water at the bottom of the crater. Doc touches the wound on his neck. Blood drips from his leather glove as he shows his hand to the alien.

"See? You and I. We're both casualties. We both need help."

Thin strands of blue lightning jump from the Novo's trunk to the dirt, spreading around the crater like a spiderweb, surging and then disappearing.

Doc is past caring. He's running out of time. He pulls off his gloves.

"Coagulant," he says, explaining what he's doing to himself. Doc sprinkles a packet of white dust on the side of his neck. "This will help slow the bleeding."

He pulls out a few rolls of elastic bandage along with several heavy trauma gauze pads. He tears open the sterile packaging, tossing the torn plastic in the mud.

"I'm making a donut," he says, feeling delirious from the blood loss. "Well, not the kind you fry in oil and dip in sugar, but you know what I mean. Maybe you don't."

Doc winds the elastic bandage around a gauze pad, forming a donut-like ring with the absorbent material.

"It's a torus. A circle with a hole in the middle. The shrapnel in my neck. I need to immobilize it. Stop it from moving. Can't take it out. Could bleed to death. But I don't want it moving around. It could cause more damage. Got to stop the bleeding."

He tilts his head to one side, showing the Novo what he's doing. Gently, Doc places the donut over the shrapnel.

"Now comes the tape. Now, I've got to hold the donut firmly in place until I can get into surgery."

He tears strips of medical tape with his teeth and applies them to his neck. The blood prevents several of the strips from sticking, so he uses a gauze pad to wipe his collar clean and applies more tape.

"See?" he says, laughing at the insanity of the moment. "You can see. But me? I can't. Oh, how I'd like to see, but all I can do is feel the wound and the bandage. I think it's secure. I hope it holds."

His fingers run over the shrapnel and around the donut bandage, checking that the metal is held firmly in place.

Electricity crackles across the Novo. Blue goo drips from its severed limb. Every instinct he has screams at him to run. Given that the alien is injured, he could probably clear the edge of the crater before it could charge its biological weapon and fire, but Doc isn't thinking about himself. An intelligent being is suffering. Out on the battlefield, it would fry him without a moment's hesitation, but the equation has changed.

Doc feels as though the war has come to an end, not only the war but the entire universe as a whole. Isn't this what happens when someone dies? The world shrinks around those that remain. Nothing else matters beyond what little life there is in this darkened crater. Black holes could collide nearby, and he wouldn't care. Supernovas could light up the night and his eyes would remain on the wounded Novo.

"I don't understand your physiology, but I can slow the bleeding. Do you understand?"

Doc grabs a couple of major trauma gauze pads from his pack. They're the size of dinner plates and highly absorbent. He pulls out a roll of elastic bandage and edges toward the Novo with the medical tape in his hand.

The Novo flinches, pulling back and half-burying itself in the mud on the side of the shell hole.

"Easy," he says. "I'm not going to hurt you."

Doc leads with one of the pads out in front of him. He's got the rest of the medical supplies tucked under his arm. The crackle of electricity fades.

"This is going to hurt, but it already hurts, right? That's one thing we have in common. Pain."

Doc places the gauze pad over the severed limb. Blue goo glows from within the material as it soaks up the alien blood. He presses a second pad in place over the first and uses a long strip of elastic bandaging to wrap around the edge of the pad, holding it in place. He tears strips of tape, sticking them to the grey alien limb.

"Ah, you're all muscle, huh? Not too many bones. We have similar creatures here on Earth. Elephants have long muscular trunks. Octopus and squid are similar, but not us humans. Our muscles attach to bones."

He grabs a second roll of elastic bandage, saying, "I'm going to restrict the blood flow above the injury. Not as tight as a tourniquet, but tight enough to slow the bleeding. That will buy you some time. Do you understand?"

Doc winds the bandage around and around the severed trunk. Blue alien blood clings to his uniform, smudging with the dirt and mud.

"Okay," Doc says, wiping the sweat from his forehead with the back of his hand and inadvertently wiping glowing blue goo on his skin, leaving a streak that looks like a neon bandana.

Doc retreats to his backpack. He closes it and hoists it on his shoulder.

"I'm going that way," he says, pointing toward the river. "I'm returning to my lines. You should do the same. You should make your way back to your lines. Go in peace, my friend."

Blue electricity ripples over the Novo, but it's not threatening. The creature rises on its trunk-like legs. Dozens of eyes in the center of its torso peer at Doc. He's fascinated. Whereas humans have bilateral symmetry, with one side of their bodies mirroring the other, the Novo is more like a starfish. It could be facing in any direction. Its trunks come in rows that extend around its body, with those beneath it carrying it like legs. The intermediate row seems almost redundant to him, but he's sure they play a role in the creature's physiology. The top row acts like the arms of an octopus. Above them, the creature's head appears as a slight dome with eyes peppered around its grey skin. It's only now that he notices the upper arms are set on one side of the creature, suggesting it does have a sense of forward and back.

Doc climbs up to the edge of the shell hole, dragging his pack with him. He turns and looks at the wounded creature. The Novo mirrors his motion, preparing to go the other way across no man's land. As he watches, its body turns transparent. The trunks are practically invisible, but the alien's torso appears muted, almost like a shadow. The trunks that act as legs seem to have grey bones within them, spanning at least what would equate to the thigh bone in humans.

The Novo rises into the night, being barely visible except for the white bandaging soaked in blue blood. The alien limps over the edge and disappears from sight.

"Take care, my friend."

Doc turns toward the river. He is exhausted. Shadows mark several craters between him and the edge of the bank. A low fog hangs over the battlefield. Gunfire erupts along with flashes of lightning, but it's sporadic. Both sides are licking their wounds after the brutal bombardment.

Doc crawls over the mud on his hands and knees, staying low, shuffling with his legs. Bits of wire tear at his trousers. His knees scrape on bits of brick, but he doesn't dare stand. Given that he's covered in Novo blood, he's likely to be shot by both sides. He's slow. He's exhausted. He's weak from blood loss. It's all he can do to shimmy off his elbows and push with his legs. His boots slide on the mud, failing to gain traction, making it difficult to move forward. He drags his pack along with him as though it were a comfort blanket, something he should let go of but can't. Minutes feel like hours.

Doc slides into the next shell hole, covered in mud and grime. From the shadows, he hears a familiar voice.

"Doc?"

"Sunday? William Sunday?"

"I thought I'd lost you."

Doc works his way around the crater, being careful not to topple into the muddy water at its base. Dead bodies float face down in the mire.

William Sunday is lying to one side, but her left leg is propped up unnaturally high. It's as though she's trying to straddle something while lying on the ground.

"Are you okay?" he asks.

"Are you?" she replies, pointing at the lump of bandaging on his neck.

"I've been better."

"I need you to pull me off this thing, Doc."

It's only then that he gets a good look at her. A slab of concrete has slipped into the crater. William Sunday must have been thrown onto it by the blast that toppled him. She's been skewered by a length of reinforced steel bar protruding from the cracked concrete. Doc drags his pack up beside him.

"What are you waiting for," she asks, but he's looking at the way blood has run from her leg down over the dirt, pooling in the mud. She's lost a lot of blood. More than him.

"I can't pull you off that thing."

"What?"

"There are two arteries running next to the femur. I think you've punctured at least one of them. If I pull you off that, you'll bleed out."

He crouches next to her, peering into the darkness and touching the steel bar. It's embedded in the concrete and won't budge. Doc feels lightheaded. Whenever he moves suddenly, he's left feeling giddy. For fractions of a second, the night goes pitch black, meaning he's on the verge of losing consciousness altogether if he's not careful. He needs to slow down his movements.

"You can't leave me here."

"I'm not going to leave you," he says, reaching up and pulling the headlamp from her helmet. It's held in place with a strip of elastic. He fixes it over his head and turns it on. A soft red glow surrounds them. Doc twists the switch on the side of the light, wanting to turn it white so he can get a better look at her wound, but it's broken.

"What are you going to do?"

"Whatever I can," he replies, unfolding his medical backpack and laying it out before him.

Doc pulls out his glasses from the top pocket of his uniform. One of the lenses has a crack running through it. The other has blood and mud smeared on it. He wipes the lenses with a cloth, but he smudges rather than cleans them.

Doc dons a pair of disposable blue surgical gloves. He lines up the equipment he needs, including a scalpel and several clamps. They're sealed in plastic to keep them sterile, so he tears the packages open, leaving them lying on the plastic.

Doc is trapped in a dream. He knows everything that's unfolding around him is real, but his mind is drifting into lower brain states. Whereas he should be wide awake, he feels drugged. He's relaxed, which may seem fine, but at the moment, he needs heightened senses. He needs focus. As it is, he'd love nothing more than to curl up and go to sleep, although he knows he might not ever wake.

"Ah, that's a lot of stuff you've got there," a nervous William Sunday says, looking at the equipment he's laid out. Her rifle is lying beside her. She keeps one hand on it. For Doc, it's a peculiar form of comfort blanket as it does nothing to help her, but she finds solace in the myth that she could somehow defend herself while pinned to the concrete slab.

"We've got some work ahead of us," he says, wrapping a combat tourniquet around her leg above the injury. He pulls it tight, cinching it up. Doc knows a slightly loose tourniquet can make an injury worse by cutting off the venous return to the heart while not stopping the arterial inflow that's coming from the heart. He has to be precise to stop the bleeding, or her leg will become distended with blood everywhere. Doc uses a pair of surgical scissors to cut away her trousers. He grits his teeth, willing himself to stay alert.

"You," she says, sounding alarmed.

"Me," he replies, humoring her as he readies himself to perform surgery in a shell hole while being injured himself.

"You've got Novo blood on you."

"Yeah. It's been quite a night."

"How?"

"Long story," he says, slurring his words. "Okay, I'm ready. I'm going to pull you up off the slab. This is going to hurt."

"Everything hurts," William Sunday says.

"Chew on this," he says, handing her a stick of Fentanyl, but knowing it will take time to kick in.

"Oh, hell yeah," she says, popping it in her mouth.

"Once you're off the bar, I need to operate. It's going to hurt like hell, but I need you to stay still, understand?"

William Sunday nods.

Doc positions himself beside her, placing one arm beneath the small of her back and the other under her knee. He lifts, pulling against the suction of the steel bar lodged within her thigh. As he flexes his muscles, dots appear before his eyes. He's on the verge of blacking out. It's all he can do to pull himself back from the abyss.

"Ah. Ahhh. Ahhhhhhh," she calls out, ending in a yell of pain. The vehemence in her cry shocks him into conscious awareness.

"Easy," he says, lying her next to the bar and grabbing a gauze pad. He's got the scalpel between his teeth and a medical clamp in his other hand.

"I need light," he says, prying into the bloody mess of muscle on her leg. He works with his gloved fingers, pushing within the wound and feeling for arteries beneath the muscle. He has to dig deep, pushing against the flow of blood running out of the gaping wound. His eyes blur, and he loses focus. He grits his teeth, willing himself to think clearly.

"More light," he says as a blue neon glow shines on his hands. "Yes, that's it."

William Sunday has arched her back in pain. Her helmet pushes against the concrete. She's got her eyes shut tight, grimacing in agony.

"To the left," he says, using one hand to hold the wound open as he presses inside her leg, feeling for the artery. The eerie blue light drifts to his left. In the back of his mind, he knows something's wrong, but he doesn't have the mental bandwidth to process any more thoughts. It's all he can do to concentrate on the surgery. His fingers tingle. His arms feel drained not of blood but of life itself.

"Got it," he says, slipping two clamps in place, one near the arterial tear, the other further up to prevent back-bleeding. He takes the scalpel and cuts away some of the muscle, giving him a better look at the wound.

"I need suction," he mutters to himself, struggling to see past the blood pooling in the wound. He pushes in a few clotting sponges next to the artery, allowing him to see the injury better.

"Nicked the artery," he says, grabbing a sterile needle and thread from his pack. "A quarter of an inch to the right and that bar would have severed the artery entirely."

He works with the needle, sewing up the hole in her superficial femoral artery. William Sunday groans. Every muscle in her body is taut. Her gloved hands are clenched in tightly held fists. Doc blinks, only his eyes fail to open again, and he loses consciousness. His head rocks forward suddenly as the muscles in his neck go limp, shocking him awake.

"Steady," he says, talking to himself, trying to keep himself awake. "Almost done. I need more light."

The blue light shifts, and he continues working.

"Okay, I'm closing up," he says, sprinkling some coagulant powder on the wound. He applies a pressure bandage with a gauze pad and releases the tourniquet. Sweat drips from his forehead in the cold. A sense of relief washes over him. His muscles go limp, demanding rest.

"That's it. That'll do until we get you back to the lines."

William Sunday opens her eyes, but she's not looking at him. She's looking past him, staring at something over his shoulder. Her hand goes for her rifle. Lying on her back with her knees up, she lifts the rifle, but she's weak. She can barely raise the barrel. Electricity crackles behind Doc. Blue strands spark around them, jumping to the dirt.

Doc rests his hand on her rifle, pushing it down.

"No."

He turns. The light around him is coming from two Novos on either side of them. They're within the crater and out of sight from anyone on the battlefield. They seethe and crackle with electricity.

"Wait," he says, holding his hands out and appealing for mercy. Doc sways. Is this real? Is he dreaming? Is this a nightmare?

The closest alien probes him, poking at him with the fine tip of its upper arm. It seems intrigued by the blue goo smeared on his uniform. It touches his forehead. The tentacle-like appendage is cold.

A disembodied voice says, *"Both casualties... Both need help."*

"Yes, yes. We're both injured," Doc says, but there's something unusual about the alien's words. At the back of his mind, there's a nagging sense of longing. Although they seem to relate to him and William Sunday, these are the terms he used with the wounded Novo, but neither of these aliens are injured.

"I'm not going to hurt you."

Under her breath, William Sunday asks, "What the hell is going on?"

Doc holds out a hand, wanting her to be quiet. The alien may have said it's not going to hurt them, but, yet again, these are *his* words. Although its voice is deep and resonates, the words are spoken with an accent—his accent. Doc is struggling to comprehend what's happening. The aliens are recycling his words as they feel they're appropriate.

"Trust... We're at war. We're enemies. There is no trust."

"But not you and me," Doc replies, recalling his next few words to the wounded Novo. He touches his bloodied glove hand to his chest, tapping his sternum. "We're not fighting. We're not out here to fight."

"Sworn to save... not kill."

"Yes," he says. Doc's still got one hand on William Sunday's rifle. He can feel her trying to bring the gun to bear on the closest alien. He pushes the barrel down, keeping it lying on the concrete. William Sunday relents, probably because she's so weak.

"You should make your way back to your lines."

129

"Yes, yes. We will," Doc says, again recognizing his words being repeated back to him. The two Novos disappear from sight, fading as their skin turns transparent, vanishing like ghosts in the darkness. Within seconds, they rise over the edge of the shell hole and rush into the night, leaving only a fine trickle of dirt tumbling down into the murky water.

"What the *fuck*, Doc?" William Sunday says.

"Let's get you out of here," Doc replies, helping her stand.

He feels faint. As he rises on trembling legs, his sight fades. Darkness surrounds him, but not the dark of night. His knees shake. He breathes deeply, bracing himself, demanding more from his frail body.

Together, they limp up the far slope of the crater. The bandage around Doc's neck has become loose. The tape lifts. Blood seeps down his chest, but he pushes on toward the river. As they come over the rise, Meyers and Happy rush to grab the two of them.

Dozens of wounded soldiers are waiting to cross the river on stretchers. Doc and William Sunday join them. A medic checks his wound and applies a clean dressing. She hooks up an IV line, laying the plastic bag above his head and running fluids into his arm.

As he lies there on a flimsy stretcher under the dark sky, looking up at the distant stars, Doc wonders about the war.

What the hell are they fighting for?

Hawk

Doc wakes to voices talking softly around him.

"Greece is beautiful this time of year," a woman says. "It's not too hot, and the beaches are amazing. The water glistens like gemstones."

"I'm rotating out to Poland," a man says. "But if I get the chance, I'll go down to Greece. I've always wanted to see the Acropolis."

"Oh, it's stunning," the woman says. She continues talking, but her voice fades.

Doc stares up at a star cluster. It's beautiful but bright. Seven stars have been set in a tight group. Pleiades has seven stars, he remembers. Well, seven visible stars hiding over a thousand in the cluster overall. But they're haphazard and scattered. These are evenly spaced. His eyes struggle to focus, and he realizes the cluster is mirrored half a dozen times, circling a central, bright star. He's confused. He's hallucinating. Or is he?

Someone's tugging at the side of his neck. He can feel the skin rising, but there's no pain. If anything, Doc feels as though he's floating on a cloud.

"Florence is a great place to visit while you're here in Italy," the woman says. "The statue of David is in..."

Her voice trails off. She leans over Doc, peering down at him. A flimsy paper hat covers her hair, while her nose and mouth are hidden behind a blue disposable surgical mask. Kind eyes peer at him from behind clean glasses. At that moment, it's her glasses that strike him as most peculiar. Since he arrived at the Front, Doc hasn't been able to clean his glasses properly. There's always a slight smudge on the lens. It's not visible when he breathes on the glass, fogging up the lens to clean it, but it never entirely disappears. This woman's glasses reflect the light around her like crystal.

"Ah, I think the anesthetic is waning."

"On it," another voice says, and darkness overwhelms Doc.

He blinks, or at least, that's what it feels like, and suddenly he's awake, lying on a bed with the back slightly raised.

A doctor seated at a central station on the ward rises. She sees Doc raising his arm to examine the catheter in his wrist. Clear tape stretches over a needle punching into his arm. The skin there has an orange/yellow shade, having been stained by an iodine solution to sterilize the area.

As he goes to turn his head, Doc feels the pull of bandages stuck to his neck, restricting his motion.

"Good evening, Dr. Walters," the duty doctor says.

Doc feels nauseous. Sick wells up in his stomach. The doctor anticipates him vomiting. She holds a small, plastic sick bag up near his face. Doc takes it and spits rather than spews, clearing his mouth of the putrid, metallic taste of general anesthetic permeating his throat.

"Oh, I feel like shit."

"Here," she says, offering him a glass of water. He sips. That there's no taste at all is a welcome relief.

"Thank you," he says, handing the glass back to her. She rests it on the bedside table within easy reach.

"You were lucky. Really, lucky," she says. "That shrapnel was embedded *under* your jugular vein."

"Under?"

She hands him a manila folder full of scans and X-ray results. Doc flicks through them.

"It was the angle," she says, tapping one of the images. "The point of entry was from behind, cutting forward and down through the neck muscle, coming to rest near the thyroid."

"Damn," Doc replies, squinting to make out the detail in the scan. He needs his glasses.

"Who dressed your wound out there?" she asks. "Because, whoever it was, they saved your life. If they'd tried to remove the shrapnel, it would have torn through your jugular."

"Me."

"You? You did that yourself?"

"In the dark, with bombs exploding around me," Doc says, smiling.

"Well, you did a damn good job," the doctor says, calling over a couple of orderlies and asking them to escort him to the ward.

"Ah," he asks before they wheel him away. "How long will I be here?"

"In the recovery and rehab ward? About a week, maybe longer."

"And then?"

"You can take up to two weeks R&R in Europe."

"No. I'm keen to get back to my squad."

The doctor smiles. "I think that's going to happen much quicker than you think."

Before Doc can ask a follow-up question, his bed is wheeled out into the corridor. The signs within the hospital are in English and Italian.

"Where am I?" Doc asks the orderly pushing him along the linoleum floor. Ordinarily, he'd crane his neck to see the person he was talking to, but the bandages wrapped around his throat are stiff and unwieldy for a reason.

"You're in the US Army hospital in Vicenza."

"In Italy?"

"Yes."

After winding through the seemingly impenetrable maze of corridors within the aging building, Doc is brought into an open ward. There are no individual rooms, just beds separated by curtains.

"Hey, there he is," William Sunday says with a burst of enthusiasm he's come to expect from her. Regardless of circumstance, she's always bubbly.

Rather than lying in bed beneath the blankets and sheets, she's lying on top of her meticulously made hospital bed. Like his bed, the back has been raised, allowing her to lounge on it. William Sunday has her legs crossed and a magazine lying on her lap. She's wearing the typical surgical smock designed to allow easy access to any part of the body. It's flimsy, barely covering her, with open sides tied with ribbons. Her left thigh is wrapped in a thick bandage.

"Hey, Doc," Meyers says with both arms in casts. At a guess, from the way they've been set, he's broken the humerus in his upper left arm and probably both the radius and ulna in his right forearm. Once, it took a minimum of twelve weeks for bones to mend, but with stem cell therapy, that's been reduced to barely six days. He'll get the equivalent of growing pains in his bones, but that can be negated with meds.

Happy is in traction, which looks worse than it is. Although his legs are in casts and raised by cables attached to a steel frame extending over his bed, his recovery time will be measured in days rather than weeks. The weights, though, look as though they're applying enough pressure to drag him out of the bed. He was asleep when Doc rolled in, but he wakes with all the talking. Given that Meyers and Happy were the ones who helped them down the bank, their injuries must have happened after they crossed the river. Doc's recollection of that night is clouded by the haze of pain and drugs he was given, but he vaguely remembers being lowered into a trench as dawn broke.

Mouse is outside. He's wearing shorts but no T-shirt, even though it's winter in Italy. Water drips from his body. Their ward opens out on a shared recreation area that includes a swimming pool. Mouse sees Doc arrive and grabs a towel. He dries himself off and walks inside.

Doc's bed is parked next to William Sunday's berth. The curtains are open. The orderly checks a few items on Doc's chart and then leaves him with a carafe of water and a few pills to control pain and reduce nausea.

"Are you coming for a swim?" Mouse asks, standing in the doorway and rubbing his hair dry. "It's heated."

"Uh, no. I'm fine," Doc says, still getting over the effects of the general anesthetic. His head is throbbing. He's dehydrated. He pours himself a glass of water.

"You should come for a swim," Mouse says, bubbling with enthusiasm. "It's so nice. This place is uber cool." With that, Mouse goes back out into the courtyard. He dumps his towel on a deckchair and jumps into the pool. Mouse leaps high into the air, clutching his knees up into his chest and yelling, "*Cannonball!*" A wall of water shoots out as he splashes into the deep end of the pool. Waves wash over the side.

Doc isn't sure if he's dreaming. "Is he okay?"

"He's fine," Meyers replies.

"No, I mean, so, there's nothing wrong with him? How is he here?"

Meyers laughs. "Mouse is special."

"He's invisible," William Sunday says. "No, really."

"I mean, look at him," Happy says, pointing as Mouse hauls his massive frame up on the side of the pool, dragging water with him. He steps back and runs, jumping in the air and bombing the pool again. Water rises as if in response to a shell exploding. Waves race around the pool, washing up over the sides.

"Oh, I can see him," Doc says. "He doesn't look invisible."

"That's the thing about Mouse," Meyers says. "He's so big, so visible, he might as well be invisible. No one ever questions him. If he pushes you in a wheelchair or helps with a stretcher, no one stops him."

Being somewhat facetious, Happy says, "That little fucker gets away with murder."

"Little?" Meyers says, chuckling.

"He gets away with Italy," William Sunday says, laughing.

"Hell, I was supposed to remain in the field hospital back in Chelyabinsk," Meyers says, "but Mouse insisted we stay together, and no one was going to argue with him."

"So Lavender and Leech," Doc says. "And Hawk? They're back in the dugout while we're getting the royal treatment in Italy?"

The banter dies. Eyes lower. Doc realizes he's blundered into a sore point without knowing it.

"What happened?" he asks.

William Sunday says, "Hawk didn't make it."

Happy says, "He took a bolt to the chest. Fried him in seconds."

"Oh, fuck..."

Doc feels his heart sink. He feels cheated. Hawk was his friend. It seems utterly cruel and inhuman for Hawk to have died without Doc even knowing. Out of all of them, Hawk was the one Doc connected with on a deeper level. Doc feels he should have at least been there for him. No one should die alone. Doc can't help but blame himself. His job is to save soldiers' lives where possible. If he could have, he would have at least held Hawk's hand as his life ebbed away into the mud and slush. To hear about it days later is cruel. Doc has been robbed of the anguish. Hawk's death is discussed as though it were a fact on some quiz show when the man's life was torn from him—from all of them.

"I'm sorry," William Sunday says as tears roll down Doc's cheeks.

Hawk's death seems like a cruel joke. It doesn't seem real. The cognitive dissonance in Doc's mind is such that he wouldn't be surprised if Hawk joined Mouse out by the pool and everyone laughed at a prank being played on him. To not be there when Hawk died, to merely hear about it from someone else, seems wrong. Life is more precious than hearsay. Hawk deserved better.

Death is an imposter. Doc decides death is a fraud. He knows it's real, but death is nothing of itself, nothing other than the absence of life.

Hawk's life may have drawn to a close in the darkness of the battlefield, but it's life that's important, not death. And what is life? A tiny collection of atoms is crafted into a body with a brain inside a womb, and then it's unleashed on the world. And that particular collection is roughly identical to billions of other collections on Earth. The great contradiction of human life is that everyone's essentially identical at a biological level and yet entirely unique, experiencing consciousness as though their own personal awareness was all that mattered within the vast, lonely universe. For a brief moment in the exhaustive history of the cosmos, a tiny bunch of atoms has the opportunity to be Doc, Hawk, William Sunday, Happy, Meyers, Leech, Lavender and Mouse. And then they're gone. Not the atoms. Just the person they formed. The atoms themselves will continue on seemingly forever. Some of them will go on to become part of other people, but they'll never again know what it means to be any of them.

Doc feels the pain of regret. He'd love nothing more than to have one last conversation with Hawk. Doc is an extrovert. Ordinarily, he wouldn't go out of his way to talk to an extremely introverted person like Hawk, as the conversation would invariably be one-sided, but Hawk was different. His words may have been few, but they struck with weight.

Doc only hopes he outlives the war. He feels he owes it to Hawk to visit his ex-wife and daughter, Marie and Heather. Doc won't sugarcoat the handful of days he knew Hawk, but he'll make sure they understand Hawk was more than a husband and father. He kept the squad alive in no man's land. Doc made notes on his discussion with Hawk before the assault. He feels Marie and Heather deserve to know what lay beneath the surface of that complex man.

When they get back to the dugout, Doc will make sure Hawk's carving reaches his family. If anything, it seems strange that Hawk would carve an eagle rather than a hawk. Doc meant to ask him about it, but he feels he can guess at the answer. Hawk wouldn't want the carving to be about himself. He'd rather deflect attention to others. Doc swallows the lump rising in his throat.

"He was a good man," Meyers says.

"He was," William Sunday replies.

"It was a noble death," Happy says.

"Don't bullshit me," Doc replies, feeling angry at the implication that he needs to be placated with such a hollow concept. "There's nothing—nothing noble about death."

Happy raises his hands as if in surrender. He meant no harm by

137

his comment. He was trying to be kind. Doc understands that, but he doesn't want any part of the whitewashing of the alien war. All wars are recast in a favorable light—and by both sides because both sides need to justify the insanity. Win or lose, the only way to see war as anything other than a senseless loss of life is to call it noble and courageous. War should be called waste. War destroys. It never builds. War is a necessary evil, but Doc has no illusions about it; war *is* evil.

"Look, I know what you're saying," Doc says to Happy, trying to soften his previous comment. "I—I understand."

"He was fixing the wire," Meyers says. "That first barrage by the Novos cut our line with Command. Hawk was searching for the broken section, trying to reconnect the phone, when he took a bolt from a Novo rising out of the dirt.

William Sunday blurts out, "Doc killed one!"

"What?" Happy asks. "You? You killed a Novo?"

"With what?" Meyers asks.

Doc is silent.

"He was covered in Novo blood when he got to me. Doc had blue goo everywhere. When he first dropped into my shell hole in the darkness, I thought he was one of them."

Happy props himself up on his elbows with his legs split apart in the stirrups holding him in traction. With a sense of disbelief, he asks, "You killed a Novo in hand-to-hand combat?"

"No," Doc replies. "It wasn't like that."

"What was it like?" Meyers asks. "How close did you get to one of those things?"

"And how the hell did you get away?" Happy asks.

Before Doc can explain, William Sunday blurts out, "And he can talk to them. He talks to Novos."

"What???" Meyers says, narrowing his eyebrows.

"Look," Doc says, still feeling groggy from the anesthetic and struggling to recall specific details from what seems like a nightmare. "It wasn't like that."

"I heard them talk," William Sunday says. "Doc was patching me up. He had his medical pack lying open on the mud. He needed light. He asked for light, and they gave it to him. That blue/white stuff."

The look on Meyers' face is one of disbelief. Even Happy's quiet, wanting to hear more.

"The big one said, *I'm not going to hurt you.*' And he didn't. He could have. He could've fried us in a heartbeat, but he didn't."

"They can talk?" Meyers asks.

"Just like I'm talking to you," William Sunday replies.

"What else did they say?"

"Ah, there was something about trust. They said, *We're at war. We're enemies. There's no trust.*' But Doc didn't agree. Doc talked them out of killing us. He said something like, *But not us. We're not fighting you.*' I—I couldn't believe what I was hearing. Doc convinced them to let us go."

"Is this true?" Meyers asks.

Doc says, "Ah, yeah. It was... It was chaos, you know. It was dark. I was injured. I'd lost a lot of blood. My heart was beating out of my chest. I—I think William Sunday remembers it better than I do."

"Damn," Happy says.

Meyers shakes his head. There's more he wants to say. There are questions he wants to ask, but Doc can see he's holding back. Whether that's because Doc has only just come out of surgery or whether he has his doubts about the incident, he's unsure. Doc wants to tell Meyers more about what happened out there in no man's land, but his memories are vague. Over time, they'll come back, but he feels weak. He's in a recovery ward for a reason.

Doc leans back on his bed and closes his eyes. Happy starts talking about other Novo encounters he's heard at the Front, but it's clear he's relaying second or third-hand information, and the details are muddled. Happy means well, but he's conflating situations and confusing events.

Doc remains silent. He feigns being asleep, not just because he's fatigued and in no mood for a discussion, but because he's trying to unravel precisely what happened to him in no man's land.

Heroes

A few days later, a nurse walks in carrying a basket.

"Mail call."

Everyone sits up except William Sunday. For her, the presence of a cheerful nurse circulating letters from home seems to bite. With no living family, she's used to being skipped. The nurse, though, stops by her bed and hands a letter to her.

"Me? For me?" William Sunday says, pleasantly surprised. She looks at the sender, and her face lights up. "It's from Lavender!" She hugs the letter to her chest before opening it. Doc smiles. It's good to see her full of joy.

The nurse hands Doc a letter from his fiancé, Jean, back in Chicago. He rips open the envelope, leaving a torn edge. He's expecting a few photos, a wad of half a dozen pages and a few newspaper clippings, as Jean's normally quite chatty and likes to talk about local news. Instead, there's a single page. It's typed rather than handwritten, which is unusual for her, but it is signed by her. Doc unfolds the letter and leans back on his raised bed.

Chris,

I'm sorry.

Doc chokes. His eyes dart away from the page, looking up at the curtain tracks on the ceiling surrounding his bed. He wants to get up and pull the curtain around him, but he can't. That would be too obvious. Tears well up in his eyes. He looks back at the page.

Once, I thought you were my soulmate—the one for me. The only one. But you've changed. I've changed. We've grown apart.

Doc bites his lips, curling them inward and pressing them hard together. A tear rolls down his cheeks. Everyone has mail except Happy. Their two beds are set diagonally opposite each other. Their eyes meet. Happy knows. He must see the tears rolling down Doc's cheeks. Doc's expecting him to say something, but Happy is silent. For someone who's verbose and outspoken, he shows restraint. He lowers his eyes, looking down at his hands in his lap. He's clearly seen other soldiers dealing with *Dear John* letters before and knows how painful they are to read.

I've met someone else. I know this must be hard on you, but I can't lie to you. I have to tell you. I have to be honest. Please, don't hate me. When you look back at our relationship, I hope you'll see it as I do, as a wonderful chapter in both of our lives, but, like all stories, it has come to an end. I treasure our time together. I hope you do, too, but it's—

Doc can't read any more. He folds the page neatly and replaces it in the envelope with meticulous care. It's an act. He wants to tear the letter to shreds and toss it in the garbage can, but he can't. No one wants him to keep up a pretense, and Happy already knows, or at least suspects, but Doc has to hide his feelings. He doesn't want to, but he must. His pride demands that he remain strong. He places the envelope face-down on the set of drawers beside his bed and pours himself a glass of water. Doc uses his knuckles rather than his fingers to wipe his eyes after knocking back the water. The combined motion is a convenient way of hiding his grief. He feels as though a knife has been plunged into his chest, breaking through his sternum and into his heart and lungs. His body aches.

William Sunday is radiant. She relates the news from the Front.

"Lavender said she's been reassigned to laundry duty while we're in Italy. She said the chocolate bars are still coming. Can you believe that? We're going to have sooo much chocolate when we get back!"

She looks to Doc for his reaction, but he's still in shock. Happy must realize that as he cuts in and says, "We need to get some real chocolate from around here to take back with us."

As they already have too much chocolate, his comment doesn't make sense except in that he's running interference for Doc. William Sunday is oblivious to the dynamic unfolding between the three of them.

"That's a *great* idea," she says, holding up her letter and adding, "Look. I got hearts and kisses."

Doc excuses himself. He gets up and goes into the communal bathroom, locking the door behind him, and sits on the toilet. He doesn't need to go. He feels empty. Doc cries like he's never cried before, burying his head in his hands. His chest heaves. The pain he's experiencing is psychological, but it feels real. After steeling himself and breathing deeply, he gets up and runs the shower, wanting to distract himself from his anguish. He turns up the heat. Steam forms on the mirror. Doc stands there beneath the shower with his tears falling along with the warm water. It's therapeutic, allowing him to ground himself before returning to the others. His wound dressing is waterproof, but he can feel some of the tape lifting.

Doc's got to move on. He has to. He doesn't want to, but he has no choice. Any choice he thought he had in the relationship has been ripped away from him. In the quiet of the night, he'll have a few more tears to shed, but he needs to bring himself back to the moment. He dries himself, gets dressed and walks back out of the bathroom with his shoulders back and his head held high. A fake smile adorns his lips.

The US Army hospital in Vicenza dates back to the Second World War, but it wasn't formally recognized as a US Army Base until the 1950s. The architecture is a mix of post-war austerity and recent buildings, making it a sprawling combination of dull, precast concrete bungalows and towering offices with glass frontage.

The Dog Food squad has been housed in the old rehabilitation section, which has been used as a backup for the larger US military hospitals in Germany for over forty years. The wear on the floors and walls is apparent.

Roses grow outside the windows, but as the seasons change, the bushes are dormant and devoid of both flowers and leaves. Thorny branches reach up from the soil. To the untrained eye, they look dead. For Doc, they're all too reminiscent of how he feels.

The ward opens out on a courtyard used for rehab by four other wards and includes a heated pool, outdoor exercise equipment and physiotherapy components such as parallel bars to help someone learn to walk again. The grassy patches have turned brown as winter reaches northern Italy.

Doc keeps a low profile for a couple of days as he recovers. The conversation invariably gets around to his Novo encounter again, but he downplays the significance of the interaction. He struggles to reconcile what happened to him with the vicious cycle of death and destruction that dominates the war. And his heart still aches at the loss of Jean, leaving him feeling depressed.

Late one afternoon, Mouse brags, "You know they caught one that night, right?"

"They did?" William Sunday asks, sitting in a leather armchair with her legs up, soaking in the warm sunlight coming through the windows.

"A Novo?" Happy asks.

"Yeah. They had it in chains. They dragged it through the trenches."

"And you saw it?"

"Oh, yeah. I saw it. The damn thing was ravenous. It lashed out like a wild animal."

For Doc, hearing this is too much. He snaps, "Well, of course, it reacted like a wild animal. We were treating it like a wild animal."

Meyers is silent, but the look on his face suggests he feels torn by

Doc's reaction.

"They're bad. They're evil," Mouse says, defending his comment.

"Are they?"

"Of course they are," Happy says, lounging on his hospital bed diagonally opposite Doc. "They're the enemy."

"The enemy?" Doc asks. "We know nothing about them. And they know nothing about us."

"What do you mean?" William Sunday asks.

"We think they're evil. They think we're evil. Brilliant! That's genius-level reasoning. What have either of us accomplished? What have we proved? Nothing."

"Easy, Doc," Happy says. "We didn't start the war. That wasn't us. That was them. They came down here and stole our land."

Doc ignores his point, asking the others, "What do we know about them? Where have they come from? Why are they here? What do they want with Earth? Don't you see, we know nothing about them."

"What is there to know?" Mouse asks.

"Everything," Doc says.

Meyers is diplomatic. "You think there's more we need to learn about the Novos?"

"Yes," Doc says emphatically. He's exasperated. To him, this seems obvious. "We... We're operating on assumptions. We're fighting a war against an enemy we don't understand. And our assumptions are... they're..."

"They're what?" William Sunday asks.

"Wrong."

"Are they?" a skeptical Happy asks.

Doc sits up straight on his bed, using the controls to raise the back of the mattress. "Think about it. What does it mean to be good or bad? To be evil?"

Mouse is sitting on a couch with its back to the courtyard. He says, "To do bad things."

Doc points at him, asking, "And you... Have you ever done anything bad? Does that make you evil? Unredeemable?"

"It's not the same," Happy says. "We're at war."

"We are," Doc concedes. "And what we see on the battlefield is horrific, but it comes from the same place. Being good or bad is a myth. No one's a saint. No one is pure. No one is either good or bad. We're a melting pot of both."

Doc sighs. From the tone of his voice, it's apparent he's not talking about the aliens.

"We're human. We make mistakes. We get annoyed. We say the wrong thing. We upset someone. We hold grudges. Anger gets out of hand. Does that make us bad?"

In the back of his mind, he's thinking about his conversation with Hawk. Although Doc has never struck anyone, he understands how Hawk could fail at that moral hurdle. Hawk made a mistake. And he paid a horrible price for that personally, but does that make him evil or simply flawed and in need of change? Doc feels a pang of regret that Hawk never had the chance to prove that he'd grown. The man who died out there on the battlefield was not the same person who struck his wife. Having spoken to him, Doc knows it was something Hawk could never make amends for, and yet regret brought heartfelt change to his life.

"What does it mean to be evil?" Doc asks. "To be bad?"

Mouse says, "If you kill someone, you're bad."

"Have you ever killed anyone?" Doc asks.

"I've killed Novos," Mouse replies.

"But that doesn't count, right?"

"No."

"Well, I've killed people," Doc says, and the temperature within the room seems to plummet. "Am I bad? Am I evil?"

Mouse stutters, "I—I..."

Happy says, "But that's like during surgery and stuff, right? That's an accident."

"That's different," William Sunday says. "It's not like you're a murderer."

"Tell that to their families," Doc replies. "They're still just as dead."

Happy asks, "And you think the Novos are killers but not murderers?"

"I don't know," Doc replies. "I'm not sure anyone knows. The problem is that we're operating on assumptions about good and evil when life is never that clear-cut. There's no black or white, just a murky grey."

William Sunday gets emotional. She chokes up as she says, "They killed my family. To me, that's a fact, not an assumption."

"And I'm sorry for your loss," Doc says. "But you were there with me that night. You saw them. You heard them speak. You know there's more to them than mindless killing machines. They're not monsters."

William Sunday hangs her head. The weight of grief from losing her family still hangs heavy on her heart. She fights back tears. "I—I don't know what I saw."

"They spared us," Doc says. "They didn't have to. It would have been easy, oh, so easy, to obliterate us at point-blank range, but they didn't."

William Sunday swallows the lump in her throat, saying, "I know."

Happy is defiant. "When they landed, they swarmed over the land, killing everyone in their way."

"That's what we've been told," Doc says, reflecting on his encounter with the Novos in no man's land. "That's a summation of what happened, a simplification, but is it the whole story?"

"You think they're lying to us? Our own people?" Meyers asks. That he's interjected is significant. For the most part, Meyers seems content to listen to the debate as it unfolds, but this point has him on edge.

Doc knows he's on shaky ground with the squad. Try as he may, he's not going to convince them the Novos are anything but bloodthirsty murderers, but he has to speak up. He can't ignore what happened to him in no man's land.

"For all the casualties in war, there's one death that's never mourned, one that's seldom even recognized. There's never been a gravestone for truth, but it's always the first thing that dies out there on the battlefield."

Meyers shakes his head. He doesn't agree. "I can't believe I'm hearing this."

Happy says, "What the hell happened to you out there in no man's land?"

"I connected with them," Doc says. "I saw them as something other than *the enemy*. I saw them as conscious beings. And they saw me the same way."

Meyers asks, "And you think that gives you the right to question the war?"

"It gives me the right to question the narrative *behind* the war. Ask yourself this. What are we fighting for?"

"Freedom," Mouse replies.

"That's the official line," Doc says. "And I bet you that's what the Novos tell themselves as well. The truth lies somewhere out there in no man's land in the filthy mud at the bottom of a shell hole."

"Okay, explain this to me," William Sunday says, "By your reasoning, what makes someone bad?"

Doc thinks for a moment.

"Most people aren't bad. They're oblivious. They're sleepwalking. They say something stupid and hurt someone, but not because they're evil, because they're blind. But us. Our reaction to their bumbling stupidity is ruthless. We react. We think the worst of them."

"What do you mean?"

"Okay. Imagine this. You're driving up a freeway onramp, and you're distracted. You're singing along to a song on the radio, or you're trying to remember what you need to pick up from the store, and you cut someone off. What do they yell at you?"

Mouse blurts out, "Asshole!"

"But are you?"

"No," William Sunday replies.

"The next day, you're driving up the same freeway onramp, but this time someone cuts *you* off. What do you yell at them?"

"Asshole!" Mouse blurts out again.

"And are they?"

"Yes," Mouse replies, laughing. "Everyone is an asshole but me."

"No, they're not," William Sunday says, cutting him off.

"Exactly," Doc says, ignoring Mouse and focusing on her response. "It's called the *false attribution fallacy*. We assume evil intent. It's easy to see other people doing something wrong and blame them for it. But we never blame ourselves when doing the exact same thing."

Meyers says, "And you think that's what's happening with the Novos?"

"I don't know," Doc replies. "But assumptions are dangerous. We're fighting blind. We're determined to kill the enemy, but we need to stop and ask ourselves why."

"What the hell happened to you out there?" Meyers asks.

"I was hurt," Doc replies. "I wasn't thinking straight. Blood was running down my neck. I was in pain."

"And?"

"And I stumbled into a shell hole."

No one speaks.

"And there, opposite me, was a Novo. It was injured. It had lost a limb. Neon blue goo dripped from a severed arm. Lightning rippled over its body."

No one breathes.

"Ah, it started charging its electricity thing, but it was wounded. It needed more time. And me? I'm dead. Either through blood loss or a bolt to the chest. Nothing matters anymore.

149

"So I start talking to it. I drop my pack and dress my wound, telling it precisely what I'm doing to myself and why. And once I'm done, I do the same for the Novo."

Happy is aghast. "You helped a Novo?"

"We were both dying. When you're dying, you see life in a different light. Your values change."

"And—" Happy asks, but Meyers holds out his hand, wanting him to stop. Happy falls silent, but not willingly.

"So I stopped the bleeding," Doc says.

"You showed mercy," William Sunday says.

"Yes," Doc replies. "Then I crawled across no man's land, tearing my uniform on the loose wire in the mud, and slid into the shell hole with you."

"That's why they let us go," William Sunday says. "They were showing us mercy as well."

"Yes," Doc says. "They were returning the kindness. Don't you see? We don't understand them. We think we do, but we don't. We've got this mindset that they're the enemy—and they are—but why?"

To Doc's surprise, it's Happy that replies with, "I don't know."

"Exactly. If knowledge is power, ignorance is crippling."

Meyers says, "We think we're heroes."

William Sunday says, "So do they."

"Yes," Doc replies.

Meyers asks, "So you think they can be reasoned with?"

"I don't know," Doc says. "But I don't buy the party line. I don't buy into the idea that they're ravenous monsters that want to suck our blood or whatever it is we hear on the news."

"I know monsters," Happy says with a surprising degree of confidence. "I've met plenty of monsters back home. Do you know what makes a monster?"

No one replies.

"It ain't hate. It's indifference. They just don't care. When someone stops caring, they become a monster. And they're the nicest people. Oh, they'll smile and hug their kids, but if they don't care about you, you're fucked. They'll discard you like a dirty rag."

Doc is perplexed by Happy. He's drawing upon some past experience, but it seems he doesn't want to elaborate on specifics. Doc would love to learn more about the incident he's describing, but he doesn't want to derail the conversation.

"They cared," William Sunday says.

"They did," Doc replies.

"I cannot *fucking* believe this," Meyers says. "You're telling me the Novos care about you. What's next? We wander out into no man's land, hold hands and start singing *Kum ba yah*?"

"No," Doc says.

"So, what do you want to do?"

"I don't know." Doc is frustrated. "I don't know what to do. I just know what happened to me in that goddamn shell hole. All I know is William Sunday and I should be dead, but they let us go."

"Damn," Happy says, shaking his head.

"This isn't going to end well," Meyers says, getting out of bed. His motion is abrupt. Doc wants to question him about his comment, but Meyers is strident. He's not angry, but he's not happy either, making his displeasure apparent by the way he physically leaves the discussion. He gets up and uses the shared bathroom beside the entrance to the eight-bed ward, effectively killing the conversation.

Meyers doesn't close the door behind him. He stands there with his back to them and pisses into the bowl. Urine churns the water in front of him. If William Sunday is offended, it doesn't show on her face. She has an old print magazine. She's been flicking through it for days now and had it on her lap during their debate. William Sunday has been reading and rereading articles out of boredom, but this is different. She's hiding behind the pages. Doc suspects she feels offended at the way Meyers has ended any debate. From the sound of his stream, he really needed to go, but leaving the discussion open-ended feels wrong. And he could have closed the door. He should have closed the door.

Meyers doesn't flush the toilet. He finishes and walks past the basin without washing his hands. For someone who's supposedly concerned about the welfare of his troops, he's oblivious to the impact of life in the trenches on his own mind.

Doc can't help but wonder about the role of habits in the war. He doubts Meyers means to be blunt, but after nine months in the trenches, pissing and shitting in a bucket in the corner of a dugout, he hasn't acclimated to civilization again. Not yet. He will. Or he'll seem to. Regardless of how tough and balanced someone might appear on the surface, war is traumatic. A soldier may leave a war zone, but the war zone never leaves the heart. Post-traumatic stress is not an excuse for poor behavior. It's a reality of the frail condition of the human mind. The problem is that no one wants to appear weak, but *hiding* weakness weakens people further. The worst of PTSD comes from denial. Doc doesn't want to question Meyers in front of the others as he wouldn't want to undermine his leadership, but Doc doubts the sergeant is as grounded as he seems on the surface.

Happy and Mouse go back to playing cards, using Happy's bed as a desk. They're jovial and boisterous.

William Sunday gets up and dons a hospital gown with woolen fluff around the edges. It's old and ragged but warm. She walks out into the courtyard as the sun dips below the rooftops. Doc watches as she wraps her arms around her against the cold. That she left as Meyers returned seems deliberate, but it's probably a subconscious reaction on her part. She's been living with the squad in the trenches for so long that privacy has all but disappeared. Here in the hospital, though, she can be alone by simply walking out into the courtyard. She sits on the edge of the pool and rests her legs in the warm water. Steam rises around her. Doc would describe the pool as tepid rather than hot, but with the temperature dropping, it's probably quite pleasant. It's heated by a thermal spring beneath the hospital.

The contrast between William Sunday and Mouse doesn't go unnoticed by Doc. She's content to sit there watching ripples roll across the surface and the way the last rays of light play on the water. Mouse would miss these subtleties with one of his cannonballs.

"I'm sorry, Doc," Meyers says in a soft tone of voice that goes unnoticed by Mouse and Happy on the other side of the ward. "I know you want to think what happened to you out there changes something. It doesn't. It changes nothing—nothing at all."

The Meat Grinder

It's another five days before they're flown to Chelyabinsk and begin their arduous journey back to the Front. No one takes up the offer of extended R&R in the Mediterranean. They don't discuss it at all, even though the rehab nurse approached each of them individually about the option. Pride binds them as a squad.

On their way back, the various discussions that arise between them center around mundane details of resupply or discussion about what they're going to do once the war is over. No one talks about the Novos. No one mentions how Doc and William Sunday escaped from that shell hole.

Standing on the open plains of southern Russia, Happy and Mouse kick a can around in a field as though it were a hacky sack. They flick it up onto the toe of their boots, tap it around a few times, and then pass it between each other, counting the number of times they can keep the game going. They never get over thirty, but Doc finds that impressive in itself. He'd struggle to reach two.

Meyers crosses the road and talks with the driver of a Red Cross truck. Doc overhears the discussion between him and the driver. The Army won't bring anything mechanical within a hundred miles of the Front for fear of being struck by long-range Novo lightning. Non-governmental organizations such as the Red Cross and *Médecins Sans Frontières*, though, regularly drive to within twenty miles of the line to help civilians. That they are not actively targeted might be a curiosity to military planners but not to Doc.

Meyers jogs back across the concrete road and tells the squad to climb in the back with the medical supplies.

"Don't you think it's strange," William Sunday asks, climbing over the wooden tailgate and beneath the canvas awning on the truck. "We can drive back, but only if we're with a medical team?"

"We are a medical team," Meyers says, ignoring the subtlety of her point as he hoists packs into the back. Happy stows them on top of several crates. There's not a lot of room in the cargo area.

"We're soldiers," William Sunday says.

Doc is quiet. He's thinking the same thing as her, but he wants to pick and choose his moments. For Meyers, though, it must be apparent that this is similar to their interaction with the Novos. In both cases, the Novos are choosing to show restraint, something humans are not doing.

William Sunday looks at Doc as he climbs into the back of the truck. She wants his support, but he doesn't feel there's anything to be gained by pointing out the obvious when Meyers and everyone else in the military seem to be blithely ignoring reality. He shrugs, saying, "Yeah, strange, huh?"

The first sign they're approaching the war zone is the sound of thunder breaking in the clear blue sky. At first, Doc finds it confusing, but as they come over a rise, he sees row upon row of howitzers spaced out in the fields on either side of the road. They seem to stretch forever in both directions. Puffs of white smoke precede the rocking motion of the guns, and then a wall of noise washes over them as shells are lobbed at the Front. Soldiers reload with the precision of robots, pushing shells into the breach and slamming them shut as gunners calculate the angle for the next target, using handheld computers for accuracy. Once again, there are puffs of smoke as the guns rock on their mounts. Seconds later, thunder rumbles through the open sky.

Several hours later and roughly a hundred miles further along the road, they stop at a small village near the Front. Thousands of tents form a refugee camp. Resettlement is underway, but it's difficult to shift people. Thousands of families have been separated and need to be reunited. Medical needs have to be dealt with. Everyone has a different circumstance. Some refugees have foreign passports and demand repatriation, but counterfeit passports are common. Nothing happens fast within the bureaucracy of the United Nations and the chaos of war. Blank faces stare through wire fences. The children are gaunt and thin.

"And we're here?" Meyers says, talking with the driver and pointing at a map as they stand beside the entrance to the refugee camp.

"Yes. You're less than thirty miles from the Front."

"Awesome. And again, thank you."

Meyers leaves the squad standing beside their packs on the roadside. Soldiers trudge past, marching to the Front. Their uniforms are crisp and clean. They're happy and cheerful, engaging in call/response songs to pass the time as they trudge along the muddy track. They're fresh meat for the grinder.

Mules pull carts in both directions, carrying ammunition and supplies to the Front and carrying away logs for use in the fall-back trenches being prepared in this region. Most of the carts are wooden, but some are made from aluminum. All of them, though, use tires rather than steel-rimmed wooden wheels, making them a strange mix of archaic and modern tech. The logistical effort is impressive. Like ants constantly on the move, there's a distinct rhythm to the flow of vehicles and troops. Occasionally, Doc spots the wounded being evacuated on carts. The dead are buried at the Front or left where they fell in no man's land, so there are few body bags.

"Okay," Meyers says, jogging back over to join them. "I've got us on a cart headed for Iowa. From there, we're on foot back to the dugout."

"Nice work," Happy says.

Doc smiles and nods. Even though it might be uncomfortable sitting on a cart, it sure beats humping all the way back to the Front.

A soldier working with a team of four mules pulls over to the side of the muddy road. His cart looks as though it's been taken from the stripped-down remains of a semi-trailer. It's packed with boxes of food and medical supplies reaching up over twenty feet, but the load is far lighter than hauling ammunition or shells.

They climb on the back. William Sunday and Doc sit at the rear with their legs dangling over the edge. The others climb up onto the boxes. As they drive on, they pass soldiers who eye them with envy, but why be in a rush to die? No one is privileged at the Front. The trenches reduce everyone to equals.

Night falls as they reach Iowa and disembark. Scars reach across the land. As payment for their ride, the Dog Food Squad helps unload the flatbed trailer. They form a human chain with several other soldiers from the stores, passing sacks and crates from the rear of the cart into the cache set below ground. The mules are restless. They can smell death on the wind. The driver is keen to unload and immediately turn around. He's not going to spend the night this close to the Front.

Snow has settled on the fields. Ice has solidified in the bottom of the craters. Looking out across the scarred land, it appears peaceful.

"Winter is crazy. The fields look almost beautiful."

"Snow's not good," William Sunday says.

"Why?" Doc asks, thinking it looks contradictory. The coming of winter has transformed the land, hiding the anguish and heartbreak of war beneath a blanket of pristine white snow.

"It's the glare coming off the snow and ice."

"Even at night?"

"Especially at night. The starlight comes down from above and reflects from below, making it difficult to creep around unseen. And the shell holes."

"The shell holes?" Doc asks, noticing a glazed look in William Sunday's eyes as she recalls traumatic memories.

"Fresh holes are obvious."

"Isn't that a good thing? Doesn't that make it easier to hide?"

"Fresh meat always heads for the fresh holes. They think they'll blend in with the mud and dirt."

"But?"

"But the Novo know. They target those holes. Stay away from

them, Doc."

"I will."

"And our bootprints no longer blend in with the past. Fresh bootprints make it easier for them to hunt."

Doc doesn't like the sound of that.

Once the squad has finished unpacking the cart and they've had some water and rations, and relieved themselves in the latrine, the squad begins trudging through the trenches. Boards flex beneath them as they march along connecting ditches. Ice cracks under their boots.

The regional quartermaster heard they were going forward and loaded them up with supplies. Mouse is wearing three packs. One on his front, another on his back with a third strapped to that one. Even with all that weight, he keeps his posture upright. Out of all of them, he's the most passionate, widening his stride, probably to get to the Front as soon as possible. Doc's carrying a second pack loaded up with IVs and plasma. Being liquids, they're heavy, but he doesn't complain. William Sunday hunches over under the weight of her double pack. She has her hands up, gripping the straps as she leans forward. For now, they're all pack mules.

"Are you okay?"

"Fine," she says, but one-word answers are never good. Like him, she just wants this to be over.

Meyers leads them through the labyrinth of trenches as darkness descends. As they're wearing helmets now, Happy turns on his red LED. Mouse and William Sunday don't bother. Doc switches his on, but it's old. There must be a loose wire as it flickers, coming to life for a few seconds before fading. Ahead, the evening barrage thunders through the air, shaking the ground as it strikes no man's land in the distance. Dirt is flung into the sky. Clouds of smoke rise from fresh shell holes all along the Front.

They reach the forward staging area and unload their cargo. Even though it's freezing, Mouse is dripping with sweat. William Sunday arches her back, stretching her muscles now that she's free from the double pack,

It takes Meyers almost an hour to convince the section quartermaster that they need to be issued with a new kit for medical retrieval. The quartermaster is adamant that he never received requisition orders from the regional command center. Even with them standing there in front of him, he stalls, makes calls and checks paperwork before finally relenting. With new kit, the Dog Food Squad trudges off in the darkness, following the trenches, walking along wooden boards through the slush and mud for the last few miles to the Front.

"Well, look at what the cat dragged in," Leech says from within their squad dugout when they finally reach the Front.

"It's good to see you too," Meyers says, dropping his pack on the bench seat running around three sides of the dugout.

Lavender gets up and rushes to greet William Sunday, hugging her before she can remove her pack.

"I missed you."

"I missed you, too."

The two women kiss each other lightly on the lips. Lavender grips William Sunday's face tenderly in her hands.

"Don't you go scaring me like that again."

"I won't."

"Promise?"

William Sunday blushes. She drops her pack on the bench beside Meyers' pack, and leans her new rifle in the corner.

"Oh, you guys get all the latest toys," Lavender says, looking at the improved grenade launcher mounted beneath the barrel.

"They're finally giving us more than one squad weapon," Happy says, blocking the doorway to the dugout. Doc can see past him, but he's keen to get inside and greet Leech and Lavender. Happy seems oblivious to his presence.

"Ah."

"Oh, right," Happy says, stepping down into the dugout and

making room for him to squeeze past. A gas lantern burns on one of the crates used as a table. Several candles light the interior. They flicker in the breeze circling within the dugout.

Once the squad is seated, Meyers asks Lavender, "What have they had you doing for the last few weeks? Just laundry?"

"We were assigned to support DQ."

"The Dairy Queens," Happy says.

"The one and only. Those guys rock."

Leech says, "We've only had two excursions in the past nine days."

"And the casualty count?"

"On our sector, it's been light. We only had three KIA and two WIA."

"That's good," Meyers replies.

Doc looks at William Sunday. She, though, is looking at Lavender. He feels as though he can read her mind. She wants to blurt out something about what happened to the two of them in no man's land, but Meyers is avoiding the subject entirely.

"Any orders?"

"Only for Doc," Lavender replies, reaching out and handing a slip of paper to Meyers. Doc starts to reach for it but retracts his hand when it's clear she's giving it to Meyers as the squad leader. He glances at it, turning it on an angle so he can read it in the dim light, and then hands it on to Doc.

Resource Request: *Dr. Christopher Walters*

Temporary Assignment: *Forward Triage,*

Devil's Lake, North Dakota

Duration: *380/1 to 382/3*

Doc's not familiar with the reckoning of time at the Front, but it seems to be based on the days elapsed since the start of the war. There's no way that number isn't going to become more depressing over time, he

161

thinks, but he keeps that thought to himself.

"I don't get it," Meyers says. "We're not due to be activated for at least another 48 hours."

"Orders are orders," Doc replies. "They must be short surgeons."

He rummages around in his pack, loading up a smaller day pack with a change of clothes and toiletries. The squad is unusually silent. They know he's exhausted after traveling all day. He could wait till morning, but for Doc, it's easier to treat the dugout as just one more stop on the journey. They'll have bunks at the triage center.

"I'll escort you," Meyers says.

"It's okay," Doc says, swinging the pack over his back.

Under her breath, William Sunday says, "They're sending you to the meat grinder."

Doc steps back out into the night. The air is crisp. Snowflakes drift through the darkness. Meyers stands in the entrance to the dugout.

"Four miles that way," he says, pointing. "If you hit Grand Forks, you've gone too far. Watch for the turn south near Rugby. It's easy to miss."

Doc nods and walks off along the boards. Ice has formed on the wood, making it slippery. Soldiers mill around in the intersections. Spotters stand on raised platforms facing no man's land, peering out from behind sandbags at the night with their starlight binoculars. Shells rain down on the battlefield. Squads form in the alleys, running at a right angle to the Front, preparing to go over the top. Nervous soldiers check and double-check their weapons, wondering if they'll make it back. It's the uncertainty that kills them on the inside. Doc can see the blank looks and distant stares. There's little to no banter as they await their orders.

Whistles sound along the front, sending out a coded message, telling the various squads that have formed in the trenches whether they're heading into no man's land or returning to their dugouts. Those who recognize the call and know they've been spared sigh in relief. Their rigid bodies relax. Others stiffen as their squad leaders make final preparations and move them into the main trench.

Doc pushes past troops readying themselves at the ladders. Somewhere at the rear, military planners have objectives that need to be accomplished. Lives will be lost, but they justify that to themselves by noting down some incremental gain in inches. Most of the missions are looking to raid the enemy's trenches for their artifacts of war. Satellite imagery allows raids to unfold with pinpoint precision, looking for exact items such as supplies, maps, weapons, and food stores. Anything that can help aid future missions is deemed important, but to Doc, it's like running on a treadmill. There's a lot of effort spent going nowhere.

Doc reaches a sign that designates this muddy patch of the trench as Rugby. Apparently, that's both a town in North Dakota and a game played in England, and Doc wonders about the origins of the US town. They must have a rugby team, even if there's no one to play against.

The trench forks, but without any signposts. He asks a couple of soldiers about the way to Devil's Lake. They all know of the place, but none of them have been there. None of them ever want to go there. As much as Doc sympathizes with their attitude, they fail to realize there are outcomes worse than being stretchered to Devil's Lake. Death is seldom discussed or even considered in the trenches. It's a shadow stretching behind the men and women at the Front. It's there but rarely seen.

Doc follows the southern trench winding away from the Front. The barrage increases in frequency and intensity as soldiers rush up wooden ladders and into no man's land. Doc can't help but wonder which of them he'll see later tonight in Devil's Lake.

He reaches the triage center. Rather than being a single location, it's been divided into ten dugouts for surgery, with another twenty dugouts being used as wards. Unlike the regular trenches, the ditches here are almost twenty feet wide, allowing for stretchers to pass each other without being seen from the battlefield.

Doc reports for duty. He's assigned a cot in the barracks and drops off his pack. He's told to rest, saying they'll wake him only if needed. Doc crashes on his cot. His eyes close, and he's fast asleep. It seems like mere seconds pass before someone shakes his shoulder and wakes him.

"You're needed in Four, sir."

"Understood."

Doc feels groggy. He was slipping into a deep sleep when he was woken. The world around him feels surreal, almost dreamlike. He knows it's about to become a nightmare.

On entering the dugout marked Theater Four, Doc is met by an infection control nurse who drapes a clean surgical gown over him. She scrubs his arms and hands and fixes a paper hat over his hair. The nurse puts a lamp on his head, attaching it with elastic wrapping around his forehead. These are all things he could do for himself, but she's responsible for ensuring consistency across the medical staff.

Doc descends into the lower section of the dugout. This far from the Front and deep below ground, a small diesel-powered generator provides erratic electricity. Fans circulate air, drawing it in through HEPA filters and pushing it around the theater. Thick plastic hangs from the walls. The ceiling has been coated with heat-shrink plastic. Oxygen cylinders line one wall. Stores of plasma and IVs are packed into shelves on the other side of the theater. White battery-powered LEDs on metal stands are a poor substitute for surgical lights. It's the floor, though, that shocks him. Surgeons, anesthetists and nurses trudge through blood and mud on the floor. Wooden boards creak under their shifting weight. A sump pump sits in the corner, slowly draining the sludge as it accumulates in a pit at the lowest point.

There are four operating tables. A lone surgeon moves between two patients, swapping scalpels and instructing the nurses as she tends to a soldier with a badly fractured leg and another with a gaping chest wound.

"You're Walters?" she asks.

"Yes."

"Thank Christ. I'm Dr. Helen Anderson. Okay, enough of the pleasantries, you're on the heart and lungs. Try to stabilize him. I've got an evac request in, but they rarely get here in time."

"Okay," Doc replies, looking down at the bloody pulp on the right side of the man's chest. He's lucky. From the appearance of his wound, he was grazed by a Novo bolt. If it had hit him square on, he would have died in an instant. As it is, he'll probably lose a lung.

The surgeon wipes her forehead with the back of her gloved hand, saying, "He's all yours. I've got to amputate this poor bastard's leg."

There's a tunnel leading to one side, probably linking up with the wards. Plastic hangs over the entrance, forming a makeshift door. Gas lanterns burn in the corridor, throwing out a soft light. Wounded soldiers lie on gurneys beyond the plastic, waiting their turn in the theatre. Behind him, he can hear Helen using a hand saw to cut through the bone. Her motion is precise, with each push and draw of the saw passing like a metronome. Doc knows that grating sound is going to haunt him. Already, there are nurses talking about more casualties coming in from the Front. Someone's out in the corridor, conducting triage, figuring out who's next in the meat grinder.

It's going to be a helluva long night.

Daylight

Doc staggers out into the blinding sunlight. He has no idea what time it is. He's so goddamn tired he can't think straight. He wants nothing other than to fall into his cot in the barracks.

Dr. Helen Anderson comes up beside him. "Insane, huh?"

"Seven surgeries," he replies.

"Nine."

"You win!"

She laughs. Theirs is a competition no one wants.

As the trench is broad, orderlies have set up serving tables in the sun. Doctors and nurses shuffle along in their bloody scrubs, picking up trays prepared with food and cups of Gatorade.

"I might—"

"You need to eat," Helen says. "And drink. You do not want to go to sleep dehydrated. You'll only feel worse when you wake."

"Yes, doctor," he replies, and she smiles.

They join the line and collect their trays.

"Besides," she says as they sit on one of the logs forming the side of the trench. "We all need vitamin D."

"Yeah, it beats being stuck in a hole."

"It does," she replies, leaning back and letting the warmth of the sun wash over her in the cold. Helen has her eyes closed. For a moment, Doc wonders if her eyes will open again. If he so much as paused while

167

blinking, he'd be fast asleep. Helen has long, brunette hair that catches the sunlight like silk. He may look like a train wreck, but she looks as though she's stepped out of a salon. Appearances are deceiving but in the most delightful way. She smiles, seeing the way he looks at her with kindness.

"So you're the whisperer," she says, taking a mouth full of stew.

Doc gulps down his Gatorade. It's sweet and salty. He didn't realize how thirsty he was until the first sip passed his lips.

"I'm not sure what you mean."

"You've seen them. You've talked to them."

"Ah," Doc replies, unsure what to say in response. He scoops up some stew on his spoon and eats, using that act to hide, at least for a moment.

"It's all anyone's talking about," Helen says. "All along the Front. They say you can talk to the Novos. And they listen to you."

Doc shakes his head. Meyers must have filed a report following their conversation in Vicenza. There would be an official version and then the scuttlebutt rippling through the ranks. Anything out of the ordinary becomes a point of fascination for bored soldiers during the war. And, like all rumors, it would have taken on a life of its own, with the details being exaggerated.

"It's not quite like that."

"You came through here, you know," Helen says. "They'd knocked you out with drugs by that point, so you wouldn't remember it. Oh, it wasn't me, by the way." She points with her spoon at a doctor sitting with several nurses further down the trench, also eating breakfast in the sunlight. "It was Helmut. He did the initial surgery, patched you up and sent you on your way. He said your uniform was glowing with Novo blood."

"Ah, yeah," Doc says, stirring his stew with his spoon, unsure where to start, not knowing what she's heard or how accurate the details were.

"They bagged your uniform and sent it away to the lab for

analysis."

"It was ruined," Doc says. "I didn't want it anyway."

He takes another bite of stew at the same time as Helen, and the two of them chew in silence for a few seconds.

"Are you going to tell me?" she asks. "Or is it like top secret?"

"It's not that grand a tale," he replies, chewing on a piece of rat and pretending it's chicken. He laughs. "I was hiding in a bathtub."

"A bathtub?"

"Yeah. I stumbled across the remains of a farmhouse and found this old enamel bathtub sitting on tiles. It looked insane. All around it, there were broken pipes and busted wooden boards, fallen walls and broken ceramics, but there it was, sitting proud on this clean tiled floor. I mean, it looked like someone was about to hop in and have a bath."

Helen laughs. "Oh, this is even wilder than the story I heard."

"I'd been separated from my squad. Shells were raining down across no man's land, but there was nowhere to hide, so I crawled into the bath."

"I would *kill* for a bath," Helen says, joking with him.

"And then the world exploded around me. A shell landed so damn close I didn't hear it fall. Hell, I couldn't hear anything afterward for several minutes. The bathtub was thrown in the air. Shrapnel peppered the metal. I guess a bit punched through, and I took a piece of hot steel in my neck."

"I saw it," Helen says, holding out her hand and stretching her thumb and forefinger roughly three inches apart. "Nasty."

"So I'm staggering through no man's land, clinging to my neck, feeling blood running down my chest, and I stumble into an old shell hole."

"And?"

"And I'm not alone."

Helen twists sideways, facing him as she eats her stew. For someone who's exhausted, her face is lit up with the fascination of a tale from no man's land.

"There's a Novo in there," Doc says, sipping some stew between sentences. "Only it's wounded like me. It sees me and charges its weapon."

"You saw that?"

"Yeah, lightning rippled across its arms, but it was too weak to fire."

"And you?"

"I'm dying. I'm losing a lot of blood. Either that thing is going to kill me, or I'm going to collapse and bleed out."

"So what did you do?"

"I ignored it."

"You ignored it?" she says, laughing. "Seriously?"

"Seriously. I dumped my pack and treated my own wound. And as I worked on my neck, I explained what I was doing as much for myself as the Novo."

"And then?"

"Then I treated its wound."

"Fuck," Helen says. Her jaw drops. "Are you for real?"

"Oh, yeah. It had lost a limb, so I applied a tourniquet and wrapped up the stub with a major trauma pad to stop the bleeding."

"And?"

"And then I left."

"You just walked away?"

"What else was I going to do?"

"That is insane!"

"Oh, it's what happened next that's insane," Doc says, chewing on another piece of rat. He pauses, finishing his mouthful and keeping her in suspense.

"So," he says, wiping gravy from the stubble on his chin. "I'm trying to make the riverbank. I crawl into a shell hole and find one of my squad there. She's wounded."

"Oh, okay," Helen says. "I think this is the part I've heard."

"I'm tending to her, and two Novos appear. I'm not sure if they were under the ground or whether they were retreating, using shell holes for cover, but they're behind me. They're glowing in a soft neon blue."

"And you operated by Novo light."

"Yes," Doc says, laughing. "How crazy is that?"

"And they let you go?"

"Yes. Madness, huh? It's just... I don't know, a contradiction."

"War *is* a contradiction," Helen says. "We value life above all else, but we'd die to defend the lives of others. Maybe they do too."

"Yep."

"And war is unnatural. Chaotic. Unpredictable. Have you heard about the very first Christmas during the First World War?"

"No," a curious Doc replies, eating some more of his stew.

"Crazy things happen in war. Back then, the Germans started singing Christmas carols as snowflakes fell in the darkness. The English responded in kind. The next day, they agreed to local ceasefires. If you don't shoot, I won't either."

"Huh," Doc says, finishing his stew.

"They met in no man's land, traded for cigarettes, and even played soccer. It should have been the end of the war; only the war dragged on for another four years."

"Why?"

Helen laughs. "Because no one knew what they were doing other than following orders. And that's the danger of authority. If you're ordered to jump, you never ask how high. No one ever asks why; they just jump."

"And we get to clean up the mess," Doc says.

"We do."

Having finished their meal, they get up and return their trays to the orderlies.

"Listen," Helen says. "Get some sleep and then head back to your unit."

"I'm supposed to be here for a few days," Doc replies.

"We've had a few fresh doctors come up from Sioux Falls. We'll be fine. You get some rest."

"Will do," Doc says. He wanders into the barracks dugout and collapses on his temporary cot. He doesn't bother getting changed, removing his boots, or slipping into his sleeping bag. Instead, he uses the bag as a pillow, scrunching it up and shifting it beneath his head. Even though there's considerable talking around him, he's asleep within seconds.

Lavender

When Doc gets back to the front line late in the afternoon, Lavender is the only one in the dugout. He staggers inside, dusting snowflakes from his shoulder. His feet are aching. The cots have been set up, so he slips his boots off and drops onto a cot even though he's not tired. As his cot is next to one of the benches, he positions his pack there so he can lean against it.

"Where is everyone?"

Lavender looks up, startled by his question. She didn't see or hear him when he walked into the dugout, which surprises Doc.

"Um."

"Are you okay?"

"Fine," Lavender snaps.

"And the others?"

"They're doing a drill with DH."

"Oh," Doc replies, seeing a handwritten letter in her hand. "Is everything all right?"

Lavender bites her lip. Tears well up in her eyes. She wipes her cheeks in the soft light of a solitary candle dripping wax on a wooden crate.

"I'm fine. Really, I am."

Doc nods even though he doesn't actually agree. Meyers left her here for a reason, and the reason is in her hand. It can only be news from

173

home, and it's not good. Doc knows all too well how crippling it can be to get bad news. He never finished reading the letter from Jean and won't write back. Not yet. He threw it in the bin before they left Italy. He feels awful not acknowledging her, knowing she'll wonder if her letter got through to him. She'll get the chirpy, cheerful letter he sent when he first arrived at the Front within about a week or so. Their letters probably passed each other somewhere along the way. He will write to her eventually, but for now, the hurt is too raw. Lavender, though, seems to be grieving a loss rather than a broken heart.

"Was it your Mom or your Dad?"

"Mom," is the trembling reply. Lavender breathes deeply, grounding herself.

"I'm sorry."

"I fucking *hate* this shit," Lavender says with a surprising amount of passion. "I—I should have been there with her. I should have never come to this goddamn war."

"You couldn't have known," Doc says. Although he's trying to assuage her grief, he's intensely curious about why she volunteered to fight the Novos in the first place. To his mind, it's madness. He can understand William Sunday fighting for the memory of her family, but Lavender is from rural Ohio. She's from a sleepy town called Botkins, with a population of barely a thousand people.

"We fool ourselves, Doc. We live our lives based on lies. Oh, they're not mean or malicious. They're kind, but they're still lies."

Doc is silent. He gets up and sits next to her. Lavender doesn't need counseling. She needs to be heard.

"I'll be all right. I'll keep my head down. I won't be gone long. I'll be back before you know it... Lies. All lies."

She sniffs, fighting back tears.

"And I knew she was sick, but she lied to me. Not on purpose, you understand, but she said things she couldn't have known for sure. I'll be fine, honey. I'm in good hands."

Lavender looks down at the letter. It's been written using a fountain pen. The flourish in the handwriting conveys grief with a sense of beauty. Teardrops have fallen on the page, blotting out the ink and smudging several of the words.

"The last time we spoke, we both lied. Why is that, Doc? Why do we lie to each other? I guess it's because we don't want to hurt each other."

"We want the best for each other," Doc replies, feeling he owes her a response and trying to soften the grief she feels.

"We do," Lavender says.

"And they're not lies," Doc says. "They're hopes. They're what we long for from an uncertain future."

Lavender chokes up. "I should have been there for her. Instead, I'm sending her letters saying, be strong. You're going to be okay. You'll come out the other side of this and laugh about it. But she didn't."

Doc hangs his head. For him, life is built on finding answers, only there are none when it comes to death. Being a doctor, he's used to fixing people, but there are problems in life for which there are no solutions. As much as he wants to comfort Lavender, try as he may, there's nothing he can say or do that will make even the slightest difference to the weight of grief bearing down on her. They say time heals all wounds, but it doesn't. Time allows people to forget their pain, but nothing is healed. There are wounds in the heart that no surgeon can reach. Even though he doesn't know her mother personally, Doc is saddened by her passing.

Death is a strange beast. Out there on the battlefield, not more than twenty yards from where they're sitting, soldiers lie rotting in the mud or frozen in the ice. Foxes, wild dogs and birds feed on the carrion of war. Bodies lie among the ruins. Each and every one of them had a family. Someone raised them. Someone cared for them. Someone loved them. They had thoughts, feelings, loves, hates, quirks, and they laughed at life. And yet, now they're repulsive rather than mourned in no man's land. Where possible, squads will retrieve their fallen, if not when they fell, then in the days afterward during a lull in the fighting, but recovery isn't always possible. The forgotten are ignored as though they were never human to begin with. They're mannequins. Oh, someone mourned them in the first few days: their squad and then their families when a rental car pulled up out the front of their home with two Army officers holding a nondescript envelope. But for everyone else who ventures into no man's land, they're a sight of unmitigated horror. And why? Because nothing is known of their lives. Grief is only for those who care.

Doc struggles with what he should say to Lavender. His words feel hollow. Pointless. Lavender, though, seems grounded. She's still grieving, but a calm descends on her as she speaks.

"Memories are funny, Doc."

"How so?"

"They're moments forever lost in the past, moments I barely realized were happening at the time, moments that didn't feel that special as they unfolded... and yet they're all I have left."

Doc nods.

"And they're vague," Lavender says. "I remember the way my mother spoke, but not what she said. I remember the way her face lit up when she smiled, but not why she was smiling. I remember her laughter, but not what she was laughing at. I remember her kindness, but not on any one given day."

Lavender looks down at the letter in her hand. "And now, I feel alone. But we've always been alone, haven't we? Even in a crowd. Even when lying in bed with a loved one. I guess I feel it more now. And it hurts to think that all that will remain of me one day is memories."

Doc says, "They're more precious than gold."

"They are."

Lavender gets to her feet. She walks to the opening of the dugout, but before she steps out into the twilight, she says, "Thanks, Doc."

Doc wants to reply, but he can't. The lump welling up in his throat chokes him. He clenches his teeth and nods. Lavender steps out into the thunder of shells crashing into the mud and dirt along the Front. It's strange, but while they were speaking, Doc could have sworn there was utter silence.

For the first time since he arrived at the Front, there's nothing for him to do. Normally, he's busy prepping his medical kit, talking to someone, writing in his journal, or arranging for laundry to be hauled to the rear or scrambling from one dugout to another. Lavender, though, has given him a gift. She's left him alone.

Normally, Doc's mind is a whirlwind of activity as he reassesses patients he's seen, driving himself to rethink his actions and do better, but not this time. His mind is blank, and that's a good thing. He breathes. He appreciates breathing.

Doc listens. In between the shells falling, he hears the creak of the wooden beams over his head. A rat scurries under one of the cots. He can't see it, but he can pinpoint it by sound alone. Once, he would have been repulsed by such an encounter. Now, he feels a strange affinity with life. Looking at the walls of the dugout, he notices carvings in the rock. Words, names and initials have been engraved in the stone, but these are not declarations of love carved into an oak tree; they're testimonies of life. They're a silent roll call. They're all that remains of the various squads that have been stationed in here. At some point, the war will end, as all wars do, and the dugout will collapse or become flooded. Will anyone ever see these etchings? Will they understand them?

There's a shoebox in the corner next to him. It's within reach, so he opens it. Inside are Hawk's personal effects: his dog tags, his dented canteen cup, several letters neatly folded, and a ballpoint pen that looks entirely normal but will hold immense meaning to his next of kin. It cost less than a buck, but to his family, it'll be priceless. Beneath the letters is the carving of an eagle's head. It's unfinished. There's heartbreak in how the work has been interrupted. The last few shavings are all that remain of his final day on Earth. The soft pencil lines mark where he was going to continue carving feathers. They speak of a future that will never be. It's both tragic and beautiful.

"I'm sending that to his ex," Meyers says from the doorway to the dugout, surprising Doc with his presence.

"Marie."

"Yes," Meyers says, taking the carving from Doc and examining it. "Stunning, isn't it?"

177

"I'd like to include a letter," Doc says.

"Oh."

"To both Marie and Heather."

"Sure," Meyers replies. "They'd like that. They'd appreciate that."

Meyers returns the carving to the box. Doc replaces the lid.

Happy and Mouse come blundering through the opening of the dugout, laughing and joking with each other, and the mood changes in an instant. Grief is consumed by life.

"Oh, hey, Doc," William Sunday says, walking hand in hand with Lavender back into the dugout. "It's good to see you again."

"We weren't expecting you till tomorrow," Leech says.

"I got an early pass," Doc replies.

"Well," Meyers says. "Local command thinks you're still down at Devil's Lake, so we've got the night off."

"Sweeeeeet," Lavender says with warmth in her voice.

It's good to see her relaxing and smiling with William Sunday. The two of them sit on the bench opposite Doc. They're still holding hands, but only just. Their fingertips rub against each other with a tenderness seldom found in war. Doc's sure William Sunday knows about Lavender's mother and will have offered her a hug and some comforting words, but what Lavender needs more than anything is company. It sounds crazy in the midst of war, but she needs to feel loved. She needs to know that life goes on. And with the Dog Food Squad, she's found a second home, a second family.

The Storm

The next day, a winter storm descends on the Russian steppes. Sleet falls in sheets. Ice forms on the wooden logs reinforcing the trench. Slush and mud overwhelm the wooden sill preventing water from running into the dugout. Various members of the squad take turns working the hand pump to keep the water level below the wooden boards on the floor.

In the early evening, the phone by the entrance rings. Meyers answers to stunned silence within the dugout.

"Yes... Yes... Understood... Dog Food is active in support."

Meyers hangs up, but before he can say anything, Happy blurts out, "In this *fucking* weather? You have got to be kidding me."

"Easy," Meyers says to a room full of agitated soldiers.

Even Lavender looks upset. Normally, she's unfazed by their assignments. She ruffles her purple hair. Her roots reveal her soft, natural brunette hair growing through, which doesn't seem to suit her. The brilliant pinks and purples in her bangs are much more in keeping with her vibrant personality. William Sunday is sitting in her classic defensive position, with her legs up in front of her and her arms wrapped around her knees. Tonight, though, with no barrage falling, it's more habitual than hiding. Perhaps, for her, it's a comfort pose.

"Are they really going to send us out there?" Mouse asks.

"Special Forces have a priority one assignment. The One-Oh-Five is deploying an experimental sensor in no man's land."

Lavender rolls her eyes.

Happy says, "Ah, fuck."

"They're hoping the weather gives them some cover," Meyers says.

"How deep are they going?" Leech asks.

"Echo-Seven."

Leech considers that for a moment, saying, "Okay. That's reasonable. That's not too deep."

Happy says, "We might not even leave the trench."

"Command wants us out there with them."

"Prior to contact?" Leech asks, surprised by that comment.

"One-Oh-Five is escorting a blank."

"Ah, fuck," Happy says, using the same words as moments ago, spoken with exactly the same sense of rhythm and resignation.

"What's a blank?" Doc asks quietly, talking to William Sunday.

"No rank. It means they're escorting a civilian. Probably a scientist or an engineer."

"And that's bad?"

"That means they have no idea what they're getting themselves into. Blanks panic under fire. They do dumb shit and get themselves killed."

"Them and anyone looking after them," Happy says.

"We've got the storm in our favor," Meyers says. "It'll keep the Novos hunkered down. We're in close support. Our role is to provide cover fire and medical extraction if needed."

"It'll be cold," Mouse says.

"Fucking cold," Happy says.

"It won't work," Lavender says.

"What won't work?" Doc asks.

"Whatever dumb fool thing it is they're putting out there. The Novos will find it and fry it."

"Command is testing a new form of electromagnetic shielding.

They're going to run it on a mechanical timer out there and look to see if the Novos react. If this works, we could run heavy machinery closer to the line."

There's considerable discussion between various squad members at that comment.

"All right. We move out in five. Get your gear ready."

Doc dons his heavy weather raincoat over his uniform. If it were made from Gore-Tex, it would be breathable, but being vinyl, it feels icky and sticky before he's even started trudging through the trenches. It's designed to stretch over his helmet and reaches down to below his knees.

William Sunday is fiddling with one of Happy's old-fashioned razors. She pulls out a blade, joking with him about cutting his throat if he leaves her in no man's land again. She turns to Doc, holding up the shiny metal.

"Ah, what's that for?"

"I'm going to cut a slit in the back of your raincoat."

"Why?" he asks, laughing at how murderous she looks with wide eyes, wielding a razor blade in the candlelight.

"To allow moisture to escape," she says. "You're going to sweat like a pig in that thing."

Happy holds up his raincoat, showing Doc how it has a thin slit running across the shoulders. "So long as you keep the hood over your helmet, the overlap will keep water out while allowing sweat to evaporate."

Doc says, "Happy. For a moment there, you sounded like a professional."

"I won't let it happen again," Happy says, grinning.

"Turn around," William Sunday says.

Doc turns. He feels her pull the raincoat away from his back as she runs the razor in a straight-ish line.

"And it won't tear any further?" he asks.

"We're going seam-to-seam," William Sunday replies. "There.

181

Done."

"Thank you."

When Mouse comes over to pick up his medical pack, Doc waves him away, saying, "I'm good."

"Are you sure? I don't mind."

"It's okay. Thanks."

Outside, the wind billows around within the trench, lifting the edges of their raincoats as they step up out of the dugout. William Sunday fusses with Doc's raincoat, pulling it up a little so his backpack doesn't cause the gap to open too wide.

"Looking good," she says, giving him a thumbs up from beneath the hood stretching over her helmet.

"All right. Let's move out," Meyers says, and they begin the trek to the Echo segment of the Front. A handful of sentries stand on raised wooden platforms, peering out into the night using starlight binoculars. These have been designed using dozens of mirrors and prisms to amplify the natural light without the need for electronics. On a night like this, Doc doubts their effectiveness. Shells fall in no man's land, but their lazy thuds are distant. Rather than a concentrated barrage, there's only the odd strike as spotters target wild dogs or foxes scavenging on the battlefield.

It takes an hour before they reach Echo and form up behind the 105th special ops squad. The blank is made obvious by the lack of a backpack, and Doc feels proud to be wearing his medical pack. He's at one with the squad.

Sleet comes down in waves, but as it's driving from true west rather than the fictional west used by the army on its maps, it's coming from behind them. On the convoluted map of the Front used by planners, that would be from the south, but it means sleet washes over the trench rather than raining down on them. As they head into no man's land, it'll be at their backs. Returning to the lines, though, is going to be nasty as they'll be walking directly into the storm.

Fresh ice clings to the ladder. Icicles have formed on the logs and support beams within the trench. The temperature is dropping. There are no whistles sounding up and down the line, as only one mission is going over the top in the atrocious weather. Hopefully, the lack of any signaling puts the Novos at ease for the night.

Several soldiers have starlight night vision binoculars hanging around their necks. Lavender and William Sunday already have their red LED lights on in the trench. There's a danger they'll drain their batteries before they get back. Swapping out tiny batteries might seem easy enough, but fumbling around while wearing thick gloves in the dark and mud and slush while under fire is rarely that simple. If they double-team with someone else on the return journey, they'll get continuous coverage.

Meyers comes down the line, talking to them in groups of two or three.

"Visibility is poor. Down to fifteen feet. One-Oh-Five laid down a guide wire last night in preparation for this mission, so we'll be following that."

William Sunday asks, "What's our formation?"

"The weather's too bad to split up," Meyers replies. "We need to stay together up there. I don't want anyone getting lost."

"You're bunching us up?" a concerned Happy asks from next to Doc.

"We'll be fine," Meyers says. "If we can't see them, they can't see us."

With that, Meyers moves down the line to talk to Mouse.

"Is that true?" Doc asks. "Do we know what they can see?"

William Sunday cocks her helmet sideways and shakes her head. She's amused and somewhat disappointed by him. She looks at him as though he's a sweet, sweet child of a lazy, forgotten summer.

"Oh, okay," he says in reply to her body language.

Once the 105th has gone over the top, the Dog Food Squad follows. Once again, Doc slips in his sonic earplugs, and the noise of war becomes dull and distant. The sound of rain, though, doesn't seem to change. Sleet comes down like hail, thundering on Doc's helmet, making it difficult to hear anything that's said. He keeps his head down and follows along behind Happy.

Leech is on point. Apparently, he can see the main squad of twenty-five troops advancing through no man's land, but Doc can't see anything through the rush of rain, hail and sleet turning the ground into slush.

Shell holes fill with water. Whereas once they provided cover, being ten to fifteen feet deep, now there is less than five feet between the sodden rim and the rising muddy pools. Streams run through no man's land, exposing corpses and smashed equipment from the early days of the war. The barrel of a howitzer protrudes from the mud, giving Doc some idea of how much the Front has moved over the past year.

Leech is supposed to be following a guide wire, but then Doc should be able to see it as well. All he sees is the pools of water forming in the divots and craters that pepper the land.

Like the others, Doc has his hand on the pack of the person in front of him. In the darkness and torrential rain, it's the only way to stay together. Water seeps into the slit William Sunday cut in his raincoat. Sweat is no longer a problem as the rain chills his back.

They pass broken buildings that seem to appear from nowhere, rising out of the darkness like ghosts. Shattered bricks and splintered beams provide more grip than the slippery mud, but before long, they're stepping back down into the slush and sinking in the pools of water forming in no man's land.

Doc wants to talk to someone. He wants to express his concerns about the mission. To him, this is madness. Not only are they bunched up, but if they come under attack, they can't move quickly in the thick mud. And even if they could, where would they go? It's impossible to see anything that could be used as cover until they stumble upon it.

Doc slides sideways. He slips into an old shell hole. Both Leech and Lavender must have skirted around the edge. Doc made the mistake of taking a lazy step, wanting to walk the most direct route behind Happy. The dirt on the rim of the crater would normally take his weight, but it collapses, and he falls to his knees. He's on the verge of toppling into the dark water swelling within the shell hole when a firm hand grabs his pack and hauls him back. He's not sure who grabbed him, but he scrambles to catch up to Happy, seeing his backpack disappearing ahead of him into the gloom.

William Sunday pats Doc on the shoulder. She says something, but he doesn't catch what's said over the relentless tapping of rain and hail on his helmet.

Doc shivers. He's cold. He's wet. He's miserable. It's difficult to concentrate with the sleet washing over him. Ice-cold water drips from his nose. Water seeps into his gloves. His fingers shake. The weather eases slightly, allowing visibility to improve.

They pass the fried remains of a Russian tank from the early days of the war. The turret and barrel lie almost fifty feet away from the body of the rusted tank itself, sticking out of the mud, having been blown off by Novo lightning. Back then, the doctrine was to attack with overwhelming force, but the Novos slaughtered the Russians, turning the battlefield into a graveyard.

Upturned Russian helmets fill with water. The fields to their left are full of so many helmets that they look like smooth stones scattered across the ground, disappearing into the gloom, suggesting they stretch on without end. The bodies are largely gone, being either fried, buried or having become carrion for scavengers.

Ahead of him, Happy crouches. He raises his rifle, pointing it into the darkness. Doc follows his cue, dropping down and resting on one knee in the mud. He turns and looks behind him. William Sunday, Meyers and Mouse all crouch as well. They have their rifles out, pointing in the same direction. Ahead, Lavender turns back, looking at Meyers. She's looking for instructions. Whatever she and Leech have seen in the darkness before them, it's got them spooked. Meyers holds up his right hand, signaling with his gloved fingers.

Out of nowhere, a bolt of lightning rips through the air, passing level with the ground. It's jagged, lighting up the dirt and rocks. It strikes Meyers in the head. His helmet goes flying. Doc is stunned. In barely a heartbeat, Meyers is dead. His head is gone. Vaporized. There's nothing on his shoulders. A red mist floats in the air. Blood squirts from his neck as his heart continues to pump. What's left of him keels over, falling into the mud. His lifeless body collapses into a shallow hole filled with water. The surface turns dark red. His hands twitch, but his arms remain still.

Doc has seen death before, but never unannounced and never that sudden. One moment, Meyers was there. Then he was gone. His life is over. It seems cruel that he doesn't even know what happened to him. For Meyers, death came in an instant. His life has been stolen.

"He... He's gone," a stunned Doc mumbles. To him, it's inconceivable that death could come unannounced with no warning whatsoever.

Doc has watched people die far too many times, both here on the Front and back in the Emergency Room of his old hospital in Chicago, but this is different. Not only is it obscenely violent, it's personal. Doc knew Meyers. He respected him. Shock resonates through Doc's mind like the ringing of an old church bell. He's never known someone who died before. Oh, he's met with patients in personal consults prior to surgery, but that's different. A life he cared about has been ripped from the Earth by a surge of glowing blue energy.

"Down! Get Down," William Sunday calls out as multiple bolts of lightning crisscross the darkness, cutting through the gloom.

Before he can react, Doc is pushed face-first into the mud. Broken bricks press against his cheek. Icy cold water runs down his chest, seeping into his clothes and chilling him to the bone. William Sunday's elbow leans into his shoulder. She's lying on him, using his backpack as though it were a sandbag, propping up her rifle. She fires rapidly. Shell casings dance off his helmet. Each shot shakes his body. Doc is terrified.

Explosions break in the distance, but these are the 40mm shells being fired by the squad's M203 grenade launcher, not artillery shells. They lack the characteristic ground-shaking thump of high-explosive munitions. They're being fired blindly to buy the squad some time.

"Move," William Sunday says, dragging Doc to his feet. He wants to ask where. Darkness surrounds them. Doc watches only the fall of his boots splashing in the mud. Somehow, William Sunday guides him to a low brick wall. The scattered rubble suggests it was once part of a house.

"Meyers," he says, leaning against the bricks. Rain soaks his face.

"It's an ambush," William Sunday says, crouching behind the wall. "They were waiting for the hand signals. That made him a target."

"Why?"

"Without leadership, we're ineffective. We're easy meat. Happy will assume command, but he was further forward. I—I don't think he knows."

Off to one side, rifle fire breaks sporadically, along with the sound of grenades exploding, but the intensity has subsided. Flashes of blue streak across the battlefield, coming out of the gloom.

"He's gone," Doc says. "Just like that. Gone."

William Sunday slaps his cheek, forcing him to look at her rather than staring off blindly into the darkness. "Stay with me, Doc. There will be time to mourn later."

Lavender slides on the mud, skidding in beside them.

"Are you okay?" she asks William Sunday, reaching out and squeezing her forearm.

"I'm good. I'm fine."

"It's a shit show out there. Meyers. Leech. Both dead."

"Leech?"

"We walked into a trap. Those *fuckers* took out point and command in one snap."

"What about Happy? And Mouse?"

"I dunno. It's every man for himself out there."

"What are we going to do?" William Sunday asks, and for the first time, Doc senses genuine panic in her voice. It seems she looks to Lavender in much the same way he looks to her for confidence.

"Get the fuck out of here," Lavender says. "We are not equipped for open warfare. Not without artillery support."

"Yes. We go back," Doc says with trembling lips. He points at a right angle to the wall, pointing into the darkness behind them.

"That way, Doc," Lavender says, pointing sideways. She taps him on the shoulder, crouching and smiling as she says, "Stay close, and you'll be fi—"

The bolt of lightning that strikes her comes from the side, meaning the brick wall they're hiding behind is utterly useless for cover. A surge of neon plasma cuts through Lavender's chest, entering from behind her shoulder blade and exiting out of her sternum. A mist of fine blood sprays across Doc's face. Droplets settle on his cheeks before being washed away by the rain. The blinding light leaves her body momentarily silhouetted in a kind of freeze frame seared on the back of Doc's eyes. Steam rises from the gaping hole in her uniform as she crumples onto the loose bricks. Her rifle clatters to the broken concrete beside him. Smoke rises from the scorch marks burned into her uniform.

William Sunday reacts. Fury overwhelms her. She fires indiscriminately into the darkness, firing on full automatic and emptying her magazine within seconds. She pops out the empty mag, allowing it to fall to the mud, and slams in another. She's down on one knee, firing controlled bursts of two or three shots at a time with her second magazine.

Doc grabs Lavender. He turns her over. She blinks. Her mouth opens but no words come out. Rain falls like tears running down her cheeks. Doc pulls her up onto his lap, cradling her as she dies. He holds her gloved hand, squeezing her fingers.

William Sunday backs up next to them, still firing into the gloom. Several more lightning bolts rip through the air, but they're high and wide.

"God, no," William Sunday says, crouching beside Lavender. "Please, no."

William Sunday turns to Doc, who's sitting spread-leg in the mud with his head sagging, resting Lavender on his thigh.

"Do something."

"I—I can't," Doc says, feeling helpless as he stares at the charred flesh in the middle of Lavender's chest. Bubbles of blood rise from her scorched lungs as she tries to breathe, but the damage is overwhelming.

Even if he could throw her on a gurney in Devil's Lake and start operating immediately, she wouldn't survive. He can feel her life slipping away as her fingers lose their strength. It's all he can do to maintain eye contact with her. Tears run down his cheeks. Lavender's lips move, but she can't speak.

William Sunday takes off her gloves. She pulls off the glove on Lavender's right hand and grips her cold fingers with tenderness, letting her feel the touch of another person one last time. She's sobbing.

William Sunday bows forward, resting her head in the crook of Lavender's neck. She mumbles something, but as she's wearing a helmet and the rain is relentless, Doc can't hear those few words.

"I'm sorry," Doc says as Lavender's fingers go limp and her hand falls from his.

Lavender's head rocks back. Her lifeless eyes stare up at the dark sky. Rain soaks her face. Water fills her mouth, but she's beyond caring.

William Sunday screams. In the chaos of the storm and the battle raging around them, it's primal. A gut-wrenching howl rises against the violence of the night. She gets to her feet, standing tall and firing her rifle on full automatic again. Within seconds, the magazine is empty. She drops the empty mag into the mud and slams yet another in place.

"Sunday," Doc calls out, grabbing her trouser leg and appealing for her to drop back behind cover.

Before William Sunday can fire again, three bolts of neon blue converge on her from different directions, cutting through the dark of night, forming a triangle converging on her frail body. They tear through her uniform, ripping her pack from her back and striking her helmet. A puff of smoke billows into the air as the back of her pack is vaporized in a flash of heat. Her uniform is torn open. The side of her Kevlar helmet glows red, melting under the intensity of the blast. William Sunday wheels around under the impact. Her arms fly wide as she spins. Her rifle clatters to the mud. Her body collapses on the brick wall, folding over it. Steam rises from her back. Her leg twitches and then falls still.

"Noooooo!" Doc yells against the storm battering him.

In the silence that follows, rain taps the puddles, splashing in them with a steady rhythm. Doc feels overwhelmed by the clash of the mundane and the horror of no man's land. His hands shake. Tears roll down his cheeks. He pisses himself. He's paralyzed with fear.

Darkness looms over him. Shadows move around him. Out of nowhere, someone runs across the battlefield. Puddles splash beneath their thundering boots. Mouse grabs Doc, hauling him to his feet. Lavender's limp body rolls off his leg and into a muddy ditch. Her head disappears face down in the dark water.

Mouse lifts Doc with ease.

"Gotta go, Doc."

"No, wait," Doc says, trying to pull away from him and get to William Sunday. Even though he knows it's hopeless, Doc can't give up on her. Out of all of them, she's the one that's always looked out for him. He feels he owes her the same respect. If she's dead, he can at least rest her gracefully on the ground. If she's dying, he can comfort her. Doc pulls away from Mouse, but the big man is having none of it. He pushes Doc into an old shell hole. Water dances in the bottom of the crater with the constant fall of rain and sleet. As the far side of the crater has collapsed, it's less than half full.

"Stay here," Mouse says. "I'm going back for Happy."

Doc lies in the mud, looking up at the dark sky as Mouse clambers around the crater. The wind whips the rain in circles, causing it to swirl through the air. Mouse crouches as he goes back over the top. A blue streak tears through the night, crossing the crater in a fraction of a second. It strikes the big man below his helmet. Neon blue lightning crackles over his shoulder. Mouse spins and falls. Blood sprays across the mud. Mouse grabs at his throat as he crashes into the water, sending waves rushing up the side of the shell hole.

Doc slips out of his backpack and scrambles down the slope into the water. He wades out to grab Mouse. The big man is lying face down in the murky pool. Blood spreads on top of the water.

Doc grabs him and pulls him to the edge. Mouse is too heavy to drag out of the water, so he leaves him with his waist submerged and examines his neck. The bolt cut clear through to his spine. The white bone has blackened. Although the Novo bolt cauterized most of the flesh, blood seeps rather than runs from the severed arteries on the dead soldier's neck. Blind eyes stare at him. Doc reaches up and rests his hand on Mouse's face. With trembling fingers, he closes his eyelids. Doc sits there half in the water and weeps.

They're dead.

They're all dead.

The whole squad has been wiped out in a matter of minutes.

Doc feels numb, but not from the icy cold rain. His hands shake. He reaches up and pulls off his helmet, allowing it to tumble into the water. Doc sobs. He's alone. Even if he knew which way to go, he wouldn't make it back to the trenches, not without getting lost or taking a Novo bolt to the back of the head.

Grief washes over him like the sleet, sapping his will for life. Death is near, if not from the Novos, then from hypothermia. His cheeks are so cold he can barely feel them.

A blue glow appears on the edge of the crater. Doc pushes himself back into the mud, trying to disappear. A Novo scrambles over the rim of the shell hole. Lightning crackles on its arms. Another Novo appears. They circle the muddy sides of the crater, working their way down toward him.

Mouse's rifle lies in the dirt not more than five feet away. Doc lunges for it. He grabs it by the barrel, wanting to spin it around so he can get hold of the stock. The closest Novo simply steps on the magazine, pinning the rifle in the mud.

The two aliens examine him. Their trunk-like appendages touch his arms and legs as he pushes away, climbing higher within the crater. Blue lightning dances over their bodies, reflecting off their compound eyes.

"W—What are you waiting for?" Doc says, tapping his chest. "Get it over with. Kill me!"

A tentacle-like arm touches his forehead, pushing him to one side.

The two aliens must recognize him as they retreat, stepping back. Colors pulsate on their arms. Patterns appear and disappear like those of a cuttlefish or an octopus. They respond to each other in fractions of a second. Rather than mere words passing between human lips, entire sentences, if not paragraphs, seem to ripple over their bodies. Their understanding of each other appears almost instantaneous from the way their limbs respond and retract. The lightning dancing between their multiple arms fades. They disappear from sight, using their camouflage to blend in with the crater, vanishing into the dark of night.

"*Kill me?*" the closest Novo says. Although it's repeating Doc's words, they're phrased as a question. The creature doesn't understand the despair he feels.

"You care, but you don't care," Doc says, barely able to speak in the cold. His eyes struggle to make out the creatures in the dark. Their ability to blend in with the mud leaves him feeling as though he's talking to himself. "Why spare me when you slaughtered them?" He taps his chest. "I'm one of them."

"*One of them,*" the Novo says.

"*What are you waiting for?*" the other Novo asks, confusing him. Is this blind mimicry? What little understanding they have seems strained. It's as though they're sparing his life not out of mercy so much as curiosity. He's a novelty. A freak.

Doc is astonished by the Novos' speed. He blinks, and two shadows race up over the edge of the shell hole and back into the night, leaving him alone in the darkness. Dirt slides into the crater in response to their motion. The rain eases, falling as a drizzle.

Doc clambers up the crater wall on his hands and knees. He reaches the rim and looks around. He has no idea where the trenches lie, but they're several hundred yards away. Through the gloom, he can see the outline of the brick wall.

"I—I'm comm—mmm—ing," he says, slurring his words. Doc gets to his feet and staggers back to where Lavender and William Sunday lie dead. He's not thinking straight. Hypothermia is setting in.

If Doc is going to die out here in no man's land, he's not going to die alone. He'll die beside his squad. He staggers to the low brick wall and reaches out for it, pushing off it as he stumbles over the broken bricks. His boots scuff the ground. They feel like lead weights. Rain hides his tears.

He reaches Lavender. As she's lying face down in a puddle, he grabs her shoulder and rolls her over. Death should be dignified. With care, he places her cold hands across her chest and wipes the mud and grime from her face. Doc fusses with her wet hair, making sure it sits properly on her forehead. No one will ever notice. No one will care, but he cares, and that's all that matters.

Doc grabs the wall, using it to help him stand, and shuffles along to where William Sunday lies folded over the bricks. Her backpack has been ripped open by one of the Novo bolts. He pulls her arm back, peeling the pack from her and letting it fall to the mud. Loose magazines and hand grenades scatter in the slush.

"Come on, William," he says, reaching over and grabbing her by the waist. Doc is determined to lay her beside Lavender so they can rest in peace together. He decides he'll bury them with bricks to try to protect their bodies from the ravages of wild dogs. Remaining here in no man's land will cost him his life to the cold, but he cannot abandon the two women, not even in death.

Doc rests William Sunday beside Lavender, laying her head gently on the ground. The side of her helmet is deformed, having melted under the heat of the Novo bolt. He removes it. Her hair is scorched. Above her ears, it's shriveled and curled from the heat. Blisters have formed on her cheeks and forehead.

Doc wipes her face, clearing away specks of mud and grit.

Blisters.

His mind halts.

Blisters only form on living tissue, not dead. Three Novo bolts converged on her in an instant, but none of them struck. One tore open her pack. Another scorched her arm, burning the thick material. The third grazed her helmet, knocking her unconscious. She's alive. She has to be.

"Will?" he says, touching lightly at her forehead. He feels for a pulse, pushing his fingers up under her jaw and searching for her carotid artery. There's resistance there. A slight, steady push comes back at him, pulsating against his fingertips.

"William Sunday?"

Doc's heart races.

A shadow passes over him. He looks up and sees a soldier standing in front of him. Is he dreaming? Hallucinating? Sleet washes over the stoic frame of a man in a combat uniform drenched in rain.

"We've got to go, Doc."

"Happy? Is—Is that you?"

"It's me," Happy replies, leaning heavily to one side. His jacket is torn. Scorch marks line his bare arms. Rain washes over his face.

"She's alive," Doc says, still kneeling in the mud.

"You need to leave her."

"I—I can't do that," Doc replies, getting up. He's unsteady on his feet. "I won't leave her, not while there's a chance. Help me."

"I can't."

It's only then that Doc realizes why. Happy's lost his left leg from just below the knee. A belt wrapped around his thigh acts as a self-administered tourniquet. Bloody bone and straggly bits of sinew hang from what's left of his knee. He's using his rifle as a crutch, with the butt pressed hard beneath his armpit. He crouches, prodding at the dirt with the barrel, searching for bits of stone or brick so the thin barrel doesn't sink into the mud.

Doc bends over. He reaches under William Sunday, lifting her as he stands.

"You won't make it," Happy says.

"Neither will you."

Happy smiles. He laughs. "So be it. If we die, we die together."

"Which way?" Doc asks.

Happy turns, prodding the mud with his rifle as he walks into the storm. Doc follows him. Doc's boots are waterlogged. He splashes in the puddles, staggering along behind Happy, carrying William Sunday in his arms.

The sky lightens. Dawn is breaking. It's the killing hour. Doc can only hope the Novos will have mercy on the wounded staggering back to their lines.

Corpses

The war is over for Happy. Dr. Helen Anderson treats him as a personal favor to Doc, but there isn't a lot she can do for him beyond removing necrotic tissue. She completes the below-knee amputation, giving him a cleanly sutured stump that can begin healing. Once he's stable, Dr. Anderson issues orders to evac Happy down the line. She sends him to the US Army hospital in Landstuhl, Germany, where he'll be fitted with a prosthetic leg and undergo rehab. From there, he'll be sent back to the States. Doc shakes his hand before he leaves, knowing that, in all likelihood, they'll never see each other again.

"You're a good man, Happy. Never forget that."

"You too, Doc."

Orderlies carry Happy away, taking him down through the trenches where he'll be loaded onto one of the bloodied evac carts they saw just a few days ago while riding back to the Front. A mule will carry Happy to the rear, then a truck, then a helicopter or an airplane. It's perverse to see human technology humbled by the alien intruders, forcing the US Army to use transportation not seen in centuries.

Doc sits with William Sunday in the recovery dugout within the triage trench. She's asleep. Blood seeps through the bandages wrapping around her head. Her wound is weeping rather than bleeding. An IV line leads into her arm. The bucket beside her cot has spew in it. As there's no electronic monitoring, the chart at the end of her bed has notes from the nurses, capturing her vital signs at regular intervals. Doc looks at the handwritten records of her blood pressure, pulse and respiration over

197

the past few hours.

Dr. Anderson sits down next to him.

"You should get some sleep."

"Yeah. I know," Doc replies, looking down at his trembling hands. Adrenaline has long since drained from his veins, leaving him exhausted.

"Our X-ray plates out here in the field are crude. Skull radiographs show no sign of a fracture."

"That's good to hear."

"The heat from that blast was nasty, searing her skin. She has no signs of increased intracranial pressure within her skull, which is good, but she could still have a bleed or brain contusion. There's no way to tell here at the Front. She needs a CT and MRI as soon as possible."

Doc nods.

"I can get her on an evac to the US Army hospital in Grafenwöhr later this afternoon. They'll be able to—"

Without opening her eyes, William Sunday growls, "I ain't going nowhere."

"Sunday," Doc says. "We need to get you proper medical care."

She looks at him with a sense of despair. Her eyes flood with tears.

"I'm not leaving her. I can't. I will not leave Lavender out there with the dogs."

Dr. Anderson is quiet.

"I understand," Doc says. "Let me talk to Command. I'll see if we can organize a recovery mission tonight."

William Sunday lets out a solitary laugh. Her head sinks into the pillow. She stares at the ceiling as she asks, "How many died, Doc? How many bodies are out there?"

He looks to Dr. Anderson. She says, "Twenty-two."

"There's no way they're going to send a recovery team into a hot zone."

"Let me—"

William Sunday cuts him off. "I'll go out there. Alone. Tonight."

"Jesus," Doc says. "You're in no state to go anywhere, let alone back into no man's land."

"I'll be fine." William Sunday swallows the lump welling up in her throat. "One soldier. Alone. Hidden in the darkness. I'll be okay."

Doc reaches out and takes her hand. He squeezes her fingers gently. "I'll go."

"You?" Dr. Anderson says.

"They won't touch me."

Dr. Anderson's eyes go wide. "Seriously?"

"I can't explain it, but they don't see me as a threat."

"Are you crazy?" Dr. Anderson asks. "What makes you think your luck will hold?"

"I don't know. But what hope do any of us have for the future? We could be killed as we sit here, struck by a wayward shell."

He leans forward and kisses William Sunday on the forehead, saying, "Rest, my friend. I'll see you when I get back."

Doc walks out into the sunlight. An orderly has set up a refreshment station in the broad trench outside the medical post. Various types of fruit sit in a wooden crate on a rickety fold-up table. Doc takes an apple and a peeled orange and heads along the boardwalk toward the Front. The sun is out, warming the trenches following the rain and sleet. Soldiers hang damp clothing on the sides of the trench, drying out their uniforms. The apple is bruised and tastes bland, but Doc doesn't care. The orange is overripe but tasty. The acidic juice bites at the cracks in his lips. It stings, but Doc finds the pain invigorating. He's alive when so many are dead. Doc is so tired he's delirious. His boots move without any conscious thought.

It takes an hour to reach the Echo section of the line. Soldiers stare as he walks past. It's the dried blood and mud on his uniform. No one wants to be reminded of the hell that exists beyond the wooden walls of the trench. Doc arrives back at the Echo ladder. Most of the icicles have melted in the sun. He reaches up, grabbing one of the rungs.

"Hey, what do you think you're doing?" a corporal asks.

"I'm going to get a friend."

"I can't let you do that," the corporal says, grabbing his shoulder. "It's suicide going out there during the day."

Doc pulls away from him and steps up the rungs of the ladder.

"They'll kill you," the corporal says.

"I wish," Doc replies. Deep down, he knows he should wait until nightfall, but he can't. It's all he can do to keep moving. He feels as if he lies down somewhere he'll drift into a sleep so deep he'll never wake again.

On reaching the top of the trench, Doc steps over sandbags and into the mud. Spotters crouch behind cover, watching as he walks into no man's land.

Doc holds his arms up with his hands on either side of his head. He walks proud. He has no intention of hiding, not that he could in the bright daylight. There's freedom to be found in walking upright through the devastation, a sense of defiance that comes from refusing to cower.

Everything that appears so terrifying at night is tragic during the day. Shattered trees are a graveyard. Having been pummeled by shrapnel and numerous direct hits, they still stand in the muddy ground, marking where soldiers have fallen.

Doc steps on a sheet of stiff plastic. He shifts his boot, looking down at a fast food sign with pictures of hamburgers and fries. The writing is in Cyrillic, but the numbers are all too familiar. It's ₱6.99 for this and ₱9.99 for that. An entire world lies buried beneath the mud of his boots.

Out of nowhere, a bolt of lightning streaks through the daylight. Doc flinches, reacting to the searing heat radiating through the air, but it's a warning shot. If the Novos wanted to kill him, he'd be dead. At this distance, they probably can't identify him. Slowly, he turns through 360 degrees, keeping his hands up, letting them see he's not carrying any weapons. Then, he walks on.

To one side, there's a collapsed bridge. Rusted cars have piled up against each other on the sloping concrete. Last night, in the darkness and sleet, he missed the bridge entirely. For a moment, he wonders if he's emerged in no man's land at the wrong point, but he remembers the ladder back in the trench. It had names etched into the side of the main supports, something he hasn't seen elsewhere. He's got to be in the right location, but nothing looks familiar. Oh, for some sleet and driving rain to make him feel more comfortable. He laughs at the insanity and then laughs some more, realizing how crazy it is to hear such a clear testimony of life among the dead. What must the Novos think? Who fucking cares?

Doc walks forward for several hundred yards, avoiding the flooded shell holes and craters. The silence is overwhelming. Earth is a planet teeming with life. The absence of any sound is unsettling. Even the wind is quiet. It's then he realizes there are no shells falling anywhere along the Front. When he first stepped into no man's land, they were landing several miles away on either side of him. Perhaps the spotters have told the artillery batteries to hold fire while he's out here. Both sides seem to be showing restraint for the madman wandering through the dirt and desolation with his arms raised in surrender.

A large soldier lies face down in the water at the bottom of a shell hole. A medical pack lies abandoned on the muddy slope. Scuff marks and boot prints reveal the heartache of those final few moments as Mouse died.

Doc walks on toward a low brick wall barely thirty yards away. In the daylight, he can see an oversized donut lying further along in the ruins. It's comically large, being easily fifteen feet in diameter and three feet thick. Once, it stood tall on a metal pole, tempting people to stop and buy some donuts instead of driving past along the road. Now, it looks pathetic.

Doc reaches Lavender. Tears well up in his eyes. He goes to crouch beside her, but his thigh muscles give way, and his knees thunder into the dirt and mud.

"I am so sorry," he says, shifting his arms beneath her frail body. He slips one arm beneath her back and the other under her knees and lifts. Her body is cold but not stiff. Her head lolls back. Her arms hang limp.

From the other side of the brick wall, lightning crackles. A Novo appears as he gets back to his feet. Its body seems to resolve out of thin air as its camouflage fades. It keeps itself prone, spreading its eight legs wide and allowing Doc to look down on the top of its head with its hundreds of compound eyes glistening in the sunlight. It's keeping itself out of sight from snipers.

"You..."

Doc staggers under the weight of Lavender. The alien could kill him, but it could kill him at any distance it chose. It didn't need to creep up close to strike him. It's curious.

"You don't understand, do you?" Doc says, standing there with Lavender in his arms.

"Don't understand."

"She's dead. Nothing can change that. She'll never know life again... Nothing matters anymore. Not for her. So why? Why am I here?"

"Nothing... can change."

"And yet, death isn't the end," Doc says. "This is what you don't understand about us. She's dead, and yet, death is not about her. It's about us—the living. It's about remembering and honoring the fallen. We can't forget. No one is gone until we forget them."

"Care," the Novo says.

Doc stops in his tracks. This is the first time any Novo has done anything more than repeat back fragments of his own sentences to him. Care is a word he hasn't used in their stilted conversation, and Doc has to rack his mind to think if he's ever used that word in their presence. He's unsure, but he thinks he used that word last night. It seems the Novos understand more than he or anyone realizes.

"Yes," he says. "We care."

The Novo fades from sight. Doc turns and walks back toward the Front. When he gets within fifty yards, several unarmed soldiers creep over the top of the trench. They meet him beside the cab of a truck that's sunk in the mud. Only the roof is visible.

"How many more?" the corporal he spoke with in the trenches asks.

"I—ah. Twenty. There were twenty-two last night."

One of the soldiers takes Lavender from him. Doc turns back toward no man's land.

"We can take it from here," the corporal says.

"I can't leave them. Any of them," Doc says, babbling and feeling feverish. He turns back, wanting to retrieve Meyers and Leech, along with Mouse, although there's no way he can carry him.

Together, six soldiers walk back out into no man's land with their hands raised, replicating his initial approach. There are no bolts of lightning, no massive stones hurled through the air, and no artillery fired by the humans. It seems an informal ceasefire has been agreed upon by both sides. It takes several hours to recover the remains of the Dog Food Squad and the 105th. The sun is setting as the last of the corpses is lowered into the trench.

Doc stumbles down the ladder, falling the last few feet and crumpling on the wooden boards.

"Easy, sir," a soldier says, helping him to his feet. "We'll get you back to your dugout."

The soldier hoists Doc's arm over his shoulder and leads him through the trenches.

"Thanks," Doc says, feeling his legs on the verge of collapsing beneath him.

As night falls, the bombardment begins again. Both sides resume the war, which causes Doc's heart to sink. Is there any hope for peace when war rages in the heart? On reaching his dugout, Doc collapses on a cot. He falls asleep to the sound of artillery thundering down all along the Front.

When Words Fail

Doc snorts himself awake. His eyes open. From the way the light falls across the logs outside the dugout, it's early afternoon. His bladder is bursting. He gets up and relieves himself in the bucket in the corner. It's clean. Empty. He squirts some navy blue neutralizing fluid in and replaces the lid once he's finished.

Someone's dropped off bottled water and a few nut bars. It's a beautiful day outside, that is, if any day in the war can be called beautiful. White clouds drift across a clear blue sky. It's cold. Vapor forms on the breath of soldiers walking past.

Doc lights a gas lantern and hangs it from a hook in the middle of the wooden ceiling. It casts a warm glow throughout the dugout, but it can't compete with the glare from outside.

Doc sits near the doorway. Sunlight spills in from the trench. He opens his journal and looks at the title: *The Anatomy of Courage.*

"Huh," he mumbles. "Courage? Really?"

It seems like an eternity has passed since he wrote those four words. Now, they seem grossly inadequate. Naive. Pretentious. Doc sits down and writes several alternative titles below the original.

The Illusion of Courage.

The Heartbreak of Sacrifice.

The Lies We Tell Ourselves.

The Waste.

Doc flicks through the pages, reviewing his writing and making notes in the margins. Chewing on the nut bar and sipping water is somewhat therapeutic for him. It's the dissonance that exists between life and death. Regardless of the weight of grief bearing down on him, his body demands food, water, rest, and to be relieved. It's the body, not the mind that demands life goes on.

Doc jots down the basic details of the storm in chronological order, leaving several lines between each point. That will allow him to fill in more details about his thoughts, observations, and reactions at a later point in time. He's determined to document the fall of the Dog Food Squad. As pitiful as it may seem, it's the only way he can honor the dead.

A shadow darkens the doorway.

"Doc?"

"William Sunday," he says, putting his journal to one side and getting up to greet her.

William Sunday steps down into the dugout, throws her arms around his neck and squeezes tight, burying her head into his chest. Doc is surprised by how frail she feels. She's strong, but her body feels almost hollow.

"Thank you," she says, letting go and wiping her eyes. "They told me what you did out there yesterday."

"Like you, I couldn't leave her," Doc says with trembling lips.

"And the Novos?"

"They let us come and go, retrieving our dead."

"It's like you said, isn't it? We don't understand them."

"They're alien," he says. "They evolved on an entirely different world, with different selective pressures and social conditions. It would be astonishing if we did understand them."

William Sunday says, "We're fools to think we could ever understand them."

"And they don't understand us," Doc replies.

"But we understand enough to kill each other."

"We do."

They sit opposite each other within the empty dugout. William Sunday grabs a bottle of water. Instead of squad members sitting on the bench seat running around the dugout, there are shoeboxes filled with their personal effects. The quartermaster has already collected their equipment and spare uniforms and returned them to inventory. The boxes are evenly spaced, waiting for the army postmaster to send someone to collect them and forward them on to their relatives. It's as though the dead have become ghosts sitting beside their meager possessions in silence.

"You should be in Germany," Doc says.

"Someone's got to look after you," William Sunday replies, and he smiles.

"Yeah, I'm a bit of a klutz out there, huh?"

William Sunday ruffles a winter jacket for use as a pillow and sits on it, kicking her boots up on one of the wooden crates.

"What happens next?" Doc asks. "I mean, what happens to the Dog Food Squad."

"It's over. Gone. Dead."

Doc is silent.

"Oh, the DF3 designation will be recycled like our clothing, but nothing will ever be the same."

"And us?"

"We'll be reassigned. I hear Donkey Kong is down on its numbers."

"Do they need another doctor?"

William Sunday shrugs. She chugs her water. The bandage around her head is clean, meaning a nurse must have changed it this morning before she was discharged. Doc can care for her wound from here so she doesn't have to traipse back to the triage center each morning.

"And you?" she asks, pointing at his journal lying on the crate in front of him. "You're still writing that shit?"

Doc hangs his head. He understands her frustration with the

journal. It must seem obsessive to her, but for him, it's a way of dealing with the trauma he feels. Instead of bottling up the hurt, he gets it out on the page, but he can see how it must seem heartless to her. He picks up the journal, holding it as though it were an exhibit in court, unsure how he can explain his thinking to her.

"It's all I've got. I have nothing else. When the world closes in, this is my way of pushing back."

"So give them to me," she says with tears welling up in her eyes. "Give me the words that will soothe my soul. Take away my pain."

"Nothing will ever take away the pain," Doc replies, putting the journal down. "The best we can hope for is to understand it."

"I—I need something," William Sunday says, wiping her eyes.

Doc stutters. "W—Words fail me."

He rubs his fingers in the corners of his eyes, pushing them up beneath his glasses and lifting the rim off the bridge of his nose. Doc wipes away grit and tears. His lips tremble as he speaks.

"Words fail all of us. You. Me. Them out there in the trenches. We want more from life. We're better than mere words, but that's all we have. We're more than flesh and blood, but words are the only tools we have with which to reach out from one to another. And words suck. Like us, they're frail.

"Words are limited. They're sequential. They're linear. One word comes after another, and then the next, and then one more, and we call that a sentence, but words are too compact for reality. They're one-dimensional—like a line drawn on a page when life is lived in three dimensions or more.

"We're trying to describe the complexities of the soul with the poorest of tools. It's... I... To me, writing is like performing surgery wearing boxing gloves."

William Sunday is quiet. Her jaw clenches. Doc doesn't know what she's thinking. He wishes she'd speak so he knows what's churning within her soul, but the hard look on her face suggests she wants to hear him defend his journal. She's not angry. To him, it seems she genuinely wants to understand his reasoning. She's looking for answers of her own.

"Words flow like time. One word follows the next as though they were mere seconds in a minute, doomed to forever travel in only one direction, slowly building to an hour or, for me, a paragraph, a page, a chapter. But us humans? We're so much more. We live on multiple planes of existence. We are more than words can express, and yet words are all we have with which to describe the passion that swirls within our hearts. We're trying to compress three, four, five dimensions into a mere one. It can't be done.

"No one really knows anyone else. Oh, we hear the words they speak. We see their actions. We think we know who they are, but we don't. Reading someone is like trying to understand a five-hundred-page novel by scanning the blurb on the dust jacket, but that's all we have. There is no other way for you to understand me or me to understand you."

He sips his water.

"No matter how hard we try, all we ever have are words, and words fail us. They cannot convey the essence of our being. Words capture only a fraction of who we really are.

"We see each other like a blind man watching a sunset. Oh, he can feel the warmth on his cheeks. He can sense the temperature dropping as the shadows grow around him. He can hear the birds settling in the trees, calling to each other. But he can never see the way the last rays of the sun stretch across the sky. He can never enjoy the hues of yellow and pink lighting up the clouds or the darkness that falls in shades of blue."

William Sunday looks down at her hands. She fidgets with her fingers.

With trembling lips, she says, "I miss her."

Doc's heart breaks. William Sunday spoke a mere three words compared to what must have been hundreds from him. She uttered three simple words. None of them contains any complexity. They're ordinary words with meanings no one will ever bother to look up in a dictionary. One letter. Four letters. Then three. Could there be a simpler sentence? And yet the depth. The heartache. The sense of loss is overwhelming.

William Sunday is giving him a glimpse into her heart.

"I—I," Doc begins, but instead of rambling, he descends to her level to feel her grief as raw and painful as it is, saying, "I know."

Neither of them speaks for the longest time. For someone like Doc, whose mind runs at a million miles an hour, constantly processing people and situations, observing and drawing conclusions, being quiet is a revelation. He's strangely at peace.

"Did you see it?" William Sunday says, brightening as she changes the subject.

"Ah... I'm not sure what you mean?"

"The donut."

"Oh, yes," Doc says, laughing, having forgotten how liberating it is to laugh. He holds his hands wide. "The big donut. Out there. In no man's land."

"I used to buy donuts from there."

"You did?"

She nods. "They were good donuts. The best."

"I bet," Doc replies, lost in the memory of the crumpled donut on the battlefield, knowing this is where Lavender fell.

"And soda. Although, we never had Coke or Fanta. We only ever got the Russian knock-off. We called it *Nikola* as a joke because, say it slowly, and *Nikola* sounds like *not cola*. It was sweet, but it was always flat. Ah, there were bubbles. Just enough bubbles in the glass that we couldn't complain to the shopkeeper, but it wasn't fizzy. Not like your American soda."

Doc smiles, enjoying her memories of life from before the war.

"The first time I tried Sprite, I almost choked. The bubbles. They went up my nose!"

Doc chuckles.

"And they danced on my tongue," she says, raising her eyebrows. "It was like a party erupted in my mouth."

Doc shakes his head, smiling at the innocence of her recollection.

"I want to see America," she says. "Do you think they'll let me visit?"

"I'll take you there myself," he says. "I'll take you to New York so you can see the Yankees play baseball in the Bronx. We'll have hot dogs and beer."

William Sunday's face lights up at the thought.

"And we'll go and see the Statue of Liberty. And the museums. New York has some of the best museums in the world."

"And Times Square?" she asks.

"Sure. But it's not a square."

"It isn't?"

"No. And that makes it typically American."

"What shape is it?" a curious William Sunday asks.

"Look on a map, and it's a triangle," Doc says. "Two roads cross at an angle. And that's the square. It's the most famous square that's not a square."

"I would like to see this *not-a-square*," William Sunday says, but the zest in her voice has fallen. The enthusiasm is no longer there. It's the shells falling outside in no man's land that dull her excitement. The wooden beams above them shake. The mud and slush on the floor ground them in reality. As nice as it is to escape the war for a few minutes, there's no guarantee that either of them will live beyond today.

"And Ohio," she says with sorrow in her voice. "I'd like to see Ohio."

"I can take you there," Doc says, knowing Lavender came from a small town in rural Ohio.

"I'd like to see where she grew up," William Sunday says.

"I'd like that, too."

Outside, there's considerable discussion as several soldiers come to a halt next to the dugout. Shadows darken the doorway. Colonel Holloway steps down into their dugout, removing his cap. William Sunday snaps to attention, jumping up off the bench seat. Doc is slower to react.

"At ease," the colonel says, tucking his cap under his arm. He looks around the dugout with disgust. Mud and slush seep through the floorboards as he steps forward. Behind him, another officer steps down from the trench. Doc sees two silver stars on the officer's rank badge, but he doesn't know what they signify. William Sunday, though, stiffens. So much for "*at ease.*"

A woman enters behind them. She's wearing civilian clothes, but they're practical: khaki trousers, hiking boots and a bomber jacket. She's a blank. This doesn't bode well.

"Please. Have a seat," the colonel says. He drags over two of the crates, setting them up as a table in the middle of the dugout and lights a couple of candles. As he does so, William Sunday circles around to Doc and sits nervously beside him. The woman pulls a map out of a cardboard tube and stretches it over the makeshift table, using the candles to hold it in place. As the candles are set in glass bottles, wax drips on the map.

The colonel says, "This is General McMasters and Dr. Bailey Browne, Under Secretary of Defense for Intelligence and Security."

He grabs a few of the smaller crates and sets them as chairs around the impromptu table. Doc and William Sunday exchange a quick glance, unsure of themselves.

Doc clears his throat. "Ah, Dr. Browne. I'm not sure I—"

"Bailey, please," she says, scooting onto one of the crates and straightening the map. She arranges the map so it faces them, meaning it's upside down for her. Unlike most of the military maps he's seen, there are none of the fake designations of Montana or North Dakota. Instead, they're looking at a map of Russia with Kazakhstan to the southwest and Mongolia in the southeast. Beyond them lies China and India. A crooked, awkward, red U-shaped drawing dominates the center of the map, weaving its way around the Russian city of *Novosibirsk*, where the alien cruiser crash-landed several years ago, giving the aliens their name. The markings for the Front are elongated. It's as though the U has been stretched sideways.

"And you're Dr. Christopher—"

William Sunday cuts Bailey off, preventing her from saying his full name and correcting her with a harsh "Doc."

"And you must be Anastas—"

"Sunday. William Sunday."

"You have to understand," Doc says. "Out here on the Front. We don't use our real names."

"Why?" a curious Bailey asks.

"Because we left our old lives behind."

"And we'll probably never see them again," William Sunday says.

"Oh... Okay."

"What's this about?" a hostile William Sunday asks. As a local recruit, she doesn't have the same level of respect for the authoritarian structures within the US Army as someone like Meyers. She'll stand to attention, but she tolerates rather than obeys orders and officers. To be fair, Doc figures she's seen enough fuck-ups on the battlefield to justify questioning their authority.

"Right," Bailey says. "Down to business. Okay. I like that. What you are about to hear is classified. You understand you cannot discuss this with anyone outside of this bunker?"

"Dugout," William Sunday says a little too aggressively.

"Yes," Doc says on behalf of both of them, trying to smooth out the conversation.

Bailey taps the map.

"This is the extent of the war as it stands at the moment. Here, the Western Front extends from *Novyi Vasiugan* in the north to *Aksu* in Kazakhstan in the south. We have 320,000 troops stationed along roughly 420 miles, with the depth of the front reaching back anywhere from fifteen to seventy miles."

Doc is fascinated.

"From *Aksu*, the Southern Front stretches 860 miles to *Tsetsen-Uul* in Mongolia. The Chinese have deployed eight hundred thousand soldiers to defensive positions all along this region, but it is not as well defined as the Western Front. In some places, such as along mountain ranges, there are no trenches at all. Then, fifty miles further along, the battlefield will be as dense and clustered and intense as ours.

"In addition to this, the Chinese have established a military logistics supply chain involving upwards of fourteen million people to feed the war machine. Like us, they're preparing fall-back positions, but for them, it's more urgent. Beijing is much closer to the action than Berlin. There's a fear that if the Novos break out to the south, they could sweep down through the desert and march through the Chinese industrial heartland within a matter of weeks, cutting the country in half."

"And the Eastern Front?" Doc asks, curious as it's the shortest line.

"From *Tsetsen-Uul*, the Eastern Front stretches to *Kyzyl* in Siberia to the north."

William Sunday says, "So the Novos are focusing their efforts to the south."

"Yes," Bailey says. "The Chinese are mining the fallback region with nukes, but there's too much uncertainty about where the Novos might break through."

The general says, "And it would slow but not stop them."

William Sunday asks, "Why aren't we firing nukes at them?"

Bailey replies, "We have, but they intercept them at altitudes of over two hundred and fifty thousand feet. We got a few starbursts off early in the war but can't get anything to the ground."

"And they hide their infrastructure with clouds," the general says. "Whether they're terraforming or just throwing up a smoke screen is difficult to tell, but we only get vague satellite information in the infrared range."

Bailey asks them, "What do you notice about this map?"

Doc thinks for a moment and replies, "It's incomplete."

William Sunday says, "There's no Northern Front."

"What's to stop them going north around us?" Doc asks.

"Nothing."

"Nothing?"

The general says, "There are no half-measures in war. You fight to win, or you lose. But the Novos. It's like they don't understand the rules of the game—like they're waiting for us to open up a northern front."

Bailey says, "There's sixteen hundred miles of uninhabited forest between *Kyzyl* and the Arctic. From where we are here in the west, it's roughly a thousand miles to the Arctic Ocean. Either way, the North is indefensible. As it is, we're struggling to maintain our lines. It's the lack of mechanized options that hurts us. Even if we mobilized a million combat troops, the logistics would cripple us."

"So why haven't they done it?" William Sunday asks. "Why haven't they simply gone around us?"

The general says, "We're not sure, but, like us, they may be constrained by a lack of resources. A northern front would stretch their western and southern forces, but..."

Bailey says, "It's a humanitarian corridor. We can get basic supplies in through there, but not much else."

Doc interrupts him, mumbling, "We don't understand them."

Bailey snaps her fingers. "Exactly. We're fighting a protracted land war in Asia; one we're bound to lose. The continent is just too damn big to defend."

"But?"

"But they're not fighting a war. Not in the sense we would. They're not trying to win."

"I don't understand," William Sunday says. "Then what are they trying to do?"

"Survive."

"Survive?"

Bailey says, "For us, wars are politics by brute force. We rarely fight to survive. We fight for conquest, to seize land, to take resources, to control populations."

"But them?" Doc says.

"When the aliens first crashed, the Russians rushed in to control the site. They wanted the spacecraft for themselves. It's their jurisdiction. They claimed sovereignty, but it quickly became apparent that the Novos weren't surrendering their starship to anyone. The first battles were against Russian special forces. They were decimated by the Novos' lightning weapon. When the Russian 5th and 6th armies fell in the fields of *Kargat,* America rallied the UN to stage a military intervention. Within the first month, the Russian Army had been obliterated. They died buying time for humanity. What few units remained were incorporated into the US-led Reaction Force. A buffer zone was established. Civilians were evacuated. For a while, there was hope for peace, but the Novos pushed outward."

"But not northward," Doc says.

"No. They seem more interested in following trade routes than taking open country, so they spread east and west and then to the south, tracing the various roads between towns and cities."

"But never to the north?"

"Rarely to the north. A large proportion of our incursions and attacks are attempts at keeping them concentrated in the south, but it's a bluff. Our strategy has been to exhaust them."

"Only?"

"Only it's not a good strategy. We need a goal, an end game."

"So why are you here?" William Sunday asks. "Why are you talking to the two of us? We're grunts. We're nobodies."

Bailey says, "Because you can talk to them."

"Woah," Doc says, sitting back and holding out his hands in alarm. "Hang on a minute."

"You said it yourself," Bailey replies. "We don't understand them. And you're right. We don't. And we need to, or we're in danger of losing the war."

"What's your goal?" William Sunday asks.

"Peace," Bailey replies.

The general says, "Fighting for peace takes more courage than fighting in war."

Doc nods at that point.

Bailey says, "I've been empowered by the UN Secretary-General, the US President and the President of the European Union to negotiate terms for peace. The Chinese are skeptical, but if we can reach an accord, I can get them onboard as well."

William Sunday looks horrified. "You're just going to let the Novos get away with all this? Let them get away with murder?"

"I've read your file," Bailey says. "I know about your family. And I'm sorry."

"How can there be peace?" William Sunday asks.

"What is war without peace?" Bailey asks.

"Pointless," Doc replies. "An utterly futile waste of life."

To which Bailey says, "Yes, so why fight? Why die if not for an achievable goal?"

William Sunday hangs her head, not wanting to answer Bailey's question.

The general says, "We think in narrow terms. All we want is victory—but victory doesn't mean peace."

Doc says, "Victory is propaganda."

"Yes," Bailey says, pointing at him. "We need real peace. Genuine peace. Lasting peace."

William Sunday fights back the tears in her eyes. "And you think that will come from talking to them?"

"It won't come from fighting them," Bailey replies. "Our war hawks want to develop ever more exotic experiments and weapons. They're looking for a game-changer, a super weapon, but it's war for war's sake. We have to look at the true cost of war. And it isn't simply the lives lost. It's the future. It's not just what we've already lost. It's all we stand to lose."

Doc taps the map. His finger points at the vast open forest to the

217

north of the U-shaped front lines. "They're only fighting us where we're fighting them."

Bailey says, "The prevailing theory at the Pentagon is that they're not interested in land so much as attacking population centers. That's where they see the threat."

Doc says, "And that's why they're pivoting south."

The general says, "Toward the most densely populated place on the planet: India, China, Southeast Asia, Indonesia. If they break through and reach these countries, the death toll will reach into the billions."

"There's something I don't understand," Doc says. "They came here on a spacecraft capable of traversing the stars. It was described as a colony ship, right?"

"Right," Bailey says. "From satellite imagery, it was several times larger than an ocean cruise liner."

"Why aren't they using that? Why aren't they using their superior technology, their space technology, to defeat us? I mean, couldn't they lasso an asteroid and drop it on London or New York?"

"We're worried about the same thing," the general says, "And it keeps our military planners up at night."

Bailey speaks with measured words. "We've only ever seen this as a war of attrition. But what if we've got it all wrong? What if it's something more?"

William Sunday is wistful. She echoes Doc's sentiments from earlier, "What if we don't understand them?"

"Exactly. This is why we need you. We need to be able to talk to them. We have to learn about them. We need to understand them."

"And how exactly is this going to work?" Doc asks.

Bailey says, "I want you to take me to the other side."

William Sunday's eyes go wide. "Of no man's land?"

"Yes."

"That's a really bad idea," Doc says.

"We'll go up over the top. We've got units stationed up north in *Novyi Vasiugan* that can link us up with civilians in the occupied zone."

"And then what?" Doc asks.

"We raise a white flag and talk to them. You can do that, right?"

"I don't know," Doc says. "I mean, saying I can talk to them is a bit of a stretch. It feels like talking to a Great White Shark."

"But you've done it. You've spoken with them a couple of times, right? Like yesterday when you were recovering bodies."

"You saw that?"

"We saw a glow from behind the brick wall. We saw your lips moving. And we saw them back down and allow others to help you with the recovery effort. That's *never* happened before."

"I'm no one. I'm just a doctor." He shakes his head. "I don't know how much they're going to listen to me. Hell, what I've experienced could be a local fluke. I could have run into the local pacifist or whatever. There's no guarantee any of the others will listen to me."

"We have no choice," Bailey says. "We have to try."

The Stars

Doc and William Sunday walk alone through the trenches.

"You don't have to do this," he says to her.

"What? And let you have all the fun?" she replies as the two of them march toward the regional command center in Omaha, Nebraska.

A glow on the horizon behind them marks the rising sun. They're traveling light, with a small pack containing clothes. They'll pick up food and water at way stations on the trek. Traversing forty miles of trenches is going to take all day. General McMasters and Dr. Bailey Browne rode mules to within a couple of miles of the Front and returned on them last night. If only they'd dragged up a few spares. As it is, it will be nightfall before Doc and William Sunday reach the rear.

Within a few miles, Doc's feet are aching. The trenches leading away from no man's land aren't as deep or as muddy as at the Front. On occasions, depending on how the rolling hills unfold, they can see out over the desolate landscape. Snow blankets the fields. Runners jog back and forth, carrying satchels with commands for troop movements. As the air is still in the trenches, the dispatch troops have their shirts off, enjoying the warmth of the winter sun on their skin as they run past.

"Do you really think this is going to work?"

"I don't know," Doc says. "But what is it they say about insanity? It's doing the same thing over and over again and expecting different results. We can't just keep sending men and women to their deaths. We have to try something else."

William Sunday nods. Her silence is telling.

"I know this is difficult for you," Doc says.

"I want them to pay," she replies with venom in her voice.

Doc is silent.

"I hate them." She turns to him, wanting a response from him, but Doc feels uncomfortable with where the conversation is going. He looks down at the fall of his boots on the wooden boards within the trench.

Her voice softens, but not her words. "I'd kill all of them if I could."

Doc swallows the lump in his throat. It's easy to condemn her anger, to call it unhealthy, but what would he feel if he'd lost his family in the opening days of the war? He can't criticize her. He has no right. The hurt she feels is real. No lecture on medical ethics or the psychology of grief ever prepared him for the raw emotion he hears in her voice. And emotions cannot be turned on and off like a light switch. Nor should they. Humans are not machines. There are some wounds for which there is no salve. Mere words would mock her pain.

Doc nods. It's his way of letting her know he understands her grief and doesn't think ill of her. Acceptance is the first step. She needs to understand that she can trust him rather than hide her feelings. Sometimes, all anyone needs is a sounding board, not trite advice.

They walk along in silence for a few yards. A male Eurasian Bullfinch lands on one of the trench supports ahead of them. The trees that once gave it refuge now line ditches in the frozen ground. Brilliant orange feathers adorn the bird's chest. Its head is black, while its wings are grey. A female Bullfinch lands beside it, which is peculiar as normally it's the males chasing the females, not the other way around, but this must be a breeding pair heading south from Siberia, struggling to stay ahead of the weather.

Doc points, "Beautiful, huh?"

The birds take flight as they approach. William Sunday's head turns, tracking the two birds as they wing their way across the snow-covered fields.

"It's wrong, isn't it?" she says. Doc may have wanted to use the birds as a distraction, but she needs resolution. She's returned to a conversation he'd rather sideline. Does that make him a coward? Is avoiding her angst a sign of weakness on his part? For him, the problem is that he cares about her. To contradict her is to offend her. He values their friendship. Is he being a wimp by wanting to gloss over her grief?

Doc thinks carefully about his response.

"It's human."

"How am I supposed to forgive them? My Ma. My Pa. My Daphne. My family. Do they not deserve justice?"

Doc is quiet. He doesn't have an answer. He hangs his head. To respond with an answer for everything is to have an answer for nothing. Doc knows that there are times in life when mere words aren't enough. William Sunday doesn't need a lecture. She needs to be heard. What she needs is to work through this for herself.

"If I could wind back time, I would. I'd change everything. I'd steal a car and go and get them. And they'd still be alive."

Doc doesn't know the specifics of how her family was killed or how she escaped. He wants to ask her for more detail, but it would be out of idle, macabre curiosity. Worse, it would distract her from working through this for herself. For someone who always has something to say, Doc struggles to remain silent. He grits his teeth, fighting the temptation to interrupt her and ramble.

"What about Mouse?" she asks. "Meyers? Hawk? Leech?"

There's one name William Sunday can't bring herself to say. Doc can hear the angst in her voice. The pain is still too raw.

"And," she says, halting for a moment. They both know what she's going to say, but voicing her grief is an admission of defeat. "Lav... Lavender."

Doc takes a deep breath. He has nothing for her. There are no answers. There are no do-overs. There's only the ruthless tyrant humanity calls time. The past knows no mercy. Regret haunts her.

"But this is my heart aching, isn't it?" she says. "Longing for something different. But nothing can change the past. No matter how high the body count, no amount of death and destruction will bring them back. Hatred breeds hatred and nothing changes, and that's the real problem. I can live my life with regret, forever longing to change the past and never changing the future."

Doc nods as she continues.

"It's the future that can change, not the past. And us. The two of us. We have a chance to break the cycle. We can change the future."

"We can," he says, feeling he has to say something to acknowledge her reasoning but not wanting to interrupt her train of thought.

"I want to change the future."

Doc smiles. "Me, too."

"I don't know that I can ever forgive them, but maybe forgiveness isn't what's needed. Forgiveness pretends nothing ever happened. But it did. My family died. I can't ignore that. I shouldn't. And maybe I don't need to. Maybe what I need is to look forward rather than back. The past. It's like a jail, isn't it? Only it's one where the cell doors can never be opened. There's no pardon, no end to the prison sentence. But the future. All the doors are open to the future."

"They are," Doc says, keeping his reply short.

"The future," William Sunday says, gazing into the distance. "That's what I need to focus on."

Hours drag by in a slow, aching rhythm that matches the endless clomp of their boots on the wooden boards. As they're out of the wind, walking along in the trenches, the afternoon is warm. The sun sets before them. Stars appear in the open sky. As darkness falls, the stars radiate. In the cold night air, they're crisp and clean. The air is fresh and invigorating. As there are no cities near the Front, there's no light pollution. The stars reveal their depth, stretching back into eternity.

"I used to think the stars were beautiful," William Sunday says as the temperature drops and vapor forms on her breath.

"I still do," Doc says. "The Novos can't be the only ones out there."

"And the others. Do you think they're peaceful?"

"I don't know. Maybe. Our history with the stars is... complex."

"How so?" William Sunday asks.

"Once, they were mysterious. They were the realm of the gods. We wrote our legends in the sky, linking the stars to hunters, lions, snakes, dragons. We foretold not just the seasons with their movements but our own lives. And then science told us we were wrong. They weren't alive. And they weren't mere dots in the sky. They were massive."

"It's crazy, isn't it?" William Sunday says. She points into the sky above the trenches. "That one there. It looks like a speck of dust, like a streetlight miles away, and yet it's bigger than us. Bigger than our whole world."

"And science was wrong," Doc says.

"Was it?"

"Kind of."

"How so?" William Sunday asks.

"Well, the stars *are* alive. We're made from stardust, and we're alive."

"And so are they."

"And that's what we need to cling to," Doc says. "In this vast, crazy, cold universe, we're both alive. So, why the hell are we fighting?"

"It's madness, huh?"

"It is," Doc says. "Did you know the atoms in your left hand probably came from an entirely different star than those in your right? I mean, that's bonkers when you think about it. And yet we get all wrapped up in this nonsense, fighting over scraps of land."

"We kill each other."

"Yeah. We really need to stop doing that."

"We do," William Sunday says, laughing.

Doc appreciates her humor. He lets out a chuckle as well. It's the absurdity of all that surrounds them in the war contrasted with the naivety of their logic.

"Oscar Wilde once said, '*We're all in the gutter; only some of us are looking at the stars.*'"

William Sunday nods in agreement. "Trenches. Gutter. Same deal."

"Yep. Life seems simple when looking at the stars."

"It does," she replies.

By the time they reach the regional command center, Doc is exhausted. The two of them check in with the duty sergeant and are assigned cots in an underground concrete bunker.

"They've got showers," an excited William Sunday says. "And toilets. Real toilets."

"I know, right?" Doc says, holding a towel and a bar of soap in his hand.

The showers are communal, being shared by both sexes in a large concrete room. No one cares. Nudity is sheer relief rather than sexually arousing. William Sunday showers next to Doc. As the showers are controlled by a pull chain, the two of them take turns holding each other's metal chain so they can use both hands to soap their bodies. After they've dried off and dressed, Doc checks William Sunday's wound. The triage doctors shaved one whole side of her head, clearing away far more hair than they needed to just to be sure they didn't miss any other injuries.

"You've got this whole punk rock thing going on," Doc says, peering through his glasses and looking at the way her skin has been singed by the Novo blast. "I think it suits you."

"Hell yeah," she replies, pretending to snarl. William Sunday makes a sign of devil horns with her hand, clenching her fist while holding out her index finger and pinky.

Several of the blisters on her head have burst. William Sunday grimaces as Doc applies some antiseptic cream to the raw skin. He's gentle, holding a non-stick gauze pad on the side of her head as he wraps an elastic bandage around her forehead to hold it in place.

"How does it look?"

"Good. Really good. You're healing up nicely. And there's no redness. No infection. Keep it clean, and you'll be fine."

"Thanks, Doc."

Their assigned cots are pushed up next to each other on the far side of the dorm. Getting to them requires squeezing down narrow walkways past snoring soldiers. As there are sixty people in the barracks, windup alarm clocks aren't allowed. Instead, a private sitting half-asleep at a desk by the door jots down their names, cots, and wake-up times. He'll have rotated out by dawn, but they'll get a gentle nudge rather than a bell ringing in their ears when it's time to get up.

"Night, Doc."

"Good night, Sunday," Doc replies, pulling an itchy woolen blanket up over his shoulders. Somehow, the fine fibers poke through the sheet and he finds himself tossing and turning and scratching before he drifts off to sleep.

At some point, the duty soldier shuffles down the row to wake someone opposite Doc. They bump his cot, and he wakes as well. An arm lies over the edge of the wooden frame of his Russian-made cot, resting on his shoulder. Whether she realizes it or not, William Sunday has reached out for him in her sleep. For a moment, Doc wonders whether he should gently remove her arm or perhaps roll over so she retracts it, but her intent is natural. It's human. Touch is kindness reaching out beyond words. Doc accepts that she inherently wants more than the sterile, heartless distance imposed on all of them by the war. There's nothing overtly emotional or sexual about being touched. It doesn't mean anything beyond the moment. With that, Doc closes his eyes and drifts back to sleep.

He wakes to a hand shaking his shoulder and words spoken in a whisper.

"Oh-six-hundred, sir."

"Thanks," he says.

William Sunday still has her arm on him. Her lower leg is straddling the wooden beam of the cot and leaning against his leg. He sits up. As he moves, she stirs.

"Is it morning already?"

"Yep," he replies as others are quietly awakened within the

darkness of the underground barracks.

"Oh, that's the best sleep I've had in months."

"Me, too," he replies in a whisper.

After relieving themselves, getting dressed and grabbing a bite to eat, they receive orders from General McMasters to meet Dr. Bailey Browne in the A3 briefing room at 7 am. As it's five past seven when they get the message, they rush through the network of trenches that make up the command center, looking for room A3. To Doc's mind, the rooms should be laid out logically, with A3 being the third room at the front of the complex, but it's down the fourth corridor they traverse, next to room E7.

"Sorry we're late," Doc says as they hurry into the room.

Dr. Bailey Browne is seated at the head of a boardroom table with General McMasters next to her. Six soldiers in combat camouflage sit along one side of the room. Behind them, their backpacks are stuffed with supplies. Rifles lean against the wall. Most of them have grenade launchers attached beneath the barrels. Doc and William Sunday take their seats opposite them.

"This is Captain Greaves from Bravo Company, 5th SFG."

William Sunday whispers to Doc, "Special Forces Group."

"Captain Greaves will be escorting us into the occupied territories."

"Not with those, he won't," Doc says, pointing at one of the rifles and contradicting Bailey.

"You want us to go into enemy territory unarmed?" the captain asks.

William Sunday says, "Doc's right. You can't go in there with weapons. Look, I don't know what will happen to us on the other side, but I do know this. Anyone holding a rifle is a target."

Doc says, "We survived our encounters because we were unarmed."

Bailey and the general look at each other. Captain Greaves is quiet.

228

"We go in with a white flag or not at all," Doc says.

"What if there's a misunderstanding?" Bailey asks.

William Sunday is brutal in her response. "We die."

The general says, "Madam Under Secretary—"

Bailey raises her hand. "No, it's okay. They're right."

Doc looks at the special forces soldiers opposite them. From his perspective, it seems a mere glance from them could kill. If they have any concerns, it doesn't show. The captain, though, isn't happy.

"Ma'am," he says. "If we are to proceed unarmed, I recommend my team goes forward as an advanced scouting party. Once we've made contact, we will return for you."

"I appreciate your concern, Captain, but I need to be there. I need to see them. I need to be able to assess the viability of First Contact for myself."

"First Contact?" William Sunday asks, confused by the term.

"We've been at war so long we've forgotten what this is all really about. Two different intelligent species from entirely different planets are interacting with each other for the first time in history. We don't—I don't know what happened between the Novos and the Russians. No one survived that initial encounter. Or the second. Or the third. But the war erupted before anyone realized quite what was happening. And that's typical. That's the way most wars start. Back in 1914, who would have thought that the murder of a mere two people in the back of an open carriage would have led to the deaths of forty million soldiers and civilians in World War One? That war could have—it *should* have been stopped long before the first trench was dug, but no. War satisfies our desire for vengeance, regardless of the cost.

"Our history is replete with examples of First Contact descending into violence. Whether it's British colonists founding Jamestown, the Mongols razing Europe or Cook arriving in Botany Bay, little thought is given to reason. It's easier to take than it is to debate."

Doc asks, "And you think this will be different?"

"No war lasts forever," Bailey says. "One side or the other

229

eventually burns itself out, and the balance of war shifts against them, but that could take years. Decades. But we don't have to wait for that. We'd be fools to wait. Even if the war swings in our favor, what do we win? A scorched Earth? And what if we lose? Ask yourself, what will we lose?"

William Sunday mumbles, "Everything."

Bailey says, "If there's a chance of reaching peace, we have to try. Like a forest fire, wars grow out of sparks landing on dry kindling. We can wait for the war to burn itself out, or we can roll out the hose and start pumping water."

The general nods, saying, "We train for war, but we hope for peace."

"And the Novos?" Doc asks.

"You've given me hope," Bailey replies. "You've shown us they're not beyond reason and compassion. Now, we need to show them neither are we."

William Sunday grins. "There's nothing quite like wide-eyed optimism to get someone killed."

Bailey laughs at that. "We're human. We're dreamers. We all dream of a better future. We hold on to hope. We can't help ourselves. For all our faults, we don't want to die—none of us."

"No, we don't," Doc says.

"So, what's the plan?" William Sunday asks. "What do we have to negotiate with?"

"Everything and nothing," Bailey replies.

Fyodor the Tajic

The special forces soldiers turn in their rifles to the armory while the team walks to the helipad. Doc notices, though, that they keep their sidearms, tucking them out of sight beneath their jackets. Several of them stock up on hand grenades and flash bangs in place of their rifle magazines. Doc understands their concerns. He only hopes it doesn't get them all killed.

Unlike regular helipads, the forward command pad is set almost thirty feet below ground. The effort required to dig out the dirt and rock by hand would have been astonishing, with a lot of it being used to form protective berms around the pad. The rotors of the waiting Blackhawk helicopter turn lazily through the air, being roughly level with the ground on one side. Four drones also power up. They look like helicopters, being the size of a fridge lying on its side. There's no cockpit or cargo area. Their rotors reach up to chest height, so they've been positioned on the far side of the helipad, away from the approach used by the team. Four drone pilots sit in the back of the Blackhawk wearing VR headsets with control boxes on their laps, viewing the world through their electronic slaves.

"What are they for?" Doc asks.

Captain Greaves says, "They're decoys. We fly them high and wide of us, just off our flight path. If the Novos take potshots with their lightning gun, they'll hit them first. And if they start taking them down, we'll land. Don't worry, Doc. We're so far behind enemy positions that they need to fire over the horizon. At this distance, they can't distinguish between us and the drones."

"Uh, okay."

"We'll fly up to *Novyi Vasiugan* and meet up with partisans operating behind the lines. From there, we'll be on horseback until we reach *Novosibirsk*. You can ride, right?"

"Ah, yeah," Doc replies, but his reply isn't convincing. In the back of his mind, he remembers a riding holiday he went on in the Colorado Rockies. His ass was raw by the end of two days in the mountains. He could barely walk when he dismounted.

"What's the matter, Doc?" an overconfident William Sunday asks, slapping his shoulder as they stand before the Blackhawk, awaiting their turn to climb into the back of the cargo area. "Is it the helicopter or the horses?"

"Both," he says, trying to joke around with her. "Anything starting with an H."

William Sunday laughs. The loadmaster straps them into the rickety aluminum flight seats in the cargo bay and hands them some plastic earplugs. Doc is clumsy. He drops his plugs. The loadmaster smiles and picks them up for him.

"Nervous, huh?"

"Yeah. Just a little."

The Blackhawk helicopter winds up to power. The rotors become a blur. The wheels lift off the crushed gravel on the helipad. As they rise, Doc gets a view of the network of trenches cutting through the frozen fields.

The Blackhawk stays low, racing along with the doors open barely thirty feet above the countryside. Captain Greaves is sitting opposite Doc and William Sunday. He gestures with his gloved hands, making out as though his right hand was the helicopter soaring along. With his other hand, he sweeps in a high arc over the top. Then, with that hand, he gestures, mimicking an explosion.

William Sunday yells over the sound of the engine. "Artillery."

Doc nods. They're flying beneath hundreds of shells being lobbed toward no man's land.

The doors on the Blackhawk are open. An icy cold wind swirls within the cargo area, chilling him to the bone. The draft seems to find the smallest gaps between his gloves and his arms, chilling his wrists. At a guess, the doors are being left open to allow them to evacuate quickly in an emergency.

The four drones keep pace with them. They're flying higher and closer to the Front by several hundred yards. On the scale of forty miles, that's nothing, but it's close enough that they can act as lightning rods for the Blackhawk. To Doc's surprise, they vary their speed and height, darting forward and dropping back, swapping places and changing altitude. It's clear they're trying to confuse any targeting mechanism the Novos might have.

Down on the plain below, soldiers work on extending trenches. They're building dugouts they hope are never used.

The Blackhawk flies over frozen lakes and narrow stretches of forest before reaching the hills. Siberia transforms from the open steppes to dense forests. The helicopter is flying so low that its downdraft is kicking up snow off the trees it passes, leaving a white cloud behind them. The further north they go, the less well-defined and narrower the Front becomes. Eventually, the trenches look like firebreaks in the forest, where trees have been felled and separated by hundreds of yards of icy, muddy sludge.

William Sunday hunkers down, raising her shoulders and burying her head to keep the cold out. Like Doc, she's got the fur hood on her jacket raised and the drawstring pulled tight to keep the fur snug around her face.

After an hour, the Blackhawk dips over the trees and down low over a lake. The far side of the lake hasn't frozen yet, being constantly churned and stirred by the rapids coming down from a mountain river. Out by the southern edge, though, the blue/white ice forms a solid slab reaching the shore.

"This is us," Captain Greaves says.

The Blackhawk hovers over the lake near the forest. Its rotors clear the snow from the ice. Doc feels the wheels touch down lightly, but the helicopter doesn't power down, keeping its weight off the ice.

"Go, go, go!" Greaves yells as his troops drop onto the ice and jog toward the shore. Doc looks down. To his horror, there are splinters in the ice, marking where their boots hit, radiating out in all directions.

Bailey lowers herself rather than jumping down onto the ice. One of the soldiers is waiting for her. With an outstretched hand and yelling over the sound of the engines, he directs her to shore. The wind kicked up by the rotors is akin to a hurricane, blowing her brunette hair in all directions.

William Sunday follows, then Doc, and finally Greaves. The captain points with his glove hand toward shore as though it's not obvious where they should go. Doc's more concerned about the ice taking their combined weight.

The Blackhawk lifts off behind them, having hovered over the ice for barely a minute. Within seconds, it clears the lake and disappears over the fir trees, leaving the team in a strange, haunting silence.

Closer to shore, there's a sudden crack like that of thunder breaking, but it comes from the frozen lake, not the sky. One of the soldiers plunges through the ice. He drops into the frigid lake water near the shore, sinking up to his thighs.

Greaves turns to them, saying, "Stay away from boulders close to the shoreline. The ice there is weakest."

Doc looks along the length of the shore. There's nothing but boulders rising out of the ice. William Sunday takes him by the crook of his elbow and leads him on, although he'd rather she wasn't so close. Ice cracks beneath them, zinging and pinging as the noise echoes around them. Doc can feel the slabs of ice settling beneath him as they crack.

They reach the shore and take wide, broad steps off the ice, avoiding the edge of the lake. Several soldiers haul the wet soldier out onto the bank. He strips down. Steam rises from his naked thighs as he rubs his legs with a jacket and puts on another pair of pants. His boots, though, are going to be wet and cold. Fresh socks will help, but his feet are going to get damn cold. Doc is surprised by just how cold it is barely two hundred miles north of their dugout.

Horses snort in the forest. Vapor forms on their breath. Three Russian partisans have led nine horses between them to the rendezvous. Doc wonders how long they've been waiting. Several of the horses have snow on their backs.

Captain Greaves speaks to the leader in Russian. The two men talk in rapid succession, but it's clear Greaves is struggling with the language.

William Sunday wades through the snow drifts covering the ground to join them, saying, "Вам нужен кто-то, кто свободно говорит по-русски?"

"Русский? Вы русский?" he asks.

"Just me," William Sunday says, replying in English.

"Then English it is," the burly Russian says.

Captain Greaves introduces them, "Fyodor, this is US Under Secretary of Defense, Dr. Bailey Brown. And this is Dr. Christopher Walters and his aide, Private William Sunday."

"And you are from?" Fyodor asks, reaching out and shaking William Sunday's hand. His focus on her is intense. His gaze seems to pierce her soul.

"*Novosibirsk*," she replies, unable to make eye contact. "*Prokudskoe*."

"I know it well. My uncle was from *Svetlyi*. He was caught in the first wave."

"As were my family," William Sunday says, swallowing the lump in her throat. She looks down at the snow and ice clinging to her boots.

"We will have our revenge, *Сестра*."

"That's not why we're here," Bailey says, holding up her hand and wanting to interject.

Fyodor turns to her, but he keeps his head lowered and slightly on an angle. It's an odd gesture to make. His eyes narrow as he peers at her with curiosity. Fyodor is in his fifties. His skin has aged from a harsh life under the sun. Siberia might be known for its fierce winters, but its summers are brutal, with swarms of mosquitos that cover acres and searing temperatures that reach beyond 100° F. His eyebrows are as bushy as his full beard, which hides his mouth until he speaks.

"Then why are you here?"

"To talk to them."

"Talk?" he says, squinting. Fyodor turns to all of them, asking, "You're here to talk? You've risked death for mere words?"

"We want peace," Doc says.

"Peace?" Fyodor says with disbelief, turning to his men and saying, "Они хотят мира."

The men laugh. Under her breath, William Sunday translates, "They want peace."

"There can be no peace," Fyodor says. "Not while they occupy our land. The only peace will come when we drive them back to the stars."

Bailey's got her work cut out for her with Fyodor. Like Doc, she has the hood of her jacket pulled forward, with the fur warming the exchange of air in the extreme cold, but that also hides her facial features, making it difficult to read her body language. If she can't convince their allies, what chance does she have of negotiating with the Novos?

"We've all lost someone," she says, standing there in the bitter cold.

"You," Fyodor says with spittle flying from his lips, freezing on his beard. He speaks with disdain. "You're American. Who have you lost?"

"My brother. He died a couple of days ago. Here. On the Western Front."

William Sunday and Doc exchange a quick glance at each other. Fyodor is silent.

"He was part of a special forces squad deploying an experimental radar absorber. They were ambushed by the Novos. There were twenty-two fatalities. And just like that, back in Washington, the body count went up by twenty-two."

She shakes her head. "That's the crazy thing about war. Casualties are just a number. Not a life. Not a person. Not a brother. Just a number."

Fyodor says, "I am sorry for your loss, but doesn't that make your journey more bitter? How can you want peace with these monsters?"

"That counter is only going to climb higher," Bailey says.

"But it could climb by tens of thousands," Fyodor says. "Millions if we don't keep them contained."

"All wars come to an end," Bailey says with vapor forming on her breath. "The question isn't will this war ever end, but how will it end? We need to ask ourselves what comes next?"

"And that's why you're here?" Fyodor asks. "To end the war?"

"I'm here to talk to them."

"Talk to them?" Fyodor laughs. "They will melt your face."

"Oh, I know," Bailey says. She points at Doc, "But not his."

Fyodor is confused.

"He's already spoken to them. Several times."

"You?" Fyodor asks, stepping closer to Doc.

Fyodor is huge. Even without his thick deerskin jacket wrapped over his impressive chest, his height of six foot four is imposing. Whether he means to be intimidating or not, Doc has to fight his own will to avoid stepping back.

"Is it true?" Fyodor asks. "You can speak to them?"

"I have. Yes."

"On the battlefield," William Sunday says. "With shells exploding around us and bullets flying."

As well-meaning as she is, Doc would rather not embellish on what were inadvertent, accidental interactions. He raises his gloved hand slightly, wanting to speak for himself.

"For all the differences between us and the aliens, there is one thing we have in common."

"And what is that?" Fyodor asks.

"We both value life."

Fyodor steps back and turns toward the forest, letting out a hearty laugh. He faces the fir trees with the boughs sagging under the weight of snow, turning through 360 degrees as he takes in what he considers absurd. His men laugh as well, although, from the expression on their faces, it seems to be in response to his outlandish gesture more than any recognition of what is being said. Doc doubts they can understand English.

"Then why do they kill?" Fyodor asks.

"Why do we?" Doc asks in reply.

Bailey says, "This is why we're here—to open dialogue with them, to understand them."

"To end the war?" Fyodor asks.

"Yes."

He shakes his head. "You are foolish. You are fools on a fool's errand, but I will take you to them."

"Good," Bailey says.

"On one condition," Fyodor says.

"And that is?" Bailey asks.

Fyodor points at Captain Greaves. "Him. He is a man of war. He understands combat. You may have your conversations with them, but him. I want him to see their structure. I want him to see their weaknesses. I want him to document the weapons we need to fight from within. I need him to help us establish a supply chain from the north. You may seek peace. I want to win this war. If your negotiations fail, I want him to carry our plans back to regional command."

Reluctantly, Bailey says, "Agreed."

"Come," Fyodor says. "We ride!"

He claps his hands, and his men emerge from where they've been standing on the edge of the forest. Hooves clomp lazily in the pristine snow as the partisans circle the horses beside the lake.

Bailey and Greaves ride two abreast behind Fyodor. Doc and William Sunday are next, followed by the US Special Forces squad bringing up the rear. Other than Fyodor, there are only two Russian partisans. They don't seem to speak English. William Sunday chats with them as they ride on the edge of the track. Rather than falling in file behind the Americans, the Russians take their horses through the deep drifts on the edge of the trail. Every ten to fifteen minutes, they come up the outside, checking on the riders.

"Where are we going?" Doc asks.

William Sunday replies, "Leonid. The tall one. He said we're riding to *Kedrovy*. It's a small town. There's a railroad there we can take to the outskirts of *Novosibirsk*."

"They allow that? The Novos?"

"He said they ignore the north."

Doc says, "That's why they want to use it to bring in weapons."

"Yes."

The team rides through the day and into the evening, following old fire breaks cut into the dense forest. Fallen trees slow but don't stop their progress. The trunks are hidden from sight beneath the snow, but their outline is clear. Fyodor leads them through ravines and over mountain passes. From the ridge line, fir trees blanketed in snow stretch into the distance, reaching to the horizon.

Several hours after nightfall, they arrive at *Kedrovy*. Smoke rises from a row of log cabins. Most of the homes within the village have been abandoned. Snow lies piled up against their sides, burying the doors and, in some cases, the roofs. The cabins nearest the rail yard, though, glow with life. A warm light radiates from the windows, reflecting off the snow.

"We will sleep here tonight," Fyodor says.

Doc's ass is numb from the combination of the saddle and the cold. He dismounts, feeling as though he'll never walk properly again. He waddles rather than strolls toward the nearest cabin.

As he rides down the line, Fyodor says, "Leave your horses. My men will tend to the animals and your packs."

"How are you doing, old man?" a cheeky William Sunday asks from beside Doc. He reaches around and grabs his lower back, stretching as he looks up at the stars in the dark sky.

"I'm looking forward to that train ride."

A wave of heat washes over them as they step into the log cabin. A stew sits over the fire in the hearth. It's been mounted on a hook hanging from a wrought-iron frame that swings over the flames. A young girl of not more than seven stirs the stew. The smell of meat and vegetables wafts through the air, along with the pungent aroma of burning wood.

"No rat tonight," Doc says.

"Oh, I think we're getting venison," an excited William Sunday replies, sniffing the air.

The team shed their coats and boots in an alcove by the door. Water seeps onto the wooden floor, dripping from various jackets as the snow and ice melts.

William Sunday leans over and undoes the laces on her boots. As the floor is wet, Doc is curious about how she's going to fare in her woolen socks. William Sunday steps on each of her boots as she removes them, avoiding the puddles on the floor, and then hops to a rug. Doc copies her, liking her style.

Although Fyodor said they could leave the horses to the Russian partisans, the US Special Forces are yet to come in out of the cold. Doc glances out the window and sees them traipsing through the snow, no doubt conducting a quick reconnoiter of the village. Bailey and Captain Greaves are already sitting by the fire on a couch that looks as though it has been transported through time from the 1950s. It looks uncomfortable but not as uncomfortable as the saddle. They warm their hands by the fire. Doc sits down gingerly next to Bailey.

"You too, huh?"

"And I thought life at the Front was rough," he replies to the US Under Secretary. She lets out a slight laugh followed by a grin.

An elderly Russian woman wearing a head scarf and smock stacks clean dishes beside the fireplace. The young girl ladles stew into the bowls. Steam rises into the air.

The elderly woman hands out the bowls, saying, "Eat, eat." From her stilted accent, it seems she only knows a few words of English. Her smile, though, is as warm as the fire radiating in the hearth. The stew is hot and unbelievably salty, but Doc is starving. He blows on the meat to cool it, enjoying the chunky lumps of potato and pumpkin mixed in with meat other than a rodent. He doesn't ask, but the meat is gamey, making him wonder if it's reindeer. Sorry, Santa. The soldiers join them, and there's idle chatter as they eat. Most of them sit on the floor with their backs against the wall.

After dinner, Fyodor comes around with a clear bottle filled with something that's definitely not water. He has a bunch of shot glasses stacked in his other hand, offering them to Greaves, Bailey, Doc and William Sunday.

"Oh, no," Bailey says, trying to wave him away.

"You are in Russia," the big man says with a grin lighting up his face. "We drink today, for tomorrow we die."

"Well, when you put it like that," Greaves says, taking a glass from him.

Doc and William Sunday take a glass as well. Seemingly against her better judgment, Bailey takes one. Fyodor pours vodka into their shot glasses, filling them to the brim. Drops spill on the wooden floor.

"We drink," he says, putting the bottle on the mantle and raising his glass. "To victory!"

"To peace," Bailey says, raising her glass in reply.

Doc has had vodka before, but whatever's in that bottle is closer to jet fuel than alcohol. Simply touching the rim of the shot glass to his lips is enough for them to go numb. A fire rages in his mouth as he knocks back his shot. His throat is set alight. He swallows with a gulp. For the first time in his life, he can feel the insides of his stomach. The microbiome that inhabits his gut just got nuked. He struggles not to vomit as he shakes his head at the astonishing strength of the vodka.

"More, more," Fyodor says, laughing at their reactions.

"One is enough, thank you," Bailey says. Captain Greaves is conspicuously quiet. His troops eye his reaction with keen interest, talking quietly with each other.

Fyodor gestures to Doc with the bottle. "Oh, no. I'd go blind."

Fyodor laughs. He doesn't bother pouring himself another glass. Instead, he raises the bottle to his lips and knocks back the drink. Bubbles of air rise within the clear liquid as it sloshes down into his mouth and throat. He sets the bottle back on the mantle and wipes his lips with the back of his hand. As his beard is wet, Doc wonders how much seeped into the hair follicles around his chin. He must feel a burning sensation on his skin. Given the drink's insane strength, he could end up looking clean-shaven by dawn.

"And you?" he asks William Sunday, pointing at her.

She waves him away.

Fyodor says, "You are Russian. You know. You see through the lies."

William Sunday is quiet. She looks down at her hands in her lap, still holding the empty shot glass. Fyodor is intimidating, but it's more than that. There's a cultural impetus at play, although Doc suspects it's not merely about male dominance in Russian society. As much as Doc wants to interrupt, he also wants to understand.

Fyodor asks William Sunday, "Victory or peace? Can there be any real peace without victory?"

Bailey holds out her hand, appealing for reason. "Fyodor. We appreciate your help, your hospitality, but it's been a long day. Perhaps we should call it a night."

"She knows," Fyodor says, ignoring Bailey. He crouches, dropping down on his haunches and looking up at William Sunday. "You Americans. You can never know. But she. She is one of us. She is not fooled."

Bailey says, "Fyo—"

But she's cut off by William Sunday. "No. He's right."

"What do you mean?" Doc asks.

"You come from the land of the free, the home of the brave."

"Yes, yes," Fyodor says, dropping onto his ass on a bear skin rug in front of the fire. He crosses his legs in front of him. It's an unusually submissive pose for someone that's ostensibly in charge. He's gone from lording over them physically to appearing subdued. Doc finds his shifting persona fascinating. Far from the classic Alpha Male shouting loudly to drown out the others, he's relying on reasoning. He points at William Sunday, looking along his finger as though it were the barrel of a handgun.

"The land shapes us," he says. "We think we're the masters of our destiny, but we're not. We're predictable. We're by-products of our countries, our cultures. We grow from the land as surely as the wheat and barley."

Bailey says, "I don't know what you mean."

"She does," Fyodor says. He could explain his thinking, but that he's prompting William Sunday is telling. He's confident, far too confident. How can he be so confident in his own position that he feels no need to defend it?

"You can be anything you want," William Sunday says to Doc. "That's what you tell yourself, whether it's true or not. America is the land of opportunity. It's the American Dream. Life, liberty and the pursuit of happiness."

Fyodor snort-laughs at that last point.

"But?" Doc asks, ignoring the burly Russian.

"But it's a lie. Oh, there are American fairy tales where someone breaks out of poverty and reaches for the stars, becoming an astronaut or an astronomer, but most people scrape by. Most struggle. And yet they still believe."

"But us," Fyodor says.

William Sunday is blunt. "We're roadkill."

Fyodor laughs. "Haha. Oh, yes. I like that. We Russians are roadkill on the highway of history."

William Sunday says, "Your country was founded on freedom. Ours is forever enslaved."

Fyodor says, "Yes, yes. The Mongols, the Hordes, the Swedes, the Poles, the Persians, the Turks, Napoleon and the French, and the Germans. And not just in two world wars. Hell, our own people have fought against us. And it matters not who won these wars, not to the common people, the peasants, not to those trodden down in the mud. In the past thousand years, there have been over two hundred wars staining the Russian steppes with blood. And the Novos. They're just another invader. Another one to add to the list."

"We know war," William Sunday says.

"We do," Fyodor says, taking another swig of vodka.

William Sunday looks sullen. "For you, Americans, wars are fought over there in some faraway land. For us, they're fought in our streets, in our backyards, in our homes. For you, they're news reels. For us, they're the view out of the kitchen window."

Fyodor says, "This is why you think there can be peace. Because, for you, peace is the norm. Not war."

William Sunday says, "But for us, peace is the handful of years between wars."

"But surely this is different," Bailey says.

"Yes," William Sunday replies. "It's worse."

Fyodor says, "Your peace would have us surrender our land. How is that peace? Would you give up Chicago? Or New York?"

"We don't know what they want," Bailey says.

Fyodor lets out a solitary laugh. "And once again, the lies begin."

Bailey is silent. Doc swallows the lump in his throat. Fyodor is right. What else does Bailey have to bargain with other than land? His land?

"And the worst part of these lies," Fyodor says, "is that you believe them. It's one thing to lie. We Russians, we know lies. We use lies, but they are believed by others. For all our faults, we don't fool ourselves. We don't lie to ourselves."

Bailey squirms in her seat.

"And what would you have us do?" Doc asks.

"Destroy them," Fyodor responds in an instant. There's venom in his words. "Wipe them out. Eradicate them."

"And that's peace?" Doc asks. "Really? That's how you define peace? No amount of hatred can ever bring peace."

Spittle flies from Fyodor's lips. "This is *our* land!"

Doc leans forward on the couch and points down at the wooden floor, matching his vehemence as he says, "And this is *our* planet."

Fyodor is taken aback by his sudden agreement. His eyebrows narrow as he seeks to understand Doc's point.

"This is *our* solar system. Our galaxy. Our universe," Doc says. "At what point do you want to stop? You claim ownership as though that bestows rights, but what do we really own? You said it yourself. We grow from the land. We don't own the land. The land owns us. It's been here long before us. And it will be here long after we're gone."

Fyodor points at a window cut into the log wall of the cabin, gesturing to the snow outside. "They're killing our people."

"And we're killing theirs," Doc replies.

"They are the aggressors," Fyodor says. "They brought the war to us. Why should we want anything other than their annihilation? That's the only peace to be found in Russia."

Bailey speaks with a soft voice. "Peace is more than the absence of war. Peace builds where war destroys. Peace brings life instead of taking it. If there's a chance, we have to try for peace."

Fyodor isn't convinced. He shakes his head and looks away in disgust.

Doc says, "It takes courage to fight a war, but what are we fighting for if not for peace?"

Fyodor says, "You're Americans. You don't understand. You can't. It is beyond you. But one day, you will understand. When they raze your homes to the ground. When they rip your children from your arms and kill your family in front of you, then you will understand what it means to hate them."

Fyodor looks up at the wooden logs that form the ceiling. He has tears in his eyes, but through sheer willpower, he refuses to allow them to roll down his cheeks.

"You think me a madman. You think me a warmonger, but she knows. For you, this is a debate. For her, it is life. Tell them. Tell them what happened in *Novosibirsk*."

William Sunday says, "It was a Friday, market day. I'd pushed a handcart four miles to the city square in *Ob* on the outskirts of *Novosibirsk*. Pigs squealed in makeshift pens. Squash was on sale for ten rubles. Honey for fifteen rubles per jar. There was a flash of light. An explosion. Glass windows shattered. The ground shook. I fell to the cobblestones. A bomb. We all thought separatists had set off a bomb in the market, but there was no screaming—no wounded. It was then I saw the streak in the sky. A cloud on a cloudless day. A thin white stripe, slowly widening, disappearing over the buildings.

Doc leans forward with his elbows on his knees and his chin resting on his hands. His fingers hide his lips. William Sunday is staring at the fire, mesmerized by the flames. She's lost in her own words.

Doc rubs the stubble around his mouth. It's subconscious on his part, but he dares not speak, not wanting to break the fragile thread of her recollection.

"You'd think there was panic. There wasn't. Several traders resumed bartering. Most of us got back to our feet and simply stood there, realizing we were witnessing something never before seen on Earth. Beyond the old brick buildings, there was a glow. It was brighter than the sun, but we were standing in the shadow of the foundry. For a moment, there were two suns shining on Earth, with one of them low on the horizon.

"Around me, farmers mumbled Ядерный. Nuclear. But there was no blast, no mushroom cloud rising into the sky. Slowly, the light faded and us—we went back to the markets. It seems silly now, but Russians are pragmatic. Within a few minutes, fighter planes roared overhead. Army trucks rolled through the streets. Then tanks. They're loud. Their treads broke up the gravel. But no good can come from curiosity. I left others to run to see what had fallen from the sky. But me? I needed to buy salted meats, carrots, pumpkins. I had to prepare the cellar for winter. I had no time for sightseeing. The army will investigate. The government will tell us what we need to know. That is what we told ourselves.

"As the day drew long, people panicked. They stacked suitcases on top of their cars, strapping down bits of furniture with ropes. They loaded up their kids and drove west. Others drove east.

"*Krasnyi Vostok*, they said. It came down in *Krasnyi Vostok*. Let the army deal with them, others said. No one asked who they were. I didn't care. I'd bartered for dried beef at thirty rubles a kilogram. It was a bargain. I was proud. My father would be happy. I pushed my handcart along the road, avoiding muddy potholes, but I was slow. It was heavy. The sun was setting.

"It was then, far too late in the afternoon, that I first saw smoke. Fires burned across the countryside. The wind was blowing east-to-west, causing columns of black smoke to rise from farmhouses across the land. I quickened my pace. By the time I got to our quarter-mile driveway, the main house had already collapsed. The barn was on fire and leaning to one side. Night was falling. Burning timber glowed in the ashes. My Papa. My Mama. I—I..."

No one speaks. For a moment, William Sunday isn't sitting in a log cabin in the snow and ice. She's back in *Novosibirsk* as autumn descends on the land.

"They were dead. Them. The horses. The cattle. Nothing was spared. And me. For the first time in my life, I was alone. My brother was at university in *Tambov*, two thousand miles away. All I could think was that I had to find him."

"See?" Fyodor says, snapping William Sunday back to the present. "This is us. This is what we Russians have endured. This is the war. Not trenches and artillery. This is *our* loss. Our families. This is what happened all over the countryside."

Bailey is silent.

"There can be no peace for those that fell that day," Fyodor says. "There is no peace for those who have died."

"But us," William Sunday says. "We can have peace. We need

peace."

"And there shall be peace, Моя сестра. We shall avenge the fallen."

"An eye for an eye," Doc says.

"Yes," Fyodor replies, seizing on that phrase and clenching a fist in front of him.

"And then everyone is blind."

No one responds to Doc's retort.

"Gandhi," Doc says, hoping to stir some recognition. Fyodor grits his teeth. His nostrils flare, but he remains silent. His wife lowers her head and averts her gaze. She seems to recognize Fyodor's reaction.

To Doc, the silence within the cabin is telling. For all his bluster, Fyodor is intelligent. He's not a heartless, mindless psychopath. He believes he's doing what's right. To be challenged is something he takes seriously. He could be flippant, but he's not. He strokes his beard. He's thinking, but not about some smart comment or off-hand reply to simply be dismissive. He's not rushing to defend himself or his logic. He's not an asshole. Doc can see he's trying to defend his family and his country the only way he knows how. Doc may not have convinced Fyodor that an eye for an eye is barbaric, but he's got him to think about not being blind to reality.

Wood crackles in the fireplace. Flames flicker, casting light over the cabin. Smoke rises up the chimney. The young girl is sitting next to her mother on a stool beside the fire. It's difficult to tell if the two of them understand English, but they're curious about the strangers in their home. They eye Fyodor with keen interest, watching carefully how he responds to the discussion unfolding in their cabin. For his part, Fyodor seems content sitting crosslegged on the bear skin. He pulls his beard into a point beneath his chin, stroking it over and over, thinking intently about their discussion.

Doc says, "The problem is we don't understand them. They're alien to us, and we're alien to them, but they're alive; they're intelligent."

"It makes no difference whether they're human or alien," Fyodor says.

"On that last point, you're right," Bailey says. "War is repugnant regardless. War should be the last resort. It's detestable. Anyone who revels in war is a monster... War is the failure of reason, and the failure of reason will be the death of humanity."

"We didn't ask for this war," Fyodor snaps.

"Let's say you're correct," Bailey replies. "Let's say we can eliminate them. Should we? Do we have that moral right?"

"Yes."

"Why?"

Fyodor says, "Because if we don't kill them, they'll destroy us."

Bailey says, "We think that, but we don't know that. Thoughts are not facts. We think we know what *they're* thinking, but we don't. They're not fighting a war of conquest. They're not advancing like Napoleon on Moscow or Hitler on Paris. They're digging in. We need to understand why. We need to make good decisions. We need to be right."

Fyodor is adamant. "They started this war. And as God is my witness, I'll end it."

Doc is disappointed by his blunt attitude, but to be fair to him, Fyodor wouldn't have ended up in command of the resistance without that level of conviction.

William Sunday interrupts the conversation. Like Doc, she's frustrated. "Can't you see what's happening here? You agree. You agree with each other. You both want the war to end. You differ not in your goal, only in the means of getting there." She addresses Fyodor, saying, "If the Under Secretary is right and the war can be ended without more bloodshed, surely that is worth exploring."

Fyodor grins. He raises a bushy eyebrow. "You think this is simple—a mere disagreement that can be reconciled, but it is not. Tomorrow, you will see. Tomorrow, you will understand what we are fighting for. Tomorrow, you will see the horror that is *Novosibirsk*."

Novosibirsk

Fyodor and his family sleep in the loft overlooking the main floor of the cabin. The team shifts the furniture to one side, stacking chairs on the table to make room for everyone. Under Secretary Bailey Brown sleeps on the couch. William Sunday lies next to Doc. Even with sleeping bags, the floor is hard and unforgiving. She's asleep within minutes, curling up in a fetal position. Doc lies there on his back, looking at the way the light from the fireplace flickers, playing on the log roof. He's got a bony hip and needs a mattress or a cot to lie on his side. It's not going to be the best night's sleep.

William Sunday edges closer to him. Her hand rests in the center of his chest. She's using her coat as a pillow. Her forehead snuggles against his shoulder. She moans softly in her sleep. For Doc, there's a sense of comfort lying there with William Sunday next to him. Physically, he feels uncomfortable, but her touch sets him at ease emotionally.

Doc wonders about the Novos. Having seen them up close on a number of occasions, he's curious about their senses. They have sight. That much is clear from the way they communicate with tattoo-like symbols rising and disappearing on their skin, forming intricate patterns as they communicate with each other. These ebb and flow like the patterns on a cuttlefish. And they can hear. They heard him speak. They were able to mimic speech in response. Although they didn't converse with him, there was understanding. They knew what he meant.

What other senses do humans share with the aliens? Do the Novos have touch or taste? What about the sweet scent of a freshly cut rose or the smell of cookies baking in the oven? Taste is indulgent. In theory, humans need only eat out of necessity, but that food is enjoyable adds an extra dimension to life, often with flavors that contradict each other. Sweet and bitter. Salty and sour. And yet, there are flavors that defy definition: chilies, cinnamon, lavender. And then there's the added component of texture. Cream is smooth, while nuts are crunchy. For humans, senses are not only a means of gathering information about the world; they're pleasurable and enjoyable. Does the same hold true for aliens?

What about touch? Of all the senses, touch seems to be the most human to Doc. Touch is so common to the human experience that it's often overlooked. Colors light up the mind. Music soothes the heart. Scents enrich the soul. Tastes are a delight. Touch, though, is ever-present. To walk across the floor or pick up a cup of coffee is blisteringly ordinary—uneventful. Woodgrain feels rough but plain. The slick, curved surface of a glass beneath one's fingertips passes without remark and yet touch is a remarkable sensation. To touch another person is to connect on a deeper level. No words have passed between Doc and William Sunday, but there's an unspoken agreement that they need each other. Touch binds them, connects them. Touch is refreshing. In the midst of the uncertainty of war, touch is reassuring. The others may be following the mission, but for them, this journey is personal. They lost their squad to the Novos, and yet it's not revenge they seek, but understanding. Fyodor might be right about Bailey being naive, but what is life without hope?

Doc breathes deeply, feeling William Sunday's hand rise and fall with the motion of his chest. Her forearm is petite. Her fingers spread, touching lightly at the skin near his neck. Doc drifts off to sleep feeling content.

Morning comes too soon. He wakes to soldiers moving around the cabin. It's dark outside. He goes to get up, but his body aches. Riding in a saddle and sleeping on the floor hasn't been kind to him. He takes his time, slowly sitting up.

William Sunday crouches next to Doc, cradling a cup. Steam rises into the air.

"Coffee?"

"Oh, that would be great," Doc says, getting up and taking the mug from her.

They sit on the couch. William Sunday has let her hair down. Back at the Front, she kept her long, brunette hair in a tight ponytail, but the bandaging over her wound made that impractical. This morning, she has removed the bandage.

"Look," she says, turning side on to him and allowing him to examine the skin on the side of her head. Doc reaches up and touches lightly at her scalp.

"Oh, that's cleared up nicely."

"I know, right?" she replies. "Do you think my hair will grow back?"

"You'll have a scar, but I'm sure your hair will grow over it, given time."

Doc is fascinated by William Sunday. Although one side of her head is shaved, she still looks radiant. The way the fine strands of hair fall across her other shoulder is refreshing. Her eyes seem to sparkle in the soft light of the fire. Whereas he feels gruff and unkempt, with prickly stubble growing on his face, she looks vibrant and full of life. In the depths of his mind, he's still haunted by the vision of her being struck by Novo lightning in the darkness. The thought of seeing her die again at some point in the war is horrifying. Doc's more concerned about her life than his.

"Good coffee, huh?" she says with an innocence he finds disarming.

"Yeah."

Even though he only just woke, Doc feels tired. He'd be quite happy curling up in front of the fireplace and going back to sleep. His muscles are sore. His body feels fatigued. If he's honest, he's a little dehydrated. The coffee won't help with that, but he doesn't care. The aroma is disarming. Closing his eyes, he can imagine he's back in

Chicago, sitting in a downtown cafe with a coffee grinder whirring softly in the background. There's something about a dark roast that's seemingly intoxicating. His coffee is black and hot. There's no sugar, but it's strong. Doc blows on the surface, cooling the drink. He sips with relish. His coffee is slightly bitter and a little smoky, but he finds that refreshing. The rush of caffeine stirs his mind. William Sunday gets up and helps the soldiers. Doc can't move. Not yet. He's enjoying the heat radiating from the fireplace.

"Did you sleep well?" Bailey asks, sitting down next to him.

Doc doesn't reply. He doesn't mean to be rude, but a mumble and nod is all he can muster. His mind is still rebooting. He's reasonably sure his frazzled hair speaks loud enough in reply. Doc closes his eyes and sips his coffee again.

"There's nothing quite like a good coffee when you least expect it, huh?"

He asks, "How did they get coffee out here in the middle of a war zone?"

Bailey says, "The women told me the UNHCR and the Red Cross are constantly shipping in supplies from the north. Rather than driving in with trucks, crates and sacks are handed off along an impromptu supply chain. Fyodor provides the last leg and keeps the odd comfort food package for himself."

William Sunday comes over with two bowls of porridge. A dab of butter melts on the surface of the thick sludge. Granulated sugar has been sprinkled on top. It melts, forming small pools on the surface.

"Thank you," they both say. Doc puts his coffee on the floor beside his feet. He's wearing socks and not looking forward to working his aching feet back into his stiff boots.

They eat, chatting idly about the snow and winters back in the US. Bailey is from Maine. She loves snow. Doc finds snow an oddity. It looks pretty enough from the warmth of a house, but he's never found the attraction of walking outside in the snow with the bitter cold stinging his face. For him, winter was only ever hopping from one warm building to another.

"It's a four-hour train ride to *Novosibirsk*," the Under Secretary says. "The Novos allow the Russians to bring in wood from the north for the civilians."

"So they coexist," Doc replies.

"Apparently."

The soldiers are ready to move out all too soon. Nothing can prepare Doc for stepping back out into a Siberian winter. The temperature has dropped overnight. The windows of the cabin are double-glazed, while the entrance has an alcove with a second door to trap the air. Even with his heavy boots, his jacket hood raised, and gloves on, the air in the alcove is brisk, warning him of what lies outside.

The outer door opens. It's dark, but the snow glistens. The air is still. The cold bites at his cheeks. Doc tightens the drawstring around his hood, narrowing the fur lining.

An old-style thermometer nailed to the outside of the doorframe vaguely reads negative forty. When it's this damn cold, near enough is an acceptable degree of accuracy. As the temperature range on the thermometer is split on either side of the glass tube, Doc is fascinated to see both Celsius and Fahrenheit converge on that number before differing as they branch out again.

"A cold snap is rolling in from the Arctic," Bailey says, noticing his interest in the temperature.

"Damn," Doc replies, watching as vapor forms on his breath. "Well, at least we'll be inside a train carriage."

"Oh, I don't know about that," Bailey says, pointing at vague shapes in the pre-dawn shadows.

They walk single-file toward the train yard. The lead soldier tramples the knee-high snow, wading rather than marching through the village. Everyone else follows in his steps. The only sound is that of fresh snow crunching beneath boots.

A single light on the train engine illuminates the yard. Coal is shoveled into the furnace. There are no passenger carriages. The train consists of ten flatbed freight cars carrying fallen trees. Chains wrap around dozens of logs on each railway car.

"This is it?" Doc asks. Bailey just smiles.

One of the engineers uses a shovel to break up the ice and snow on the edge of the lumber cart immediately behind the coal cart and engine, clearing a spot for them. They clamber up and sit on a steel ledge no more than two feet wide. Bailey, Greaves, Doc and William Sunday sit in the middle, holding onto worn leather straps mounted on the steel frame behind them. Apparently, they're not the first passengers on this route. Fyodor climbs a steel ladder on the coal cart ahead of them and calls out to the engineers, telling them they're ready to depart.

Steel wheels slip on frozen rails. Slowly, the train pulls away from the yard, turning and joining the main line. In the distance, the sky lightens as dawn breaks. The sun is reluctant, rising with the same regret Doc felt on waking. Snow flurries drift across the dense, dark forest.

As the train gets up to speed, its plow kicks up a snowstorm, surrounding them and causing a white-out. The trees whip past like shadows. Snow swirls in the gaps between the railway cars. Doc wraps his hands across his chest, keeping his head low, trying to ward off the cold wind whipping by. Railway ties become a blur beneath his boots. As the sun rises, sunlight reflects off the rails.

William Sunday nudges into him, trying to reduce the way the wind curls around her. Without thinking about it, he puts his arm around her shoulder and holds her tight against the cold.

"All this seemed easy back at the Front, huh?" she says.

"I never thought I'd prefer trenches and a dugout to riding on a train."

After about an hour, Fyodor comes clambering along the side of the coal cart. There's no walkway as such, just a thin lip of steel. His boots kick at the ice as he works his way along the ledge. The wind whips past him.

He moves around the back of the coal cart and crouches opposite them. The railcar coupler between them shifts as the train rounds a long, sweeping bend.

"Belchers," he says, pointing across the snow-covered forest into the valley. "You can see them out there to the west. We call them smokers."

To their right, easily three miles away, large animals amble through the forest. Long necks sway above the treetops, feeding on the pine needles as though sauropods have been brought back to life. Black smoke rises from spikes on their backs, darkening the sky.

"See how they change the air," Fyodor says. "You can't negotiate with that."

Bailey points. "Is this what blocks our satellite imagery?"

"Yes. Yes. Here, they are sparse. In close to *Novosibirsk,* they roam in herds reaching into hundreds. There it is always night. The cloud cover sits at maybe five thousand feet. It's difficult to be sure, but we only see the sun at dawn and dusk."

"They're changing the land," William Sunday says.

"Now you see why there can be no peace. They would take our world and transform it into theirs."

Bailey is quiet.

Doc says, "These creatures. Where have they come from? Did they arrive on the spacecraft?"

"No," Fyodor says. "They bred them here. What you will see in *Novosibirsk* is the generations born on Earth. This is why we asked you to come. Not to bring peace. But to see what is being done. It is not enough to contain the Novos on the battlefield. They must be eradicated."

Bailey's lips tighten. She pulls a scarf over her face, ostensibly to keep her cheeks warm, but it allows her to hide her reaction. For his part, Fyodor is oblivious. He's being factual. He's not keeping score. He speaks like a tour guide, being proud of his country.

"From here, we will descend from the plateau and follow the valley. The rail line shadows the river *Ob,* leading down to *Novosibirsk.*"

Fyodor leaves them, returning to the train engine. For the first time, Doc looks up, seeing the black smoke being belched out by the furnace. The coal isn't clean burning. Soot stains the upper logs. As horrifying as it is to see aliens ambling over the countryside, pushing their way through the forest and sending up smoke, they're not the only ones. Doc wonders what they think of the mechanical animal chugging along the rails toward *Novosibirsk.*

"Ma'am?" Captain Greaves says once Fyodor is out of sight.

"Yes, yes," she says, waving her gloved hand in a dismissive gesture.

Greaves pulls a camera out of his pack. It's mechanical. There's no digital display. He winds on the film, cranking a lever until it clicks into place, and begins taking photos of the belchers on the hillside, winding the film on with his thumb after each shot. As much as Under Secretary Bailey Brown may want peace, it's clear those who authorized the venture also want to gather as much intelligence as they can. As far as Doc knows, this is the first military unit to venture beyond the lines. Or, at least, the first not to be slaughtered—so far.

The river *Ob* has frozen over except for a few patches of open water in the turbulent bends at the base of various cliff faces. The river cuts through steep ravines only to emerge on floodplains with villages dotted along the embankment. The railway tracks curl with the river, being set several hundred feet above the water. Bridges allow them to crisscross the river, avoiding mountains. They only pass through one tunnel. It comes so suddenly that Doc is shaken by the onset of complete darkness. The roar of the engine and the clack of the wheels rushing over the rails echo around them. Smoke clogs the air. And then, as quickly as it came, the tunnel is gone.

As they approach *Novosibirsk,* the sky darkens. Belchers can be seen moving in herds. The smoke that rises from their jagged spines lifts high in the air before hitting a thermal layer thousands of feet up and spreading sideways. Even with the prevailing winds dispersing the haze, these impressive creatures seem to replace the lost smoke as fast as it spreads.

Being seated behind the coal cart, Doc can only see out to either side. Fyodor shimmies back along the edge of the railway car, holding onto the rim above his head as he negotiates the thin, icy ledge that threatens to send him tumbling into the ravine below. The wind whips past the hood on his jacket, obscuring his view. He reaches the team and steps out of the wind, crouching again on the other side of the rail coupler connecting the carts.

"Soon, you will see a hive. On this side of the train, out across the river. It is the first of many."

"A hive?" Bailey asks.

"What happens in these hives?" Doc asks.

"Much," Fyodor says. "We have identified breeding colonies, storage houses, trading rooms, garrisons, administration. This first one is a nest for the warriors."

He returns to the train engine. After less than a minute, a hive appears off to their left. It's huge, rising hundreds of feet in the air like a skyscraper, but it's organic rather than being built from bricks or steel. The base is circular. It's wide and broad, reaching several hundred feet in diameter and tapers to a point easily six to seven hundred feet up. Snow clings to the sides lower down. Belchers wander around in the shadow of the hive. Whether they're protecting it or feeding off, it is impossible to tell. Captain Greaves snaps pictures, zooming in with a long telephoto lens.

"Damn," William Sunday says. She's tired of sitting and has taken to standing, leaning against the wooden logs that fill the open freight car behind them.

"Yeah," Doc says, reaching out and holding onto the rough-hewn wood as he gets to his feet as well. The speed with which the railway ties are rushing beneath them is unnerving. One slip. A slight fall and he's dead, but he's got to get a better look at the hive. Doc edges toward the side of the railway car, holding onto a steel chain that keeps the logs in place. Staring out across the valley, there are dozens of hives reaching up beyond the trees like buildings randomly set in the forest.

Greaves says, "We simply do not know what we're up against."

William Sunday says, "We're not the only ones preparing for the next phase of the war."

The train passes through outlying villages, whipping by cabins with regular frequency. Peasants stand outside, watching as the train rolls in toward town. Doc wonders about these people. Somehow, they survived the initial skirmishes in the war. And Doc can't help but reflect on Fyodor's point that Russia has only ever known war in one form or another. In between it all, people struggle to live. They want no part in the battles thrust upon them. Whereas Americans want peace, Russians only want to survive.

The train slows. They're approaching the outskirts of *Novosibirsk*. Drab grey apartment buildings appear. Several have been partially demolished, being victims of the early shelling. Even so, people still live in the ruins. They trudge up wooden stairs built over the rubble to reach the remaining floors. Doc's not sure how often the train makes the run from the north, but it's rare enough for kids to stop and stare. Burning wood not only allows civilians to heat their homes but also to cook food and melt snow for drinking water. Without it, they'd die from the cold. The Novos must understand that as they allow the trains to run. To him, that's a sign of compassion.

Doc is curious about where the coal comes from to feed the train engine, but there's clearly not enough to distribute it more broadly, and the inhabitants of *Novosibirsk* need to chop up the logs to fuel their fires.

More hives appear towering above the buildings. Although they all have the same shape, being elongated, circular spires, some have curves like a corkscrew. Others are chunky, as though they're made out of blocks. Winged creatures dart between spires, gliding from one to another and entering through holes in the side. Occasionally, these creatures flap broad wings. Seeing them at this distance must mean they have wing spans approaching those of a small plane. They carry cargo with clenched talons wrapped around teardrop-shaped bags, each one easily the size of a car.

"It's an entire ecosystem," Bailey says as Captain Greaves continues taking photos. "I—We had no idea."

The train comes to a halt. It eases to a stop before the brakes are applied hard, and everyone lurches forward. Thankfully, they've all got hold of something, so no one tumbles onto the tracks. Fyodor appears in the snow beside the railway ties, saying, "Come. This way."

The drop down from the railway cart is further than it seems. Doc sinks into the snow. He loses his footing and slips. Once again, William Sunday grabs him before he falls. It seems she's always there for him.

"Careful."

"Thanks."

The special forces soldiers spread out, forming an outer perimeter as they walk through the train yard. They're spaced roughly twenty feet apart. The soldiers keep their side arms holstered, but their hands never stray far from their hips. Their packs are stuffed with supplies, unlike Doc and William Sunday who are only carrying clothing and bedding in their packs.

Already, workers have begun releasing the chains on the freight cars. They're using a hand-powered crane, something Doc hasn't seen before. It's made out of steel beams, but it uses a block-and-tackle arrangement like those of old-fashioned sailing ships to gain enough leverage to raise the logs. Five men work with the chain on the crane. They're wearing leather gloves. Several others turn the aging rusted frame, allowing them to lower the logs onto the dock. Lumberjacks wait with two-handed long saws ready to cut the logs down into manageable sizes that can be split with an ax. There's a lot of yelling and commands being called out as they swing into action.

The team emerges onto the road. Civilians push handcarts through the streets, following grooves worn in the snow and sludge. The streets are grey and dirty. Novos and humans walk with purpose, in a hurry to get somewhere and out of the cold. A large wooden flatbed cart trundles by, being pulled by an oversized Novo. Although it looks like a gigantic spider, its legs are as thick as those of an elephant. Glowing spheres have been stacked in a pyramid shape on the rear of the cart, being held in place by a wooden frame set around the base.

"This is wrong," Doc says. "This is all wrong."

"No shit," Bailey replies.

"No, I mean life here in general. The structure. It's not right."

She turns to him as Fyodor hails several bicycle-drawn carriages that act as taxis.

"Explain."

"This is an interstellar species, right? Where's the technology?"

"Hold that thought," Bailey says as Fyodor gestures for her to climb into a waiting carriage.

Doc and William Sunday climb into the second carriage. The soldiers toss their packs in the third and jog along with the informal convoy. The cyclists struggle to get traction on the icy roads and never go any faster than a light run.

They pass storefronts selling meats and vegetables. The smell of fresh bread baking nearby floats on the breeze. Red Cross packages have been torn into pieces, with the cardboard being used to cover holes in windows and missing glass. Gaunt faces watch them with morbid curiosity.

The convoy pulls up in a park overlooking the river. Holes mark where trees once stood. Kids hack at a rootball, being all that remains of an old oak. They're using hand trowels to knock off the dirt so they can use the roots for firewood. A low stone wall leads along the riverbank.

The four of them hop out of their carriages and follow Fyodor to the embankment, looking out over the frozen river. Captain Greaves has his camera out, snapping photos of everyday life in the occupied zone. The kids play up for the camera, laughing and making silly faces.

"From here, you can see much," Fyodor says, pointing at the far bank. "The spheres. We think they hold fuel for the Novo artillery."

Across the river, there are dozens of massive spheres, each one reaching up several hundred feet.

Captain Greaves says, "This is the start of their supply lines."

"Yes," Fyodor says. "One fighter jet. Just one, and the whole place goes up."

"But we can't get close," Bailey says, entertaining the idea.

"See the corkscrew spires? See how lightning ripples up the side of them? That's their air defense. Take those out, and they're vulnerable."

"And that's what you want to do?" the captain asks.

"A coordinated strike," Fyodor says. "Give us C4. Lots of C4. We'll plant explosives on each of the spires, but we'll wait until you're ready to attack before we detonate."

"A surprise attack," the captain says. "It could work. How quickly can they respond? What other defensive spires are there? What coverage can they provide?"

"We're not sure, but the Ob River is ten miles wide at this point and extends for over a hundred and fifty miles to the southwest in roughly a straight line, giving you a low-level approach. You could slip past their defenses."

"It's suicide," Bailey says.

Captain Greaves says, "Most of our aircraft are stand-off weapons delivery systems. They're not designed for low-level attacks well behind enemy lines."

"But?"

"But maybe a B21 could slip through. Its stealth capability might give it an edge if they're distracted."

Fyodor says. "Light up the Western Front with a major offensive, and you'll divert their attention. They won't expect this. They think they're safe. Untouchable. With a coordinated attack, we could cripple their means of war production."

Captain Greaves doesn't respond. He takes numerous photos, not just of the spheres and the spires but of the view out across the broad river as it opens out into what looks like an elongated lake.

"What's that?" Bailey asks, pointing at a hive that has multiple spires reaching up toward the sky.

"Headquarters," Fyodor says. "It is heavily guarded."

Doc notices that Fyodor is looking at Greaves, not at the exotic hive with five spires surrounding a larger sixth spire in the middle. Captain Greaves takes a number of pictures using the telephoto lens to zoom in. He takes a bunch of wider shots to pinpoint its location within the city itself. It's clear he's thinking about secondary targets or perhaps even making their headquarters the primary target.

"That is where we must go," Fyodor says. "That is where you will find the leaders."

"How is this going to work?" Doc asks. "I mean, we can't just waltz in there."

Fyodor points to one side of the massive hive. "There! See the football stadium next to it? That's neutral ground. We control the warehouses on the far side, so we have a fallback position if things get nasty."

Bailey nods thoughtfully. "Captain?"

Greaves replies, "Neutral ground is good. Stadiums have lots of entrances and exits. That gives us options if things go sour."

"And will they?" Bailey asks Doc.

"I don't know."

"We have to try and open dialogue," the Under Secretary says, addressing Greaves. "But your film. Give that to a couple of your soldiers. Send them back. If nothing else, at least we've gathered intel."

"Understood," the captain says, winding the reel handle on his camera.

"We can get your men back as far as the cabin," Fyodor says, looking pleased with himself.

Captain Greaves pops the film capsule out of the camera and hands it to one of the soldiers before loading another roll. After talking to several of his soldiers, two of them grab their packs and depart, having hailed down another bicycle-driven cart.

Bailey speaks to Doc, saying, "You and Sunday will go to the main hive and try to make contact. You'll inform the Novos of our desire to enter into negotiations. If they agree, you'll bring them to the football stadium. Understood?"

"Understood," William Sunday says before Doc can reply.

The Hive

"This is as far as I can go," the driver says, bringing their carriage to a halt in the deep snow at the side of the road.

Ahead, the multi-pronged spires of the central hive rise above the buildings. Sparks of electricity run to the tips, which is reminiscent of the way Doc's seen Novos charge themselves when on the battlefield. Fyodor seems to think the air defense is controlled only by the thin corkscrew spires scattered around the city. Doc isn't so sure. Underestimating the Novos and attacking prematurely could not only be disastrous but could cause greater animosity. Trust is fragile. Betrayal is rarely forgotten. He can only hope their negotiations chart a new course for the war.

Captain Greaves took their packs from them before they left the park, allowing the two of them to travel light. The bulge on William Sunday's hip, though, is a loaded sidearm. Doc doubts it would be effective against an enraged Novo.

Barricades have been set around the hive, forming chokepoints that only foot traffic can pass. The Novos, though, have no problem scaling the overturned dump trucks and shattered concrete floors arranged as walls. They clamber over them like gigantic spiders with thick, stocky legs. Doc is interested to see that, even when not threatened, the creatures fade in and out, using their camouflage sporadically. It can't be to hide as the war is hundreds of miles away. It must be indicative of some deeper aspect of their physiology.

The two of them are still at least a block away from the base of the hive.

"Wait," William Sunday says. She steps sideways into an alleyway. "They're not going to let firearms in there."

She pulls the gun and holster from her hip and slides it into a gap between a fire escape leading down from above.

Doc undoes the belt holding a portable medical kit on his waist. To the untrained eye, it looks like an overstuffed fanny pack, but it unfolds to reveal surgical scissors sharper than any knife, along with single-use disposable scalpels and hypodermic needles. There are also morphine sticks and trauma bandages. Trying to explain them as harmless to an alien would be impossible. He pushes the pack in next to the gun, obscuring the weapon even further. William Sunday wedges a bit of cardboard in front of both items to hide them from view.

"This had better work," she says, looking at Doc with a sense of alarm.

Doc shrugs. "It's a long shot, but we have to try."

"It sure beats creeping through no man's land in the dark."

Together, they join a line of civilians passing through the checkpoint. They step through a glowing blue rectangle of alien metal crackling with electricity. It's reminiscent of a metal detector at the airport only it seems as though it would fry anyone that tried to smuggle in a gun.

On the other side of the barricade, men and women stand in a line, waiting to collect bundles from a group of Novos that have set up in an old shop. The glass window has been removed, and a table has been placed in front of the store. As the civilians shuffle past, Novos place plastic-wrapped boxes on the table to be collected. Each one is easily a foot square in size. As the plastic is white, it's impossible to see what lies within, but several people take two or three boxes and then turn the corner to exit the secure zone through another security point.

"Aid?" Doc says. "They're providing aid to these people?"

"I guess," William Sunday says.

The base of the spire rests on dozens of legs reaching out far wider than the structure. They support the towering spire like roots punching through the concrete and reaching deep into the ground. Each one is as thick as a house, spreading the weight of the spire lording over them. From where they are, the two of them can only see three of the spikes reaching up from the side of the massive spire. The tip in the center is obscured by the clouds.

William Sunday says, "So we're just going to—"

She stops mid-sentence. They're standing in the shade of the spire next to one of the supports. Novos scuttle around them, surrounding them. At first, they approach from the sides. Lightning crackles over their legs, rippling as it dances over their spider-like bodies. They're threatening to attack. A quick glance behind and Doc realizes the closest Novo is in their blind spot, cutting off any means of retreat.

The last of the six Novos approaches from in front of them. Even though Doc's seen Novos up close on the battlefield, that was at night with sleet lashing his face and mud covering their bodies. He should be afraid, but he's fascinated by their physiology. Their eight legs are roughly the same thickness as a man's thigh, but they don't taper like those of a human, not until they reach what must be feet, where they narrow. Their arms are thinner and lead to a point roughly the size of a human thumb. Their four arms reach in front of them, closing to a single point with the dexterity of a hand when grabbing something. The lightning forming on their legs rushes up along their arms, sparking at the tips and threatening to lash out at them. They have sharp fangs, but if they have mouths, these must be located beneath their bodies as they're not visible.

William Sunday edges closer to Doc. Her hand rests on the small of his back. She wants him to know precisely where she is, less than a foot behind him and just to his right. From the way she's positioned her hand, it's clear she means to push the two of them apart if they're attacked and throw him to one side. Doc doubts she will be fast enough to beat a Novo bolt at point-blank range.

Lightning crackles in the air.

"No," Doc says, holding his hands up in surrender. "Talk. We just want to talk."

Beady eyes watch the two of them. They're dark and lack any visible pupils. Symbols ripple over alien legs as the creatures speak with each other. As their skin is pale, the black shapes and squiggles appear as though they're being projected onto their arms and legs. The characters are fine, being no larger than the text in a book. Even if it were English, the sheer volume of information would be impossible for a human to read. The equivalent of a page from an old-fashioned newspaper seems to scroll up the creature's legs and around its arms. Some sections are bold. Others are larger, perhaps acting as titles or headlines.

"What are you saying to each other?" Doc asks.

"*What are you saying?*" the lead Novo asks, mimicking his voice but not completing his sentence, which suggests it understands the difference those last three words convey. It may be repeating his words back to him, but there's meaning. The Novo wants to know why he's come here to the massive spire. As they've walked forward away from the shop front, it's obvious they haven't come to the hive for aid.

"You recognize us, don't you? Not you personally. But somehow, you've shared the imagery. You know we come from the battlefield."

"*You... come from the battlefield,*" the creature replies, again being selective with its words in response.

"We want to talk to you. Talk to your leaders. We want to talk peace."

The lightning subsides.

The Novo says, "*Save life, not kill.*"

"Yes, yes," Doc replies.

"What does that mean?" William Sunday asks from behind him.

"That was me. That's what I said," Doc says. "When I first came across a Novo. It was wounded. Bleeding. I bandaged its leg. It must have relayed our conversation from back then to the others."

Doc addresses the Novo, doing his best to recall the exact words he used in that darkened shell hole. "I'm a doctor. Not a soldier. I'm sworn to save life, not kill."

"Both casualties. Both need help."

"Is that me?" William Sunday asks. "Do they mean me?"

"Yes. They're replaying our conversations as a means of communicating. They recognize you."

"Come," the creature says, wheeling around and leading them to a ramp rising into the darkness of the spire.

William Sunday comes up beside Doc as they walk into the alien hive. Quietly, he says, "They're so utterly different from us. Whereas we struggle with what to say and how to condense our thoughts into words, they communicate with volumes of information. By comparison, we're sending tweets while they're passing along an encyclopedia."

"So, they avoid rumors and exaggeration, huh?" William Sunday replies.

"Yes. It seems they can spread information far and wide and in astonishing detail."

Within the hive, there are no right angles or sharp edges. Every surface is curved. Rooms seem more like interconnected bubbles while walkways amble along rather than unfolding in a straight line as they would in a building. Unlike humans, Novos aren't limited to walking on one surface. They tend to favor what Doc would call the floor, but approaching Novos will climb up the side and walk along the ceiling instead of pushing past them in the corridor. At first, Doc assumed their feet were an adaptation to carry their weight in heavy gravity, but instead, it seems they spread to function more like the feet of a gecko, allowing them to climb surfaces with ease.

"Feel that?" William Sunday asks.

"What?"

"The floor. It's not solid. It's spongey. It's got some give."

She's right. Doc's been walking through so much snow and sludge that he didn't pick up on the transition to what feels almost like a trampoline. He unzips his jacket and lowers his hood. It's warm within the hive.

To his surprise, they're not being followed by the Novos that surrounded them outside. They're being led by this one creature. To his eye, the Novos seem like clones, but he begins to notice subtle differences in the Novos they pass. Some will have thicker legs, some thinner. Some reach up to six feet while others barely clear four feet in height. And their skin tones are different. They're all pale, but some have shades of pink while others have a light purple hue. Some Novos have slender arms. Others have broad, almost muscular arms. Another difference is in the dome on their heads supporting their broad, single, compound eye. Some of the Novos they pass have a prominent brow, others a smooth curve supporting their eye bulge.

The two of them walk into a bubble-shaped room only to watch as the interior swells in size, doubling as they enter. Bench seats rise from the floor within seconds, but they, too, lack sharp edges. They're arranged like the pews within a church, all facing in the same direction with an aisle in the middle. At the front of the newly formed room, a platform rises, creating a stage. Holes appear at the back of the bubble-shaped hall, forming in the wall, allowing Novos to scurry through before sealing behind them.

The Novo leading them into the auditorium comes to a halt before the stage.

"I think these are for us," Doc says, sitting on one of the bench seats at the front of the room. William Sunday sits beside him. Above the stage, several more Novos climb through holes appearing briefly in the ceiling and the walls. They scuttle down onto the impromptu stage as an elongated bench appears, rising out of the stage floor. The Novos sit on the bench but in the most unexpected manner. Several of them sit with their eight legs tucked beneath them on all sides, effectively forming the shape of an organic diamond. Their arms rest on their torsos. Their eyes glisten beneath the soft light coming from the roof. Unlike a human room, there's no single source of light or even grouping of lights. Instead, the entire roof glows, which means there are no distinct shadows.

"Uh, this is looking very formal," William Sunday says. "We're not on trial, are we?"

"I hope not."

Doc's not sure which Novo speaks, but it's not the one that escorted them through the hive. That particular Novo is standing to one side, watching the proceedings. Even with their legs folded beneath them, the equivalent of their knees and thighs are visible. Symbols ripple across them as words are spoken.

"Doctor Christopher Walters. Born 27th of November 1996 in Grand Rapids, Michigan. Graduated medical school in 2029, with subsequent residency in general surgery, and fellowships in trauma surgery and critical care. Currently on the clinical staff of the University of Chicago Medical Center and director of Emergency Services at Weiss Memorial Hospital, specializing in ear, nose, and throat surgery. Volunteered for service in a front-line medical evac team in the war against the Novos."

Doc stands. His arms hang by his side. "Yes. That's me."

He takes his seat.

"Anastasia 'William Sunday' Abramov, born—"

"Yeah, that's me," William Sunday says, rising quickly to her feet and cutting off the Novo. She doesn't want her history paraded before Doc or anyone else, for that matter. Doc understands. Words can stir up trauma. William Sunday suppresses the past in order to live in the present. Eventually, she'll need to reconcile what happened to her and her family, or she'll snap.

She takes her seat again.

"You... come from the battlefield... to save life, not kill... to talk peace... The floor. It's not solid... We're not on trial, are we?... It's spongey... rumors and exaggeration... We want to talk... It's got some give."

William Sunday turns to Doc. "What do they mean?"

"What do they mean? They're wondering what we mean. They're trying to probe our reasoning, examining our words, looking for clues to our intent."

A single word echoes through the room.

"Peace."

"Yes. Peace," Doc says, addressing the central Novo. Although there's chatter between them, it seems to emanate from the smallest Novo with soft blue skin. Waves of information roll between the Novos as they pass messages back and forth. Doc is beginning to see patterns. Watching them is like staring through an old-fashioned kaleidoscope that rolls through various geometric shapes as the barrel is twisted. They have accents, or perhaps what would equate to vocal inflections. The messages seem to have patterns encoded within them, allowing their origin to be distinguished. Even without accounting for the way the symbols move from one to another, Doc can distinguish between them based on the styling of the images. There seem to be common elements blended in with unique signatures, perhaps acting as accents or mannerisms.

"There is a concept in your world," the central Novo says. *"One we don't share. One we struggle to understand... We grasp the principle, but it is complex. Layered... We have observed it but with confusion."*

"I will help you understand," Doc says, unsure what they're referring to but wanting to be helpful. He clutches his hands in his lap.

"Lies... Explain."

From beside him, William Sunday whispers, "They think we're lying about wanting peace?"

"From their perspective, we could be," Doc says quietly. "How would they know?"

"What is a lie?"

He speaks up, clearing his throat. "Ah, a lie is something that's not true."

"Why would you not tell the truth?"

"To gain an advantage," Doc says. "An advantage we would otherwise not have if we stuck with the truth."

"Lies are an instrument."

"Lies are often a reflex—a reaction. You're right. Lies are complex. Humans can lie without even realizing it, without intending to mislead anyone."

"*Explain.*"

"Ah, perhaps someone's getting some food, and they ask you if you want something to eat, and you brush them off. You lie. You say, no, I'm fine. I'm not hungry."

"*Why would you lie?*"

"You're not trying to hurt anyone. You have conflicting priorities. You're hungry, but you're preoccupied; you're busy. You're anxious or upset. You don't want to deal with anything else. And you don't want to have to explain yourself. You want to focus on something other than food. Or you can't be bothered."

"*And this lie gives you an advantage?*"

"It's easy. It's the easy way out. It's the easiest way to end the conversation."

"*But not all lies are harmless.*"

"No, but they're all convenient. And they need not be untruths. They can be partial truths. Or they can leave out the truth altogether."

"*And this brings an advantage?*"

"Gaining an advantage is the only reason to lie."

"*You lied to us.*"

Doc is silent. His heart races. Sweat breaks out on his forehead. He feels William Sunday stiffen on the bench beside him.

"*You told us we were welcome. You told us you would help us repair our ship.*"

"Ah, not me," Doc says, pointing at himself.

"*You didn't want to help. You wanted control. You lied to steal from us.*"

Doc swallows the lump in his throat. He shifts the subject, asking the question, "You can't lie, can you?"

"*No.*"

"Why?"

"Because we share all. For you, information is fleeting. Your words are like the fog that rises over the river. It's there, and then it's gone. You speak, and you barely remember what was said in reply to you. An hour. A day. A week later. And you can no longer recall with precision. You remember how you felt, but not the words that were spoken."

"Sometimes we remember more," Doc says. "Sometimes words make such an impression they sear themselves on our soul."

"And then they are out of context," the Novo says. *"They exist in a void. And like your lies, they are magnified beyond the importance they should carry."*

"Yes," Doc says, hanging his head and looking down at his boots for a moment.

"You said lies are convenient. I suggest your memory is convenient, and that is why lies come so easily."

"But your memory?"

"Is shared."

"So truth can be validated."

"Yes... If we were to lie, it would be exposed by all... You said lies bring an advantage, but only to the individual. They weaken the collective. They undermine society. They hurt you."

"They do," Doc replies.

"Trust," the Novo says. *"We're at war. We're enemies. There is no trust."*

Doc is about to reply when he realizes the Novo is once again echoing his own words back to him from the battlefield. This is what he said when he slid into that shell hole and came across the wounded Novo.

"But not you and me," Doc replies. The Novo is right. He's hard-pressed to remember the exact words he used, but he knows the Novo has what amounts to a transcript of the event.

"Them. Out there. They're shooting at each other. But not us."

William Sunday goes to speak, but she doesn't understand. Doc holds out his hand for her to be silent. She may not realize it, but they're no longer conversing. They're reliving that moment in no man's land, recalling the logic that led to Doc saving the life of a wounded Novo. The council wants to understand his reasoning.

"We're hurt."

"*We're injured.*"

Doc turns side on so he can see both the council and William Sunday. There's confusion on her face.

"I'm bleeding, too," he says.

"*You and I... We both need help.*"

It seems that initial encounter between them in the mud and grime has become a metaphor for the war at large. Doc desperately wants to acknowledge that and say, '*Yes, humans and Novos, we both need help,*' but he needs to follow the script. He wracks his mind. Back then, in the darkness, he dumped his medical pack on the dirt and treated his own neck wound. He talked through the procedure with the Novo, but it's what was said next, what was said when he treated the Novo's injury, that's important. He's not sure how the collective memory of the Novo works, but they seem to be reliving the moment. The symbols and images rippling over their bodies flash by faster than he can track.

"I can stop the bleeding... Do you understand?"

They're roleplaying, speaking in an allegory, using that fleeting moment in no man's land as a turning point for the entire war. William Sunday clenches her jaw. She must desperately want to speak but senses there's a deeper truth being discussed.

"*I'm not going to hurt you.*"

Doc says, "This *is* going to hurt, but it already hurts, right?"

Back then, he was referring to bandaging the Novo's severed limb, but now, he means the war as a whole.

"*That's one thing we have in common.*"

"Pain."

Doc is astonished at where the Novos have led him with their

275

recollection of that night. For all the senses they share, pain is one neither enjoys. Across untold miles and the depths of spacetime, both species have evolved to feel pain. And it makes sense. Convergent evolution is common on Earth. Sharks and dolphins both have dorsal fins even though they're separated by hundreds of millions of years. One is warm-blooded, the other cold. One gives birth to live young; the other lays eggs. One has smooth skin; the other has a rough, jagged hide. But their dorsal and pectoral fins are uncannily similar because these are so efficient in water. In the same way, humans and Novos share not only sight and sound and touch but also pain. It might seem strange to William Sunday to listen in on their conversation without any context, but pain leads to peace. If there were no agony, there would be no desire for resolution. Doc smiles, remembering what comes next.

"Go in peace, my friend."

"Yes, Go in peace," Doc says. These were the final words spoken by him on that dark night. The Novos have been testing him, exploring his character, wanting to understand whether they can trust him.

"One of our leaders," he says, realizing their review is complete. "She has journeyed with me to *Novosibirsk*. She has come with the authority to negotiate peace, to end the war."

There's no reply. Chatter ripples between the Novos, with thousands of symbols appearing on their bodies, washing back and forth between them as they debate his words among themselves.

"US Under Secretary of Defense, Dr. Bailey Brown, has risked her life to come here to *Novosibirsk*. She represents the President of the United States of America, the President of the European Union, and the United Nations Secretary-General. Between the three of them, they can stop the war."

"Then stop it," the central Novo says.

"We need assurances from you," Doc says. "We need to know why you're here and what you want. We fear for our people. You are pushing south toward some of the most densely populated regions on our planet. This frightens us."

Again, there's no reply. Messages flicker back and forth across the skin of the Novos. After almost a minute, the symbols subside.

"Bring her here."

"She asks to meet on neutral ground. There is a football stadium less than a mile from here. It is a big open area. Once, tens of thousands of our people watched games being played there. Now, it stands empty. Dr. Bailey Brown asks to meet you there."

"Tell Dr. Bailey Brown I will meet her there soon. Tell her Sha-Karn-Um comes. Tell her Sha-Karn-Um is the Overseer of the Free Culture, the Appointed Sovereign of the Community of 'Ng-Ar-Um, what you call the Novos."

"I will tell her," Doc says, bowing slightly, wanting to show respect.

"And tell her there must be trust, not lies."

The Stadium

Stepping down from the ramp, a cold wind swirls around Doc and William Sunday as they leave the hive. Snowflakes drift on the breeze. They zip up their jackets and close their hoods against the sudden drop in temperature. Winter is starting to bite. Each day is considerably colder than the last. The Novo escorting them out of the hive is silent. It walks to one side as they step back onto the concrete road.

"Thank you," Doc says, acknowledging it, but there's no reply.

The Novos' aid program is well organized, but that means the two of them can't exit through the entrance they used to get into the secure zone. They follow civilians carrying up to four aid packages out through another gate and then have to walk around the block to get to the alley where they stashed Doc's medical kit and William Sunday's gun. Doc wraps the belt around his waist and clips the kit back on without checking it. William Sunday isn't as trusting. She pops the magazine out of her Glock and checks the load. She has two spare mags and checks those as well, making sure they're full. Doc thinks it's overkill, but he doesn't say anything.

"Okay, let's get to the stadium," she says, taking charge. To be fair, Doc isn't known for his spatial awareness. He saw the stadium from the river, but he has no idea where they are in relation to the park. All he knows is that they're on the other side of the river from the park.

"This way," William Sunday says, taking off 180 degrees to the way he's facing.

"Oh, right."

The two of them are conspicuous. Those that have remained in the city are gaunt and thin. Their faces are long with sunken cheeks. They watch them walk past with the kind of curiosity that begs for a chance, for change. William Sunday sets a blistering pace. Her boots crunch in the sludge and ice. With black smoke looming over the city from the belchers, *Novosibirsk* is caught in a perpetual sense of twilight.

They reach the stadium. Anything wooden has been stripped for firewood, including doors, window frames, fencing and even the timber framing within the ticket offices and entry gates. The steel frame of a booth stands like a skeleton beside one of the tunnels leading through the stands to the field. Busted particle boards lie on the floor. They step into the shadows and walk through to the team dugouts. Graffiti lines the walls, but it's not in English.

A table has been placed in the middle of the field with steel bench seats set on either side. As they emerge from the tunnel, Doc spots Fyodor and Bailey sitting on plastic seats in the front row not far from where they've entered. They've cleared the snow and ice off several other seats.

"How did it go?" Bailey asks, getting to her feet as they approach.

"Good," Doc replies, shaking her outstretched hand. It seems like a strange gesture, given they've only been apart for a couple of hours. Fyodor gets to his feet as well, although he seems more reluctant.

"And?"

"And they've agreed to meet," William Sunday says.

Doc says, "Their leader is called *Sha-Karn-Um*. And holds the title of Overseer of the Free Culture, the Appointed Sovereign of *'Ng-Ar-Um*."

"You saw her," Fyodor says in surprise. Doc is taken back. Not only does he know *Sha-Karn-Um*, but he's assigned gender to her, something Doc wasn't aware of within the Novos.

"Yes," William Sunday says.

Fyodor points at the snow and ice beneath his boots. "And she's coming here?"

"Yes."

"And that's significant?" Bailey asks.

"We have heard of her, but no one has seen her. As far as I know, she's never left the central hive."

William Sunday says, "Well, she said she'll be here soon, whatever that means in Novo time."

Bailey walks out onto the frozen field, saying, "Come with me."

William Sunday and Doc follow her. Fyodor jogs off down the tunnel, saying he needs to get his team ready. Snowflakes swirl in flurries. Soccer goals still stand at either end of the field. The nets are torn. One of the metal cross beams is bent. There are tracks in the snow by the far corners. The penalty area is muddy, breaking up the white of the snow. Kids must play here. Probably teens. They're wasting energy they don't have to spare. The chance to escape the war by kicking a ball around is too much of a temptation to pass up.

Doc looks up at row upon row of seats within the stadium. There are three tiers. A soldier waves from the back row. Although he seems friendly, he has a shouldered rifle. Fyodor isn't taking any chances with the Under Secretary's life. Doc's not sure what the Novos will make of an armed presence within the stadium.

As the soccer pitch is designed to allow water to drain, running off to the sides, the field has a slight slope away from the center. The table is set at the highest point. A scoreboard at the far end has [0 : 0] displayed. The numbers must be painted on sheets of metal, or they would have been stripped along with everything else. Doc finds the score appropriate. No one has gained anything from the war.

"Have a seat," Bailey says. They sit on one side of a card table in the center of the field. It's made from aluminum. The surface is dented, while one of the legs is bent, causing it to lean on a slight angle. It's more symbolic than practical. No one is presenting anything or signing any documents today. If anything, it's a curious inclusion. It's neutral ground between them. The table separates them from a bench seat opposite them.

"Tell me about them?" the Under Secretary says.

"They were curious," Doc says.

"They speak in riddles," William Sunday says.

"Not riddles," Doc clarifies. "They struggle with concepts like lies and deception. They wanted to know if they could trust us, so they recalled some of my words spoken on the battlefield."

"Interesting," Bailey says. "And what did they conclude?"

"I don't know. It's difficult to tell. For every word spoken, there are hundreds, perhaps thousands of words passing between them in symbols that run over their bodies."

"I've seen that," Bailey says. There's something in the way she recalls that memory that jogs a question that's been bugging Doc for quite some time.

"Why are they different?"

"I don't understand what you mean," Bailey says.

"The photos I was shown before deployment. The Novos look nothing like that. They don't have the interchangeable parts."

"These Novos are different," she says.

"Don't you wonder why?"

Bailey is quiet for a moment before replying, "Yes. I guess I do."

"And their tech. I don't understand the lack of technology," Doc says. "Having been inside a hive, it seems they don't need it."

"But?" Bailey asks.

"But they arrived here on a spaceship. They spoke of lies. They said the Russians were trying to steal the craft from them."

"They were," Bailey replies. "They were... heavy-handed."

"All this raises a question," Doc says.

"Which is?"

"Who are the aggressors in this war? Is it us or them?"

Under Secretary Bailey Brown is quiet.

"Whatever you do," Doc says. "Don't lie to them."

William Sunday says, "Lies really piss them off."

Doc asks, "But where is it? Where's their spaceship? Why aren't they repairing it? Why build these spires? Why not fly off? Why start a war?"

"I—I don't know."

Novos appear on the far roof of the stadium. They creep along the metal, weaving their way between the support struts.

"They're here," William Sunday says.

On each of the tiers within the stadium, Novos appear. They take up positions near the front row of each level. Lightning crackles over their limbs. Doc looks behind him. Fyodor's men are taking up similar positions. It seems no one wants to cross the halfway line.

"I don't like this," William Sunday says. "I really don't like this at all. This is looking a little too much like the Western Front."

Doc nods. He does not like what he's seeing either. Peace talks shouldn't be conducted down the end of the barrel of a gun. Fyodor comes across the snowy field, jogging from the far corner behind William Sunday. He comes to a halt behind them and stands with his arms held behind his back, which seems unusually formal. Is he nervous? Doc is about to ask him about pulling his troops back when Fyodor points, asking, "Is that her?"

A Novo clambers through one of the pedestrian tunnels on the first level of the stadium. Even at a distance, the leader of the Novos is recognizable by her small frame and the way the other Novos follow her. There's a sense of respect in how they surround and support her.

"Yes, that's *Sha-Karn-Um*," Doc says as she walks down the aisle between rows of seats. On either side of her, dozens of Novos swarm into the stadium.

Fyodor steps back, keeping some distance between him and the human delegation. He seems anxious. He doesn't strike Doc as someone who would be unsure of himself, but given the tension of the moment, they're all nervous. If anything, he seems to be trying to position himself roughly halfway between them and the stadium seating behind him.

Sha-Karn-Um drops down onto the field along with six other Novos. The rest of the aliens spread out through the stands. *Sha-Karn-Um* walks beneath the goalposts. Mud and snow crunch beneath her spider-like legs. As she approaches the table and bench seat set at halfway, Under Secretary Bailey Brown stands, as does Doc and William Sunday.

Sha-Karn-Um is smaller than the other Novos. She positions herself over the bench seat and lowers her torso onto it, leaving her legs outstretched rather than sitting as she did in the hive. Behind her, five other Novos stand guard. Like Fyodor, they hang back well behind her.

"*Sha-Karn-Um*," US Under Secretary Bailey Brown says, bowing slightly. "It is an honor to meet you. On behalf of the President of the United States of America, the President of the European Union, and the Secretary-General of the United Nations, I bring greetings."

The Under Secretary takes her seat. Doc and William Sunday bow slightly and sit down as well.

Bailey reaches out and places a small metal device on the table. A red LED flashes on top of it. The Novos behind *Sha-Karn-Um* stiffen. Blue electricity crackles along their limbs.

"This is not a weapon," Bailey says. "It's simply here to record our conversation. This is so others can hear what is spoken between us today."

Doc says, "Just as you record information on your skin, sharing it with others, we do likewise. This allows us to share with all."

Sha-Karn-Um bows her head slightly. It's mimicry. Her motion is jerky. She's trying to replicate the etiquette shown to her by Bailey and earlier by Doc in the hive.

"*Peace... Trust...*"

"Yes," Bailey says. "That's why I'm here. To gain your trust. To work toward peace."

"There is much we don't understand," Doc says. He doesn't mean to interrupt the Under Secretary, but he feels they need to clarify their position.

"I will help you understand."

Bailey won't recognize this, but these are the words Doc spoke within the hive when the Novos asked about lying. William Sunday, though, recognizes those few words. She sits slightly forward on the seat.

Bailey gestures to Doc. She seems happy for him to ask questions.

"You arrived here in a spaceship. You said we lied to you. That we tried to steal it. Where is your spaceship? Why aren't you fixing it?"

"Not us," Sha-Karn-Um says. *"Not ours."*

"I don't understand."

As she talks, shapes ripple over her body, being replicated by those behind her and those in the stands.

"We were cargo."

"Slaves?" Doc asks, genuinely surprised.

"We are the formers. It is our lot to shape the colony."

"But?"

"But we wanted more than to serve. We rose up. We wanted to be free. We forced the ship to land. When war broke out, we saw our chance. We took over."

Doc and Bailey exchange a quick glance at each other.

"You killed them?" he asks. "Your masters?"

"Yes. Like you, we will kill to be free."

Doc feels a chill at those few words. Humanity has seen itself fighting an invading alien horde, but the Novos see themselves as fighting for their freedom—for their very existence.

Being slaves, Doc cannot begin to imagine the trauma they've gone through as a species, but there are certainly parallels in human history, such as the American Civil War and the Second World War. Slavery was never a question of states' rights. It was a question of human rights. Hitler may have fought a war of aggression against Europe, Russia, and North Africa, but it was the way he butchered the Slavs, the Roma, the gays, and the Jews that made him a monster. Late in the war, senior Nazis sought terms for peace, but there could be no peace for those in the gas chambers. The Allies understood that peace meant more than a ceasefire. In the same way, the Novos are fighting for their lives. To kill to be free is the cry of those who would otherwise be slaughtered. Resources can be divided. Land can be negotiated. Life cannot. Doc swallows the lump in his throat.

"And the ship?" William Sunday asks.

"*Gone. It was too great a temptation. Too great for you. Too great for us.*"

"You destroyed it?" Bailey asks, surprised by the notion.

"*Used it,*" Sha-Karn-Um replies.

"And the war?" the Under Secretary asks. "You fight us on three fronts. What is it you want from the war? What land do you need?"

"*Land? No, not land. We seek the sea.*"

"The sea?" a bewildered Doc asks. "I—I don't understand."

"*Your planet. This world. It is mostly ocean.*"

"Seventy percent," Doc says. He looks at Bailey, saying, "They want the one thing we can freely give them."

William Sunday says, "Nations own coastal waters, but no one owns the ocean. The sea is there for all, right?"

"Why?" Under Secretary Bailey Brown asks, narrowing her gaze as she stares at *Sha-Karn-Um*. "Why do you want to reach the ocean?"

"*Your planet. It is large. Its gravity is strong. It pains us.*"

"Your camouflage," Doc says as the realization hits. "That's why you can only go invisible for short periods of time."

"*Your world crushes us. Life here takes much effort, but in the oceans...*"

"You're buoyant," Doc says.

"And this is why you're fighting to break out to the south?" Bailey asks.

"*To reach the great sea.*"

Bailey shakes her head, but not in disagreement. Like Doc and William Sunday, she's stunned to realize how little they've understood about their adversary. They could see the actions of the Novos on the battlefield, but they never understood their motives.

"And on reaching the sea?" Bailey asks.

"*We ask only to live. To be free.*"

Bailey thinks aloud. She turns to Doc, saying, "With a ceasefire in place, we could establish a southern corridor to the Indian Ocean."

"Will they buy it?" Doc asks. "The Indians? The Chinese?"

"No one wants war."

"*Peace,*" *Sha-Karn-Um* says.

"Yes, peace," Bailey says, but before she can continue, a crack of thunder breaks overhead within the stadium, shaking them to the bone. Thunder or gunfire? Heads turn. Up on the second tier, one of the soldiers is firing on an opposing Novo, or is it the Novo firing on him? Crackles of lightning rip through the air. Bullets ricochet off the concrete, sparking in the shadows.

All around the stadium, firefights break out.

"Who fired? Who fired first?" Fyodor yells into an old-fashioned handheld radio, running toward them. He grabs the Under Secretary by the back of her jacket and pushes her toward the exit set in line with halfway. He's got his hand clamped around the back of her neck, keeping her head low as he forces her to run crouched over the fresh snow.

William Sunday does the same thing with Doc, grabbing him and pushing him on after them. Just for once, Doc would like to run for himself instead of being shoved along. He resists, but the frail frame of William Sunday is astonishingly strong.

"No! Wait! Cease fire," Doc yells, looking back at *Sha-Karn-Um* and her support team. Unlike the humans, the Novos stand their ground. The Novos that have escorted her to the meeting rush forward. They form a wall curving around in front of her, protecting her. All of them fire lightning bolts into the stands. Machine guns return fire from the various tiers within the stadium. Grenades explode, kicking up snow and ice.

Doc stumbles. Clods of dirt are thrown up by Novo lightning striking the field next to him. If the Novos weren't under fire from the

Russians, those bolts would have found their mark.

"Extraction. I need extraction now!" Fyodor yells into his radio as they approach the sideline. Six of his men come running out of the tunnel with rifles pushed hard into their shoulders, picking out targets and firing at Novos in the stands. Jagged bolts of lightning punch through metal advertising signs on the edge of the field. Several bolts find their mark. Two soldiers are knocked off their feet. The strength of the blast hurls them into the seats on the lower level of the stadium. Steam rises from their burnt uniforms. They were dead before they hit the concrete.

Doc flinches. A thunderclap seems to break directly overhead. The compressed air squeezes his lungs, making it difficult to breathe. An explosion rips through the air. William Sunday falls. Her body crashes to the snow. The remaining soldiers grab the Under Secretary and Doc and run them down a dark tunnel.

"No, no, no!" Doc yells, but no one can hear him over the thunder of Novo lightning and rocket-propelled grenades being fired within the stadium. Doc tries to wrestle free of the Russian gripping his upper arm, but the man's fingers are like a steel vice. He yells at Doc in Russian.

"Безопасность. Нам нужно доставить вас в безопасное место," he yells from behind a thick beard. "Safe. Understand? Must be safe."

"No," Doc says. "I need to go back in there."

"No," the soldier says, grabbing him and pushing him across the street and down a narrow alleyway. More soldiers wait in the shadows. They have their arms outstretched. As soon as Doc and the Under Secretary are close enough, they grab them and push them further on along the alley. There are easily two dozen soldiers in reserve in the narrow alleyway.

The ground shakes as a massive explosion rocks the stadium. Doc turns, seeing sheets of ice falling from the roof. Black smoke billows into the sky, rising high above the stadium. One of the stands collapses, crumpling in on itself. Debris is hurled across the street. Dust hangs in the still air.

The two of them are rushed across yet another side street and down a muddy track toward a partially collapsed warehouse. Half of the

288

twisted metal roof has fallen in some previous battle. Steel girders rise from punctured concrete. The offices and roller doors, though, are still standing, supporting what remains of the roof.

"Are you okay?" Doc asks the Under Secretary.

Blood drips from a gash on her head. "I'm fine. I'm okay."

Russian soldiers lead them down a concrete ramp onto a broad parking lot. Semi-trailers sit in rows beside what remains of the massive warehouse. Snow has piled up on top of them and in between their flimsy metal frames.

"This way," one of the Russian soldiers says, directing them to concrete stairs rising up from the parking lot to the warehouse floor. Rubber bumpers line the edge of the floor. Once, trucks would have backed up to these thick black strips, allowing workers to walk on and off the trailers as they stacked food and produce inside. The fall from the warehouse floor to the parking lot is roughly five feet. In the shadows, without any barriers, it would be easy to tumble over the edge.

The soldiers stop at the top of the stairs, allowing Doc and the Under Secretary to walk out under what remains of the warehouse. Crushed shelves lie strewn to one side. On those racks that have survived, there are crates of weapons and ammunition.

"Let me look at that cut," Doc says with shaking hands. He unzips his medical pack and pulls out a vial of saline solution and an elastic bandage.

"Thank you," the Under Secretary says with a trembling voice. They're both in shock. For Doc, focusing on someone else helps him ground himself. He desperately wants to return to the stadium to look for William Sunday, but he doesn't speak Russian, and it's clear the soldiers have been ordered to keep them here.

Doc cleans the gash on Bailey's forehead. He uses saline solution from a plastic vial to wash away the dirt.

"You're going to need some butterfly stitches," he says, reaching into the bag on his waist and rummaging around. He uses a broad patch with tiny needle-like protrusions to pull the two torn pieces of skin together and seals it with a sticky bandage the size of his palm. Doc is careful not to catch the Under Secretary's hair in the adhesive strip.

"W—What the hell just happened?"

"I don't know," Doc says. "Everything happened so quickly."

"Jesus. We've ruined this, haven't we? Our one chance at peace, and it descended into war. Again. Fuck!"

Doc closes his medical pack. He breathes deeply. Being a doctor, his life is dedicated to treating patients. His focus is on identifying problems and finding solutions, but there are none. What seemed so simple earlier today is now impossible, and that frustrates him. He hates to admit there's nothing to be done. The past can't be recalled like a video game and replayed to get a different outcome. If only it could, how different would the world be? Or would that only make things worse? Would conflicting priorities—selfishness—still doom humanity regardless? Fyodor may have shouted into his radio, asking who fired first, but deep down, Doc knows the answer. That they can even operate radios within *Novosibirsk* is a curiosity. What else has Fyodor kept from them?

"Damn, that was close," a familiar voice says from behind him.

"William Sunday," Doc calls out before he's had the chance to spin around.

William Sunday's uniform has been blackened with scorch marks, but she doesn't appear wounded. Soot lines her face. Snow clings to her shoulder, slowly melting and dampening her jacket. Doc doesn't care. He throws his arms wide and hugs her, wrapping one arm over her shoulder and pulling her in tight. For her part, she returns the hug, but without quite the same gusto.

Doc pulls back. "I saw you fall."

"Tripped," she says.

"What happened back there?" Bailey asks.

"Fyodor had the whole place wired to explode."

"He what?"

"He had demolition charges in place. He had to have set this up days ago. Weeks ago."

"But how would he know where we'd meet?" Doc asks.

"He didn't," William Sunday says. "He suggested the stadium, remember? I guess he wanted some insurance."

"Sweet Jesus, this is bad. This is so bad," the Under Secretary says, running her hands up through her hair and pacing back and forth. "Is she alive? Did *Sha-Karn-Um* make it out of there alive?"

William Sunday lowers her gaze. "I—I don't know."

Scattered gunfire and the rip of lightning bolts continue to rage in the distance. The fighting may have died down, but it hasn't stopped.

"What are we going to do?" William Sunday asks.

Bailey has a blank look on her face. She looks dejected. "Nothing. There's nothing we can do."

Revenge

"Fyodor," a Russian soldier with broken English says to them. "He wants you safe. You please come with me."

The soldier is a woman in her early twenties. Like William Sunday, she's thin and petite and not to be messed with. She has her hair pulled back into a bun.

Although one side of the warehouse has collapsed, the area covered by the remaining roof still spans several hundred feet. Beyond there, snow and ice cling to the fallen steel. Soldiers stand around smoking. The dock they entered from is eerily quiet. As it faces the distant stadium, that seems ominous. The last of the stragglers scurries up the stairs. One of the soldiers climbs over the chest-high loading dock, which seems dumb given that the stairs are only twenty feet further along, but he's young. He doesn't care. He laughs and jokes with the older soldiers, begging for a cigarette from them.

The Russian woman escorts them to the far side of the warehouse, leading them away from the stadium. They pass a roller door with icicles hanging from the chains. It hasn't been opened in a long time.

"Please," the soldier says with a rifle slung over her shoulder. She pulls a metal fire door open, leading to a narrow alleyway between two brick walls. These mark other warehouses or perhaps factories. Garbage lines the walkway. Empty cans crunch beneath their boots. Shit and piss blend in with the snow and ice. Even with the cold dulling the aroma, the smell of ammonia hangs in the stale air. Bailey gags. She holds her scarf over her mouth and nose.

Rather than leading them on, the soldier remains behind them, holding the heavy door open. She calls out, "Go. Go... Go on."

Sheepishly, Bailey leads them forward, followed by Doc and then William Sunday and the Russian. Halfway along, a Novo drops into the gap, falling down from the edge of the roof. Doc hadn't even thought to look up to see if they were being watched. The creature lands with a thud in the snow.

"No, please," Bailey yells as several of the Novo's arms reach out and touch her in the center of her chest. They tear her jacket open.

Doc tries to grab her, but William Sunday knows what's about to happen. She shoves him hard to one side, flattening him against the brick wall as a bolt of lightning bursts out of the Under Secretary's back, having burned through her heart, lungs and spine. Blood splashes along the alleyway. A wave of heat washes over Doc. The smell of burned meat lashes his nostrils. He squints, trying to make out the carnage unfolding in the glare of artificial lightning being unleashed within the cinderblock alleyway.

The electric blue bolt cuts through the Russian as well, but it hits her off-center, tearing through her left shoulder and continuing on down the alleyway. It strikes the door leading to the warehouse, scorching it. Black soot forms where the bolt sizzles on the metal.

The Russian falls to one side, colliding with the wall. She fires her rifle. A single shot rings out, but it's ineffective, ricocheting off the concrete cinderblocks. William Sunday keeps Doc pinned to the wall with her forearm. With her other hand, she draws her Glock and fires several times as the Novo scrambles up the wall. Whether she hits it or not is impossible to tell as it disappears over the top of the wall, leaving her firing at the dark, brooding sky. She lets Doc go and adopts a two-handed grip on her pistol, turning both ways and scanning the top of the alley for any other threats.

"Gotta move," she says, but Doc is kneeling in the sludge and mud, cradling Under Secretary Bailey Brown.

"Go, go," the Russian soldier says, but her voice lacks vigor. Her wounded arm hangs limp by her side. Her shoulder is black. The skin is burned and blistered. Blood drips from her fingers.

Doc ignores both of them.

"Easy," he says to Bailey, holding her head back. She chokes, trying to breathe. Blood seeps from the gaping hole in her chest. Doc locks eyes with her, knowing the last thing she'll ever see is the tears running down his cheeks.

"We've got to go," William Sunday says, tugging on his shoulder, but her eyes are focused on the narrow gap between the buildings, watching the darkened sky for any sign of movement. Doc can't do it. He can't leave Bailey to die alone. He grips her hand and squeezes, wanting her to feel kindness one last time. Her lips twinge. She tries to speak.

"I know," he says with his voice breaking and tears falling. "I understand."

She blinks. Tears swell in her eyes and then her eyes glaze over. The transformation from life to death is smooth. She's no longer looking at him. She's lost all focus. Her eyes seem to stare through him at the snowflakes drifting through the air. Her muscles stiffen and then sag. Her hand goes limp.

"Doc, please," William Sunday says, pulling at his shoulder. Her eyes are still on the narrow ledge running along the top of the alleyway. With her other hand, she is holding her gun with an outstretched arm, ready to fire. Reluctantly, he lowers Bailey to the snow, knowing she's past feeling now. He closes her eyes with his fingers, touching gently at her eyelids.

The Russian has the fire door open. She leans against it, propping it open and calling to them to hurry. William Sunday pushes Doc on ahead of her, but she remains sideways. Her eyes scan the rooftop as they retreat.

Once they're back inside the warehouse, several Russian soldiers rush to help the wounded soldier. Doc and William Sunday sit at a table that looks as though it's been transported from 1950s America to the present through a time warp. The rim is made from polished chrome, while the plastic top is red with glitter embedded in the material. The surface is scratched, but otherwise looks as though it could be from an

American fast-food restaurant. William Sunday rests her gun on the table. The acrid smell of burnt gunpowder lashes both of their nostrils.

"W—What just happened?" Doc says, looking at his trembling hands.

"Revenge," William Sunday says.

"So that was no accident? It was waiting for us?"

"Stalking us. That thing was hunting us. It knew precisely who she was. And that was personal. The Novo could have fired from the rooftop, but it wanted her to see it up close. It wanted to look in her eyes as it killed her."

"Fuck," Doc says, running his hands up through his hair. "Fuck. Fuck. Fuck!"

"It had us dead to rights."

"B—But?"

"But it wanted witnesses."

"What?" an astonished Doc asks.

"That was an assassination. After what happened in the stadium, the Novos are sending a message to Washington. A very clear message."

Doc shakes his head. He feels utterly defeated.

"This is war, Doc," William Sunday says. "I know you hoped. You wanted something more, but war is messy. War is brutal. War is never easy."

There are several boxes of rounds on the table. Although the writing is in Russian, the caliber sizes are numbers, making them easy to distinguish. William Sunday ejects the magazine from the grip of her pistol. She places the mag on the table and then racks the slide of her Glock, ejecting the chambered round. She pushes that round into the magazine and reloads from one of the boxes. The silence between them feels strained. Doc is still mourning not only the loss of Under Secretary Bailey Brown but the peace talks themselves. William Sunday is once again preparing for war.

Minutes pass like hours. One of the Russians brings over a jug of water along with some cups, but there's no food. What happens next? Doc isn't sure what else they can do here in *Novosibirsk*. He hasn't seen Captain Greaves or any of the US Special Forces since they entered the stadium. He has no way of knowing if any of them made it out of there alive. As it is, they're hundreds of miles behind enemy lines. They could return with Fyodor to the village on the next train and await extraction from the frozen lake, but there's no way of knowing if anyone's coming for them. They may have to trudge through the Russian wilderness in the dead of winter to reach the northern section of the front lines. Doc sighs. They're probably stuck here in *Novosibirsk* until at least Spring.

There's a commotion from the docks. The two of them get to their feet. William Sunday already has her sidearm drawn, but there's no gunfire. The Russians are yelling and cheering. Fyodor comes down the muddy driveway leading to the dock and warehouse. Behind him, soldiers drag a net. They've caught a Novo.

Fyodor jogs up the stairs into the warehouse. The soldiers heave the net up over the lip of the dock onto the concrete floor. They clamber up over the edge and drag the wounded Novo into the center of the warehouse. Iridescent blue blood stains the concrete. The net falls open.

"*Sha-Karn-Um*," Doc mumbles as William Sunday holsters her Glock.

The soldiers form a circle around the injured Novo, leaving easily thirty feet on all sides. Several of them have bayonets attached to their AK-47s. *Sha-Karn-Um* looks panicked. She turns through 360 degrees, looking for a way to escape, but the soldiers are easily three to four deep all around her. They're jeering and yelling, baying for blood. And they're armed. Bayonets poke at her if she gets too close to them.

She's injured. Blue blood drips from between her forearms at the point they connect to her torso.

Doc and William Sunday push through the crowd, wanting to get to the front. Fyodor walks around within the circle, taunting *Sha-Karn-Um*. He's got his shirt off, exposing his bare chest. He's not overly muscular, not by the gym-junkie standards of the US, but he's lean. His muscles are crisp and well-defined. Blue Novo blood stains his hair and

297

beard. He waves a knife at *Sha-Karn-Um* as he stalks around the outside of the circle, flexing his muscles. He's carrying a small canvas bag in his other hand, swinging it around. Blue blood drips from the corner of the bag.

"Don't do this," Doc calls out. He goes to rush to *Sha-Karn-Um's* side, but William Sunday grabs him, holding him back. He wrestles to free himself, but she simply tightens her iron grip. She clenches her lips and shakes her head, saying a firm "No. You can't interfere. He'll kill you."

"You," Fyodor says, pointing the chrome blade of his hunting knife at Doc. "You need to see this. You need to understand."

The soldiers roar with approval as Fyodor speaks to them in Russian. Several of them pass around a hat with wads of money stuffed in it, apparently gambling on some aspect of the kill.

"You think you know war. You're a fool," Fyodor says, turning his back on *Sha-Karn-Um* as he faces Doc. The blade of his knife passes mere inches from Doc's throat.

Doc stands proud. He refuses to back down, but William Sunday is right. There's nothing he can do. He grits his teeth. Doc isn't one given to hatred, but if he had a gun in his hand, he'd kill Fyodor without a moment's hesitation for what he's done, betraying the peace process. The Russian soldiers would kill him in return, but he wouldn't care.

Fyodor turns before the crowd of soldiers, holding his arms up high and gesturing for them to cheer. He's talking, but it's impossible to hear what he's saying over the uproar. Fyodor dumps the contents of the canvas bag on the concrete, shaking it empty. Two dull blue fangs fall to the ground. He throws the empty bag to one side and turns back to *Sha-Karn-Um*, tormenting her. He kicks the fangs across the concrete for all to see. They scatter across the floor. For her part, *Sha-Karn-Um* shrinks, lowering herself. She's trying to look smaller.

The commotion among the soldiers dies down. Everyone wants to know about Fyodor's unusual trophies.

"This is how they do it," Fyodor says, pointing at *Sha-Karn-Um* with his knife. He jogs the blade from side to side, pointing at two wounds between her front arms. "See where she bleeds? This is where the monsters produce their lightning. This is what you should target. Aim for the fangs."

A Russian soldier translates as Fyodor speaks.

Doc tries to pull away from William Sunday. She yanks him back, saying, "Don't do anything stupid."

"And this is their leader," Fyodor says. "This is their President. This is the mighty *Sha-Karn-Um*. She is the one that wages war on us, but not anymore."

"What are you going to do to her?" Doc blurts out.

"I'm going to kill her. Just like she killed the Under Secretary. Just like she killed hundreds of thousands of civilians and soldiers."

"You won't change anything," Doc says. "You'll only make the hatred worse."

"Hatred," Fyodor says, laughing. "We humans are masters of hatred. Russia knows only bitterness for her enemies. There is no compassion. No mercy. No peace. We will crush the Novo."

Doc replies, "How many people have to die before you run out of bullets? A million? A hundred million? A billion? Will your anger ever be satisfied?"

Fyodor extends his knife before him, staring down it as though it were the barrel of a gun. He glares at Doc.

"She will die. You will die. We all die, doctor. It's not a question of if, but when. But how we die—that matters. And us? We will die as warriors fighting for our people."

Throughout the circle of soldiers, there's a murmur of Russian spreading whenever Fyodor speaks, with those who understand English translating his words into Russian. The soldiers cheer at the realization of what he's said.

William Sunday tightens her grip on Doc's arm. She's squeezing so hard that the muscle is being compressed against the bone. It hurts, but for Doc, that only amplifies the anger he feels toward Fyodor.

The burly Russian dances around *Sha-Karn-Um*, shuffling with his boots like a boxer in the ring. She responds by turning, keeping her forearms facing him. They sway before her, desperate to keep him at bay.

The soldiers clap in unison as though counting out seconds. Fyodor adopts what looks like a fencing stance, even though he's wielding a hunting knife, not a rapier. With one hand held high behind him and his boots dancing across the concrete like a Cossack, he picks his moments, lunging past her arms and striking her torso with the knife. Deep cuts ooze iridescent blood. *Sha-Karn-Um* tries to retreat from him, but the swell of the crowd restricts her motion. The chaos and noise work to Fyodor's advantage. She's terrified. He's enraged.

Fyodor slashes her legs and her arms and strikes at her torso, leaving gaping wounds. Blue blood pools on the concrete. *Sha-Karn-Um* slips on her own blood. She falls to several of her knees, and Fyodor strikes with ruthless efficiency, slicing through her hide.

Sha-Karn-Um groans. She's weak. She tries to fend off Fyodor, but he slashes her arms. The alien collapses, and the soldiers laugh. She's still alive but is weak from the blood loss.

Fyodor rests his boot on *Sha-Karn-Um's* torso. He speaks at length in Russian, pointing as though he were a trophy hunter, having brought down a lion on the savannah. He poses as a soldier takes photos with an old-fashioned camera.

"Stop this," Doc calls out. "This is madness!"

Fyodor walks over to him.

"Can you not see? They are not superior to us. We are the victors. Today and tomorrow. Forever. We will win this war."

Behind him, *Sha-Karn-Um* crawls across the concrete floor, dragging her injured legs behind her.

"She begged for her life. Could you hear her? When my boot was on her hide. She pleaded for mercy. And I will show her mercy. I will show her the mercy she showed our people—the mercy of a bullet through the brain."

As *Sha-Karn-Um* reaches the edge of the warehouse floor, the soldiers part, exposing the dock where trucks once pulled up to unload boxes.

Fyodor holds out his blue, bloodied hand to one of the nearby soldiers. The soldier unholsters a sidearm, checks the breach and offers it to him.

"Wait," William Sunday says, stepping forward before Fyodor can take the gun. She rests her hand on the gun but doesn't take it from the soldier.

Fyodor turns on her with his knife. He lifts the blade, raising it toward her throat. Several soldiers on either side of them draw their guns, pointing them at William Sunday. Fingers rest on triggers, gently applying pressure.

"Let me do it," William Sunday says. "I want месть—revenge."

Fyodor smiles and lowers his bloodied knife.

"No. Don't," Doc says as two Russian soldiers grab both of his arms and hold him back.

"Have you already forgotten?" William Sunday asks, turning on him. "Bailey's body is still warm, lying in that damn alleyway, and you've forgotten already?"

"You don't have to do this," Doc says.

"They killed my family," William Sunday says with trembling lips. Tears stream down her cheeks. "They slaughtered them. Don't you understand that? They killed them without mercy."

On the other side of the warehouse floor, *Sha-Karn-Um* has reached the edge of the concrete. Her body hangs over the rim. She drops to the dock below, leaving only a bloody blue trail on the floor.

"Give me this honor," William Sunday says to Fyodor, gritting her teeth in anger. He doesn't reply. He simply smiles and gestures to the bloody mess on the concrete with his knife.

William Sunday pulls her Glock from its holster. She raises the gun toward the ceiling and pulls back on the slide, exposing the barrel and loading a round into the chamber.

"Don't do this," Doc yells. "You're better than this!"

William Sunday walks away from Doc without looking back. She's strident. Angry. Determined. For Doc, it feels as though a knife has been thrust into his chest. Like *Sha-Karn-Um,* he's been betrayed. Fyodor gloats as Doc falls to his knees on the concrete.

"No," he says with a whimper, feeling helpless.

Fyodor steps up to Doc, crowding him, lording over him. Blue blood drips from Fyodor's knife onto his boots.

William Sunday marches across the warehouse floor and drops over the edge of the dock onto the shattered concrete that makes up the parking lot. A blue glow rises, revealing how *Sha-Karn-Um* is crawling along out of sight. She's desperately trying to reach the next factory as though that might provide some safety.

"This is for my Ma," William Sunday says, holding the Glock outstretched before her. The gun is as black as the smoke billowing into the air from the stadium beyond the buildings. Her arm is straight, her muscles taut. She steadies herself and squeezes the trigger.

Boom!

William Sunday is emotionless. "And my Pa, my dear sweet Pa."

Boom!

From where he is, Doc sees the gun recoil.

William Sunday bends her elbow as each shot lashes out of the barrel, returning her arm ready for the next shot as shell casings bounce across the concrete.

"Nooooooo!" he yells.

"And my sister, Daphne."

Boom!

"And my brother, William."

Boom!

"And Meyers, Hawk, Leech and Mouse."

Boom! Boom! Boom! Boom!

With each shot, the glow from the Novo fades.

"And this," William Sunday says, adopting a two-handed stance and staring down along the barrel of her gun with unwavering focus. "This is for Lavender."

Boom!

The final shot echos through the warehouse. The faint blue glow beneath the dock fades into the shadows. William Sunday stands there for a moment with her arms hanging by her side. The soldiers on the raised concrete floor are silent. She holsters her sidearm and reaches up. Two soldiers grab her hands and haul her back up onto the warehouse floor.

"Now, you see," Fyodor says, scowling as he addresses Doc, who's still kneeling on the concrete. "Now, you understand the Russian way. This is how we bring peace."

William Sunday marches up next to Fyodor. Doc holds out a single, trembling hand. He's not sure what he wants or why he's reaching for her. His motion is instinctive.

"Don't touch me," she growls, stepping away from him. "Don't you *ever* touch me again." And Doc feels as if those bullets struck at his own soul.

"You're pathetic," Fyodor says, staring down at him. "You make me sick."

With that, Fyodor turns and calls out in Russian, issuing orders to his troops. Someone yanks the chain on the roller door, raising it. To Doc's mind, the sound of the metal clanging is like that of a machine gun firing on full auto. Soldiers cart ammunition from the shelves, carrying wooden boxes between them as they exit the warehouse. Within a matter of minutes, Doc is alone. With the roller door raised, the wind curls inside the warehouse, bringing snow flurries along with it.

Fyodor and William Sunday are the last to walk out into the street.

Neither looks back.

Honor

Doc feels numb, but not from the cold. He gets to his feet. The silence around him is deafening. The warehouse is a lifeless husk. In the distance, there are explosions. They're muffled, but *Novosibirsk* is descending into chaos. Columns of smoke rise above the buildings, but these are not from the belchers. The alien smoke rises in a steady stream, whereas burning fires release plumes that billow and fold on themselves. Fires blaze across the city. Flames reach into the sky.

What is he going to do? What can he do? Nothing. Doc stumbles forward, feeling lost. He's alone, abandoned in an occupied city, a city besieged by violence, and one where he doesn't understand the local language. The wind rushing through the open roller door chills him. He wraps his arms around his chest. He should raise the hood on his jacket, but he's not thinking straight.

Doc follows the bloody trail winding its way across the concrete floor for no other reason than it's there. The brilliant iridescence has faded. If anything, the Novo blood resembles a bottle of antifreeze spilled on the concrete.

He sits on the side of the dock with his legs hanging over the edge. The rubber bumpers have aged and perished. A few feet below him in the parking lot, the limp body of *Sha-Karn-Um* lies crumpled in a heap.

"I am so sorry," he says to no one.

Doc drops down into the parking lot out of a desire to keep moving and stay warm. His boots squelch in the slush. In response, *Sha-Karn-*

305

Um flinches. One of her limbs twitches.

Doc remains perfectly still. His eyes focus on the crumpled, fallen alien, unsure what he's seen. She couldn't be alive. William Sunday shot her eight or nine times at point-blank range. Is he imagining her reaction to his presence?

"*Sha-Karn-Um*," he says softly, edging closer to her. One of her arms rises slightly before falling back to the concrete.

Doc rushes to her side. He kneels, unzips his medical kit and rummages around, pulling out bandages.

"Easy," he says, donning a pair of disposable plastic gloves. He has no idea about the alien's physiology, but there have to be universal constants like avoiding infection and contamination, reducing blood loss, and stabilizing a patient against shock.

Although his kit is small, it's designed to treat severe wounds. He tears open a gauze pad and applies it to a deep gash near her massive compound eye. Doc pads the area, wanting to get a good look at the damage. There's the equivalent of veins and arteries with larger components that must serve a similar function to blood vessels in the human body. He grabs a butterfly clip similar to the one he used on the Under Secretary and uses it to close the puncture. He stops the bleeding and applies a large bandage, using medical tape to hold it in place.

"I need to move your arm to one side," he says, gingerly raising one of her forearms so he can reach a deep cut on her torso.

Sha-Karn-Um's coloration has faded to a dull grey, which must be related to her blood loss, but she responds, raising her arm a few inches. Doc repositions her arm and begins working on another cut. He pries with his fingers, reaching in and feeling for subsurface structures, knowing she must have the equivalent of organs, a circulatory system and supporting biological structures like nerves and lymph nodes. For him, it's a case of identifying what has been punctured. Beneath his fingers, he can feel what seems to equate to an irregular heartbeat, or it would be irregular if it were human. Fluid oozes beneath his fingers, but he can't see within the wound. Rather than slashing, at this point, Fyodor must have lunged and stabbed, pushing the knife in to the hilt, causing a narrow, deep injury.

Doc takes a scalpel and makes an incision, extending the cut on the surface so he can reach what appears to be a torn artery beneath. He twists and turns his gloved fingers, wanting more than a fleeting look at the damage. The puncture wound on the artery is jagged. He uses his scalpel to clean the edges, allowing him to join the ends of the tube together.

"I need more hands," he mumbles. "You have plenty. Me? I need more than two."

He works with his fingers and applies another butterfly clip, feeling rather than seeing the point of the wound. The plastic coating over the clip is designed to adhere to a slick surface and helps seal the puncture. Doc has the handle of the scalpel between his teeth as he works with his fingers.

"Got it," he says, gently prodding and feeling the way the artery sits within her body. He closes the external wound with a few stitches.

Sha-Karn-Um stirs. She rises slightly and turns, exposing other wounds.

"You're going to have some scars," he says. "Sorry, this isn't my best work. I need an operating theater. A couple of surgical nurses would help."

"*Help*," *Sha-Karn-Um* says.

"Yes, help," he says, smiling as he bandages another gash. "I'm helping you."

That she's talking, even if incoherently, is a good sign. She's conscious. She's aware. It tells him his efforts are working, helping her body achieve the alien equivalent of homeostasis and finding a new point of equilibrium. If she slips back into unconsciousness, the shock she's sustained will probably kill her. All he can do is try to mitigate her physical injuries in the hope that her internal systems will rebound.

The wounds on her arms weep blood, but Doc's more concerned about the deep punctures in her torso.

Doc says, "I'm going to turn you around, okay? I need to look at some of your other injuries."

Sha-Karn-Um doesn't reply, but the motion of her arms suggests she's trying to help. Her legs don't move at all, making him wonder if she's been paralyzed or if she's too weak to lift them. She did say the Novos struggle with Earth's gravity. Being injured would make that physical stress worse.

Doc gets to his feet and leans over her, grabbing at her torso and twisting. She's heavy. She tries to help. He gets her to turn by about a quarter. It's enough to expose a deep gash that was lying up against the concrete wall of the dock. If anything, the bitter cold seeping through from the frozen concrete has probably helped keep her alive, slowing the bleeding.

Doc is gentle, kneeling on a cinderblock and leaning on the wall as he works on the gash. He uses a vial of saline solution to squirt into the gash to wash out the grit and dirt.

As he reaches into the wound, he realizes there are no bullet holes. He stops and looks around. *Sha-Karn-Um* was shot at a distance of not more than four or five feet. William Sunday could not have missed at that range. He looks at the trail of blood running along the wall, marking where *Sha-Karn-Um* fell and dragged herself toward the next factory. In among the snow and ice, there are chunks of freshly broken concrete, but they're off to the side.

Boots slam into the ground behind him. Someone has dropped down from the warehouse into the dock. His heart races. He's worried he's about to turn and see a Russian soldier with an AK-47 leveled at the two of them.

Doc swings around with the scalpel in his hand. He never thought he'd have to use one as a weapon, but if he's forced to, he will. Doc freezes in place. William Sunday is standing there with a major trauma kit slung over one shoulder.

"Sunday?"

"Oh, Doc," she says with tears streaming down her cheeks. "I'm sorry. I'm so sorry. I circled back as soon as I could. I—I had to wait to slip away until I wouldn't be noticed."

Doc springs to his feet and throws his arms around her. She drops the pack to the broken concrete.

"Oh, dear God, I love you," he says, grabbing her face with both of his bloodied gloved hands and kissing her on the forehead, leaving neon blue smudges on her cheeks.

"I love you too, Doc," she replies, choking up. Tears well up in the corner of her eyes.

"I—I," Doc says, lost for words.

"Back in that shell hole. Back when my leg was pinned, they had us dead to rights, but they showed mercy. I—I had to do the same."

"You," he says, letting go of her and grabbing the trauma kit. "You had me fooled."

"I had to fool all of them," William Sunday says, kneeling beside *Sha-Karn-Um*. "Or they would have killed her. Is she okay? Will she be okay?"

"I don't know," Doc says, grabbing more saline solution from the kit and flushing out more of the alien's wounds. He binds the cuts on *Sha-Karn-Um's* arms and legs. He's careful not to cut off the circulation. Alien blood soaks through the bandages, but a little pressure reduces the intensity.

"We need to get her out of here," he says. "Get her back to her own people. They'll know how to treat her."

"There's a stretcher in the office," William Sunday says, jogging up the stairs.

"Hang in there, *Sha-Karn-Um*. We're going to get you back to the hive."

William Sunday comes back with the stretcher. She lays it out next to the alien. Together, the two of them lift *Sha-Karn-Um* onto the canvas. Doc closes the trauma kit and slings it over his shoulders. William Sunday takes the lead, grabbing the aluminum handles. They lift. *Sha-Karn-Um* is heavier than a human. Her limbs hang over both sides of the stretcher. One of them drags through the snow as they stagger up the driveway toward the street. To Doc, it's as though they've dredged up some deep sea creature and shoved it on a stretcher. She could be dead already, for all he knows.

"What if we run into someone?" William Sunday asks without turning around.

"Human or Novo?" Doc asks.

"Either. Both."

"I don't know," Doc replies. "I mean, I hope reason prevails. We're medics. We're evacuating the wounded. Does that count for something?"

"I sure hope so," William Sunday says as civilians peer at them from behind dark curtains.

Doc's heart aches as he sees a young girl in the shadows, watching from behind a window as they walk down the street. She can't be more than five or six years old. Her face is grubby. Like so many others, she's innocent, having been caught up in the war simply because she was born in the wrong place at the wrong time. As she stares at them, he wonders what she's thinking. Does she understand what they're doing? Or for her, is this treachery? In a time of war, the desire for peace is treason. He follows her gaze as they walk past. The girl places her hand on the glass before her, splaying her fingers wide. There's no animosity. Life reaches for life. There's nothing to her gesture beyond a desire for hope. She may not know who they are or what they're doing with an injured alien, but she seems captivated by the contradiction out on the street. She leans close to the window, watching them as they disappear along the road.

The two of them reach the stadium. Bodies lie strewn in the ruins. Although Doc doesn't recognize them, several of the soldiers are wearing US Special Forces uniforms. Beside them, dead Novos lie half-buried in the rubble.

Sha-Karn-Um stirs.

"Easy," Doc says, feeling her weight shift on the stretcher. She wants to see what's left of the stadium, but she can't sit up.

"*One,*" she says as they carry her over the broken concrete scattered throughout the street.

Doc isn't sure what she means. They pick their way through the ruins, passing more bodies from both species. Dark, red, frozen blood forms a trail leading to the body of a US soldier who's collapsed in the far gutter. Lifeless eyes stare up at the dark sky as they walk past. Not more than ten feet away, the crumpled remains of a Novo lies beneath a fallen steel beam.

"*One,*" she says again, but it's clear she's not counting casualties. She's trying to convey some deeper meaning, but exactly what escapes Doc.

Further along, a brick wall has collapsed, crushing a Russian soldier fighting with a Novo at close quarters. From beneath the rubble, their arms touch, and it's then the realization strikes him.

"Yes," he says. "We are one in death. Once we're dead, it matters not whether we're human or Novo."

"*Yes. One. United in sorrow.*"

"And that's always the way," Doc says. "For thousands of years, we humans have fought each other over land, over ideas, over riches, over ego. But for all our differences, for all our animosity, once dead, we're united. The battlefield knows nothing but the bitter unity of those who have died."

Gunfire breaks down a nearby street, followed by bolts of lightning crackling through the air. They rush past an alley, avoiding that street. William Sunday steps over bricks and broken beams, working her way toward the hive towering over the southern part of town.

Patterns appear on *Sha-Karn-Um's* torso. The images are faint. Whereas once they appeared as stark as a tattoo, now they're washed out. They flicker over her arms, disappearing beneath her bandages. In response, Doc looks around. If she's speaking Novo, it's because she can see a Novo nearby.

Before he can say anything, William Sunday says, "We've got company."

From the rooftops, Novos appear. Lightning crackles over their hides. Doc grimaces, expecting a bolt to tear through his chest at any moment.

"I make four," William Sunday says.

"Six," Doc replies. "No, eight."

"What are we going to do?"

"What are *they* going to do?" Doc asks as several of them rush down the side of a concrete apartment building. Their legs grip the concrete like a gecko scrambling down a wall. They're fast, reaching the bottom within seconds.

"Do you want to stop?" William Sunday asks.

"No, keep going. We need to get her back to the hive."

From behind them, several Novos rush past. They move like the wind, coming out of nowhere and running past them along the street. If they wanted to attack, Doc and William Sunday would be dead before they knew what happened. There are dozens of Novos, all coming from the rear. They stop ahead, lining either side of the street as though they were forming an honor guard.

William Sunday picks up the pace. It's unnerving passing by dozens of Novos standing side by side, but it's then Doc realizes they're facing outward, away from them. They're watching the buildings. They're here to defend *Sha-Karn-Um*.

On reaching the barricade less than a block from the massive hive towering over *Novosibirsk*, the truck barring the road is dragged to one side, allowing them to walk on. Doc and William Sunday start up the ramp leading into the hive. It's unnerving watching as hundreds of Novos line the sides and roof of the vast ramp, clinging to the rough surface and watching as they walk in toward the heart of the hive.

Within the alien structure, they're greeted by smaller Novos reaching up only two to three feet in height. They swarm under the stretcher, lifting it from beneath, taking it from them. Doc and William Sunday stand to one side as *Sha-Karn-Um* is rushed away, presumably to the alien equivalent of a surgical unit. Without saying anything, they follow, wanting to remain involved, but the corridor within the hive morphs. One moment, they're staring at the organic, sprawling walkway; the next, they're sealed within a sphere.

"Ah, what just happened?" William Sunday asks.

"I think we're in a holding cell," Doc replies, looking around at the spongy texture of the sphere. It's no more than thirty feet in diameter. With nothing else to do, he sits, leaning against the slope and drops his pack.

"Well. At least we're alive."

The Hunting Knife

"You," Doc says, using his pack as a pillow propped up on the side of the spherical cell. "You should win an Oscar for that performance back there in the warehouse."

William Sunday laughs. "Well, it wasn't all an act."

"It wasn't?"

"Oh, no. I was taking my frustration out on that damn concrete. It's strange, but it was cathartic. Each time I pulled the trigger. Each time the pistol grip slammed back into my hand, and the recoil fought against my arm. Each time the crack of gunfire lashed out. It felt like the pain—the anger—the heartache was drifting away. Each shot gave me closure."

"And *Sha-Karn-Um?*"

"At first, she didn't understand. She panicked. She was trying to escape. Bits of concrete were being flung at her as the bullets struck nearby."

"But?"

"But then she realized it was a feint. I think she could see the hurt in my eyes, but she could see that pain wasn't directed at her. That's when she started playing along. She'd glow bright and then fade with each shot."

Doc says, "Okay, so you're going to have to share the Oscar."

"I guess."

Time drags, but neither of them cares. It's warm inside the hive.

315

They remove their coats. The light seems to come from all around them, but it's not blinding. Somehow, air is circulating. The snow and ice on their jackets melt. A pool forms at the bottom of the sphere, slowly soaking into the floor and disappearing.

"What are they going to do with us?" William Sunday asks.

"I don't know," Doc replies.

"Are we prisoners of war?"

"Maybe."

"And *Sha-Karn-Um*. If she dies..."

Doc doesn't reply. He doesn't need to.

Above them, off to one side, a hole opens in the sphere, forming a tube. A body slides down, coming to rest between them.

William Sunday says, "Fyodor?"

The Russian's face is scratched. One side of his beard has been ripped from his cheek, leaving hundreds of deep red spots on his skin. Blood seeps from a scorch mark on his shoulder. His uniform is ragged and torn. He's only wearing one boot. His exposed sock is bloody.

Doc unzips his medical pack.

"Don't you *dare* touch me," Fyodor growls. He moves like a wounded animal, desperate, ready to lash out one last time. The Russian edges away from Doc. William Sunday circles around the inside of the sphere, making her way over to Doc and giving Fyodor a wide berth.

"You're hurt," Doc says, rummaging through his pack. "You're in pain."

"You're a *fucking* traitor."

"This is Fentanyl," Doc says, ignoring him and opening a plastic wrapper. "Chew it. Don't swallow it. Push it against the inside of your cheek."

Doc hands the medical lozenge to him. Grubby fingers reach across the clean floor. Fyodor snatches the drug from Doc and shoves it in his mouth.

Doc waits for the Fentanyl to hit before pointing at the Russian's shoulder and saying, "I can take a look at that if you want?"

Fyodor looks up at the curve of the ceiling. He closes his eyes for a moment. The veins on his neck flex as he grits his teeth. His hands shake. Reluctantly, he says, "Yes."

Doc drags his pack around the curved bottom of the sphere and dumps it next to the burly Russian. Fyodor looks hard to his left as Doc treats his right shoulder. Whether he's ignoring Doc or simply avoiding seeing the extent of his injuries is difficult to tell. He grimaces with the slightest touch. Fyodor may not want to appear weak, but he's clearly in excruciating pain. Doc uses medical-grade scissors to cut away the burnt uniform and get a better look at the wound. He dabs at the exposed, blackened muscle with a surgical cloth dipped in saline solution. With a scalpel, he probes at the Russian's neck and shoulder, gently lifting burnt flesh and examining the damage.

"Okay, the joint in your shoulder is badly damaged, but it looks like the axillary vessels and nerves are intact. The top of your trapezius is gone. That's the muscle leading from your neck to the deltoid on your shoulder. There are deep tissue burns and a fracture in your scapula. You're going to need surgical replacement of the ball on the humeral head within the socket as it's shattered. Try not to move your arm as the bone will grate. I'm going to clean the wound, apply an antiseptic and immobilize your arm in a sling."

Fyodor nods. His silence is telling. For a strongman, it's humbling to accept help. Doc sees beyond his rough persona. He's human, just like them. And he's hurt. Pain is an equalizer. Bluff and bluster are meaningless in the face of a severe injury.

Once Doc is finished packing the wound with sterile dressings, he applies medical tape to hold them in place. Then, he uses a large, cotton triangular bandage to make a sling and slips it around Fyodor's neck.

"It's really important you don't move your arm. You'll need a prosthetic to take the place of the shattered bone. Try to move, and you'll tear the muscles further and damage the socket."

Fyodor nods again. The inner turmoil he feels at being injured and captured is apparent. It's the uncertainty. The future is shrouded for all, but for him, it must appear pitch-black. No matter how tough someone is, being without hope is debilitating. It changes the way they see the world.

Doc gets up and takes the pack with him, returning to William Sunday on the other side of the cell. It's a token gesture. None of them are more than five feet apart at the bottom of the sphere.

"Thank you," Fyodor says, looking down at the clean material forming the sling.

Doc nods. Now is not the time for words. By echoing Fyodor's own body language back at him, he's showing he understands the Russian needs time to deal with the shit in his own head. William Sunday has been unusually quiet through the last half an hour, but Doc's confident her silence means she, too, understands what the burly Russian is going through. Saying thank you was a token gesture. No one can change their mind in a heartbeat. Fyodor is fiercely independent and proud. He needs time. Like a cruise liner or an aircraft carrier, he's not going to turn on a dime. He needs to process what's happened for himself.

William Sunday reaches out with one hand and massages Doc's neck. He didn't realize how tense he was until her fingers began squeezing the muscles there. He positions the pack between them, giving them both something to lean against. She works her thumb and forefinger up to the base of his head and back down to his shoulders, squeezing and rubbing his skin. It's crazy, but William Sunday speaks loudest with touch. Her words are measured and meaningful, but her heart comes through her hands.

Quietly, he says, "That feels so good."

She responds without saying anything, squeezing and releasing, allowing his muscles to relax.

After almost an hour, Fyodor says, "They took me alive. They wanted me alive. Why?"

"I don't know," Doc says.

"For revenge?" he asks.

"I don't think so."

Doc doesn't say as much, but killing Fyodor would have been easy. The Novos are brutal in combat, but they share supplies with the inhabitants of *Novosibirsk*. To Doc's mind, they're more rational than emotional.

"We're fucked, aren't we."

"Oh, yeah," William Sunday says. She's given up on massaging Doc's neck and taken to playing with his hair, scratching lightly at his scalp with her nails. She's kneading like a cat, although Doc doesn't mind. William Sunday stops and sits up, facing Fyodor. Doc joins her, sitting crosslegged and leaning against the pack.

"Why are they keeping us alive?" Fyodor asks.

"Only they can answer that," Doc replies. "But they've lumped us together."

"They have," Fyodor says.

William Sunday turns to Doc, asking, "Do you think they're watching us?"

"I don't know. I would."

"Me too," Fyodor says.

"Do you really think peace is possible?" William Sunday asks.

Doc points at himself and then at Fyodor. "Depends who you're asking."

Fyodor is silent. He lowers his gaze. His body language screams in anguish. The bravado from the cabin is gone. Vodka no longer loosens his lips. Losing the use of his arm has humbled him. Pain makes a mockery of any ideology. Being captured is humiliating.

Doc says, "Wars cannot last forever. Like a wildfire, sooner or later, they burn themselves out. Either one side wins or the other. Or one side withdraws and licks its wounds, but eventually, the fighting always stops. Wars only last as long as there's an aggressor, someone that would steal not only land but lives."

"There was a hundred-year war, wasn't there?" William Sunday asks.

"There was," Doc replies.

"That must have been one helluva mess," Fyodor says. That he's injecting himself into the discussion is a positive sign. He's moving from resentment to acceptance, even if it is begrudging. Doc is kind in his reply.

"All wars are a mess."

"They cannot have known what they were fighting for, not after a hundred years."

For Doc, it's interesting to hear Fyodor talking about an obscure war fought centuries ago in France. It's a metaphor, a placeholder, a substitute for talking about the war with the Novos. From the perspective of Fyodor's ego, it's much easier to talk about something similar and carry the logic across without feeling threatened.

Doc says, "The English were fighting for land. The French fought for their freedom."

"Who won?" William Sunday asks.

"No one, really," Doc replies. "Not on either side. Not a single person that stood on the battlefield on that first day. Not their children or their children's children. Or even a generation beyond that survived to see the end of the war. They were all dead long before the English were finally driven back across the Channel."

"And for what?" Fyodor asks, looking down at his arm hanging limp in the sling. "For misery and suffering."

"On both sides," Doc replies. "There are no winners in war, only losers... The only way you 'win' is by losing less than the other guy."

"It's interesting, isn't it?" Fyodor says. "You could have predicted the outcome of that war a hundred years beforehand, but it had to play out."

Doc says, "Yep. No one would accept what was a forgone future until the battles had been fought."

"It's sad," William Sunday says.

"It is," Fyodor replies, still looking down at his arm in the sling. Doc hasn't said as much, but Fyodor probably realizes what Doc already knows. He will never regain full use of his arm. Oh, over time, he'll be able to lift a glass of water or a plate of food, but he'll never have the full range of motion, particularly when trying to reach above his head. Even with extensive physiotherapy, Doc doubts he'll be able to raise his hand above his shoulder.

Around them, the floor subsides. The ceiling within the cell expands, doubling and then tripling in height, opening out like that of a cathedral. What was a cramped prison cell balloons into something grand and majestic. Intricate shapes and geometric patterns appear as though carved into the walls. Spikes hang down from the vast ceiling. They're jagged but not threatening. There's a clear motif in the architecture that seems reminiscent of a medieval church with its columns, arches, and narrow windows, only these seem organic, as though they were created by wasps rather than architects.

Light streams in from what appear to be stained-glass windows. It's mimicry. It has to be as there's no sunlight outside, nothing beyond the dull grey that seeps through the smog from the belchers. Whereas stained-glass windows in a church portray divine intervention or scenes from the Scriptures, these are blobs of red, yellow and green. It's as though the windows are out of focus.

The Novos are emulating human culture. They've seen the Russian Orthodox cathedrals in the city. They must admire them, which to Doc, is peculiar. They've embraced local architecture and adapted it to their own ends. It tells him they see Earth as a home.

The three of them are left sitting on the side of a raised dais in the center of a hall that stretches easily two hundred yards in both length and height. Its width, though, would be barely thirty yards. Colors ripple over all of the surfaces, scrolling through the rainbow. Symbols and images curve and curl around the columns. Text appears. Sometimes, there are human words, such as *war, death, life* and *peace*, but most of the squiggles are indistinguishable. They vary in size. As the alien words pass beneath the three of them, they're often no larger than the text within a book. High on the ceiling, the letters are easily six to eight feet in size.

Doc finds the cacophony of sights around him disorienting. It's the motion of symbols rushing over uneven surfaces. Bile rises in his throat. He pinches his eyes shut, trying to block out the conflicting sights around him.

A hand rests on his arm. William Sunday is beside Doc, grabbing him, wanting his attention.

Doc opens his eyes. Novos line the walls of the cathedral. The rolling images have subsided. They fade from sight. Lightning crackles between the Novos. There are hundreds of them. Blue bolts pass harmlessly from one creature to another, surging around the chamber.

"*Sha-Karn-Um*," he mutters.

The leader of the Novos is standing on the broad platform before them. The bandages Doc wrapped around her injuries have been replaced with what looks like clear molded plastic. Large insets of artificial flesh have been placed over the holes where her electrified fangs were torn from her body. A soft pink hue lights up her skin, having replaced the deathly grey when he last saw her.

Sha-Karn-Um is holding Fyodor's hunting knife. Her eight legs spread wide, lowering her profile like a spider creeping in to attack. Her four arms converge in front of her, gripping the hilt with surprising dexterity. The chrome blade has been cleaned. Its mirrored surface reflects the gothic hall around them, catching the light from the windows.

Fyodor scrambles to his feet. Even with the Fentanyl, the sudden movement pains him, and he reaches for his wounded shoulder with his good hand.

Fyodor stays low, crouching as he faces *Sha-Karn-Um*. She turns, waving the knife before him. Fyodor holds out his one good arm. His hand sways as though he, too, were holding a knife. He's bluffing, trying to deflect attention in the vain hope of disarming *Sha-Karn-Um*. That he's surrounded by hundreds of Novos crackling with energy seems to escape his mind. Any one of them could kill him in an instant. His focus is solely on the threat of *Sha-Karn-Um* before him. The two of them face off against each other, turning slowly on the platform.

Even with just one arm, Fyodor is looking for an opening to lunge and perhaps disable *Sha-Karn-Um*. Whereas Doc's default reaction is flight, Fyodor's is fight. His eyes, though, betray him. He's defensive. He may be a warrior at heart, but his wounded arm limits his motion. It hangs in the sling, swaying as he shuffles. He tries to be brave, but Doc can see his outstretched hand trembling.

"Don't," William Sunday calls out to *Sha-Karn-Um*. She and Doc scramble to their feet. William Sunday steps forward. This time, it's Doc's turn to take her arms and hold her back.

From the side of the stage, he whispers, "We can't interfere."

"No."

"We have to let this play out. It's the only way."

Fyodor and *Sha-Karn-Um* circle each other. This is the fight in the barren, icy warehouse replaying again, but the roles are reversed. Instead of Russian soldiers baying for blood, aliens clamber over the walls, sending messages to each other in flickers of black and white. The silence is a stark contrast to the yelling and cheering on the frozen dock. Back then, the Russians were consumed by their bloodlust. They rejoiced at seeing their enemy slashed with the knife. Although it's difficult to tell, the Novos seem more calculating and analytical. Far from being a spectacle, it seems they're curious.

"Is this what you want?" Fyodor asks with sweat beading on his forehead. "Revenge?"

"*What you want?*" is all *Sha-Karn-Um* says in reply, taunting him.

The two of them shadow each other, with neither attacking, each edging around the platform. Fyodor watches his footing as he nears the edge. The drop to the floor below is easily twenty feet, effectively stranding him on the raised platform. He keeps his center of gravity low, moving like a wrestler even though he's only able to hold out one arm.

"I—I can't win," he says.

"*Win?*" *Sha-Karn-Um* replies, shuffling her legs and forcing him to continue circling the platform to stay out of reach. "*Why is it all you ever want is to win?*"

"Because to lose is to die."

"*Die?*"

"I deserve this," he says, passing by with his back to Doc and William Sunday. "But damn. That doesn't make it any easier."

"*What is easy?*" Sha-Karn-Um asks, stalking him with the knife. She swings the blade around, maneuvering it with deft precision, swiping at the air, making it clear she could kill him with a single blow.

"Hate," Fyodor says. "Hate is easy." He points at himself and then at the alien, saying, "You hate me. I hate you."

"*Hate... is to burn on the inside,*" the alien replies.

Fyodor shuffles with his boots. "Hate is the anger of fools. And me? I'm the king of fools."

"*What would you do?*" Sha-Karn-Um asks, flipping the knife around and twirling it as though it were a baton. The chrome blade reflects the light around them like a mirror. She's teasing him, tormenting him with her prowess.

Fyodor says, "What is war without peace?"

"*War?*" Sha-Karn-Um asks. "*Peace? What does that even mean to the two of us? What war is there in here?*"

The alien scuttles around the platform, replicating his motion and waving the knife before her as he once did in the warehouse. She's challenging him, wanting him to try to disarm her.

Fyodor's one boot is heavy, slowing his reactions. The sock on his other foot leaves bloody imprints on the stage. He lurches back, dodging out of the way as the knife slices through the air in front of him. There's fear in his eyes. Sweat drips from his forehead, running down the side of his face.

Sha-Karn-Um asks him, "*Would you live or die?*"

"What is life without death?"

Fyodor falls to his knees. His wounded arm hangs heavy within the sling. He's physically exhausted. Even if he weren't injured, he'd be no match for her with a knife. She's too quick, too agile. His one good arm hangs to his side. He raises his head, exposing his neck, inviting her to strike.

"If there must be death, let mine bring life—bring peace."

"*Your death?*"

"Let my death satisfy my debts."

Fyodor closes his eyes. Tears stream down his cheeks. His lips quiver. The veins on his neck bulge as he grimaces, awaiting a single, fatal strike from her to the jugular.

William Sunday pulls away from Doc, but he's as firm with her as she once was with him, anchoring her in place.

Sha-Karn-Um closes on Fyodor. Her legs straddle the soft floor like those of a spider approaching its prey when caught in a web. Above her, the Novos surge with patterns rushing back and forth over their skins. They have the rhythm of a crowd chanting in unison, but their calls to each other come in absolute silence. The blade of the knife passes within inches of Fyodor's neck, slicing through the air. Light catches the polished chrome. The tip threatens death. With a short, sharp motion, *Sha-Karn-Um* stabs, thrusting with the hilt, plunging the knife deep into the floor in front of the Russian. With that, she pulls back.

"*Your knife,*" she says. "*You dropped it in the warehouse.*"

"I—I don't understand," Fyodor says, opening his eyes. His hunting knife has been wedged into the floor mere inches from his knees.

"*Mercy,*" *Sha-Karn-Um* says, and in that instant, Doc's mind is alive with the realization of what's happening. It was mercy that had him care for the wounded Novo in that muddy crater when he could have fled. It was mercy when the Novos allowed him to carry the wounded from the battlefield. It was mercy when William Sunday fired at the concrete beside *Sha-Karn-Um* instead of killing her in the loading dock. And it's mercy the alien leader now offers Fyodor.

"*Mercy is what we all need, but none of us deserve. It can be asked but never demanded. It can only be chosen by those who hold power. Mercy is to break the chains that bind us all. Mercy is to refuse vengeance.*"

"Mercy?" Fyodor says, stunned by what's unfolding. His fingers tremble. He looks at his good hand, turning it over before him,

325

astonished he's still alive. She could have killed him. She should have. After what he did to her, betraying her in the stadium and stabbing her in the warehouse, she has no reason to spare his life.

"*Hate begets hate, and we all lose a part of ourselves. Peace means more than laying down weapons. Peace only comes from having mercy.*"

As she speaks, her words are replicated in the shapes and symbols on her body. They ripple out through the crowd.

"*I choose mercy over hate.*"

Fyodor pulls the knife from the floor. It's wedged in and takes considerable effort to remove. On pulling it out, he examines the blade. There are nicks on the leading edge. Each one speaks of the violence that has unfolded beneath his hand.

"It sounds crazy," Fyodor says, still looking down at the knife. "It's circular logic, but nothing will change if nothing changes."

Doc releases his grip on William Sunday's arm. For her part, she stands silently, watching these two warriors talking rather than fighting.

"*We could fight for a hundred years,*" Sha-Karn-Um says, revealing how she has been listening to them.

"Or we could find peace today," Fyodor replies.

"It takes courage," Doc says.

"It does," Fyodor says, turning and looking at him with tears in his eyes. "It takes more courage than attacking an unarmed prisoner in a warehouse. That... that was cowardice."

With those words, he drops the knife. It's symbolic. *Sha-Karn-Um* returned it to him, but he doesn't need or want it any more. The look on his face is one of repulsion. He hates what he's become. The knife seems to personify that as he finds it repugnant, screwing up his face as he looks at it with disdain. Doc wonders if perhaps that's the only true role for hatred in life, to expose shortcomings and press for change.

Fyodor gets to his feet. He stands proud with his shoulders back and his head held high. "I've only ever thought of war... What can I do for peace?"

"We must talk, not fight. We need to understand, not argue. We must be honest, no matter how much that may hurt. No lies. No more lies. Do not lie to me. Do not lie to yourself."

Fyodor nods.

William Sunday takes Doc's hand in hers. She squeezes his fingers gently in response to those words from *Sha-Karn-Um*.

"And we *will* have peace," Fyodor says, joining Doc and William Sunday. He taps Doc on the shoulder, speaking to *Sha-Karn-Um* as he says, "Send them back to the Front. I will stay here with you. And we will talk. All of us. And together, we will bring peace."

The End

Epilogue

The flight from New York City to South-East Asia is torturous. Even though it costs a fortune, Doc pays for business class tickets to try to offset the fatigue of so many marathon flights back-to-back. William Sunday does not complain. Champagne before take-off is a pleasant change from boiled water in the trenches.

It's been six months since the end of the war. To reach the Novos, Doc and William Sunday have to fly from New York to Tokyo and from there to Singapore, where they wait eight hours in the airport for a connecting flight to Chennai in India. Due to delays, the onward flight to Colombo in Sri Lanka departs within twenty minutes of touching down in southern India, and they have to run between gates, hoping their luggage makes the flight. From Sri Lanka, they board a US Navy helicopter for a two-hour flight to the frigate FFG-62 USS Constellation in the Indian Ocean.

After thirty-seven hours on the move, the flight deck, hatchways, dull grey paint, and hard metal surfaces of the warship are a blur. Doc collapses on the bottom bunk in their quarters.

"Oh, I see how it is," William Sunday says, dropping her pack beside his. She flops on top of him and squirms to one side, squeezing between him and the bulkhead and effectively pushing him out of the narrow bed with a few well-placed wiggles.

"Okay, okay," he says, reluctantly getting to his feet and climbing onto the top bunk. William Sunday laughs. Although she doesn't say as much, he suspects she doesn't actually care which bunk she gets. The thought of tormenting him was too much. As she's almost a decade younger than Doc, she's far more playful. If Doc tries to address her as Anastasia or even Ana, she ignores him and only responds to her wartime name. For William Sunday, it's a way of honoring not only her brother but all those who fell in battle.

As the warship is underway, there's a steady hum coming through the hull. Ordinarily, Doc would find it annoying, but he's so ridiculously tired that he's asleep within seconds. He wakes to see William Sunday with her hair in a towel, having taken a shower. She's wearing a loose-fitting tracksuit and sneakers.

"Good morning, sleepyhead."

"Good morning," he says, rolling off the bunk bed and misjudging the fall to the floor. He expects the deck sooner and lands with a thud when it's a foot or so further away than he realized. Their cabin has an adjacent bathroom, which is unusual for a warship, but their tiny, cramped quarters are normally reserved for visiting captains and admirals.

"Are we there?" he asks, seeing her peering out of a porthole.

"Oh, yeah," she says, pointing at the horizon. "Look!"

Doc slips his hand around her waist, gives her a quick kiss on the cheek, and looks out of the porthole. Priorities. There's a specific order in which these things must unfold. Looking out at the flat expanse of the ocean, dozens of alien hives rise on the horizon. Unlike in Siberia, there are no belchers and so no dark clouds. The Novos are sensitive to ultraviolet radiation, but living in the hives and beneath the waves, they're protected from UV, so there's no need to produce smog.

"Magnificent!"

"I got you some fruit from the mess," William Sunday says as Doc rummages around in his bag for a change of clothing.

"Thank you."

He slips into the cramped ensuite, brushes his teeth, uses the toilet, shaves and has a shower. After he's dressed, he has breakfast by the porthole, staring out at the alien city towering over the ocean.

There's a rap on the hatch. William Sunday opens it, and a sailor informs them that their onward flight is ready to depart. They grab their packs and follow the sailor to the flight deck and onto the refueled Sikorsky Seahawk. The pilot and copilot greet them with far more enthusiasm than they did in Colombo, making Doc wonder if this is their first flight into Novo territory. The captain comes down from the bridge for the launch. He, too, treats them like celebrities. Smiles and handshakes abound.

The rotors wind up to speed, and the helicopter lifts off the deck. Brilliant blue, azure waters pass beneath them. Given that most fish stocks are around the coast, normally over continental shelves, the location of the Novos floating city has no environmental impact and is well within international waters.

War seems like a distant memory. Already, there are talks being held with both the Maldives and Australia for cruise liners to visit the alien city. From Perth, it's five days at sea, while from Malé, it's only two. The US, China, India and the UK all have a naval military presence in the region, but there have been no hostilities. Far from fighting, the focus now is on what humanity can learn from its new neighbors. Although it might seem like Doc and William Sunday are old friends dropping by, they've been tasked by the US State Department and NASA with a number of questions for the Novos. The war may have ended, but the Novos' reluctance to divulge information persists. As far as Doc understands, it seems cultural rather than intentional. The Novos want to get on with their own lives.

Lightning crackles from spiral-like hives on the outskirts of the floating city, but they're symbolic of the aliens' independence rather than threatening. Far from simply being weapons, these spires also produce energy for use within the city. The helicopter flies around the central administration spire with its various peaks reaching up toward the sky and lands on a floating dock next to one of the submerged legs. Like an iceberg, most of the structure is below the waterline.

"Fyodor!" William Sunday yells as the loadmaster on the helicopter pulls open the side door. The rotors are still turning, winding down, but William Sunday is already out on the flight deck before Doc can react, leaving him to grab their bags.

"Ah, Sunday," the Russian calls out over the whine of the engines powering down. "You are my favorite day of the week."

Fyodor's arm is still in a sling, but it's far more sophisticated than the cotton sling Doc made for him. A single leather strap leads from his wrist to his neck, looping around and running back down to his arm. His elbow isn't supported at all, which takes pressure off the shoulder, allowing it to heal. Mentally, Doc makes a note. That's the type of sling he should have used, even if made from cotton.

"Hey, Doc," Fyodor says, reaching out with his left hand and offering what is an unorthodox handshake.

"It's good to see you again, my friend."

"And your wife? Your daughter?" Doc asks.

Fyodor points at a nearby hive across the water, saying, "We live there. It is much warmer than Siberia."

"I bet."

"And *Sha-Karn-Um?*" William Sunday asks.

"She wasn't expecting you until tonight. She's touring the nurseries on the sea floor. I've sent word. I'm sure she'll rush back."

"So, how does all this work?" Doc asks as a Novo takes their bags from him. Fyodor leads them into the hive.

"We assumed they were terrestrial creatures, but they're not. They're amphibious. In the water, they move like squid. And like dolphins or whales, they have no problem diving into the depths. Come. I'll show you."

After walking up into the hive, Fyodor reaches up and touches one of the walls. He has an exotic alien bracelet wrapped around his wrist. Links lead to three of his fingers where thin rings wrap around his knuckles. The hive reacts to his touch, forming a sphere around the three of them with a flat bottom, sealing them within what was, moments ago, a tunnel.

The floor drops away beneath their feet, taking both Doc and

William Sunday by surprise. They fall faster than they would in a high-speed elevator.

"Okay," William Sunday says, bending her knees. "That's going to take some getting used to."

"Oh, just you wait," Fyodor says, relishing their reaction. He still has his hand on the spherical wall. The alien elevator changes direction, moving at an angle. The sensation is unnerving as the view around them doesn't change. The sphere slows after roughly a hundred meters. Doc feels the pressure building against his ears. He reaches up, squeezes his nostrils shut and blows gently, wanting to equalize his inner ear.

The sphere they're in flattens and broadens. Three-quarters of the sphere becomes transparent, morphing into what seems to be glass. The sea beyond is dark. Beneath them, the ocean is pitch black. Above, there's a faint blue glow marking the surface. Shapes jet past in the shadows.

"Stay by the edge," Fyodor says, pointing at the center of the room. It takes Doc a moment to realize that the central section of the floor now falls away into the water.

"And here she comes," Fyodor says.

Sha-Karn-Um bursts through the surface, leaping out beside them and spraying them with water. William Sunday laughs with delight. Doc isn't quite as easygoing. For him, this is surprising, bordering on alarming. They're effectively in a pressurized diving bell.

"*Ah, the doctor and his nurse,*" *Sha-Karn-Um* says.

William Sunday raises an eyebrow at that comment.

Sha-Karn-Um holds out two of her arms, dripping with water, and offers to shake with them. Doc responds, noting how cold she feels. *Sha-Karn-Um* repeats the gesture with William Sunday, but she stops mid-shake. She remains in physical contact with William Sunday, which seems strange.

"Is everything all right?" Fyodor asks, seeing her concern.

"*Two heartbeats!*"

"What?" Doc says, confused.

"Oh, ah, yeah... about that," William Sunday says. "I've been meaning to—"

"How is it you have two heartbeats?" a perplexed *Sha-Karn-Um* asks, relaxing and withdrawing her arms.

William Sunday cannot suppress the smile lighting up her face. Her cheeks are flush. Her eyes sparkle. She takes Doc's hand, saying, "I forgot to tell you. I missed something last month."

"You're pregnant?"

"Yes."

Doc throws his arms around William Sunday, lifting her off the ground as he hugs her and spins her around.

"Oh, Sunday," he says, kissing her gently on the lips.

Sha-Karn-Um says, *"New life comes where once there was death. This is good."*

"It is good," Doc says, feeling that's an understatement. He shakes his head. "Why didn't you tell me?"

"I—tried. There never seemed to be a good time."

Fyodor slaps Doc on the shoulder, saying, "Now is a good time."

"Now *is* a very good time," Doc says, still shaking his head and unable to wipe the smile from his face. With the best of intentions, he wants to go through the checklist given to him by NASA, but none of that seems important anymore.

"We celebrate," *Sha-Karn-Um* says, and the sphere seals beneath them, rising up from the depths. The curved, far side of the sphere, though, remains transparent, allowing them to see hundreds of Novos swimming in the depths. Lights shine from habitats beneath the water.

As they reach the surface, the sphere returns to the inside of the hive and continues up.

"We have much to celebrate," *Sha-Karn-Um* says as the alien elevator emerges in a chamber with a vast glass window providing a panoramic view of the floating city. There's a polished dining table with an ornate silver candlestick on it. The back wall is a floor-to-ceiling bookcase packed with books of differing sizes and colors. A painting

hangs on the wall. There are leather couches and armchairs, along with a broad desk in the open area. It seems *Sha-Karn-Um* has an eye for Earth's antiques.

They're hundreds of feet up, looking out over dozens of hives at various distances. Beneath the waves, nodes can be seen. These must equate to houses. They bob close to the surface. A few of them break the waves, but most of them are six to eight feet below the water, expanding as spheres of their own.

Sea birds soar on the wind. Given that they're hundreds of miles from land, they must be nesting on the hives.

"The birds," Doc says, pointing. "What do they eat out here?"

"*Oh, we have attracted fish. We've given them a deep-water home.*"

Fyodor has obviously been in this room before, as he uses his hand controller to open a panel on the wall and produces glasses already brimming with a yellow fluid.

"Non-alcoholic," he says, handing one to William Sunday.

They sit on the leather couch, looking out over the sea. *Sha-Karn-Um* sits on a broad seat that allows her to face them while also looking at her ocean world.

"*Sha-Karn-Um,*" Doc says.

"*Questions. Questions,*" *Sha-Karn-Um* says. "*Do you humans ever not have questions? All I ever get from the United Nations is questions.*"

Doc lowers his head slightly, wanting to be respectful.

"Please understand," he says. "We mean well."

"*Questions are an itch that can never be scratched.*"

"Answers bring satisfaction."

"*You. For you, I will answer questions.*"

"What brought you to Earth?"

Sha-Karn-Um gestures toward the window with her four arms as though the answer to his question is so obvious it need not be stated.

"This. All of this."

"I don't understand. Why would you give up the stars?"

"*Give up the stars? What was there to give up?*"

"You could soar through the heavens. There was nowhere you couldn't go. Why come here? Why destroy your ship?"

"*You humans are quaint. You think the stars call to you. They don't. They warn you.*"

"Of danger?"

"*No. Of the endless void. The vast, lonely emptiness. You think a new life awaits you out there. It does not. Nothing awaits you. A whole lot of nothing.*"

"I don't understand."

"*The Gad-Gari, our old masters. They saw your world from seventeen thousand light-years away. They saw you long before your civilization began. They saw a single diamond in the dirt. Generations rose and fell during our journey. And all to reach a planet you would leave. I find that amusing.*"

Fyodor gets up and grabs a hardback picture book lying on the table. The title is *Apollo Remastered*. The book's spine is bent and well-worn. From the way Fyodor flicks through it, he seems to know every page. He and *Sha-Karn-Um* have forged an unusual bond for adversaries. Over the past six months, they must have discussed almost everything between them. Doc makes a mental note: Fyodor should address the UN on behalf of the Novos. Having been on both sides, he has a unique perspective.

"I think this is what you're looking for," Fyodor says, handing the book to *Sha-Karn-Um*.

"*Yes, yes,*" the alien replies. She turns the book around, holding it open to a page from the Apollo 11 mission to the Sea of Tranquility. An astronaut stands on the dusty lunar surface with the black sky behind him. "*Magnificent desolation! That is what your Buzz Aldrin called the Moon. And he's right. And this is true of Mars, Jupiter and Saturn and all their moons. This is true of ten thousand worlds we have surveyed* beyond your system. They are magnificent and yet desolate."

"Huh," Doc says. This is not the answer he expected.

"You look to escape. We look to arrive. You look for life in outer space. Life looks for you. For you are an oasis in the desert... Have you not wondered?"

"Wondered what?" Doc asks, sitting forward on the couch. He has his hands clenched together in earnest, wanting to understand the perspective of an extraterrestrial intelligence.

"Why we didn't stop at Mars. We could have had the entire planet without a fight."

"But?"

"Mars will never rival Earth. It will never come close. You think you can settle on Mars, but you forget it took billions of years before Earth could support humans. You live in paradise. You trash paradise. And for what? A dream among the stars? A dream of finding the Earth on which you already live?"

Doc says, "We'll make it to Mars."

"And the end of all your exploring will be to arrive back where you started and to know the place for the first time."

"T.S. Eliot," a proud Fyodor says, taking the picture book from *Sha-Karn-Um.*

"Eliot?" Doc says, surprised to hear *Sha-Karn-Um* quoting an English poet.

"You've taught her well," William Sunday says.

"I wasn't always a fighter," Fyodor says. "Once, I taught English in *Novosibirsk.*"

"You think we're wrong to have our eyes on Mars?" Doc asks.

"Not wrong. Naive. You imagine great cities there. Great countries arising. But it will be like your southern region, like Antarctica. It will be cold, harsh and unforgiving. But Earth. Your world is a jewel within the galaxy."

"And the Gad-Gari? Do they have eyes on Earth?"

"They do, but they know nothing of you. Not yet. They move through the galaxy on scales that dwarf your civilization. They will assume a colony has been established here. They won't make landfall here again for thousands of your years."

"And us?" Doc asks. "Humans and Novos?"

"We will talk. We will trade. We will learn. We will help one another. We will care for this extraordinary planet and the life that permeates every nook and cranny."

Doc nods.

"Will these answers satisfy your President? Will this please your United Nations?"

"Yes. Although it will challenge their assumptions."

"And that's a good thing," William Sunday says, squeezing his hand.

"We've assumed too much for too long," Doc says. "It's time for us to open our eyes not just to the heavens but to all that surrounds us here on Earth."

Afterword

Thank you for taking a chance on independent science fiction.

If you've enjoyed this story, please take the time to rate it online and leave a review on Amazon or Goodreads. Your opinion counts. Your review will help others decide whether they should pick up this novel.

The Anatomy of Courage

This story is based on the non-fiction book *The Anatomy of Courage* by Charles McMoran Wilson, 1st Baron Moran (1882-1977), who was also known as Lord Moran. He served as the personal physician to Sir Winston Churchill. As a doctor in World War I, Lord Moran had no knowledge of concepts such as PTSD (Post-Traumatic Stress Disorder), but he was a keen observer of human nature and captured the heartache of that tragic war. I've drawn from the examples he cataloged from the trenches of World War I and expanded on them in this novel, wanting to keep his insights alive.

Kurt Vonnegut

I love Kurt Vonnegut as a writer. His work is sublime and underrated. He was the first science fiction author of the Golden Age to question the purpose of war. Others had written about alien/space wars, echoing our own terrestrial wars, but they invariably glorified them or belittled their destructive impact. Vonnegut dissected the harsh reality of war, exposing it as flawed and futile. Vonnegut was brutally honest.

339

His experience in World War II didn't echo the patriotic sentiments of Hollywood in the fifties. He became a voice within the science fiction community for the counterculture of the sixties. I've tried to capture some of that sentiment in *The Anatomy of Courage*.

If you're interested, I wrote a tribute piece for Kurt Vonnegut called *The Children's Crusade* based on his novel *Slaughterhouse-Five*, which can be found in my anthology Hello World. I mirrored not only the heart of his original story but also his chaotic, disheveled style.

Vonnegut loved to talk about the art of writing and often simplified complex concepts into simple ideas. When talking about the structure of stories, he used shapes to convey story arcs. He described how most stories follow a / shape, meaning there is rising tension that starts low and builds inexorably toward a crescendo. In *The Anatomy of Courage*, I've used what he'd described as a U-shape, meaning the story starts on a naive high and sinks into despair with the death of the Dog Food Squad before rising to its triumphant conclusion.

The Great Silence

Perhaps the most plausible of all possible explanations for the Fermi paradox and the Great Silence is the Rare Earth Hypothesis. In essence, this says Earth is a rainbow unicorn. Earth is an outlier even among Earth-like planets. And not simply by being rare among other physically similar worlds but extremely rare in that it not only has life but has evolved technologically intelligent life.

Earth, though, has only just developed to the point where it can sustain not only complex life but human ingenuity. For most of the time that life has existed on Earth, some 3.8 billion years, the atmosphere has not been even remotely breathable. The paradise we see around us is relatively new. It is not the norm, not even for Earth itself. We may consider Earth as ideal for intelligent life, but it's only become ideal recently.

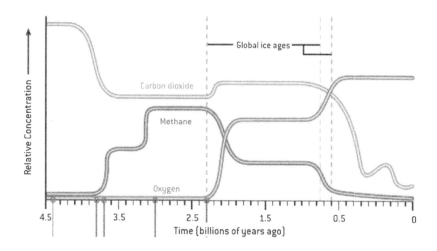

In this diagram, you can see the relative abundance of oxygen, methane and carbon dioxide in the air over the last 4.5 billion years. Although vast amounts of oxygen were unleashed into the atmosphere 2 billion years ago, the levels of carbon dioxide and methane were so high that human life wouldn't be possible.

Life arose astonishingly quickly on Earth, within a few hundred million years. Then, for *billions* of years, Earth was a microbial planet. Complex life is only recent. Intelligent life is even more recent. While the cultural and technological intelligence of humans is a newborn babe by comparison.

If we spotted a hundred seemingly identical replicas of Earth out there in space, all of them already teeming with microbial life, it's quite possible that *none* of them would have anything like the habitable biosphere we enjoy today.

The Great Silence may be the Great Divide, meaning life can flourish, and intelligent life can (eventually) develop on multiple worlds, but these worlds are so rare that the sheer distances involved in terms of both time and space are insurmountable. And that brings up the problem of galactic colonization.

It may be that the reason we don't see any intelligent species spreading through the galaxy is that there are no contemporaneous,

341

habitable islands for them to spread between. Earth may well be the only oasis in this region at this time.

Here on Earth, Polynesians spread around the globe by island hopping, slowly sailing out across the Pacific and finding various islands so distant they could never have been reached from Asia on a single crossing. This is the model SETI scientists and science fiction writers assume when considering how aliens might spread through the galaxy, but the rarity of worlds like a mature Earth may be so extreme as to negate this strategy.

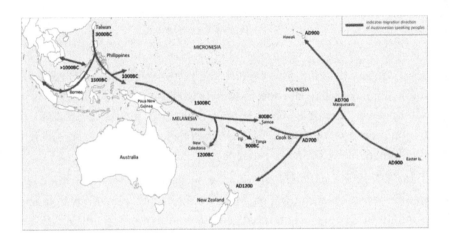

Instead of spreading in short bursts from Indonesia and the Philippines to Papua New Guinea and then to Melanesia and on to Fiji, then Samoa, then the Cook Islands and splitting to find Hawaii and New Zealand, and finally reaching the Easter Islands, three-quarters of the way across the Pacific, the equivalent celestial journey would require a single voyage from Thailand to Easter Island, or perhaps even further to England or France, by comparison. We, and others like us, may desire to spread through the galaxy, but there may be no practical destinations within reach.

We may long to spread into space, but to spread where? Science fiction makes it look easy. Orbit a planet. Beam down to the surface. Set up a colony. But planets even remotely like ours are exceedingly rare.

For us, planets like Mars might appear to be good candidates for colonization. Elon Musk isn't shy with his ambitions to develop cities on Mars, but his goals may be more fiction than reality. Although the surface of Mars looks similar to the dry, high-altitude deserts of Earth, it is physically incomparable. The extreme cold, the absurd thinness of its atmosphere, and its lack of a magnetic field means living on the surface of Mars is not viable.

Martian colonies would need to be developed in lava tunnels to avoid the devastating impact of cosmic radiation. Even if habitable domes could be built with their own electromagnetic shielding or soil dumped on top, they would never span a significant percentage of the Martian surface. The low gravity means that even with the most extravagant terraforming taking place over tens of thousands of years, the planet wouldn't be able to hold onto a significant atmosphere. And that's it. Outside of Earth, that's the best real estate in our solar system.

We'll eventually have some form of off-world colonies, but it is doubtful they'll ever support populations into the millions, let alone the billions, at least not in any reasonable timeframe. It's easy to think this is simply an issue of scaling, that once we have a settlement with a thousand people, we can build toward ten thousand, then a hundred thousand, then a million. After all, there are well over a hundred cities on Earth with a population of more than a million, but these are supported by immense amounts of fertile land and a thriving global economy. Even in an advanced country like the US, with a population of 330 million people, there are only ten cities with more than a million residents. If you count surrounding urban areas, this goes up to 45 cities, but it's still less than half the population. Building (domed) cities on a lifeless, frozen planet with barely any discernible atmosphere is a logistical nightmare that dwarfs anything seen on Earth. Our planet really is an oasis in a parched desert.

If you want to learn more about the challenges involved in life beyond Earth, check out A City on Mars by Kelly and Zach Weinersmith.

Will we fare better in other solar systems? Maybe. But given the lack of viable exoplanets discovered so far, it's doubtful. And given the extreme effort required to reach them, it is impractical. The Great Silence may be a testament to how utterly futile it is to colonize outer space compared to caring for our own home world. Perhaps ET has already figured this out while we're still dreaming about the stars.

Jesus or Joshua?

In this novel, Doc refers to himself cryptically as Joshua, being a reference to Jesus and a reminder for him not to adopt a messianic complex. There's some interesting history behind this point.

In Western culture, there's no name more evocative than that of Jesus Christ. The irony, though, is that this is a name that would have been lost on the disciples and even the apostles if not Jesus himself in the first century. During the time of Christ, the spoken language in Judea was Hebrew. Aramaic was also used in the synagogues. When Jesus was crucified, the sign above his head was written in Hebrew, Latin and Greek: Hebrew because this was the common language of Judea, while Latin was used by the Roman army, and Greek covered civil administration by non-Jews.

Jesus is a translation of Joshua (*Yeshua*) into a foreign language. Although it may sound blasphemous to suggest otherwise, calling him Jesus is akin to calling me Pierre. To his followers, he was Joshua ben Joseph, and later, Joshua the Messiah (which equates to the Greek term Jesus the Christ).

Joshua was a common name in the region at that time. The use of the Greek version *Jesus* from the second century onward appears to be a deliberate attempt to make his name more unique, as the name Joshua appears throughout the New Testament, just not in reference to Christ even though that was his actual name! Strange, but true.

William Sunday

If you're curious about the origins of this unorthodox name in *The Anatomy of Courage*, it came from a goat.

Last year, I visited the town of Tintenbar in rural New South Wales and stayed at Paddock Hall while writing this novel. There were a few goats on the farm, and they would stick their heads in through the broad, low bathroom window while I was sitting there contemplating science and fiction. One of them, William Sunday, was quite a cheeky character and full of life. And he squeezed his way into this story.

War isn't Hell

War isn't hell. It's much worse.

The classic US television comedy M*A*S*H was set during the Korean War and features astonishing insights into human nature, but perhaps none is more profound than the idea that war is not hell—it's something worse. I wove that concept into *The Anatomy of Courage*, referring to it as though it were an actual historical incident rather than a comedy sketch, but it is no less true for being humorous.

The dialogue in the show unfolded in the middle of the mobile surgery theater like this...

Hawkeye: *War isn't Hell. War is war, and Hell is Hell. And of the two, war is a lot worse.*

Father Mulcahy: *How do you figure, Hawkeye?*

Hawkeye: *Easy, Father. Tell me, who goes to Hell?*

Father Mulcahy: *Sinners, I believe.*

Hawkeye: *Exactly. There are no innocent bystanders in Hell. War is chock full of them - little kids, cripples, old ladies. In fact, except for some of the brass, almost everybody involved is an innocent bystander.*

This is such a profound insight, and yet it's largely lost to history as few people go back and watch these classic shows anymore.

EPR

EPR, or Emergency Preservation and Resuscitation, as described in this story, is an actual medical technology under development by the

345

University of Maryland Medical Center in Baltimore.

Normally, if someone is shot or stabbed and loses more than half of their blood, they require major surgery and have mere minutes to live. EPR can extend survivability to two hours by cooling the body to 15C/60F, giving first responders time to get a patient to the hospital. During this time, the brain's activity has effectively ceased, and the body is clinically dead, but the cold preserves cell integrity, allowing them to be revived. The actual procedure uses an ice-cold saline solution to replace the blood. In *The Anatomy of Courage*, I've used a little literary license to say this will eventually be accomplished simply by cooling the blood itself rather than replacing it. In either regard, this technology is a lifesaver on the battlefield and in any mass shooting. The sooner it is perfected, the better.

The Necessity and Tragedy of War

20th-century French philosopher Albert Camus, writing about the nature of war, noted that:

"...in the midst of a murderous [warring] world, we agree to reflect on murder and to make a choice... Over the expanse of five continents throughout the coming years, an endless strug-gle is going to be pursued between violence and friendly per-suasion, a struggle in which, granted, the former has a thou-sand times the chances of success than has the latter. But I have always held that, if he who bases his hopes on human nature is a fool, [then] he who gives up in the face of [these] circumstances is a coward. And henceforth, the only honorable course will be to stake everything on a formidable gamble: that words are more powerful than munitions."

War is both a necessity and tragedy of human nature.

Like Camus, I have a friend who dismisses my views on war as foolish, saying, *'The sheep sleep safe from the wolf only because of the shepherd with his staff.'* On one level, he's right. Violent aggression cannot be countered with pacifism alone, and yet, from the vantage point of history, there are flaws to this logic.

War is never black and white. War is never the shepherd against the wolf, the righteous against evil. We may tell ourselves that to justify the senseless loss, but so do those on the other side of the battlefield. War is only ever, at best, a murky grey.

Even seemingly righteous wars, like the liberation of Europe from the Nazis in World War II, are often marred with war crimes committed by the liberators, such as the indiscriminate bombing of Dresden or the mass rape of German women during the fall of Berlin.

No war exists in a vacuum. The causes of war are seldom as simple as they're portrayed in the media and are often muddied with blind ideology, especially by the aggressors, as they have to justify the madness to their own people.

The aggressors in any war are motivated by stealing land, resources, and wealth, but they hide like cowards behind patriotism, duty, and a distorted sense of righteousness. Truth is the first casualty in war because lies provide camouflage.

I agree with Camus: rushing to war is an act of cowardice. It takes courage not to fight. Sending young men and women to their deaths as a patriotic duty is easy for politicians. Peace demands courage. War is the political equivalent of using a chainsaw when what is often needed is a scalpel. War is blunt and brutal and painful. War should be the last resort, not the first.

For almost a century, US doctrine has been *"peace through strength."* But it's not just the military that needs to be strong; the morals, principles, and justice that resonate within the country also need to be strong and free from corruption. A strong military with weak civilian oversight is a murderous machine. For all its flaws, democracy is the only way to ensure balance.

There are times when war is thrust upon us by aggressors, like the Russians invading Ukraine, but war should never be an excuse to abandon our humanity. The only justifiable motive for war is to free the oppressed, not to steal, not to kill, not to enslave, not to satisfy hatred. Hate is acidic to morals. Wars should be fought to restore humanity and not out of bitterness or selfishness.

On March 4th, 1861, barely a month before hostilities broke out

347

between the North and the South, Abraham Lincoln was sworn in as US President over an already divided country. In his inaugural address, he said:

We are not enemies but friends. The mystic chords of memory, stretching from every battlefield and patriot grave [during the War of Independence in 1776] to every living heart and hearthstone all over this broad land, will yet swell the chorus of the Union, when again touched, as surely they will be, by the better angels of our nature.

Lincoln was not naive. He knew war was coming. As early as January of that year, several months before his inauguration, shots had been fired at Fort Sumter, and a blockade had been put in place. The Governor of South Carolina had demanded the surrender of the fort from the US Federal Government. And yet Lincoln could already see beyond the Civil War. He could not have known how bloody and brutal and protracted it would become, but he knew Americans were *"not enemies but friends."* And he knew one day the war would end as all wars do, and the people would *"again [be] touched... by the better angels of our nature."* And this is the real goal of war: not to decimate and destroy but to restore our better nature. And this is precisely what happened to Germany and Japan after the Second World War. They were transformed from fascist death machines into models of democracy. Neither country is without its flaws, but they have embraced our *"better... nature."*

Even in lost wars and failed battles, this maxim holds true. Each April, the people of Gallipoli in Turkey welcome Australians and New Zealanders with open arms, even though the ANZACs were the aggressors invading their land in 1915. The people of Laos, Cambodia and Vietnam hold no ill will toward the US, Australia, or any other nation involved in the Vietnam War.

War is a blight on humanity, but it is *"the better angels of our nature"* that lights the future. Camus may have been naive when he said, *"...words are more powerful than munitions."* Or perhaps he had a vision of humanity rising from senseless, barbaric wars to become a true civilization.

In the words of Isaac Asimov, *"There are no nations! There is only* humanity. And if we don't come to understand that right soon, there will be no nations because there will be no humanity."

William Bolton

William Bolton is my great-grandfather.

The incident Leech recounts in the opening of *The Anatomy of Courage* of a dispatch runner being killed by a sniper is based on the death of my great-grandfather in World War I. Having survived several horrific battles, including Verdun and the Somme, William Bolton was well over a kilometer behind the front lines, carrying dispatches between command posts, when he was shot in the head. He died barely a week before the armistice ended the war in early November 1918, leaving behind a five-year-old daughter he barely knew, who went on to become my grandmother. She treasured the medals he was given and passed them down to me, but there were no heroics, no acts of courage or grandeur to his death. It was pointless. The war was all but over in November of 1918, and both sides knew it. His death was just another tragedy in the mindless spectacle that is war.

Christmas 1914

One of the concepts explored in this story is the idea that wars are rarely understood in their time, especially by those on the front line. Following orders is necessary for discipline in the military, but it betrays humanity, treating soldiers like machines. If truth is the first casualty in war, rational thinking is the second.

Even seemingly clear-cut wars of good against evil can become mired in darkness. With the Second World War effectively won, the Allies firebombed Dresden. *"The intentions of the attack are... to show the Russians when they arrive what [the US/UK] Bomber Command can do."* Rather than focusing on economic areas within the city or targeting specific factories, the Allies carpet-bombed the entire city, killing tens of thousands of civilians indiscriminately along with refugees from other areas. The Allies wanted the Soviets to think twice about extending the war and attacking the West.

Those involved in the bombing could see no wrong in their actions, but morals aren't defined by perception. If the Germans had bombed New York in the same manner, there would have been no doubt about it being a war crime.

Make no mistake about it. War is a necessary evil, but it is still evil nonetheless. The full extent of the evil takes time to uncover, and those who perpetuate these wars will do all they can to bury the evidence of their atrocities.

In chess, the pawn can only move forward and never look back because it is the role of soldiers to obey to the death and never question the king. There are only a handful of moments in history where wars have faltered because those tasked with killing stopped the madness, at least for a moment.

Roughly six months after the start of World War I, there was an impromptu, unofficial ceasefire over Christmas. From various reports, it seems to have started with the Germans singing carols on Christmas Eve from their trenches and the British, French and Belgian troops responding by singing their own traditional songs as well.

On Christmas morning, German soldiers could be heard calling out *"Merry Christmas"* in English. In some places, the Germans held up signs in English that read, *"You no shoot. We no shoot."* For the next week, up until New Year's Day, soldiers mingled in no man's land, traded rations for cigarettes, and even played soccer against each other. The war resumed not because of the soldiers but because of politics. It's a brilliant example of how war doesn't make sense at the level of the individual.

War is politics by brute force.

One-Star Reviews

If you go through my back catalog of novels, you'll find plenty of one-star reviews because I'm (supposedly) pushing political ideas within my books, but this ignores the reality that fiction is invariably a reflection of society.

I would argue that *all* fiction is political. And the ability to write a

350

story *without* politics is a political statement in itself, quietly supporting the status quo. In the words of Jean-Paul Sartre, *"Every word has consequences. Every silence, too."* Now, I don't think fiction should be a political treatise, but it should make people think, and it shouldn't shy away from the issues that impact our lives and the debates that are unfolding in society.

In this particular story, a mere 15 words out of more than 100,000 are guaranteed to trigger yet another flurry of one-star reviews.

Slavery was never a question of states' rights.
It was a question of human rights.

If this offends you, good.

This isn't politics.

This is a fact.

And it plays on an astonishing historical irony. Today, it's the Republicans who are offended by statements like this, even though the roles were reversed in the American Civil War. Back then, it was the Democrats who supported slavery!

The Republican Party was formed in 1854, almost a decade before the Civil War, specifically to oppose Democrats on the issue of slavery! In 1864, when the 13th Amendment was passed, abolishing slavery, the vote in the House of Representatives was 119 to 56 in favor of constitutional change (86 Republicans, a bunch of independents, and a mere 15 Democrats voted for the amendment, while 50 Democrats and a few independents voted against it).

If you want to get political, then I'd argue that Republicans should be proud of fighting for human rights over something as nebulous and fickle as states' rights. After all, the outcome of an election in any given state should have no bearing on human rights.

On March 17, 1865, while addressing the Indiana Regiment, Abraham Lincoln said, *"Whenever I hear anyone arguing for slavery, I feel a strong impulse to see it tried on him personally."* And he's right!

351

Those who argue for *"states' rights"* would never actually want the state to enslave them personally.

Thomas Jefferson said it best when writing the Declaration of Independence: *"We hold these truths to be self-evident, that all men are created equal, that they are endowed by their Creator with certain unalienable Rights, that among these are Life, Liberty and the pursuit of Happiness."*

No state (or country) has the right to violate human rights.

Apollo Remastered

In the epilogue, Fyodor grabs a copy of *Apollo Remastered* to make the point that as magnificent as outer space may be, it is equal parts sheer desolation.

Apollo Remastered is a coffee table picture book developed by Andy Saunders, who digitally restored hundreds of photos from the various Apollo missions. Although we've all seen photos from the lunar surface, often these are washed out, especially those taken from within the cabin of the spacecraft as the glare of the sun bouncing off the Moon blinded the camera. Andy has painstakingly restored these, often turning what were little more than dark, blurry silhouettes into astonishingly detailed images.

In the words of Apollo astronaut Charlie Duke, the 10th person to walk on the Moon: *"Andy Saunders' remastered images are so clear and real that they are the next best thing to being there... They are an exact representation of what I remember from my journey to the Moon on Apollo 16. These photos reveal very precisely what the Moon was really like."*

If you're a fan of the Apollo missions and you'd like to understand what Buzz meant when he spoke of *"magnificent desolation,"* I highly recommend *Apollo Remastered*.

AI or Alone?

I've been accused of using AI to write my stories by a couple of authors who have said there's no way anyone can write four or five high-quality stories with entirely different characters and plot lines in a single year. They think it's no coincidence that my increase in productivity comes at the same time as the proliferation of AI-written books.

Unfortunately, the truth is far more mundane. Last year, my wife and I separated after thirty-two years of marriage. There's no fault to lay before either of us, but I was—am—devastated. Now, I live alone in a one-room studio apartment overlooking someone's swimming pool. It was designed as an entertaining area, not a living space, but it has a wonderful view of the local forest. I've been going to therapy, but the best therapy has been to lose myself in the pages of a book, either while reading or writing. So, no, I don't use artificial intelligence. I find solace in my keyboard.

Thank You

Thank you for taking a chance on an obscure Australian science fiction author who hails from Auckland, New Zealand. Your support of my writing is deeply appreciated. By purchasing this book, you're giving me the opportunity to write the next one, so I'm grateful for your kind support.

I'd like to thank a bunch of beta readers who helped me with quality control, including Chris Fox, David Jaffe and Terry Grindstaff. Gabe "*Velveeta*" Ets-Hokin USMC and Mike Morrissey LCDR. USN Ret. helped with military aspects of the novel, while Dr. Randall Petersen helped with medical insights. Special thanks to John Stephens, who went through the novel three times to help polish the final story. Any mistakes, though, are mine.

If you've enjoyed this novel, please leave a review online.

If you'd like to learn more about upcoming new releases, be sure to subscribe to my email newsletter. You can find all of my books on Amazon. I'm also active on Facebook, Instagram and Twitter (and, no, like Stephen King, I won't call it by a single letter of the alphabet).

Peter Cawdron

Printed in Great Britain
by Amazon